CU00871823

ORPHAN PODS

BRITTA JENSEN

ALSO BY BRITTA JENSEN

First published in the United States in 2025 by Murasaki Press LLC
Copyright © 2024 by Britta Jensen
Cover illustration and design by Sarah J. Coleman

First Edition—2025/Designed by Murasaki Press, Map by Britta Jensen, Editors: Nancy Knight and Heidi Asundi

Murasaki Press LLC
PO Box 152313
Austin, TX 78715
School and bulk sales of this book can be purchased for business or promotional purposes. Email info@murasakipress.com for more information.
Join the author's mailing list and read bonus materials at britta-jensen.com

This book has been catalogued for libraries as follows:
Names: Jensen, Britta, author.
Title: Orphan pods / Britta Jensen.
Description: Austin, TX : Murasaki Press, 2025. | Summary: Two orphaned teens strive to rescue their friends and family from their city's evil casino bosses. | Audience: Grade 7 & up.
Identifiers: ISBN 978-1-7363835-4-4 (hardcover) | ISBN978-1-7363835-9-9 (paperback) | ISBN 978-1-7363835-8-2 (ebook) | ISBN 978-1-7363835-5-1 (audiobook)
Subjects: LCSH: Young adult fiction. | CYAC: Homeless children--Fiction. | Siblings--Fiction. | Quests (Expeditions)--Fiction. | Romance fiction. | Science fiction. | BISAC: YOUNG ADULT FICTION / Action & Adventure / General. | YOUNG ADULT FICTION / Family / Orphans & Foster Homes. | YOUNG ADULT FICTION / Social Themes / Friendship. | YOUNG ADULT FICTION / Science Fiction / General.
Classification: LCC PZ7.1.J46 Or 2025 (print) | LCC PZ7.1.J46 (ebook) | DDC [Fic]--dc23.

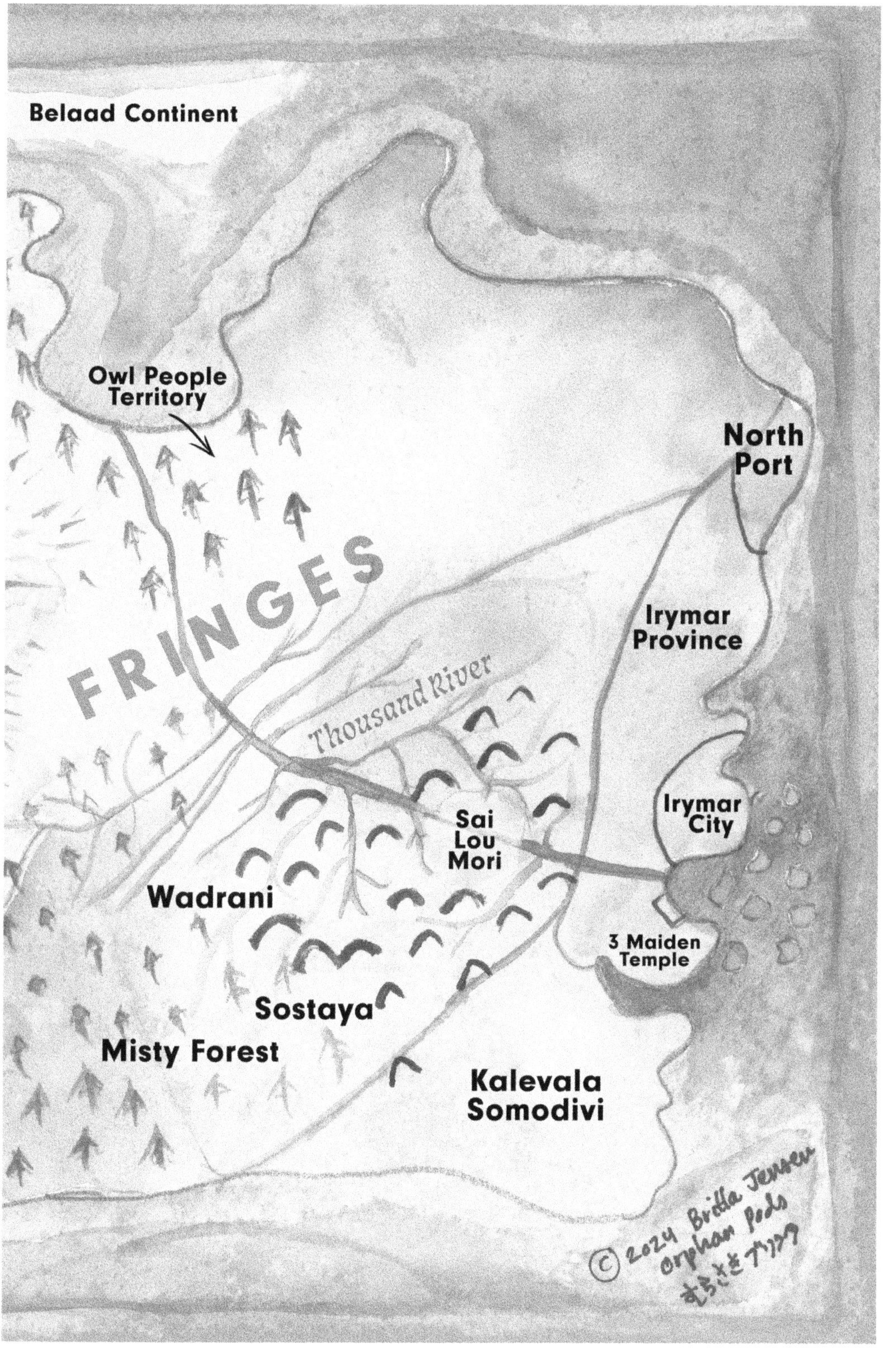

Belaad Continent
Owl People Territory
North Port
FRINGES
Irymar Province
Thousand River
Irymar City
Sai Lou Mori
Wadrani
3 Maiden Temple
Sostaya
Misty Forest
Kalevala Somodivi
© 2024 Britta Jensen
Orphan Pods

For Woolery, Fairbanks, Vance, Houston, & any kid who feels lost.
There is a home waiting for you.

Chapter 1

Idris

Age 15

The time had come and I didn't feel ready. Today the ruby goddess's smooth glass felt warmer in my palm than other chilly mornings in the factory. Dread crawled up my throat, pushing me forward, away from the weaving machines starting up.

Take the first chance you're given, Idris. My father had said that to me before he fell ill.

Pray to the goddess and save yourself, Little One, my mother whispered before she died. *Do it for both of us.*

As their only daughter, their words echoed inside my head louder than the clacking of looms and shouting of overseers around us workers.

Yes. Today I am done being a slave.

I rubbed the palm-sized glass statue of the goddess, the last thing of my mother's. I whispered a quick prayer.

My tail flicked back and forth in anticipation, and I tucked the goddess back in my uniform's thigh pocket. My wrists ached from the heavy shock bracelets and the bruising they gave me when I wasn't flying cargo hovers. The stench of onion soup followed me from the weaving room, where I liked to hide from Wiid, the overseer, and dissipated on my arrival in the cavernous hover transport bay.

"Idris, what you got in your pocket?" Wiid's bellow rose over the looms' racket, startling me. He glared at me across the rows of stacked crates of fabric.

I couldn't run from him. There was too much riding on today. I pretended I didn't hear him, willing my tail to be calm while I followed my petrukian's black-winged flight pattern across the factory floor. Pinu flew past the whirring and wheezing looms and over a spinner that had been out of commission for weeks.

Good girl. I had hoped she'd lead me to some morsel of food, because they never gave us anything other than liquid before cargo runs. Insurance to make sure we came back. My stomach was pins and needles, but I pressed on.

I ran to keep up with Pinu, skirting the dye vats where two workers wore face masks to protect them from the stench of ammonia. The rest were bare faced and coughing from the vinegar-scented air. Face masks had to be earned. Usually that meant snitching on your fellow slaves for stealing food or slacking.

I pushed my black, unbraided hair out of my face, my private form of rebellion for not being allowed to cut it. Refusing to braid it, per factory regulation, bought me an extra fifteen minutes of sleep. My only luxury.

My tail flicked back and forth as I surged forward beyond the rows of large black-and-silver-winged petrukian birds spying on all of us. Like our lives weren't hard enough in Brailesu Factory.

I looked up to where Pinu perched in the metal H-beams above me. She flapped her enormous black wings, before tucking them primly behind her. So she hadn't led me to food, like I'd hoped. My body started to deflate as my stomach felt like it was going to digest itself. Standing here wasn't going to get me to food any faster. Judging by the cargo clock, we had three minutes to get to my hover before I'd have today's rations docked.

"Pinu!" I called. She soared down and landed on my shoulder

before nipping at my earlobe, her large bill snapping in her sound of endearment for me.

"You two better be ready for the next run," the Ungar overseer growled, her furless skin gleaming in the morning light, nervous pink eyes darting back and forth, watching the pilots prepping in the hangar bay.

"Idris! Stop!" Wiid bellowed, curling his finger back for me to come closer. The Ungar overseer attended to another hover, and I wished I'd called her back, made her stay like she had other times. Instead, Pinu tutted on my shoulder, acting like she was waiting for instructions.

"Not you, Pinu. Go!" Wiid waved his arms, but Pinu stayed, flapping her long wings at him.

"I don't like waiting, Idris." Wiid's hands slid up my arms, dipping into the wide neck of my uniform.

"I have a rash. It's catching." I shrugged him off, but he held onto my shock bracelets. My arms were still sore from the last beating I took from him for being late for my cargo run two days prior.

"Who says?" Wiid glared.

"Don't I, Pinu?" I asked my bird.

"She's going soft. I need to give you a new one." He tugged on my bracelets and leaned in, his wild purple mane grazing my cheek. If I shoved him, he could take me off this run.

When I was younger, I had hoped his disgusting mane would get stuck in one of the looms or catch fire from coming too close to a hover's engines. It was a shame no one had shoved his useless carcass into the dye vats. Because my hatred of him was so obvious, he'd made sure I was stuck with the oldest, clunkiest hover that held more crates than any of the newer ones. All his mercurial posturing hadn't changed my mind about never letting him anywhere near me. He'd taken my mom from me.

I'd rather he beat me than do what he did to her.

"Cheep, meep," chirped Pinu.

The warning alarm blared for the next group of hovers to line up.

"Hurry up!" Dina, Wiid's daughter, shouted to the Ungars loading the goods inside my hover's boxy cargo hold. Their thin bodies strained to keep the wire crates from toppling or undoing the careful folding of the more delicate fibers that would fetch a nice price on the outmarket, if they weren't bound for Stencil's casino.

"We're not finished here." Wiid licked his lips, staring down at my chest. "I still remember your mother," he whispered.

I started to gag and tried to smile to cover it up. It was all I could do not to vomit on him.

My mother had assumed he would get better after the war ended.

She was wrong.

His yellow eyes narrowed, his cat-like snout twitching.

My tail flicked out and I stopped myself before I hit him with it. His hand grasped at my elbow as I wrenched away from him and climbed into the squat cockpit, Pinu soaring in after me, her black, silky wings tucked in for landing. The long, egg-shaped cargo hover had been mine since I had started flying at age eight, and my mother's before me. I shut the four side doors before he could get close and turned over the switches for the engines. The ancient, silver hover, originally seating eight passengers instead of cargo, roared to life.

I rolled down my pilot window and extended my wrists for him to remove the shock bracelets. He was one of two in the factory with the key. The bracelets emitted a shock if you got too far away from the Brailesu Factory where I'd lived my entire life. Not enough to kill. Just enough to keep you compliant and afraid. Yes, I'd definitely tried. Multiple times. The beatings afterward hurt worse than the shock.

This is the last time he's taking them off.

This is what it looks like to leave it all behind, I told myself, restraining myself from grinning with the joy bubbling up inside me. *I'm finally going to be free.* I rubbed the statue of the goddess in my pocket, murmuring a quick prayer before revving up the engines, impatience burbling and making my stomach fizz. *Can I escape where so many hadn't?*

Wiid leaned in, standing on a rolling ladder, burnt onions on his breath in the stifling, dry heat of the hangar. "Hands further out." I let him take off my shock bracelets. Once they were gone, he held my wrists lightly. "I own you—every inch. Like your mother." He sneered, his teeth yellow and already rotting.

"No, you don't." I said, the goal always for my tongue to sour everything he touched. "The disease that's eating me alive owns me," I lied.

"Stop being dramatic." He held on firmly to my wrists.

"Watch. It'll kill me, just like it did my parents." I looked at him, dead serious, ready to bite through his hands if he held them any longer, but I couldn't act too eager to leave. I had to keep a bored, detached look, just a moment longer.

"I'll be waiting for you when you return."

"Happy, glad day, then, Overseer Wiid. Pinu, we can't wait, can we?" I said with a twisted smile on my face. *You're never going to see me again.*

"That's what I like to hear," he murmured and released my scarred wrists.

I kept my eyes on the distant movement of hovers pulling out of the hangar. His daughter, Dina, waved us through as the next to take flight. Flutters of nerves started in my stomach. *Only a little while longer.*

"I have an hour to get back from Bliss, correct?" I asked Dina. Pinu clicked into her harness beside me in the co-pilot's seat, her bill ready to peck at the buttons to free up the landing gear.

"Food bonuses if you make it back sooner," Dina said, watching me carefully from her perch next to the bay doors, her haunted yellow eyes always following me, before flicking warily to her father, Wiid.

I leaned against my pilot's chair, adjusting the pitch to accommodate my longer legs. The greasy marks on the wheel made me suspect Wiid had used my hover earlier.

He popped his head into the window of the cockpit, just as the last hover was airborne. "Give it to me, Idris."

"What are you talking about?" I asked, genuinely puzzled.

"The goddess statue. You're not allowed to have it." He smiled, the acid joy in his eyes burning molten hatred through my chest.

"You can't have it," I said evenly.

"Oh yes I can."

I glared at Dina, assuming she'd told him, because she'd seen me praying earlier that morning.

"Hand it over, and I'll give it back to you when you start playing nice." His yellow teeth bared.

I took it out of my pocket, glancing at the last reminder of my mother. I wanted to chuck it at his head, anything but give it over.

Whatever you can do to be free, do it, Little One.

Idris, do it for us.

My hands were shaking when I handed over the ruby figurine, so worn with age that her face was no longer distinguishable. I wanted to tell him it would curse him, bring him a short life, turn his only daughter against him.

I couldn't say any of those things because I had to get free of him, even if it meant giving up the last physical object belonging to my parents. The last item that had brought me any measure of hope.

As soon as his hands snatched at the statue, I realized maybe I didn't need hope anymore. If I had freedom and could leave this accursed valley, perhaps that was better than some piece of glass that had never made my life any better. If the goddess was really all-powerful, why had she left me here for so long with Wiid's burning hands? I dropped it onto the ground, as it echoed and rolled away, forcing his daughter, Dina, to chase it. I rolled up the window before he could say anything else.

My chest still searing, I steered the hover out of the dock carefully as Dina unlocked the overhead metal door which coasted upward. The entire hangar buzzed with the next batch of deliveries. If this was the last time I was seeing this, I needed something more final than tired grey and blue uniforms shuffling like ants, with no real purpose other than surviving a life we weren't sure we wanted, because the casino bosses needed revenue more than we needed decent lives.

I cranked up the radio, a disgustingly loud and annoying Myrel song with an electronic synth track.

Sal monga jyet sal,	*Love hits you like it does,*
qil bak chef sal yuu.	*its chains surrounding your desires.*

A cold sweat broke out across my back and arms.

Could I really do this?

Will Pinu stay with me like we'd practiced the last few months?

I hadn't endured all Wiid's beatings for "accidentally" leaving the flight path to wait another miserable day. I looked over at Pinu, ever alert, thankfully not hopping with the joy welling up inside me prematurely.

Escape first. Celebration second.

I scanned the skies for a sign that today wasn't the day to try this. Rain, clouds, something. The hanger's open-door alarm jolted me back to my flight controls. "Pinu, landing gear up on five." Once the hover in front of me cleared their flight path, I gunned us airborne. The sky was a pale blue and the surrounding desert so crisp I was sure this was the day I wasn't coming back. I watched the flight path indicator, alarms ready to blare the moment I was a few meters off the flight path. *So long Brailesu Factory!*

Pinu cheeped once we cleared the factory complex, the worn, blue buildings standing out from the dry ground littered with sage brush and stunted trees. Our natural water source mostly diverted away to provide enough water to power the casino bosses' enterprises.

"We're almost free, girl!" Below us, the packed desert earth was pitted with pockmarks from the war that had devastated most of the valley. The surrounding hills of red rocks bore the marks of more than ten years of fighting for control of the valley.

I searched the ravines and fields ahead for a good place to land in order to disable the locators each factory hover was equipped with. I could taste freedom somewhere beyond the towering red rock hills surrounding Zeto City. If I had my way, I was going to get out to the prairie the first chance I had, even if it meant risking death. Anything was better than going back.

I yanked the throttle, gunning forward on the flight path until I saw the ground change from dirt and cacti to neat green fields and trees. If I could get beyond the trees, it might be the perfect spot to land and disarm the locators. Fields lay to the east of us and I veered to the right, to the fallow fields so I wouldn't disturb any crops. Alarms immediately blared.

"Off course! Off course!" A metallic voice droned. "Altitude adjustment in 10 seconds. Re-route!"

Pinu jumped up and down as we plummeted in altitude, more agitated the further off our flight path I got. My entire back was drenched as I struggled to keep the hover's nose up, the blaring of the navigational sensors filling my empty stomach with acid.

"Off course!" The alarm blared.

"Pinu, get ready to rip out the locators!" I tried to find the alarm speaker so Pinu could snip it, but the hover was already juddering in the air. I landed us with a bump, turning off the engines. I let out a low, guttural sigh before jumping to action. I had to snip all the locators to deactivate the AI and prevent it from notifying the authorities. I opened all the panels where we'd identified the locators on previous cargo trips. "Get that one." I yelled at Pinu.

Pinu pecked at the locators under her side of the cockpit while I tore at the wires on the locator to my left.

"Off course, off course!" It yelled, the volume increasing.

I nervously glanced up for drones that might intercept us.

"Fifteen seconds 'til conn...ect..." The voice faded away when Pinu ripped the last wire from her copilot's console.

There was still one more locator on the front radar console. I hopped out and took my screwdriver to the side panel in the nose of the hover, rummaging for the blue-green locator wire. I couldn't find it. A drone soared overhead, and I almost paused to look up. It hovered over us for only a few seconds. I dug amongst the wires, tempted to snip as many as I could find, but if I wasn't careful, I might cut important navigational tools, or a coolant line. Pinu landed on the nose and cheeped at me.

"Not now, Pinu. I still can't find the last locator."

She jumped up and down, fraying my nerves. I sliced through one line, only to find the correct locator wire—more blue than green—then ripped out the red diode that had faded to a dead maroon. Pinu had the rest of the locators in her beak and threw them onto the warm, black soil beneath us.

"We have to get out of here, girl." I held out my arm for her to jump on as I ran back to the cockpit. When I looked to the left, where her head was cocked, a group of children and teens approached from a neighboring orchard. They were watching us. *Oh, no, that's the last thing we need, more witnesses to my escape!*

I pulled my wet uniform from my lower back. I had to get my bearings for where I was going next, and fast. Old hangars loomed in the distance. It was strange to see so many kids. I'd been one of a handful that survived past the age of eight in the factory. But these kids seemed older than my fifteen years. Pinu squawked, flapping her black wings.

"Stay. Don't even think about saying 'hi'," I warned.

We had to get away. I hopped into the cockpit, and Pinu remained on my lap, transfixed by the approaching kids in green uniforms. I fired up the engines, my heart thudding in my chest. I shut the door and rolled the window up halfway so it would be harder for Pinu to get out.

An older boy approached, his orange hair long and shaggy. A frame of shiny scales illuminated his grinning face. "You here to be registered?" he asked, folding his arms casually across his chest.

"Registered for what?" I asked, my heart dropping. We needed to get out of here, fast.

"Orphan Pods." He looked astonished when Pinu hopped into her seat. "You fly that thing by yourself?" He came closer.

"Yes, now get away from my hover," I said, putting the hover into gear for takeoff, my heartbeat thudding in my ears.

"Why not come to the pods? Free food, a pod to yourself. It isn't much, but better than what's waiting for us out there." His smiling face was saying something else, a strange glimmer in his dark eyes. "Besides, we need more sexy girls like you here!" He bounced an eyebrow at me before grinning.

"Shut up, Rusty! Leave her be." A red-haired girl hobbled behind him, struggling to walk on metal legs. More kids milled behind them.

"I have to go." I revved the engines, guilt swimming through my veins. My uniform was cold and clammy against my skin. My first taste of freedom, and I'd lingered where a bunch of idiot kids could report me back to the factory. *Stupid, stupid, stupid.* I urged us upward and back toward the prairie.

If they told someone, I'd see more than the business end of an electrocoil. My whole body stiffened as the surprised faces of the kids craned upward when I flew over them. The orange-haired kid waved at me before the hobbling girl pushed him into the dirt.

Whatever you have to do, get out of Zeto Valley, as soon as you can.

I heard my mother's breathy voice in my ear and increased our speed. Beneath us was only sagebrush and pitted red earth. I didn't know how far the hover's batteries would take us. Pinu fidgeted in her seat, her wings half-flapping. I was entranced with the flow of the Ong River, its yellow, silt-laden waters rushing by. I'd never seen the river from this viewpoint, having spent all my routes shuttling back and forth to the casinos operated by the two main war heroes turned casino bosses: Whip and Stencil.

All the water exiting the city was thick and grey, like a swollen slug inching along. Beyond the city limits the water changed: almost clear and blue, sparkling. I followed its path toward the looming red rock enclosures that framed the valley where the Ong cut through. I needed those waters to lead me away from Zeto's towers and wastelands forever.

The engine choked, and I looked at the battery gauges. We still had 60 percent power, but a thin trail of smoke was billowing out the back and a temperature warning flared. Pinu jumped up, pressing on the coolant gauge, but nothing changed.

No…this can't be happening, not after everything…

We lost altitude again, the hover shuddering in the air. I brought us closer to the desert, but was afraid to land in that desolate space. Beside the river, past the surrounding coral rock hills, stood a large white compound sticking out of the border between the desert and the start of the prairie. A gust of wind blew the hover closer to the river, and I overcorrected, bringing us back in line with the compound. Pinu hit the stabilizer button, but the wind blew us off course again. One engine cut out, then another.

Panic swelled in me like a tidal wave. "Goddess! Not Now!" I fought the spots clouding my vision, hearing my mother's voice.

Don't give up, my daughter.

CHAPTER 2

TOREF

AGE 16

He had to find more metal somewhere. *I just have to.* Toref leapt over the side of the dirt-and-rock ravine, craning his neck to look up at the cloudless sky rimmed at the horizon with blonde hills and the towering red rocks of the Scraggs beyond. Sweat poured down his dark face and ran down his arms, forming rivulets over his dusty brown skin. He'd left at first light, after a fight between him and his two sisters and his mom.

"You have to stop taking those pills, Mom!" Lena, his oldest sister, had shouted.

"Get away from me, you ingrates!"

He leaned over to catch his breath, trying to exhale the memory from that morning while scanning for anything shiny on the ground. *I'm not certain I can find scrap metal here, but I have to try.* They were out of food.

Mom isn't doing anything to change the situation, that's for sure. His heart sank just thinking about it. He focused on clambering up the ravinescape, which reached his shoulder and was too high to hop over. *There's nothing here, not a single patch of metal.* He remembered the earlier days when he'd enjoyed the scent of the hot earth and hiding in the comfort of the dried-up runnels of yellow rock that were a common site in Rif City's badlands. More rock and earth than anything green.

Maybe that's why all the city's buildings were green and covered in organic-looking graffiti that spanned multiple stories. Much of the graffiti had cropped up after the war had laid waste to most of the natural greenery. Elaborate forests, oceans, and sometimes jungles flourished in the Ungar artistic style on every flat surface that was larger than a few square meters after the Ungars lost the war with the Hybrid factions. *Probably to show that we wouldn't be so easily defeated,* Toref thought.

He took one more cursory look, the sun beating down on him, before gauging the distance to the wavering bulk of the scavenging yard. *Nothing more to do here.* He buttoned closed the pocket of his trousers containing the few coins he'd earned that morning. It was enough for only one day of water rations, but he needed to get to his sisters before the heat made him thirstier than he already was.

Could he tell his mother that he was going to stop sharing water rations with her if she didn't start helping them and get off the pills she was taking?

He wiped the sweat off his brow as he made his way through the ravine and climbed up the sloping earth onto the dirt road, a shortcut to his block of green flats.

He glanced up at the metal railings over the long stretch of awnings rising nine stories high. Along the sides there used to be elevators that ran. "Back in the good old days" his dad used to say. No one lived up that high anymore, at least not that Toref knew of.

He stopped to catch his breath, remembering his dad's reverberating voice. "I'm ho-ooome!" The way he'd sing in the mornings before his shift, waking them all up, always apologetic when Toref wandered sleepily into the kitchen.

He passed the schoolyard and tried to keep from looking at his old classmates, pausing in their lessons under an oiled canopy. Once he was close enough to spot their quizzical faces, he sped up, eager to see if his sisters made headway with Mom. His mom hadn't gone back to teach school, so he and his sisters didn't have the tuition to go. *I have to stop walking by here hoping for things to be different.*

As he followed the curved road to his side of the flats, yelling echoed around the building's yard. That wasn't unusual this time of day, right before the water and electricity was turned off at the peak afternoon heat to allocate all resources to the factories. After most retreated indoors to escape the heat, the fight would die down, he thought.

The cries got louder. *Penny and Lena!* Despite the heat, he sprinted toward his sister's voices, rounding the corner to the sandy lot in front of his building. A small white hover, accompanied by a woman with waist-length hair and purple, gleaming skin, held onto his sisters Lena and Penny. They struggled against her grip.

"Let go of them!" Toref rushed toward them.

"You can't do this to us!" His oldest sister Lena yelled, struggling against the Hybrid woman's grip on her arm.

The purple woman snapped an electrocoil whip around them, binding them together, making them cry out against its sting.

Toref stumbled in the sand, spotting his mother sitting on the building's steps.

"You think life is so hard here? See how it is on the other side," she seethed.

"What are you doing?!" Toref shouted.

"Mom, please!" Penny begged, her small body huddled against Lena.

Toref surged toward them, desperate to reach the hover in time. "Let them go!"

He was a few yards away and his legs felt like jelly. A new cramp was slowing him. "No! No, don't take them! I have coin!"

The woman shoved his sisters inside the hover and hit a latch on the door. The doors sealed right as he reached the passenger side, his sisters still yelling and banging on the windows noiselessly.

"Don't take them!" He pulled at the passenger side door, but it was locked from the inside. He grabbed onto the co-pilot's door handle instead, tugging and prying at it.

The purple woman hopped into the pilot's side, completely unfazed, and slammed her door shut, revving the tiny vessel's engines before the round hover was floating with Toref still holding onto the door handle. He had to let go, but he didn't want to. He banged on the window with his other elbow, before having to hold onto the handle again as the hover kept raising higher. "Lena, try to break the glass!"

Lena clawed at the window, distress distorting her long face.

"Noooo!" Toref's reflection layered over Lena's in the glass, terror streaking his dark, round face. If he didn't let go now, already as high as the second story of his building…his arms gave way and he sunk to the burning earth.

Penny's hands pressed against the glass. Toref reached upward helplessly as the hover disappeared from view. It was gone before he knew what else to do. He didn't have any weapons, nothing to over-power whoever that was. A warm breeze blew dust in his face, and he was afraid to turn around, a terrible anger licking its flames at his insides, threatening to spill over and claim his mother. He took sips of breath, trying to calm down, to find his words.

He finally twisted toward her, a slip of who she used to be, her brown face ashen.

"It's better this way…they kept complaining, kept saying I need to work when I can't. So, I've found a better place for them." She struggled to stand, her whole body shaking. "Plenty of food there—"

"—What did… you…do?" Toref asked, still out of breath.

"You want to join them?" Her anger was back, her expression no longer pained. "Do you?"

"Where did…you…send them?" Toref kept his distance. He wanted to shake her out of this crazy state that had gone on too long. He was afraid he'd kill her, break her bird bones that got thinner every day she refused to do anything other than sleep and drug her life away.

"It doesn't matter now. They're going to a better place." A small smile played at the side of her mouth. "A place where they'll *appreciate* everything I've taught them."

Toref came closer. "Where?"

Her face flickered for a bit, a touch of her old self coming back. "Orphan Pods. Why? You want to go, too?" Her face got mean again, reminding him of Lena when she was in a bad mood. "Loyalty always has a price. There's a reason you're here and they're gone."

Toref stepped away from her and roared, shrinking onto the steps, horrible sobs contorting his body. "You're lying. You better tell me where they're going." He held out the coins in his hands, tears streaking his cheeks. "I won't give you any of this unless you tell me."

Her expression changed, a horrible twist to her mouth. "Fine, have it your way. I'm sending you the same place I sent them. The Pods. Like I said." She held out her hand for the coins. Toref flung them away from her, the coins quickly lost in the sand.

He was going to find his sisters if it killed him.

"Get going. You aren't welcome here anymore," his mom yelled, kicking sand in his tear-streaked face before digging in the sand for the money.

Toref spotted the gleam of one of the coins and beat her to it, pocketing it and sprinting away for the water station.

CHAPTER 3

IDRIS

We were only functioning on two engines. Sweat dripped down my face, and I fought to keep the nose up as we lost elevation. "Tafla!" I cursed. We were moving too fast for me to stay on course and make it over the river dams. My hover's last engine was going to cut out soon; the cabin was warming up from whatever was making the batteries overheat.

"Pinu, we're landing."

"Cheep, cheep." Pinu hit the landing gear and pushed the emergency window release.

"Wait, why did you do that?" I yelled. I struggled to stay parallel to the ground, circling closer to the white and terra-cotta compound. The wind rocked the hover again. I held on tight to the steering wheel, my hands throbbing from the effort to keep us level, shifting downward, which was useless. The last engine sputtered and died as I heard the crunch of gravel beneath the hover. Pinu soared out the copilot's window toward a sprawling, white multibuilding complex. I was out of breath and rested my head on the steering wheel. We weren't far enough away from Zeto. Not by a long shot.

So stupid, thinking we could just waltz out of there and onto the prairie.

I pushed my head off the steering wheel, inhaling deeply to try to calm my unsteady pulse.

After a few minutes, Pinu hadn't returned.

"Pinu, come back!" I yelled.

She was still flying above the terra-cotta roof of the whitewashed two-story building. A handful of Hybrid men in tan jumpsuits were gathered around, apparently not in any sort of hurry to apprehend me, which had to be a good sign. I took a few steps toward where Pinu was circling and stopped.

What if this is a fleshmarketer outpost?

I scrambled back to the hover, kicking up gravel.

A woman in flowing yellow robes stepped out of double glass doors, smoking a feratik stick that made my mouth water. I froze where I stood while she sauntered toward me, her robes undulating pleasantly, her hair swishing free to her waist. The softness of each step that brought her closer to me was so natural I couldn't help staring as she moved forward in silky waves, her grey skin sparkling in the sunshine.

I tried to collect myself, make some plan, but the woman held me in a trance. *Why didn't I feel more afraid of this stranger?* I couldn't move, even if I wanted to. I didn't want to abandon my hover, since it was all I had, with Pinu flying the coop.

Would this woman send me back? Or try to harvest my organs, or worse? My heart thumped so hard that I had to lean against the hover. I wanted to run but was too weak. I hadn't eaten for over a day. I was parched, my tongue threatening to stick to the roof of my mouth.

The woman was an arm's length from me. "You fly dat ting? You too skinny and starving."

When I didn't answer her in Stan, she switched to Hybrid Kesh.

"I understand both," I interrupted in Stan.

"Yes, yes. 'Course." Her voice continued in its melodic flow. Every movement from her billowy, fabric-laden arms so elegant and soft. *Why is she so calm?*

Pinu soared above us before circling slowly, her wingspan as wide as my arm width.

"Pinu, come back!"

A large grey man, appearing to be one of the Myrel, or rock people, approached. I took three long steps back. I wasn't about to let him get anywhere near me. Pinu alighted on his shoulder, and I was too petrified to reach for her. *Please don't let him take her from me.*

"Been long while since I see petrukian in wild," his voice rumbled in a low bass.

I could leave without Pinu, technically. And if they were going to capture and send me back, this would be the time to make a run for the prairie, but I felt so stuck, so rooted to where I was. I didn't want to run without Pinu, especially if she trusted them enough to land.

"She's mine." I held out my arm.

Pinu wasn't moving. I felt that tug, the deep pull to run, until the man spoke again.

"My family raised dem before the war." The man stopped walking toward me when he saw me back up. His mineral skin glistened in the sun. Before my family was captured during the war for factory conscription, my father had written about the Myrel and chronicled Hybrid history. There was a softness to this Myrel man that made me want to come closer. This also frightened me, my ease toward him and the yellow-robed woman. All it took was one swipe of his meaty fists and I would be down, unable to run.

I took two more steps back.

"I see you need some repair?" His low, resonant voice calmed me. Pinu snapped her beak pleasantly, and I kept my hands outstretched for her to fly to me. Whatever happened, I couldn't let them take her away. The man stayed frozen, his wrinkled grey face turned up in a toothy smile. I wondered what made him grin like that. It had been so long since I'd seen anyone genuinely smile.

My mother's face floated in front of me for a second, her round yellow eyes blinking, her mouth turned up like it did when my father sang to her. The prairie grass swished around me and carried the memory of her away.

I knew I had to make a decision.

"You run from factory, yes?" he asked.

When I didn't answer, he continued, "I Shakratel, this my daughter, Yura. We not speak Stan or Kesh so well, but we say enough for coin and help people." He grinned, revealing round gaped teeth.

"I'm Idris… I don't have coin," I admitted, remembering the fabric cargo in my hover. Would they steal it, if I showed it to them?

I squinted at the red rock hills behind me. I didn't have a choice. I had to hope that I could get repairs in exchange for the exotic fabrics that I'd be lucky to ever feel on my skin.

I glanced back at Shakratel, standing next to Yura. Both of their grey faces mottled from the mineral elements that were a part of their heritage. *What had brought them all the way out here*? Their bodies stilled further as they watched me debating my options. *I was going to have to try to trust someone, wasn't I?*

"I have fabrics here. They'd fetch a good price." I walked gingerly to the back, the gravel crunching under my bare feet that were tough from years in the factories. Pinu flew to my shoulder, and I unlatched the back of the hover, all those neat stacks of fabric upended from our emergency landing. Pinu whistled at the turquoises, fuchsias, and teals. Only one stack of violet fabric in the whole sea of beautiful colors. I had often looked away from them because I knew they were something I couldn't have.

Pinu, on the other hand, started toward the violet fabric, eager to rub her beak in it. Now that there was no one watching our every move, I was going to have to be firm with her.

"No, Pinu, stay."

She squeaked, but didn't move.

I reached for the turquoise stack first, the silky fabric pleasant. It was a hue too close to my factory uniform. I lifted the violet fabric and Yura approached, her cedar scent alerting me before she was beside me.

"Violet the most expensive cloth." Yura ran her fingers through it. "Ooh, silky, come look Shak-ra-tel." She separated each consonant in his name, her tongue rolling on the "r".

I clutched the violet cloth to my chest. "I'm keeping some of this." I gestured toward the remaining piles of fabric pouring out of their wire framed baskets. "You can have the rest for hover repairs and a place to stay until it's ready. I'll need food, too."

Shakratel raised an eyebrow at me and walked toward the cargo hold. "These will get you a lot of coin, but you can't sell them all at once. If you do, someone will tell factory."

"Will you?" I asked.

He looked at Yura and she started to laugh with a tinge of disdain.

"Why we tell doz people? We not in Zeto limits. We have own laws out here," Shakratel said, his voice booming.

Could I believe him? There was something in the way that Pinu flew to him and how he held himself, watching, not grasping like Wiid or the others in the factory. There was no desperation. The wind buffeted my long black hair around me.

I didn't have a lot of options.

I'd been free for all of twenty minutes, and here I was trying to bargain.

When I handed over the first stack to Yura, though, my breath loosened like I'd done something right for the first time that day. I had to make sure they understood how much was riding on this exchange.

"I can't go back to the factory. I'd rather fly this hover and myself into the Ong River than ever go back," I said. "I won't stay long. I'm heading out to the Fringe territories when I have enough coin."

Yura sighed, putting a hand on Shakratel's thick, muscular shoulders. They nodded to each other and said nothing.

At that moment, I felt the weight of my parents' deaths, of never having a friend, other than Pinu, and spending so much of my life without a choice. I looked at my tall, thin body next to their radiant health. I felt the smallness of me. The terrible weight of not being able to defend myself like I had needed to. I wanted their hard skin and the inner softness that they exuded effortlessly.

Yura winced and held out the fabric again. "That not happen. We get coin for this and find safe place to stay. Yes, Shak-ra-tel?"

"We firs' get hover repair and food in belly. You stay here. No question." Shakratel called out to two men in grey jumpsuits hanging out at the compound. I stepped closer to Yura, making sure not to touch her. Shakratel spoke to them hurriedly in another dialect that was mixed with Kesh, and they opened compartments at the front of my hover, attaching a tow line to the axel on the bottom to move the hover closer to the orange-roofed hangar where other smaller hovers were being repaired.

Yura put a hand gently on my shoulder. "What your name again, Little One?"

Only my mother had ever called me that. "Idris," I said, halfway hoping she'd call me "Little One" again.

"It good name. We call you Idi, yes? Come inside out of the sun." Yura took all the violet cloth and a smaller pile of the teal fabric, then called out to a group of women who were approaching. She snapped her fingers and they unloaded the back of the hover while the tow rope hauled it in.

Pinu flew inside ahead of us, cheeping cheerily. I yearned to feel so carefree. I hadn't expected freedom to feel like this, like a weight of choices that I had to sift through.

"Oh, petrukians," Yura exclaimed, clapping her hands. "I always wanted one."

"Are they valuable?" I asked.

"Oh yes. Very, very valuable. You take care with her. She fetch much, much coin." Yura looked at me with captivating almond-shaped grey eyes. I followed her into the cool of the thick-walled building, our footsteps echoing on the orange tiles. The room was full of light and large windows that overlooked a green patio with enormous flowers. Yura held out her hand to Pinu, but she flew back to me, settling into my lap as food was offered by women in blue and grey robes, long and flowing like Yura's.

I didn't know then what those long robes meant. If I had, I probably wouldn't have let them serve me my first savory rice stew of my new, free life.

CHAPTER 4

TOREF

THREE WEEKS LATER

The voices of Toref's sisters harmonized and echoed in his mind.

Sing way down low
Where your voice don' wanna go...

The memory of them singing temporarily distracted Toref from the slow build of morning heat in the harvesting field. He found himself humming along with the memory of them, his voice squeaking on the high notes, forgetting there were other kid pickers around him that could hear him making a fool of himself.

He still didn't know why he was here after three weeks. The first week he'd been sick with dehydration from trekking all the way to the Pods. Now, sweating in the sun, picking endless rows of zucchinis and purple parabelas while he bided his time, he was determined to ask every Monitor in the enormous Orphan Pods complex where his sisters were. He kept hoping every day he was assigned to a different harvesting field that he'd be able to hear their voices singing or complaining about picking fruits and vegetables in the blistering heat.

From what he could gather, the Monitors were in charge, knew everything, and made sure that everyone worked and ate. If he caught the attention of a roving Monitor, floating by on their hover disc, they'd scan his arm chip, check his vitals, and ignore his questions before zooming off to handle another crisis in a place that seemed to be 90 percent people ages seventeen and younger, and only 10 percent adult. He was left alone with all the other listless, age-sixteen specimens, trying to ward off the hopelessness of being abandoned.

He reached for another zucchini, keeping the scratchy sides of the velvety leaves from irritating his skin. He hadn't worked enough shifts to be eligible for overtime, leaving him without the coin to buy the time-off the rest of the older kids earned to leave their shifts before the midday sun scorched them all.

He hadn't minded at first. It allowed him to search the fields for his sisters when the fields emptied of workers. Peering through the vine leaves at the other kids still working their shifts, he realized he was one of the few over-fifteens on harvesting duty. Green uniforms indicated they were assigned to the fields. The only Ungar on his shift, Toref was as dark and smooth-skinned as the day he was born, unlike several of the Hybrid kids who had fur, scales, or tails. Some had added fashionable mods after arriving, with mixed results. *I wonder if people would speak to me if I had some mods?*

He glanced skyward to catch the next Monitor whizzing overhead on her hover disc. The shiny metal plate emitted a whine, which Toref suspected meant they were badly in need of service. *Maybe I can fix it and get intel on my sisters.* He didn't understand why—in the cavernous space that housed thousands of children, ages infant to seventeen, scrupulously documented and embedded with arm consoles—it was so hard to find Penny and Lena?

Speak up man, or you'll get nothing, his dad used to say, when he was alive.

Toref released his collecting basket's waist strap, wiped the sweat off his brow and watched the other Hybrids, silent, resigned, almost alien-looking next to him. "Hey, have you seen two girls who look like me around here? Named Penny and Lena?..." He waited a moment while the kids blinked at him and shook their heads. "They're my sisters. Can you tell me if you do, maybe?"

The kids just shrugged and walked off with their tools, tails flicking behind them.

He was definitely the only Ungar for rows around. At least no one had called him names. But they hadn't been eager to talk to him either. There was a certain listlessness in their eyes that he recognized.

It was the same way his Mom's eyes had grown unfocused and all the light extinguished when the news about his father came from the factory in Rif City four months ago. He'd heard the explosion, and later found out about the chemical fire, but it hadn't stopped his family from waiting for their dad, wondering when his booming voice would enter their small, two-room flat again. Maybe that's what had driven his mother to the edge: all that waiting.

A familiar whine buzzed overhead and Toref jumped up and down, waving his hands at the Monitor soaring above him on her disc.

"Monitor, please, over here," Toref called.

The Monitor slowed down; her shock of blue hair clashed with the dusty, cloudless sky. She hopped off her disc where it wobbled midair for a few seconds before falling to the dirt.

The Monitor scanned his forearm console, the long thin indentation still red around the edges on his forearm where it had been embedded a few days ago, the chip inside lighting up, showing his vitals.

"No, it's not that—I'm looking for my sis—" he started before she interrupted.

"You're approaching dehydration. Get inside for your midday meal."

"My sisters…Penny…Lena—"

She hopped on her disc and was off before he could ask anything else. The rest of the row of pickers watched him coolly, a few tails flicking back and forth, scales shining in the sun. He didn't have scales, or a tail, or anything that made him even remotely cool. Was that why this third Monitor had ignored him?

Penny and Lena'll be there waiting for you, his mother had said. So, why, in the entire three weeks he'd been at the Orphan Pods, had he been unable to find them? The afternoon meal bell rang out and he took his baskets and passed them along the assembly line. A few of the kids watched out for any Monitors before slipping bits of parabela fruit into their pockets. Nobody seemed to want the zucchinis, which made Toref wonder if it had something to do with their appearing in every meal he'd been served since arriving.

He followed the row of light-green uniformed kids back into the chow hall, the heavily graffitied space echoing with voices. He looked at the elaborate murals, depicting lush vegetation he'd never seen. Beyond him, a line snaked around the school's learning bungalows. The Monitors there were listening to the kids in line with a certain rapt attention that Toref hadn't seen anywhere else. In the lines of Hybrid and Ungar kids, mostly tens and above, each Monitor was taking their time, nodding their heads, tapping at screens built into the tables.

They weren't running away from anyone's questions here, though a few took frequent glances at the thick woven canopy hung over them while fans blew from the cavernous ceiling. The whole space had been converted from hangars the Hybrid forces had used during the civil war.

Toref tried to determine which lines led to which purpose. There was a mix of ages, each line twenty or more kids deep. He spotted a few Ungars, like him, with purple or pink irises that marked them as unmodified humans. He studied everyone who walked by who matched either of his sisters' height, gait, or dark brown skin. Whenever a girl turned, he'd find scales or fur that immediately cancelled the little hope he had in finding them.

After stumbling through the sea of kids, he chose the back of the shortest line. Unsure if this was really where he was supposed to be, he cleared his throat. "Which line are the age sixteens supposed to stand in?"

A fox-like girl turned around, her white tail swishing, the fur around her brow wet. "I don't think it matters, yeah?" She snapped her tail in annoyance, and Toref kept cautiously studying the sea of teens

27

approaching the chow line beyond them, his emotions feeling like they would erupt into boils on his skin at any moment.

You all can be a family again.

Could he trust anything his mom had said after Dad died?

He sighed and glanced up at the moss-covered wooden beams in the converted hangar. It was larger than any other indoor space he'd ever seen. Even his father's factory could fit inside. The south wing of the hangar housed an array of hundreds of sleek white pods, shaped like elongated eggs, suspended in the air by a multilevel metal suspension pattern which rearranged itself for the next crew of kids starting their shifts. The noise of them tromping down the metal steps almost drowned out the voice of the Monitor calling out to Toref's line. He wasn't eager to go back to his pod, where he only slept, and just barely. It was too lonely and dark in the windowless, cramped space. *It's the first time I've had to sleep anywhere by myself.*

"That's all for today, folks." The short Monitor with blue hair jumped on her hover disc to move over to them, tucking her notepad into her shorts pocket. Groans ensued.

"I been waitin' for weeks…"

"Not as long as me."

The fox girl threw her hands in the air and trotted off.

"Sorry. Try again tomorrow." The blue-haired Monitor watched them with concern, her thin mouth drawn in a line, her pink eyes flicking over them. Toref recognized her from the fields earlier. *So, she was Ungar too.*

He made a beeline for her, hoping she'd recognize him. "Wait, Monitor…"

"Whatcha doin'?" An orange-haired Hybrid boy stepped in front of Toref, and the Monitor was gone. Toref exhaled noisily, tempted to push him out of the way. His mane of orange hair was a finger's length from touching Toref's cheek.

Though he was trembling, Toref stood his ground. Lena, his older sister, had always said, *"Either act crazy or kick ass, but don't let them know you're soft."*

"School." Toref folded his arms, keeping his face stony.

The kid's arm scales gleamed in the midday sun below his cutoff sleeves. His mouth turned into a grin. "Man, I've been looking all over for you."

"For me? Why?"

He thrust out a hand. "Rusty."

No one in the desperate complex had been this friendly, and Toref was immediately on his guard.

Rusty gestured to the dissipating line. "Third day I've seen you wandering around here."

"So?" Toref caught a whiff of something earthy and pleasant from Rusty's clothing.

"There's an easier way of getting into school, if that's what you're waiting for." Rusty smiled at a gaggle of Hybrid girls in white uniforms, two who waved and one who leaned in and gave him a kiss on the cheek before taking off. Rusty turned his attention immediately back to Toref.

So a few girls know him, it doesn't mean I can trust him. An image of Penny and Lena swam before him, appearing lost and forlorn, not knowing he was looking for them. *Maybe Rusty can help.*

"I'm Toref." He took Rusty's hand, the cool scales soothing on Toref's calloused palm. It was the first time he'd touched anyone in weeks. He looked at Rusty's smiling face and there was something there he couldn't quite place, a curve to his thick, brown eyebrows.

"I know how to cut your line waiting in half. But it means you have to earn some coin with my crew." Rusty gestured toward a group of older mammalian Hybrid teens, their jumpsuits folded down at their waists, tails flicking, playing the first stage of Ruga, a multistage gambling game.

A girl with bright red hair hobbled by, and Rusty sprang to catch up with her. Toref studied their interaction carefully. Rusty's voice went especially low. He didn't look at the red-haired girl the same way he had the girls in the white jumpsuits. There was a wobble to his face.

"Come on..." he pleaded. "It's only an hour of your time, I promise. I'll make it worth your while..."

The redhead crossed her arms. "No way, I'm too busy today." She stumbled along and Toref wondered what made her walk so stiffly.

"It's not for me...just come talk to..." Rusty dropped his outstretched hand and watched the girl continue to hobble away, her bright hair bursting out of the two ponytails at the nape of her pale, freckled neck. "Minny, I got coin for you...Tor...ef..."

Toref was surprised that was the last enticement Rusty was offering. He turned back to Toref, grinning, but the shine was gone. "A little testy, but heart of gold." He clapped a hand on Toref's back. "We'll catch her tomorrow." Rusty glanced over at the game, nodded at one of the older girls watching, and focused all his attention back on Toref. "So, what's your story? Who sent you here?"

"I came from Rif City," Toref said.

"Why?" Rusty turned his body away from the game. From this close, Toref noticed the dark purple freckles that lined the edges of Rusty's mostly human face.

"Dad died." Toref looked behind him for another Monitor, just in case he could snag them.

"What about your mom?" A corner of Rusty's mouth turned up in a way that made him no longer appear like a kid to Toref. His dark human eyes contained a grief tucked away in a pocket of his otherwise sunny disposition. Was that a look Toref could trust? He was afraid those very eyes would betray him the way his mother's had only three weeks ago.

Rusty shifted his weight, still not looking away when the noise from the game escalated. Toref had nothing to lose. He was already completely on his own. What would Rusty's knowing change?

Toref glanced up at the sky, so he didn't have to see Rusty's expression. "She sent my sisters here. I need to find them." When he looked back, Rusty was still there, arms folded, his mouth twisted in thought.

The yelling behind him was now frantic, one blonde, furred girl grabbing a younger boy. Rusty swiveled around as each player in the circle removed the sticks and dice, the crowd already taking sides, issuing judgments. "Stop cheating, Ruthi!" Rusty yelled. "Usha, I'm leaving you in charge to sort them out." He handed over a few coins to Usha, the white-maned wisp of a girl with a very deep voice.

"Go on, I've got this." Usha said, waving him on.

Rusty gestured toward the orchards at the opposite end of the complex. "I gotta get away from here."

Something was troubling Rusty, and Toref suspected it had nothing to do with the game. He wasn't sure he could trust this kid, yet it appeared others did.

He kept his distance, though, watching for signs of problems as their boots kicked up the fine silt between the rows of trees. Bees buzzed between blooms. The light from the sun danced across Toref's dark arms, and he folded down his uniform's sleeves, the heat searing when they reached an opening in the clearing before entering the next row of mature fruit trees, yellow apples dangling deliciously.

Rusty stopped, his arms wide. Toref realized they were the only two kids around in the oppressive heat that cooked the top of his head.

"Look, everybody was sent here. Most were lied to." Rusty dropped his arms, gesturing for Toref to follow him to the end of the orchard where tall vines climbed trellises in the distance. The smell of the peaty earth was pleasant and Toref relaxed, his heartbeat no longer a dull thud in his ears. Small brown sparrows flitted from tree to tree.

When Rusty slowed his pace, Toref noticed how the orchard formed a recognizable V-pattern instead of the rectangular shapes of the vineyards. Rusty put a hand on the trunk of the nearest tree, his stare moving past Toref. "Most kids told their siblings are here, learn they ain't here at all. If we don't find them in a few weeks…" He held his palm facing up, before dropping it and gazing at the dirt.

A terrible clutching started in Toref's chest. He hoped it would pass. But, as sweat dripped down his face, the heat burned him from the inside out, his thoughts choking out all reason. What if they truly were lost and that everything that had happened, that terrible unraveling of his family, was not over yet? He didn't know if he could bear that unknown. He tried to catch his breath, but his chest tightened and he was scarcely able to exhale without gulping for his next breath.

"What is it, Toref?" Rusty asked, crouching down, hands out but seemingly afraid to touch him.

"Leave me be," Toref said. "I'll be fine in a little bit." *I hope.*

"Naw. I'll stay. Make sure you're alright." Rusty took a step back and stood there, hands outstretched, like he held a lifeline Toref wasn't sure he needed or wanted. What had his mother told him about favors? *Do I want to believe her now, after all that's happened?*

CHAPTER 5

IDRIS

I watched Reggi, one of the teen mechanics, install the new coolant lines. His large hands gripped the turquoise blue cords, feeding them through the existing loops where I attached them to the tank that surrounded the battery mount on the roof. His red cap fell over his eyes, making his wild curls flop before he righted the cap and grinned at me with a wide smile, shoving the cap back on. For the past three weeks, since I arrived, I'd felt good working in this way, feeling useful, but also having a choice in it. No Wiid breathing down my neck, or crappy rations. Nobody yelling at Pinu for perching on my shoulder.

Most of all, I could wear whatever I liked, cut my hair too. There was so much choice, but I'd settled for chopping off my hair and shaving it on the sides as I'd seen some men do.

"Your hair look like some racer," Yura said with a smile after I'd done it.

"I don't want to be easily recognized."

"There so many escape slaves, they not find you easily, not with new Gnasher ID Shakratel set up for you. No worry, worry so." She touched my now spiky hair and her smile looked a little sad. "Your hair so beautiful. But I understand." Her face didn't show she understood at all.

I wore flowing purple pants and a short-cropped top that allowed the dusty summer wind to cool me off more easily than my uniform ever had. But I also felt so bare.

"You're lucky you didn't fry your whole electrical system when you cut the coolant operating system's wiring," Reggi said, looking up at me, keeping his hazel eyes steady on my face before dropping them down to my waist, his long, pale freckled face blushing before handing the wiring up to me, our hands briefly touching. I didn't understand why he turned red when he got close to me.

"How old are you?" I asked him.

"What?" He stopped what he was doing. "Why do you care?"

"I don't. You just seem young." *Maybe he was older than I thought.*

"I know what I'm doing," he insisted.

"I'm not saying that." I crossed my arms, hopping down from the top of the hover to where he was. "I'm fifteen, if that makes it easier to tell me."

He stared at me, his eyes going wide before his jaw locked, a tension in his round, freckled face. "I'm fifteen, too. Been here since I was eight." He looked sad as he said it, like there was a story he was waiting to unburden.

"Shakratel's is a good place to be."

"So, you'll stay?" he asked, his eyes going wide with hope. "I mean, I understand if you have other places you want to be."

"I want to leave the valley. First chance I can get." I rested my hand on the battery mount.

"On your own?" He sat back on the rolling bench.

"With Pinu." I watched him relax a little, his eyes busy searching my face before turning back to the coolant lines.

"No one leaves here by themselves, Idris." It was the first time he'd said my name and it felt different to hear him say it— a friendliness in his tone that was different from Shakratel or Yura. "It's dangerous out there in the Fringe territories. You never know what you'll find." He tapped the side of my hover. "Besides, this girl needs some serious overhaul for that kind of travel."

I nodded tersely at him. Yeah, I had all sorts of learning to do that I was sure I wasn't ready for. I was determined, once the hover was ready, to discover what life would be like, relying only on myself and no one else. I met Reggi's gaze, a softness to his hazel eyes that I liked.

Yura stopped me on my way to the dining hall. Her crimson robe swished as she walked, several racers tracking her with their large owl eyes, their head feathers twitching. She paid them no mind and took my arm. "Reggi say your hover almost ready for flight?"

"Probably by tomorrow, once we do a few test flights and make sure the batteries hold a charge."

Yura sat me down on a bench in the hallway, waiting for the racers to pass by. "You know you can stay here, long as you want, earn coin, fly people where they need to go, make cargo runs. You safe here, Idi."

I didn't believe I was safe anywhere, except where Pinu and I could be out in nature, just the two of us.

"At some point, won't they come looking for me?" I asked.

Yura's almond eyes were wide and unblinking, her mouth pressed in a line. "Zeto a pretty big place, five districts, plus Rif City to the north. That's lot of ground to cover for an escape slave."

"Even one who stole a hover?"

She folded her arms, the wide bell sleeves swinging. I wondered what it was like to be so elegant and powerful? A large Hybrid man swaggered by, his boot heels making a clinking sound against the wood floor. He turned back to her and stopped in his tracks. "Yura, you never change, do you?"

"Maybe not. Maybe so. Go inside, I'll see you in a few minutes." She had a different smile with him. More practiced, less warm. Something else passed between them that I didn't understand. Singing started in the dining hall and the sounds of people using the gambling tables on the outskirts of the large dining area.

"The hover is old, it not valuable." She leaned into me, venturing to put an arm around me, her sleeves soft against my bare arms. "I not say it never happen, but I see many, many come through here. Most escaping with more injuries than ones keep you up at night." She looked at my wrist scars pointedly.

So, I had been talking in my sleep. All the more reason to be on my own.

"We can help you here. You out on your own and there no guarantee. You still want leave to Fringes? When you old enough and strong enough, we help."

I looked at her and didn't understand why she was doing this. Why, after knowing me for so little time, with so little chance of compensation was she willing to take me on? Not like a project, and not like a friend, but something higher and without definition.

"I have to be able to pay you back," I insisted, leaning into her.

She kissed my cheek and patted it. "Of course. Now come get something to eat."

I followed her into the dining hall, a trio of her performers singing in soft green robes while a group of men and women watched. On the outskirts stood the man with the noisy boots, his bright red hair spiked on top of his head, similar to the other racers. His beard had swirls carved into it that he kept running his fingers over.

Yura snapped to attention, nodding to the women performing a soft ballad that they usually reserved for dinnertime. I sat at the table, Yura taking in the room, secure in her domain, most of the male eyes on her, but especially the red-haired man. As she finally sat next to him and he took her hand, a collective groan seemed to ensue through the room.

I knew then, without really having definitive proof, that Yura was more than an entertainer, more than her father's right-hand woman. There was a reason there were so many men with stun sticks patrolling the grounds and it wasn't just to protect the compound's earnings. When the man stroked Yura's arm and she cozied up to him, my stomach dropped.

No Yura. Not you.

I couldn't watch anymore, flashes of my mother and Wiid under my eyelids. I took my steaming dinner of rice and curried mashed yams topped with aili berries out to the hanger and sat in my hover with Reggi. Silently eating until Pinu flew in to join me and peck off my plate.

"Something wrong?" Reggi asked, his mouth twitching a little while he screwed in the bolts at the top of the battery cover on the hover.

"Just hungry," I lied, and refused to look at him until my face relaxed from its state of shock.

Once my hover passed all its test flights the next day, I insisted to Shakratel that I was ready to live on my own. I'd already been shuttling passengers back and forth for him since I'd arrived. I knew all the routes. He sat across from me, heaving his barrel chest, his grey belly flapping over his leather skirt-like pants. "Idi, it not safe out der for you."

Yura came in, all in a flutter, and sat next to me. "You not leaving?"

"It's better on my own. I can't keep being in your debt." *Or watching men paw at you.*

Shakratel exhaled loudly. "We been over dis before, Idi. You earn much, much coin with fabric. You work hard. You not burden on compound."

Yura looked at me sideways, inspecting me carefully. "It not something someone said or did? If so, we not let them back." She looked so fierce I was afraid to tell her the truth. I couldn't get to where I needed to be if I was dependent on them. At some point, I was going to leave and if I stayed with them it would be that much harder to strike out on my own. Plus, Yura's everyday conversations with those men brought back too many bad memories, shadows darkening my every thought.

Shakratel held out a small medallion. "This you Gnasher ID. It give you different name and make it so no one say you hover stolen. Stick it to your pilot's wheel in case security drones raid you while you on a run for me." He stood up like the matter was settled.

"There's a cave…" Yura said.

Shakratel groaned and glared at her.

"It close to here. It perfect for her." She clapped her hands and Shakratel and I followed her outside. I wasn't certain if I wanted this alternative to staying at the compound. I felt that twisting of changing my mind again and wished that my parents were back here. I could almost feel the breath of their ghosts on my skin, and I jumped out of the leather chair in Shakratel's office, running back to his hangar to see if there was another cargo run. Not because I liked flying, but because I liked running from my emotions a lot more than I did facing them.

I was certain I could find the cave on my own, but Shakratel and Yura had insisted on coming. We made our way toward the Scraggs, a collection of tall rock cliffs that surrounded Zeto City, some still bearing pockmarks and blackened bottoms from the war.

I slowed down the engines so we were floating, the new couplings making it possible without stalling out. The early morning sun lit a short ledge of rock that led into a cave opening just big enough to fit my hover, with a few feet of clearance on each side. Pinu released the landing gear. She spread her black wings high, knocking into me, then folded them back, cheeping cheerfully.

Once we landed, a few touch lanterns came on, which must have been installed despite my asking them not to make a fuss.

"Oh, look those lantern look good," Yura exclaimed, like she was surprised.

I felt bad for judging her. Her long braids trailed down her back and swished as she reached up to hit a switch that made the rest of the cave's interior lights flicker on. I saw my reflection in the pilot mirror: short black hair, pale yellow, round eyes staring out at me. I had to look away so that I couldn't acknowledge the fear of finally being on my own.

"Reggi make solar panels up top. You charge everything here. Easy, easy," Shakratel said, pointing to the thick cables that dangled from the rock ceiling. He stretched before clutching his cane and opening the passenger door to head toward the back of the cave. There was a faint sound of gurgling, his shadow dancing along the stone walls.

I followed him, unaccustomed to the uneven, rounded stones underfoot. It was different from walking on cement floors. The rounded stones felt gentle under my boots as I approached a small table and bedroll that had been set up at the back corner, close to a ringed cluster of lights much brighter than the landing lights. I picked up the bedroll. It smelled like Yura's musky perfume.

I was ready to go back to the compound then, though I didn't want to admit it.

"I won't need this. I'll sleep in the hover." I tossed the roll into the cargo hold, getting ready to take Shakratel and Yura back.

"Wait while, Little One," Shakratel said, one hand outstretched like he was going to touch me, but then thought better of it. "You might change your mind. It get mighty cold here at night."

Yura's face squished, her displeasure clear. "Too stubborn, you are Idi."

They had always had enough. They didn't know how my debt to them was pressing on me, weighing my every step in the boots they'd insisted I'd need, but I couldn't pay for. Not to mention the rest of this: lights, solar panels, and repairs from Reggi who was so friendly and eager to help. I was waiting for something to turn, for it all to fall apart, like it had so many times before. I still didn't know what they wanted in return, because I had never seen anyone doing anything just because. Except my parents.

Look how they'd turned out.

I followed the sound of water at the back of the cave, a cleft in the rocks I could easily fit through. The darkness felt familiar, a large succession of boulders leading down to the water. A few breaks in the rock ceiling allowed light in, but my raccoonish eyes easily adjusted to the dark. The undulations of shadows felt familiar and cool, like it could insulate me from the outside world. *So, this is what freedom tastes like.*

"You got plenty a water here. Two streams, dependin' on rainfall," Shakratel said.

Yura folded her arms, looking down at the two of us, her long nose elongated in the dim light. "You too young to be here on your lonesome, Idi." She rubbed her arms, looking very cold. "What if someone follow you here, or you run out of food? Or, if your hover break down. You can still change mind." She looked at me hopefully, like she'd sorted out that I wouldn't enjoy it here, but the light in her eyes shifted when I remained quiet, whisking me back to a place I never wanted to return.

"Can you give me a moment?" I staggered back to the cave from the water cavern, trying to catch my breath as the memory hit me full force.

"Just a few weeks more, when they pay us," Dad said to Mom after almost six months had passed after the war ended and still no coin from the factory's "release program" to get us across the desert to the prairie.

"They're never going to pay us, Guyin, don't you see that?" She hissed back at him, her orange tail flicking back and forth. "This is no place for our daughter."

His failing health made it hard for him to stay upright for his entire shift, so I lingered by Dad's side, rubbing his back while he coughed blood into his sleeve. I dabbed at the stain in his faded blue uniform with cold tea before Mom saw. I tucked the thin cotton blanket around his bony shoulders, only a few fur patches remaining on his thin neck. I couldn't stop his coughing with warm red beetle-broth soup.

I scuttled back and forth, fetching as many cups of warm tea as possible, the black-winged petrukian birds glaring and squawking at me for "wasting resources." Dad kept looking more spent as I wiped away the fresh sheen of sweat from his bald head. One petrukian swooped down and pecked at the bowl, like it wanted me to give it something. Unlike the rest, there was a calm to its blue-rimmed eyes.

"Get your mother, Idris," Dad said finally.

I ran off down the corridor that connected the weaving room with the hover bay, dodging the few hovers coming in for a landing, their massive engines touching down with a menacing growl. I darted over to the repair wing at the edges of the hover hangar where the pilots and mechs congregated. Overseer Wiid stood over my mother, his foot on the edge of her wheeled trolley where she was repairing an elevated hover, its mechanical guts exposed. Wiid wheeled her toward him with a flick of his boot, his mane of purple hair emphasizing his unpleasant, squashed face while he flicked his hairless tail. The closer I got, the more the reek of garlic poured off him.

"You want that family of yours out of here quickly? Do what I say." He bent down and his hand grazed her cheek.

She flinched, pushing him away to wheel herself to standing. Her large, dark eyes beheld me, stress lining her mouth, orange tail flicking back and forth. "Idris…"

"It's time the kid learned a thing or two." He grabbed the lapel of her uniform. She shoved him back.

"I love my family."

"Love ain't nothin but a word for them radio songs. You want out? You know what to do." He thumbed behind him where I'd come from. "That man of yours ain't getting better in Brailesu's poisoned air." He grabbed her from behind and she yelped before he slapped her and she fell to her knees. I ran to her, and the same petrukian from earlier swooped down. Wiid fed it crumbs from his pocket and he stomped off with the enormous black bird on his shoulder, his boots echoing on the cement flooring.

A thin trickle of blood ran down the corner of Mom's mouth. She dabbed at it with a rag from her pocket, smearing engine grease over the wound.

"Don't tell your father," Mom insisted.

"Dad's worse. Please hurry." I grabbed her hand, leading her to where he *was slumped over his tool bag, his eyes closed and breath shallow. His skin was so pale, I was afraid all the blood had been sucked out of him.*

She held him close to her. "Don't leave me, Guyin, do you hear me? Don't leave me here. Tomorrow we'll go, I promise." She rocked him back and forth, holding his head to her chest. I put my small arms around the other side of him while he shivered.

He opened his yellow eyes and smiled weakly at her. "Make sure Little One has a better start in life." He slumped against the loom.

"Idris, take care of him. I'll be back."

"Mom, don't."

I snatched at her uniform, but she was too fast, heading back to the hangar.

A gentle hand grasped the back of my arm and I startled away from it, falling onto the stones below me.

"What happened, Idi?" Shakratel asked, helping me up from the floor of the cave.

"Just a…bad memory. We all have them…after the war…right?" My breath came in gasps as I tried to calm myself, to will them to see me as strong.

Yura enveloped me in her arms, holding me close to her. "You not ready to stay night here. Come back home with us."

She held onto me, and Pinu landed between both of our shoulders, her talons digging into my jacket.

"I think Pinu likes this idea." I smiled weakly, eager to leave before another memory hit me. I let Yura guide me back into the hover, letting my breath settle before I fired up the engines to go back to Shakratel's compound.

CHAPTER 6

TOREF

Toref glanced up in wonder at the golden apples hanging from the trees, dusty-blue sky peeking through. He would have died weeks earlier to see this much food, to know that it could save his mother from starvation. *All I have to do here is reach out and pick it.*

But he didn't want to. Everything was too garish and unreal. He stood up, wiped his hands on his jumpsuit and met Rusty's unsmiling face, his orange mane now soppy in the heat.

"We'll find them. If they're here," Rusty said.

"What do you want in return?" Toref asked, his body still flooded with unspent emotions.

Rusty exhaled and looked toward the hangar where the individual pods were housed, now small and insignificant in the distance. "I get enough coin from running all the games around here." He ran his hands through his mane. "What you good at?"

"Fixing mechanical things, some circuit board bugs, mostly."

Rusty's freckled face brightened. "Really?"

Toref wasn't sure he liked the flicking motion of Rusty's black eyes as he looked beyond the two of them before rubbing his scaled hands together, a whispering sound issuing from the friction. "Brilliant, man.

Just brilliant," Rusty said, and clapped a hand on Toref's back. "Come on. You gotta see the Reserve."

A small trail of green, white, and yellow uniforms, tails swishing back and forth, traipsed past them toward the hangar bay. One Ungar girl with long black braids stopped when she saw Toref. "Kalish, move it!" Her friends called out to her.

She was off before Toref could ask anything.

Giggling rose behind the grove of trees and two girls in white uniforms, their hands dusty from picking apples, waved at Rusty. "Oh Rusty, how are youuuu?"

The other girl, a Hybrid cheetah with dark spots dotting the places where she had skin instead of fur, wrapped her tail around Rusty's thigh.

Rusty's face put up a mask of delight while he slowly extricated himself. "Ladies, it is a pleasure, as always, to see you." He clapped an arm on Toref's shoulder. "Here's my man, Toref, a new arrival."

They smiled at him, until they saw Toref's violet eyes, he was certain, then clocked their attention back to Rusty.

"We were hoping…" the cheetah girl started.

"Sorry, we have projects calling us elsewhere. If you're looking for a good game, Usha's running things on the outskirts of the cafeteria. See you in a few."

They giggled and ran off. Toref watched Rusty in amazement. If anyone was going to help him find his sisters, it had to be him.

"Come on man, you gotta see the Reserve, best place around here," Rusty said, gesturing down the orchard path, picking at one of the golden apples along the way.

Toref struggled to keep up with Rusty who sped ahead, dust kicking up in his wake.

A hovering sound whooshed above them through the trees. Toref looked up, but the sunlight blinded him when he tried to find the source of the sound. He ran to catch up with Rusty, following his orange mane through to the edge of the trees. In the dusty clearing, where a new field of crops lay, Monitor Dolxi touched down and was laying into Rusty, whose head was bent in submission. Toref recognized Dolxi as the beefy adult who'd checked him in on his first night at the Pods.

"That's a 50 coin fine, Rusty. You know better than to let the under-eights play. They've got learning to do."

"Not one of my games. Promise." Rusty looked almost earnest, his gaze meeting Dolxi's broad face without a waver.

Dolxi stepped onto his disc, hovering above them in all his shirtless bulk. He seemed to be one of the calmer child-minders. Toref usually only saw him patrolling and cruising on the late shift. He often waved to kids instead of actively avoiding them like most of the Monitors who only got involved if you were fighting or sick.

"Rusty, I know you fix all the games around here." Dolxi crossed his heavily muscled arms. "Pay up, or I close you down."

Rusty stared at Dolxi for a few seconds before reaching into his pockets reluctantly. Patting one pocket, then the other, a tinkling sounded. He looked defeated and small, his thin back curving as he counted out the coins into Dolxi's palm.

"It's only 40." Dolxi stepped off his hover disc while it floated to the ground before snapping into his hand.

"That's all I got." Rusty emptied the rest of his pockets.

Dolxi turned to Toref. "What about you?"

Toref turned out his empty pockets and Dolxi pointed at both of them. "I don't want to see you fixing anymore games for those young'uns." He nodded and sped off.

"Wait!" Toref called out, but the distant whine of the disc was all he heard.

"You got coin after all?" Rusty asked, his face flushing in patches of purple and red.

"He might know where my sisters Penny and Lena are."

Rusty took off his boots, unfolding his socks. A few coins slipped out and Toref looked at the shiny, round pieces spilling into the dirt. Rusty tossed a few up to Toref, which he caught.

"What's that for?" Toref asked.

"You'll see." Rusty said, winking.

"You lied?" *I need information, not coin.*

"Course I did."

What else is he lying about? Toref thought, then a bigger question came to mind as he watched Rusty count his remaining coin. "How do kids earn coin here anyway?"

Rusty looked at him sideways, like this was common knowledge. "After 30 days of shifts, you get coin. The longer you work, especially if you take extra shifts, the more you earn. Kids who go to school even get some coin."

Toref was genuinely puzzled. "Really? Why?"

Rusty folded his arms, digging his boot in the dirt. "Teach us responsibility, to manage money when we all graduate and leave this blessed place." He started through the field toward a large, dilapidated wood barn in the distance. "Come on, we can't stay out here."

Rusty continued on the path toward the filtered shade where larger vines of grapes and parabela grew, their long purple fruit succulent. Rusty picked one and handed another to Toref. "Fresh stuff is always better."

"Won't we get in trouble?" Toref asked.

Rusty's mouth was set in a grim line. "No rules here, only coin and more coin."

"But—" Toref started.

Rusty cut him off. "The rules that sent me here after the war and don't let me know where my parents are, or why they sent me here? The rules that keep you waiting in impossibly long lines for school or the rules that say Monitors..." his voice trailed off. He stretched, but Toref could feel the anger pouring off him, how it pulled at his freckled skin and made his mane look deflated. Rusty drew back his orange hair into a thick cord, his scaled hands shining in the fading sunlight. Toref felt like it was the first glimpse of his new friend without the razzle dazzle.

"If we don't at least try to follow the Monitor's rules, I won't find my sisters."

"My coin is going to find your sisters, not the Monitors." Rusty looked off in the direction Dolxi had flown over the vines. "Though Dolxi or Xiu are our best allies for finding information." Rusty threw him another coin. "But, even they require a little money to jog their memories."

So, coin was going to get information… He felt a bit of resentment that this place was no different from Rif City.

Rusty finished off the fruit, picked another and handed it to Toref. Toref bit into the soft flesh. The purple juice was sweet and warm. He wiped the juice with his sleeve.

"What do your sisters look like?" Rusty asked.

Toref paused before describing them. He'd seen how Rusty looked at all the girls. "Lena is two years older than me, tall, thin, but a little paler than me."

"The other?"

Toref watched him scan the skies like he was looking for something in the golden streaks of the setting sun.

"Penny is a year younger. She's shorter, like…" like his dad was. That gentle softness their mom said made them pleasant to look at. "She looks almost like my twin, except for her bushy hair and even rounder cheeks."

Rusty held his gaze. "If they're here, we'll find them."

Toref felt warmth spread through his heart, just that prickle of hope lifting him.

Rusty led Toref through the fields to the barn that had its front door blasted off. Bales of hay and cord were coiled up along with sheets of discarded cloth rolled into bundles. Rusty took a seat on the tallest bale and invited Toref up. He kept looking out at the sky, like he expected to find something there, before turning his dark eyes back to Toref. "I haven't seen anyone like them, especially not Ungar." He kept staring at Toref. "Three weeks, you think?"

"It can't be longer than that. I came here a day after a small hover came to pick them up."

Rusty took a thin stick from his pocket and popped it into his mouth. "Small hover?"

Toref nodded.

"Anything else you remember?"

"You can't do this to us!" Lena screamed.

The purple woman snapped an electrocoil whip around them and they cried out louder against its sting.

"Mom, please!" Penny begged.

"Get them out of here, they aren't my daughters anymore."

Toref was sweating when he stopped talking, afraid he'd cry more than he already had. He wiped the moisture away from the corners of his eyes.

Rusty pulled a stick out of his mouth. "What did the hover look like?"

"Really modern, barely fitting the three of them," Toref replied, his breath catching when Rusty's gaze fell.

"How did you get here?" Rusty asked, his eyes focused and flinty in the dim light.

"Walked up to the gates."

Rusty's freckled face widened in awe. "You're bad-ass man. Nobody walks here unless they're asking for the Hybrid gypsies to harvest their livers."

Toref was about to ask how Rusty got to the Orphan Pods, but Rusty plopped onto his side. "Might as well tuck in here for the night, since both our shifts are before dawn." He looked at his arm console, tapping once.

Through the barn entrance, the fields spread out in one long stretch of green and purple rising above the red soil.

"Why don't you sleep in your pod?" Toref asked. The old barn lacked the privacy the pods provided. But he wasn't going to venture through the fields if he didn't have to, not alone.

Rusty's eyes took on a hard glaze. "Can't be in confined spaces."

Toref caught a glint of unease in the way the afternoon light reflected off Rusty's eyes. Rusty turned away from him, and soon he was snoring softly.

What was it like to feel so comfortable that you could drop off in seconds like that? I wonder if I'll sleep better once I find Lena and Penny?

Toref settled back on the bales of hay, spreading the blanket so that the straw didn't poke him in the face when he laid down.

Rusty's breath was uneven and he sat bolt upright, patting his pocket and looking around the abandoned loft like he needed something. When he'd turned completely around and settled back onto the bales again, he stuck a twig in his mouth, arms under his head, looking beyond Toref. "You'll know in three days or less, promise. Between Minerva, me, and your fixing skills, we'll know." Rusty kicked up his feet, spreading a blanket over himself. "Just don't tell me you didn't want to know…when the truth comes out."

"Okay, thanks."

Another thread of pain wound through Toref, settling into his half-empty stomach. Rusty settled back on the pallets, the crickets kicking up and frybugs lighting up around the field. Their rhythmic insect sounds felt eerie. Toref jumped off the bales and trotted out to the vines, picking two more fruits. One for now and something for later. He climbed to the back of the loft and slept on the lowest pallet, away from Rusty's snoring.

Toref dreamt of his sisters picking fruit.

"Penny, Lena! Over here!"

They didn't seem to see him at all. He shouted again, clutching at their light green jumpsuits while they dragged him across the soil to the next row.

"Why can't you see I'm here, I came all this way so we can be a family again."

Toref was finally at the front of the queue after a week of waiting, despite Rusty's offer to help him cut in line. He'd had enough favors from Rusty. Toref needed to feel like he could do this on his own. Plus, he didn't want Rusty watching him fumble over his words. He waited for the Monitor to acknowledge him. Behind her, a flash of red hair caught his eye. The girl Rusty had called Minnie hobbled along.

Monitor Xiu looked up at Toref, her bright pink eyes complimenting the aquamarine feathers growing out from her hairline. *Ah, she'd bought gen-tweaks to try to blend in.* "What is it, Toref?" she asked.

He felt his eyes go wide, his voice wobble and he figured speaking fast would help him stop this shy nonsense.

"My sisters. They're supposed to be here—"

"—Yeah, Rusty already harassed me about it earlier this week. I told him the same thing…" She scanned Toref's arm patch. "I have to go stop a fight in the south fields, so tell me their names real quick."

"Lena, Penny…" he spluttered, so anxious his words were leaving him. "My mom told me…they came before me…but I've been here a month now…I can't find them."

"Full names?" she connected the scanner to her stylus and tapped rapidly at the screen, then shook the tablet. Toref inched closer so he could see the screen. She didn't stop him.

"Penny and Lena Baldashian," he finally exhaled.

"Ages?" She scrolled across the screen with her finger, leaving the stylus on the table.

"Penny's fourteen and Lena's eighteen."

"Hmm…" She kept scrolling, tapped through a few more screens. "Nobody with those names or ages have come through in over a year. Any chance they gave different names when they received their patches?"

Toref knew they would be too scared to do something like that.

"They Ungar like you?" She asked as if she weren't Ungar herself. She didn't wait for him to answer, but showed her screen, the search results pulling up a zero on all fronts. "Nothing even remotely close. Don't have a ton of Ungars anyway. Maybe 200 of you out of the 8,000 we have here."

He felt his whole body go cold, a deep iciness in the pit of his stomach. He didn't know what to do next, everything in him frozen.

"Xiu, your shift change was five minutes ago. Get on it, Ungar!" Monitor Briggs yelled, her green face turning paler as Xiu patted Toref's shoulder before stepping onto her hover disc to zoom off.

Thankfully, she wasn't a witness to Toref crumbling in the dirt, his face covered so no one could see his tears. Everything in his mouth tasted like chalk as every hope inside of him eroded.

My sisters aren't here.

The incredulity of the situation kept him frozen to that spot until someone pushed him over and laughed, kicking dirt in his face.

"Hey! Leave him alone." A familiar female voice yelled at Toref's aggressor.

Toref wiped his face quickly, trying to calm his breathing so it wouldn't look like he'd been crying. He glanced up at Minnie, her flaming red hair a giant halo bursting around her freckled face. He couldn't stop looking at her like there was something in her gentle, pink eyes that would save him from the situation he was in.

"Give me your hand," she said.

Without thinking, he gave it to her, and she pulled him to standing, though he regretted it when he realized how hard it was for her to stay upright.

"It'll get better, you'll see," she said, her hands moving like there was more she wanted to say. "I know where Rusty is. If you want, I can take you there?"

Toref looked away from her, not wanting to be caught out in this private moment, which he knew was stupid. He lived with thousands of other kids. There was no privacy. But he wasn't going to hang around and let anyone witness him in his misery.

"Thanks, I'm going to get back to my shift."

He took off through the orchards, with no intention of returning to his shift.

"Didn't it already end..." Her voice faded away as he picked up his pace.

He had to do something to stop the burning ache that had been eating away at him for too long. There had to be another way to find them.

~

"You sure you want to go back to Rif City?" Rusty asked the next morning, the smattering of dark purple scales along the edges of his slightly reptilian face making him look younger in the dawn light. He'd been watching Toref carefully, almost too close for comfort as they made their way to the north fields after Monitor Xiu had roused them from Rusty's barn where they'd slept that night.

Toref tossed Rusty a length of cord to wrap around the hay bales. "I have to know where my sisters are." He kept watching the two-lane dirt road behind Rusty, waiting for the Monitors to whizz by on their hover discs so he could make a clean escape.

"It's pretty easy to bust out of here. Most don't try it 'cause it's too dangerous out there." Rusty held out a hand for Toref to wait.

"What? I can get back, right?"

Rusty waited until a Monitor hovered past them. "You get three chances, or escapes, if you will. Kids can leave for legitimate job-seeking activities, or to see family, but if you get caught by Hybrid gypsies and you aren't near one of the retrieval tunnels that leads back here, good luck."

Toref considered that this one escape would only give him two more chances to find his sisters before he'd be kicked out, or "graduated" as some of the kids referred to their being thrust into the world at age eighteen.

"I'm going to wait here for an hour in case you change your mind." Rusty threw a burlap bag at him with three precious breakfast rolls: the kinds only the upper-tier kids got after months at the Pods.

What had Rusty traded to get these?

"Whatever you do, if you see Hybrid gypsies or fleshmarketers, press the retrieve button on your arm console." He pointed at tunnels in the distance. "You see all the tunnels around here?"

Toref nodded, the concrete tunnels standing out from the dry earth past the harvesting fields.

"They're leftover after the war, used for rapid transport of troops. If you're near one of their entrances, they'll suck you back here quick." He smiled in a way that sounded like it wasn't a pleasant experience.

Toref looked down at the console in his left forearm. "If I get caught escaping, I'll get quarantined for a month or something, won't I?"

"Better that than someone harvesting your organs and leaving the rest of you for the coyotes." Rusty's eyes were flint.

He pointed back toward the Pod's hangar bay. "You remember Minnie, the redhead?"

Toref nodded.

"Doesn't have any legs 'cause of those fleshmarketers."

So that's why she walks that way, Toref thought. For a moment, he hesitated, the emptiness in his stomach growing and filling with terrible, unsettled nerves.

No, I have to get answers from Mom. It's only a two-hour trek. I've done it before and with far less supplies than this.

He hauled the burlap sack with his water flask over his shoulder and started on the road. He glanced back once at a worried Rusty staring at him.

CHAPTER 7

IDRIS

I had been taking on double shifts, sincerely believing that if I didn't have to sleep, I'd get out of Zeto a lot faster. Have my own cabin by the ocean, you know, all the dreams that foolish teenagers like me dreamt when they didn't know any better.

I woke up late that afternoon to the sound of Yura's voice crackling through the radio, "Idi, you there?"

I shifted from the bench seats at the back of the hover where I'd fallen asleep, Pinu curled up on my lap. I could not understand how an enormous bird, so light in the air, could feel so heavy in her sleep.

The radio crackled again. "Little One, let me know you're alive."

Pinu slid off my belly to the floor and flapped her massive black wings. I stumbled over to the radio in the cockpit, my legs feeling like jelly. "I'm here. What you need?" I asked, mimicking the cadence of her voice.

"We need cargo run to Bliss casino."

I threw Reggi's red hat on over my mussed hair, pulling it down tight in the cooling afternoon air. "Big shots, huh?" I asked.

"They need recycling and pay top coin for us to take their garbage away."

"Really, Yura? Can't someone else do it?" I hated making their recycling runs, half the stuff not cleaned and full of flies so I had to hose it down before I let it into the hover. I'd rather deal with drunk partygoers than haul trash. Though, I got a cut of whatever the casino paid Shakratel and Yura.

"Idi." Her voice was firm.

"I know, I know. I'm going." Plus, this meant my first hot meal of the week.

"How long?" she asked.

"Ten minutes till I'm in the air, and I'll radio when I've got the cargo, unless I have to wash any of it down."

"Thank you Idi. We have nice platter waiting for you and Pinu."

"Yeah, yeah. Thanks, Yura."

Pinu jumped up and down about the hot food.

I tucked in the radio headset, checked the battery levels after recharging. We were at 50 percent, which was enough until we returned to Shakratel's. My stomach grumbled and I knew the longer I waited, the less I would want to make this trash run.

"Come on, Pinu, time to go."

She squealed with her hungry cry, and I fed her the last of our nutbars. I had to satisfy myself with a neutrino drink until we reached Shakratel's. My escape savings had to stay safe from my daily needs coin stash, which was currently empty.

Pinu flew into the open windows and pushed the button for the windows to roll up, and I revved the engines. We were airborne, the city's towers and magnetic bands with their busy traffic already lit up at sunset.

"Strap in, girl."

Pinu pulled on the harness with her beak and tugged until it popped into place. Petrukians were busy birds, and she was wiggling with glee after several days of not flying. Thankfully, she rarely ventured out of the cave on her own. But I was worried a day might come when she'd try and wouldn't come back.

I guess that was what everyone feared on some level: that the thing they loved most would never come back. I saw it in Shakratel's eyes, his grey eye folds turning up when he watched Yura with a new man. Not sure he wanted her to be doing that thing, but also knowing that there was no way he could stop her.

I wondered if Yura loved anyone besides her father? And when it all started or if it would ever stop? If the day would come that she'd decide she'd had enough of men touching her and never committing to her in a way that meant anything.

I shuddered to think of it and steered us toward the bright blue tower of Bliss casino, rising out of the poorer districts to the north of the city, half of the buildings still bombed out after the war, but still full of occupants who couldn't do any better.

I let the hover's magnetic underbelly get pulled into the bands that were created for traffic to seamlessly travel between the five main casinos in the Central District. Bliss, the glitziest casino in the whole area, was almost more glass framed in white stone than anything else. The first time I'd seen it I had almost crashed into two other hovers, and a security drone pulled me over to check my Gnasher ID. I was sweating bullets because it was my first cargo run alone.

Now, I was a pro, shifting down as we coasted along the magnetic bands, keeping to the outer, slow lane so it would be easier to float over to Bliss after passing Stencil's gaudy and grandiose casinos: Flame, Garnet, and Amber. Emerald came next with its green steel tower and gorgeous Ungar murals. They had originally been a form of protest in the aftermath of the Hybrid Wars for the casinos being built before anything else, but in true Whip fashion, she'd just had them touched up and integrated into the elegance of the casino.

The minute we landed at Bliss, the cargo steel doors opened and two cat Hybrid women in light grey uniforms came out to check my Gnasher ID. I hopped out to inspect whatever they were going to stuff in my cargo hold.

"Taxi, taxi!" A young Hybrid woman in a long billowy red gown called out to me, running barefoot. Her dress was stained at the hem, her tail swishing, trying to keep her balance as she stumble-ran. Her makeup was smudged away to reveal skin that glistened like Shakratel and Yura's. Once she was closer, I noticed she was much younger than I'd estimated. Her hair was long and curly, similar to Yura's, with a bounce that I could only dream of.

"There are other taxis around the front." I said first in Stan, then in Hybrid Kesh. She ran into my hover's open cargo door and bolted inside.

Already the workers were unstrapping the containers of recycling I needed to make sure didn't need washing. An acrid smell filled the hover. I needed to get this woman out.

"To Shakratel's now, please," she pleaded, tears streaming down her face.

That was a first.

I had picked up enough fares of women like Yura, except not so classy or clean. Cuts often on their shoulders and tails, bite marks along their necks, sometimes missing fingers and toes from prior incidents. I turned around to look at her and Pinu cheeped. I glared at Pinu who made a sorrowful sound that hopefully the woman couldn't hear. I wasn't eager to cut out on the recycle haul, but I also knew that I couldn't ignore whatever had happened to this girl. "You got coin for that long distance? It costs at least 30 silver."

"I pay now. Go. Please." She threw a bag of coins at us that Pinu picked up in her bill.

"I'll give you the change when we get there," I said, watching the workers making their way slowly down the gangplank. "Hey, I'll be right back, I need to recharge my batteries, they're running low."

"You're slated to take this stuff, either take it now, or lose the coin," one worker called out to me.

Yura would be pissed if I missed this run.

"Load four crates in then." I rushed out to help them, bits of muck still sticking to half the stuff in the plastic crates. After everything was loaded in, the vinegary sweet aroma of the garbage made me want to gag.

"Just go," the girl said, now shivering when I strapped back in.

"Grab the blanket in the back," I said to Pinu who hopped over to help her.

In the rearview mirror I caught a Hybrid cheetah man in a suit chasing after us. The dark contour of his suit fabric and sculpted beard told me he was somebody important. If I didn't move quick he'd have the security drones coming after us.

When we were almost aloft, an object thunked against the copilot's side before we coasted toward the magnetic rings. He was getting ready to throw another bottle at us. I gunned us forward, floating us on the rings and aiming us toward the lights of the Os Dam's tower. Once I was certain we weren't being chased, I looked behind and the girl was keeled over, not even strapped in. Pinu was still beside her, spreading the blanket over her.

"Hurry, please," she said faintly. Pinu wouldn't leave her side, which meant something was definitely wrong.

I got on the radio. "Yura? Is Yura there? Radioing Shakratel compound."

It took several minutes before anyone answered. "She's busy, you gotta message?"

"Yeah, I'll be there with the recycling delivery, but I got a sick passenger in tow that needs help. She specifically asked for Shakratel."

When we landed there were an abundance of guys, some traders, others racers or fleshmarketers all gathered around smoking their pipes. One of the taller ones sneered. "Look who's back. Loser taxi and her stupid bird."

"Get Yura," I said to one of Shakratel's squat body guards. He ran in and seconds later Yura darted out.

"She asked for Shakratel. She's really hurt," I said, opening the cargo door, Reggi darting out to help unload. Pinu was still tutting over the girl shivering on the floor, blood seeping out of the corner of her mouth. I rushed over to her, dabbing a corner of my pocket hand-kerchief at her mouth. She coughed and more blood came out as Yura helped me sit her up.

Reggi was calling out instructions for the recycling.

"Oh, Samrah. Why?" Yura said to the girl.

So, she knows her.

Yura continued murmuring to Samrah in Myrel, bits about her not leaving and other things I couldn't understand.

"Get Shakratel now," Yura ordered, and I ran inside to find him limping toward me with his heavy staff. I had never seen him look so worried.

"Idi, is it our Samrah?" he asked, his large wrinkled face turned down in a worried frown.

"Yes…there was a guy…a suit…he came after us."

Shakratel quickly spoke in Myrel to two of his bodyguards who went to the back hangar bay, cranking up the radios. "We in for a long day. Come get something hot to drink, Idi. It best you put the hover in the bay for whole day." A look in the set of his eyes said I wasn't to argue because there was more he was going to say when we didn't have a crowd watching.

"I can help carry her, then I'll eat," I said. I had tended to my dad all those years, hadn't I?

I helped the bodyguards carry Samrah as Yura spoke softly to her in Myrel. Pinu settled on Shakratel's shoulder while he smoothed down her feathers. I almost didn't notice my hover being towed into the bay and the awful silence that settled over the compound that was normally almost too lively for my taste.

Two more women came in royal blue robes that swished as they helped us carry Samrah through the dining hall. I followed them behind the silk divider to the area that usually only paying customers came through. It was eerily silent as they cut off Samrah's robe to cleanse her light purple flesh where she had been bitten in multiple places on her shoulder and chest. Her eyes were closed and her skin so ashy that I wasn't certain she was going to make it. Yura barked orders, and we all followed. I got into a rhythm of cleaning the wounds, refreshing the water, back and forth until I was dizzy from hunger.

"Go eat. Come back in half hour," Yura said.

Reggi appeared in the doorway. "I've saved your favorite spicy yams and chicken," he said, winking. I followed him into the dining hall. I needed to believe it was easier to concentrate on food than worry about why Samrah's wounds filled me with dread.

Reggi and I sat in the hangar bay, away from the noise and bustle. It felt good to be there in the flickering work lights, away from everyone whispering about Samrah. Didn't they all see such things everyday outside the compound?

"Who is she?" I asked Reggi.

He shrugged. "I think I heard Shakratel say something about her being his niece."

"And working at Bliss?" I asked.

He smiled a little. "Loads of people leave here to work at Bliss. They think they can earn more, get more famous, whatever stupid reasons they have. Some of them come back, the lucky ones, but most don't." There was a sad look on his face, and I felt a personal note to his tone.

"You worked at Bliss?" I asked. "I mean, you got skills fixing stuff that could make you famous." I smiled and then remembered myself.

Reggi grinned back. "No, I'm smart. I know a good thing when I see it." He watched me a bit too long.

Voices were loud along the corridor behind us. We'd left the door open between Shakratel's back offices and the hangar bay. The people came closer, and I heard Stan interspersed with Myrel that I could understand.

"She didn't want this…" Shakratel said.

"I tried stop her…but that's the one she choose. They offer much much coin…it too much to resist."

Shakratel let out a groan.

"She perform for hundreds 'stead of small crowd here." Yura sniped back.

"You know...how she was...that this not good life for her!" Shakratel bellowed in Myrel.

"We try save her. No good arguing will do," Yura stomped off, and the door into the hangar swung shut.

Reggi scooted his wheeled stool closer to me. "You caught some of that?" His large hands looked useless as he fidgeted, grabbing a bit of copper wire and looping it through his hands, coiling and recoiling it.

"So, she went against Shakratel's wishes...to become what?" I asked.

Reggi leveled his dark eyes with mine. "Probably a singer. I heard she had an amazing voice. Good painter, too. All the art here was done by her."

I looked at the nearby wall mural and thought about what could make someone leave such a good life at Shakratel's.

He scratched his head and put the copper wire down, coming just close enough that I felt something in the air change between us. "She started out as a singer-artist, but the casinos always ask for more. They aren't satisfied with your work. They want all of you, and when they're done with you..." he gestured outward. "You see what happens."

He was so quiet that I felt this moment of understanding pass between us. I took his hand, squeezed it twice before getting up to go to the bunk I usually stayed in on the west side of the compound. Pinu flew over to my shoulder as I made my way through the dim light, still conjuring Samrah's pale face, and vowing that I would never let anyone do that to me.

Never, never, never. I repeated over and over while Wiid's hands reached for me in the dark. I took out a knife, swiping for his face in my mind.

Then, I tried to imagine they were Reggi's hands reaching for my waist, but my mind wouldn't let go of its fixation on my past. I exhaled as I opened my eyes and called out to Pinu. "Come on girl, it's time for rest."

CHAPTER 8

TOREF

Sweating from his two-hour trek, salty perspiration dripping down his dark face, Toref stood in front of the dilapidated block of green flats that he had grown up in. He knew he had to confront his mother, no matter how much he was trying not to be afraid. He took another swig of water, letting the water slowly trickle down his throat, small rivulets streaming down the sides of his face, unable to move from where he stood in the sand. This was where he'd last seen his sisters.

"You can't do this," Lena screamed.

If he'd been faster, he could have stopped all of it. But, would he have been a match against the sting of an electrocoil whip? He'd seen the scars on his father's arms and legs from his service in the Hybrid Wars.

He trudged up the stairs, his feet leaden and heavy. Each step beat out a thud, thud, thud accompaniment to his racing heart. He unrolled his old shirt, full of holes, and shook it a few times before slipping it back on. He left the water canister out in front of him. He'd start with that.

"Where did you send them?" he asked the empty air.

He kept practicing this question to himself while he waited at his mother's locked front door. The entire breezeway was empty, the sun now at its apex in the sky. He rapped his fist on the metal latticework door to the flat where he'd lived his entire sixteen years, until three weeks ago.

No response.

He beat again, shaking the frame.

Still nothing, not even a flicker of movement from the neighboring flats. He knocked louder again, wanting to shake the metal door loose from its rusty hinges. Sweat beaded on his forehead, his canister of water warm now against his leg.

He wondered if his mom had gone or…*no, I can't think that. I have to find my sisters. Someone must know something.* He went along the entire floor, knocking on doors, waiting and repeating the action until he realized no one was coming out.

He started to descend the steps, making sure to avoid the rusty holes in the wobbly steel stairs. A squealing echoed behind him stopped him. The bolts on a door squeaked and banged against the wall.

"Toref? Is that you?" His mother ambled along to where he stood in the breezeway. "My boy." Her eyes were so bloodshot that her purple irises glowed. Skeletal hands reached out for him. "I knew you'd never leave me."

"You sent…me…away…" His voice caught, and he wiped his nose on his shirt. He was afraid to touch her. *She might fall apart.*

The minute she crouched down, clearly exhausted by the effort of staying upright, he ran to her, careful when they embraced. She smelled like dust and sweat.

"I have water and food for you…" He held out the water and she snatched it without saying a word, immediately chugging.

"You always were so good to me."

"Mom, where are the girls?" *So much for easing into that.*

Her face immediately darkened, the shadows under her eyes engulfing her cheeks and neck, pulling her back down to a place where he couldn't reach her. "Ingrates, *tafla*…" she cursed in Hybrid Kesh. "They're where they deserve to be."

He fought to keep his voice from wobbling. "But…you said… they're at the Orphan Pods…and they're…not."

She reached for him, catching hold of his arm, her raggedy nails digging into his flesh, bringing her face so close their noses almost touched. "Loyalty has a price, my son."

"Tell me where they are." He fought against her hold on him, remarkably strong for her frail state. *I'll topple her if I move too suddenly.*

"Forget about them. They're fine, living the high life…nowhere you need to worry about." Her mouth turned up in a sour smile, and he knew then: she wasn't going to tell him anything. The woman who had raised him was dead. Some part of her had disintegrated with his father in the factory accident. He reached for the canister, but she held fast to it. She caught sight of something, her eyes widening.

"Your chip…" She clawed at his forearm, dropping the canister, which clunked down the stairs, rolling off into the sand.

"Tell me where they are! I can get you food, water, anything you need," he pleaded, sweat pooling in his lower back.

Before Toref could withdraw, she released his arm, wrapped her hands around his neck, squeezing. He fought against her, trying to keep from breaking her frail body. If he accidentally killed her, he would be at fault. No Orphan Pods, no trying to make his way as a scavenger of electronics. He'd be sold to the hungriest fleshmarketers and all of his organs harvested until his last breath.

"Give the chip to me!" she growled.

"No. It's not possible…" He twisted away from her, stars appearing before her face dimmed.

Yanking against her hold, he dropped his body weight against the railings, hoping he didn't tumble down the metal stairs. She let him fall. He rolled to the side, the railing bowed, but held his weight.

He kicked out, his vision returning, and she fell in a heap on the landing. His satchel had fallen beside her and he left it, darting down the stairs three at a time to get away, grabbing the water canister before she did.

"You can't leave me. I've got no one," she croaked.

Toref stopped in the sand, backing away, watching her crawl on her knees to the edge of the railing. Her thin, light brown face so similar to his older sister, Lena's.

"Don't deny me…the chip's enough for both of us."

"Tell me where Lena and Penny are," he yelled, his voice breaking.

She clutched at the sack, riffling through it, and bit into one of the rolls, ignoring him. Was this how it was going to end between the two of them?

"If you don't tell me—" Toref started before seeing a door open.

An elderly Hybrid neighbor opened his door gingerly, thin reptilian tail wagging before he saw Toref's mother. Then he slammed and bolted his door.

Toref didn't want this to be the last thing he remembered about his mother. She sighed, burped, and slunk back up the stairs, not looking back, saving him from being the one to walk away.

CHAPTER 9

IDRIS

Yura laughed a little too loudly at the gambler's jokes—his spiky hair making him look like a porcupine, his heavy cologne wafting down over where I sat. I had to take a step back and accidentally knocked the chair against the table too loudly, jostling his malt drink at the other end.

I hadn't intended to stay but couldn't help watching the gentle circling and how it seemed to happen effortlessly for some men with Yura, and for others not at all. The gambler stopped to look at me, and I rushed outside through the doors of the dining hall, out to the patio in the back where Yura kept her prized orchids and aili berry bushes. *I can't watch Yura pretend to like this guy and imagine what will come next.*

The moon was full on the horizon of the dark prairie, the shadow of the red outline of the second waning moon like a sore spot in the clear night sky. I smelled Yura's burning feratik stick before she called out to me.

"Idi, he harmless." She approached me carefully, her heeled sandals slapping against the pea gravel. She put a hand on my bare shoulder. "Why it bother you?"

I looked up at Yura's grey eyes, ringed in worry. I had been dreading this conversation, hoping Yura didn't notice how I felt about the men she paid attention to, never mind the ones Shakratel had to haul off the premises. "Something happen you not tell me?" she hissed lightly, exhaling smoke over her right shoulder, away from me. "You knows him?"

I shook my head, stepping closer to her. "No, I don't know him. I just—"

How did I explain to her that I knew the type?

"I don't understand how you can let him touch you, then next week...it's someone else." For other girls who worked with Yura it was sometimes a new guy every night and there was very little discernment, if they had the right amount of coin and weren't hideous.

I recalled my mother's face after an encounter with Wiid, how each time she seemed paler, more withdrawn, and eventually died of the disease I was sure he gave her.

Yura put the stick into a holder on the patio, its spicy scent curling around us. "I not let them all touch me. Shakratel definitely not let them all. Over his dead minerals."

I couldn't help laughing, but then I spotted the serious look that softened when Yura embraced me. There was more to it as she took my hands, her soft white robe sleeves falling over both our palms. I wondered, had my mother lived, if this would have been the sort of conversation we'd have had.

"I not like a lot other. Some of the girls, they not stay here, they not want see many men. They find one and they leave dis place. But, I not give my heart away." Her voice had a hitch and she squinted before continuing on, looking around me, but not in my eyes. "My heart taken during the war, and when that love died and we need entertainer and sometimes sleepers, then I do that. It easier than every day same man, same story and me not free." She exhaled and looked at me, her pupils wide and dilated, the rest of her pristine, chiseled face drawn, her mouth in a tight line.

"I must be free, and you understand dat. But I also need a little love —not much—just a little, and then I happy to send him away." She smiled a little, but the mirth didn't travel to her eyes.

She put her arms around me, her soft robes soothing against my bare arms. "It not easy life, but I choose it, and it keep me from thinking about my dead soldier."

I put my head on Yura's shoulder, not sure how much I could ask, since it was the first I'd heard about him. "What was his name?" I asked, holding Yura closer.

"Yizdi," Yura looked so sad then, all the light gone out of her eyes. She took my hand and walked us back to her feratik stick, taking a long drag before exhaling again. I was half tempted to ask for a drag myself, but knew that Yura would tell me I was too young.

"You not worry, Idi. It be different for you, my love. Little One has different life, a different freedom, you'll see." She winked, kissing me on the cheek. "You not fully grow up in middle of war." She took a drag of the feratik. "It mos'ly over when you still little, yes?"

I watched her finishing the last of the stick before its end went from bright red to ash grey, and we stood in the rising moon, so much unsaid between us.

"Yizdi must've been someone very important, Yura."

"He was the best man I know, except Shakratel. But he my dad, so it easy to say so." Yura smiled and brought me into her shoulder, though I was taller.

"It's still hard to not worry for you, Yura," I said, thinking of my mother, wishing that there had been some sense of closure there.

Reggi popped through the awning and bowed to Yura.

"I go back to him now," Yura winked at me. "We talk again tomorrow, yes?" She cupped my chin before sauntering off through the double doors.

I did not want to be alone with Reggi after that revelation. Yura stepped away before I could ask her for a few more minutes. I knew Yura had to be free to earn coin in her own way. Even if it felt like there was something more noble out there than having to entertain every lowlife, racer, or gambler that made their way through the compound. I had to hand it to Yura, she never showed any indication of disgust. *I would never be able to manage that.*

Reggi took off his hat, his head fur mussed. He shuffled back and forth, and one of Yura's white giant orchids swung in front of him, startling him. He took a step back and laughed a little, but I could tell it was a nervous laugh, not a laugh of genuine amusement.

"So, I took a look at the landing gear..." he started, his hands twisting in front of him.

"I told you it was fine." I didn't need to spend more coin on my hover than necessary. Reggi was always trying to find ways of making it fly more efficiently until I could afford a major upgrade.

"Pinu didn't think so." He arched a thick black eyebrow.

I like those eyebrows a lot. I took a step back in the pea gravel, the crunching sound giving my retreat away, startled by the thought of his eyebrows, almost unable to not look at them.

"So, you're talking to each other now?" I asked.

"Yeah, you know, she has a special vocabulary, just for me." He smirked and blew dust off his hat.

I wished he'd stop fidgeting and step closer to where I could see his eyes.

"Pinu only talks to me, you know." I took that first step to him, my heart racing. Unsettling me but driving me forward.

"That's what you think." He stood there, his hazel eyes shining in the string of patio lights, his grin so wide each freckled cheek was round with mirth. He spread his hands, opening and releasing. They were cleaner than I'd ever seen them. In fact, he wasn't wearing his coveralls, I realized. He wore a simple embroidered tunic and fitted shorts.

I looked down at my jumpsuit, the arms cut off and the front open to my navel, revealing my red chest band. I folded my arms protectively around my skinny body. I was hungry again, even though I'd just eaten. But this hunger resided in a subbasement layer I wasn't fully aware of until Reggi stepped closer, the aroma of wood scent and something delicious on his skin. Like he was a forest, and I was just there, somewhere beneath all his branches.

"So, I can show you, if you like?" It didn't quite sound like he was talking about the landing gear, and he held out his hand like he expected me to take it. I contemplated the thick, furred fingers, my gaze traveling up to his broad chest and his round, pleasant face. But could I trust him? I looked through the dining room, already bustling with Yura's girls singing in Myrel harmonies, their skin glistening as they sang the haunting atonal tunes the rock people were famous for.

I wouldn't be alone, not really, with so many people around at the six-day's end. I went through the patio double doors and looked behind me as he held the door open. Reggi searched me with his eyes. He put a hand gently on my shoulder, and it felt natural for him to follow me through the crowd, his hand releasing when the music was no longer audible, players concentrating over their Ruga tables. Shakratel nodded to us as we headed down the white-walled corridor and out to the repair hangar.

I shut the hangar's metal door, and all the bustle of the compound whooshed silent behind us, our boots echoing on the cement floor. Reggi's station looked different. Everything was in its place and yet newer, shinier. "What did you change?" I asked.

"You like it?" His freckled cheeks flushed, and he ran a hand through his hair. The ends curled back, and a flash of crimson ran along his center part. I felt a rush through my navel and tried to look away to calm myself because the urge to touch his face was over-powering.

"So, the landing gear is just over here. I'll stay quiet so we don't wake Pinu," he said softly, pointing to where she was snoring in her copilot's chair.

"Yeah, she sleeps all the time. I'm not worried about it."

His expression changed, like he'd said the wrong thing, and I instantly regretted how I sounded.

"The wheels, um, here…come closer…" he shone the work lamp on the wheel shaft. "The shocks are worn thin and the wheels as a result are starting to crack under the strain. I can…" he stopped and just stared at me, his gaze falling on my lips.

"You're right—Pinu has been complaining about my shoddy land-ings. But, I can't afford new gear yet." I crossed my arms, then felt too businesslike and tried to adopt a more casual stance but decided on folding my arms again instead. I couldn't afford more gear. I could barely keep both Pinu and me fed and keep up my savings for flow batteries to leave the valley.

"Shakratel said you can live on site and save some coin. Probably pick up more fares that way." Reggi lit up a little when he said it.

A fresh breeze blew by, and for half a second, I wanted to consider it, to surrender my hard-won freedom to be here where loneliness would be the farthest thing from my mind.

"You can think about it. You don't have to decide today, next six-day or even in the next thirty-day. I can fix this in the next two days, if you like? You'd need to stay on site, though, to test it." He looked hopeful when he said it.

"I can't. I have to start an early shift, Reggi, you know that."

He took a step toward me, his hand closing over mine, my back resting against the hover, the metal still warm on my spine from part of the hover peeking out from the hangar into the sun.

"Please, Idris, let me do this."

His hand traced my bare arm, his large hands soft against my arms, moving so slowly in soft circles, my nerve endings singing softly against his touch. "Oh…"

"I've liked you since you first came Idi, weeks back… please…" He took one step closer, his face within a few inches of mine, eyes focused on my lips.

I felt a shudder go through me. I closed my eyes only for Wiid's face to appear in my memory, his voice replacing Reggi's, superim-posed over Reggi's gentle whisper.

You'll never be free of me. I own you. Always.

My eyes snapped open, and Reggi startled when I stumbled back, releasing his hold on my hand.

"No, no, no, Reggi." I backed away, eyes filling with tears and doubled over on his stool, trying to knock Wiid's voice out of my head. Heaving sobs wracked my body, and Reggi hovered around me—not touching me, but also not leaving me. I was surprised he hadn't run.

"Bad memory from Before?" he asked.

"Yeah…"

"Can you tell me?" he asked.

"Nah, just stupid *tafla*." I waited for the shuddering to subside, to get my breath again. "I'd burn him down with the best flame torch if I could." This was where I felt safe, in the violence of destroying versus having to resolve what had happened and the feeling that Wiid was responsible for far more than he'd ever be able to account for.

"Cut him up with a six-sided facet knife," Reggi offered.

"Then, what's left of him can be skewered by Shakratel's bodyguards."

"Even better, I'd kill him myself, feed his carcass to Stencil." Reggi grinned.

"Let's do it, next six-day, huh? Bust into Brailesu, unless someone else's already done it for me." I hunched, trying to keep the clacking sound of the looms out of my memory by saying its name, the crashing of overwhelming memories trying to stay at bay. The image of killing Wiid over and over again was simpler than easing myself into the deep responsibility only he could carry, but I managed to remain burdened with.

Reggi stood by my side under the work lights and gently, almost as if asking, hovered an arm around my shoulder, barely touching my skin. He waited until I nodded and pulled me into him. The wood smell dissipated and the memories burst from me.

"You don't have to stay so far away. Not from me. I know how bad Brailesu was," he whispered.

"No, you don't," I whispered back. "Nobody does."

We sat in the light, and he said nothing as I hummed the song I'd sung to my father as he'd lay dying in the factory.

I woke up hours later in my single bunk in Yura's women's section of the compound. Reggi's red hat lay next to me. Except for Pinu, I was alone.

CHAPTER 10

TOREF

By now, the Monitors would know Toref had escaped. His mom's violet eyes swam before him, and he had to refocus on something else. His exposed skin baked in the desert sun with no vegetation tall enough to offer shade. He stamped his feet, dust clouds rising, to try and keep himself from rehashing the memory of his sisters being carried away, their flailing limbs reaching toward their cowering mother. *Wherever they are, I'm certain they weren't stupid enough to cross the desert in search of her.*

From a distance, the dirt-packed highway looked like it could holdup in a rainstorm, but when his bare feet touched the cracks, the packed earth crumbled. The sky was a deep, hazy blue—no chance of rain—and he still had ten kilometers left to walk. If Lena and Penny were there, they would have sung to him, urging him onward.

Fool you once,
fool you twice
three times
blind as mice.

He repeated his little rhyme to keep his mind busy during his trek back to the Orphan Pods complex, scanning the barren landscape for shade. It only worked for a few minutes.

Toref pressed a button in his console: it read out the time (15:47), his distance from the next source of water (1.3 km), and the closest town (Skez). Nothing there about how to mend his aching heart, or where his next of kin might reside. Or how to banish his circling thoughts, coming back like predatory vultures, from his mind.

Mom is past redemption. He hung his head, sweat pouring off his neck, only to evaporate halfway down his back. With only a few hours of daylight left, he had to keep a clear head. *I have to stay alive for Lena and Penny. They have to be out there, somewhere.*

He looked for any security drones that could be following him, but the sky remained a painful aquamarine. He glanced at his forearm console, glowing an electric sapphire that showed he was moving too slowly. He glanced behind him: only red stone hills beyond. The sun was setting, and the coyotes called to their packs. He had maybe two more hours of hiking and that wouldn't get him to the Orphan Pods before sunset.

Crap. Why did I trek all the way out here?

He crouched in the red dirt, hands over his head while his thoughts crowded all reason out, his heart trying to burst from his chest. *I have to do something…think, think.* His skin felt unnaturally cool, the image of his mother's swollen face, and her skinny arms strangling him, popping into his mind yet again.

His console flickered again. There was a distress button. Didn't Rusty say something about those tunnels he could use to get back? He didn't know if it would work this far out, but he could try. A swell of drums and bagpipes rose in the distance.

Hybrid gypsies. His heart thudded loudly in his ears. *I have to get going, but where?*

He could either die of thirst, get eaten by coyotes, or get in trouble at the Pods for skipping out. Their quarantine sentences were pretty severe.

The drums got closer, the bass pounding a beat in his chest.

I'm better off being quarantined than dying.

Sorting through the menus on the glowing blue console in his arm, another gust of dust halfway obscured the screen while he found the retrieve option and depressed his finger.

Before he could release the button, wind stirred up all around him, an opening swirling a few feet ahead of him. The noise of the Hybrid gypsies was too close for comfort. He darted into the tunnel. *Here we go...*

He was sucked downward and engulfed in darkness. "Ahhhhhh!" he yelled while a spray of water doused him, making it hard to breathe. Grit abraded his arms as he sped through what appeared to be the container for a concrete well. The noise was deafening as he picked up velocity. He closed his eyes, the shuddering increasing around him, curling his body further into a ball. *Moons above, make it stop.*

He came to an abrupt halt, the tunnel dumping him out onto a cement basin. He lay sprawled before two Monitors and several older teens in grey uniforms. They must've been the ones maintaining the transport tunnel. One of the Monitors zoomed off, and Rusty stepped forward with a girl on each arm. "Looks like the old retrieval tunnels still work, huh Briggs?"

"That's Monitor Briggs to you, young Rusty." Monitor Briggs chided, two antennae sticking out of either side of her hairless head as she inspected her tablet. She levitated over on her hover disc, close to Toref. She was his least favorite. He had a feeling that the sentiment was mutual from the look on her pale, lime-green face.

The girls on either side of Rusty leaned over to look at Brigg's tablet, their green- and purple-haired heads bobbing in unison. Why had Rusty brought them?

"Yes, Ma'am," Rusty finally said, voice tinged with rudeness.

"No." Briggs continued to stare at her tablet.

"Sorry?" Toref was confused. Did she think he was someone else?

"I am not a ma'am. Lutana Hybrids don't have a gender. Remember from your arrival tutorials?"

Toref was about to point out that the arrival tutorial said something different, but decided against it.

"You were found out of bounds. Missing for approximately five hours. Please present your chip."

Toref handed it over reluctantly, afraid he would get punished for keeping it inside his cheek. Could they see all the places he had been?

Her antennae emitted a yellow light that scanned the surface of the chip. Then, her yellow eyes lit up, her human face settling into a satisfied expression as she placed the chip back in Toref's console.

"You went far, Baldashian. I am surprised you survived. Your dehydration levels are exceedingly high, and you will need to recover your body mass loss. You're confined to your quarters for four weeks, or until your case can be reassessed."

"Four weeks?" Toref was astounded. He'd expected ten days max. He groaned and covered his gritty face. At least he could have a shower whenever he wanted if he was stuck in his pod.

Rusty was stifling a laugh, and the two girls weren't too far behind.

Briggs lifted an eyebrow. Instead of hair, she had a long snakelike bulk of flesh that rearranged its mass on either side of her shoulders. "This is a light sentence considering the danger you could have brought with you in the transport tunnel." She nodded toward Rusty and company. So he had turned Toref in. He was too numb to feel any anger toward Rusty.

"If you satisfactorily pass all tests and tutorials while confined to your pod block, you may begin classes in four weeks, unless the Head Monitor decides to give you leniency after two weeks. However…" she leaned into him, whispering, "I don't think you deserve it, Ungar." She zoomed off, her hover disc whisking her away with an electronic whine.

He'd hated it when people had seen his purple irises in Rif City and acted like he was lesser than them just because his family were among the few who hadn't bought mods to upgrade themselves to look like Hybrids. There were all sorts of complications that resulted from Ungar taking the cheap stuff that gave them fuzzy ears and a small tail but didn't quite align with their DNA, so their bodies started to reject the mods. His parents had known it left them all at risk from the fleshmarketers, who made money by creating new Hybrid mixes from Ungars bought or captured.

What does it matter now I'm here?

He followed her out as water flowed back into the basin. Rusty rejoined him at his side, running a hand through his mane of orange hair. It looked a little more tame than usual. He slung one arm around the green-haired girl and the blue-haired one walked apart from them. The brown awnings of the hangar bays lay ahead and for the first time, Toref felt glad to be there. A hush fell over the group as they walked through the hangar and the Individual Orphan Pod Array where Toref had slept before Rusty invited him to the barns.

The setting sun cast a golden glow on the vines hanging down from the ceiling of the hangar bay. He would have liked to have eaten in the cafeteria with everyone else, to enjoy the last few hours of daylight, knowing he was safe. He was lucky if he spent seven hours a day in his pod before he'd met Rusty, and that was only for sleeping. Now, the communal shower, toilets, and eating facilities he enjoyed were off-limits during quarantine. More like prison, he thought darkly.

"Well, Bud, I'm sure you'll appreciate the barn even more now you're stuck in your pod." Rusty shivered, clapped a hand on his shoulder and took off. "Don't worry, we'll figure something out." He flashed Toref a wry smile.

"Thanks," Toref muttered, feeling even more dark inside, watching Rusty's departure. His mind turned back to his family.

He knew he should feel lucky, being far better off than his mom, and possibly his sisters as well. But when he looked at the IOPA system, District 93, he felt doomed to a frustrating fate. He watched the system rotate and reconfigure for a new kid going back to their pod, and he didn't know how he could stay in that 12-by-12 foot space with no windows and a shabby skylight for the next month. As much as he liked being a rule follower, the injustice made him want to figure out a way to rig the system in his favor. *Especially to escape the punishing thoughts my mind will give me once I'm fully alone.*

CHAPTER 11

IDRIS

AGE 16

"Why did I do this to myself?" I exclaimed, my eyes stinging. I had forgotten to wipe my hands clean on my overalls before touching my face. I was sweating so much that my vision blurred while I attempted to screw the last bolt in place for the new hover blades I'd installed. *I should have waited for Reggi to do this.* I felt a greasy smear across my nose and crawled out from under my hover to wipe it off. *Why did I do this on my birthday, of all days?*

Three days without solid food was catching up to me. The emergency protein tablets weren't giving me enough juice to keep me fully lucid. I threw the remaining tablets into the water canister. *At this rate I'd have another hour to get my hover in the air to pick up enough fares for solid food.*

Or, you can fly to Shakratel's for a decent meal and tell them you turned sixteen today.

But that would mean seeing Reggi and feeling all of that again. No, it was better to stay away. To avoid him at all costs, to keep from the over- whelming feelings I had tried to keep at bay by staying busy, fixing, working double shifts that meant I only slept when the hover abso-

lutely needed its batteries charged and keeping to the back of the compound when I did have to do a cargo run for Shakratel.

Would it be so bad? I'd asked myself again and again. But, then the feeling of touching him and Wiid's words surfaced. *No, I'm better off staying away.*

"This had better work," I muttered, starting the engines, listening to the purr of the engines for H1 and H8. I rested back against the pilot's chair, making sure not to pinch my tail as I scooted back. My hover's narrow long nose at the front and wider rear seats dated it before the Peace Pact that had ended the Hybrid Wars. I inhaled deeply, trying to fight the fatigue that crept over me in a sticky, thick fog. *Gotta get going. Sleep when you're dead, girl.*

I jumped down and stowed my tools in the cargo hold, whistling for Pinu to wake up. I caught my reflection in the glass: black mohawk grown out and no longer spiky, my yellow eyes bloodshot.

"Pinu, come on." I had to lift her onto the copilot's seat and strap in her safety harness. Pinu hit the switch to drop the chain barrier that separated the cockpit from the rear of the hover. That barrier kept quite a few drunken passengers from stealing the coin they'd just paid us.

Once my sunshades were in place, I caught the sun peeking over a far distant outcropping of hills opposite the Scraggs, the burst of light warming me. Usually, I only worked the night shift, but I didn't have a choice today.

I patted my empty pocket. *Not a coin to my name.* My dreams of leaving Zeto City had never been further away than at this moment.

"We've got a long day ahead, Pinu."

Pinu nodded with her bill and engaged the locks. I coaxed back the throttle, checking the eight engine lights before going airborne. *Someday*, I told myself, *I'll take off for good.* Instead of heading for the tall blue and red casino towers, I'd veer sharp to my left and make my way to the plains that led to the Fringe territories beyond the River Ong's silt waters.

But today wasn't that day.

I tried to get the dispatcher radio to pick up any hails. After a few seconds of static, and no voices, I turned on the radio that Reggi had installed months ago. Pinu pressed her bill to the music station on one of the three channels the old radio picked up. A tanaloon strummed with a light percussive sound of clapping hands and tambourine.

Ah kyenti, kyenti, malou-

I relaxed as the singing began, the tune a favorite. Yura had introduced me to this song months ago.

Oh kyenti, kyenti, malou

Closing into the magnetic bands, I veered toward the ashy yellow colored buildings of the Whizz District where the poorer partygoers tended to gather. They weren't bothered by my old hover. I sang along to the song,

So-shik sub yuuu
So-shik suba luu-uu-uu

It was one of the Ruckle Snits songs. The wheeze box and tanaloon were much louder in this version of "Kyenti Malou" or "My Dirty Dearest." *Or was it "Dusty Dearest?"* Unsure of the exact translation from Hybrid Kesh to Stan. Pinu bobbed her bill along to the music.

"Whizz Stand 1, hovers needed. Whizz Stand 1." My first hail crackled over the dispatcher radio.

"Pinu Courier here, I'll be there in sixty seconds, over," I confirmed.

I pulled back the throttle and veered toward Stand 1, which was outside Papa Motos, almost running into two sleek, black security drones that darted around me. I tried to stay calm. They probably wouldn't pay me any attention—

A hail interrupted the music, and Pinu turned down the dial.

"Pinu Courier, come in. This is Security Rover 567-931, pilot confirm identification."

I cursed. They were coming after me because I'd almost hit their stupid drones. Great. I pressed the ID console, hoping my Gnasher ID would go through, and they'd leave me alone. There was static on the line, the music almost audible, or maybe it was hunger playing with my mind.

"Something's wrong with your ID. We gotta take you in," the security drone's metallic voice came over the radio.

Before I could reply, a magnetic cable attached to my hover, and I was no longer steering. *Tafla!* My only escape would have been to throttle back hard enough that I broke the cable, but then they'd follow me. The newer drones would catch up in no time. I looked around for another way out. Could I radio Shakratel? They would hear me, if I did.

Pinu jumped up and down, clearly feeling my distress.

"Girl, there's got to be a way out of this," I said, gritting my teeth and wracking my brain for options.

I considered letting Pinu fly to Shakratel, but I wasn't certain she knew the way or had enough energy in her to make the flight. "What am I going to do?"

Pinu cheeped back plaintively. She knew we were in deep tafla here.

There was always the danger of capture, too. I broke into a sweat, despite the cool morning. I should've stuck to the night shift, like always. Or gone back to Shakratel's. *What was I thinking?*

There had to be another way. Anxiously searching Whizz District's yellow lights and jagged pillars passing below, bile rose in my throat as I stressed over all the missed coin. Wherever they were taking me was undoubtably worse than my cave. *Do I just jump out the window and save myself the trouble of whatever is waiting for me below?*

My limbs shook when I realized we were headed directly to the big casinos. I wasn't sure which crime boss was worse: Stencil, who owned the majority of the casinos, or Whip. Both were former generals of the

Hybrid Wars, who had traded their war personas for running casinos built out of the rubble of the city they'd helped destroy. *Stupid tafla all around.* I rammed Reggi's red hat back on my head and buttoned up my sleeveless jumpsuit, slipping on the pullover I kept under my seat.

Another cheep from my bird, and Pinu's black feathers were puffed up and alert. In a few minutes, we'd be within view of the blue and green towers of Bliss and Emerald, Whip's territory. She had earned her name from carving her initials into her rival's people with her electrocoil whip.

Opening the hidden compartment that I'd built into the copilot's deck for stashing coin, I coaxed Pinu into the narrow opening, helping her scoot inside. Pinu spun around, her dark eyes pleading with me, beak lowered in subservience.

"Stay put until I let you out. If someone takes the hover, break out and fly to Shakratel." I put a hand on Pinu's head. "You understand?"

Pinu nodded once and sat down to roost in the compartment. I closed the hatch, opening the vents so she would get plenty of air. "Don't make a sound until I get back."

I steeled myself for the worst. *Will they send me back to the factory? I'll make a run for it, or die trying.*

I tried not to imagine what would happen if I didn't come back, or if Pinu were abandoned and forced to fly to Shakratel's on her own, sharing airspace with hovers and security drones. I detached the connection to all the eight central lines in the engine compartment. They weren't going to drive my life away without having to reattach each line in the same configuration Reggi and I had created.

A young woman in a maroon outfit knocked on my window. She was surrounded by two grey uniformed Hybrids with a mix of human and reptilian features. I hopped out and slammed the door. Like me, they were more human than animal, but they were much wider and with more mass than my willowy body towering over them. The girl had a shock of purple hair that was familiar, her eyes a soft brown now that were no doubt artificial lenses or later gene tweaks. "Whip wants to see you, Idris."

Her face came into focus, her snout just like her father's, except with none of the menace. Her brown eyes were hiding something. The shock of my past coming up to greet me made my knees buckle. Dina motioned for me to follow her inside the casino. My legs were stiff and sore as I followed Wiid's daughter up the steps, shaking as I sifted through what she had in mind for her father's old victim.

CHAPTER 12

TOREF

Toref glanced up at his pod district. It had been awhile since he'd slept there, but it felt like weeks. The last thing he wanted was to have to mentally rehash everything with his family in the tiny space all by himself. *At least in the barns with Rusty I had his banter to distract me.* Above him, in the hangar, several pods were open and kids talked to each other across the steel frames that kept the hundreds of pods suspended twelve levels in the air. Toref tried to locate his pod among the homogenous white, oval-shaped containers and eventually found it: IOPA 93-TB. His number and initials were stenciled on the rust-caked seams of the otherwise white container. It had been moved to the top level, as if to emphasize the impossibility of his escape.

The IOPA 93 Gamma operator scanned Toref's retina and arm console before he operated the pod lift. The kids were forced back inside their pods as the top hatches closed and the pod capsules reconfigured.

The screen flashed "platform F2," and Toref rushed up the stairs, his aching calf muscles straining to make it past the second set of stairs. He had two minutes before his pod moved to another platform.

He was panting when he arrived, his pod already open. A wave of exhaustion hit him as he stepped inside.

Was his journey all for nothing? *Will I ever find Lena and Penny, or am I stuck here at the Pods?*

The capsule automatically shut over him, sealing him from the outside world. "Starting decontamination sequence," a robotic voice announced. Steam filled the shower console above him, hot water drenching him, his muscles relaxing, even if it was a touch on the hot side.

It isn't fair. They couldn't give me answers about my sisters. Now I'm being punished for taking initiative. The feelings of anger and hurt dulled a bit in the short-lived warmth. His old clothes disintegrated when the water stopped, draining through the floor panels, and a red jumpsuit dropped out of the airlock chute next to his bed. Something about his bed looked wrong. The coverlet was different, which was strange, because there hadn't been any variations in any designs between pod units that he'd observed. He grabbed the crimson jumpsuit, the fabric starchy and stiff. After putting on the undershorts, he zipped up the loose jumpsuit that hung from his lanky frame.

"Red matches your eyes very nicely."

He whipped around. A familiar flame-haired girl pushed her way out of one of his stowage hatches and struggled to stand. *Is it Minnie or Minerva?* He stepped forward to help her, and she batted him away, hobbling to get onto her feet.

"Minnie?" he asked. *I hope she didn't see me naked.*

"Minerva," she insisted, her red curls bouncing when she shook her head, smirking at him.

"How did you...why...we'll get in trouble!" He panicked. Being caught with her would extend his quarantine. *Why hadn't the system sensors picked up her vitals?*

"The system in your pod is old; it doesn't pick up life signs, just your chip. Don't worry, I talked to the system a bit before you arrived." She held up a cord that connected to the wall panels, the other end affixed to her tablet.

"You're not supposed to be here…I mean…it's sealed. There won't be enough—"

"Once again, I'm Minerva." She extended her hand, and he ignored it. "And you are?"

"Toref." He didn't want her seeing him like this.

"Rusty sent me. You'll need my help getting out of here." She hobbled over to the plexiform settee.

"Do you need help?" he asked, and she threw a tool at his feet.

"Come on down." She settled and raised up one of her pant legs to get comfortable. Instead of a leg there was a metal rod attached to her boot. "What? You never seen someone without full legs? Stop looking and help."

He averted his gaze. His face warmed from her chastisement as he knelt down by the electronic panel at the front of the pod, keeping his eyes trained on her face for instructions.

"Rusty said you're good with fixing things. I'm good at talking to electronics. Between the two of us, we should get your pod open in no time."

He liked the confidence in her face, a certain mirth around the corners of her lips.

"What about the Monitors?" he blurted.

"That's the least of your worries." She whisked a wire out of the pocket of her white uniform, threading it through her tool. "I've got some tech needing your handiwork. We'll call it a fair trade when I get this thing open." She handed the other tool to him and typed into what looked like one of the Monitor's tablets.

"Where'd you get that?"

"Stole it." She was teasing him. "Okay. Now try the other lever."

He turned the locking mechanism counterclockwise, adjusting the bolt to loosen it. She leaned in closer, looking uncomfortable, and pulled out the electrical interface on the door to inspect its innards. Their gazes locked, and he noticed her pink irises.

"Stop staring. I know you're excited I'm Ungar, but can we get a move on? I don't want to stay the night." Her voice was softer than before, her face flushing.

The tension he hadn't realized he'd been holding onto dissipated. He felt calmer than he had in months and wasn't sure why. *I'm not going to question it.*

Handing her the tool, he moved closer to help, her curls tickling his cheek when she leaned in closer to inspect the panel's grid. Toref wanted to ask her about her legs, how it happened, anything to make her talk. But he felt that sensation that came over him whenever there was a tense moment and his words failed him.

"Toref is a shy guy!" Penny used to tease.

Courage, man, he told himself, *say something, anything.*

"It looks like we'll need to find another way out, maybe through the skylight?" he offered.

Minerva just grunted and kept tapping at the tablet before leaning back on the stool. She swiveled her legs over. "Your turn."

He took the tool with the spiral end and made contact with the door panel's circuit board. Sparks flew, but he felt like he was making headway. Then, the entire panel's lights went out and the pod shuddered and groaned. The only light came through the skylight.

"Well, I guess that's that." Minerva sighed and leaned against the foot of his bed. "Time for a system reboot."

Toref's muscles felt like rocks, everything creaky and burning. It had been an uncomfortable night in his pod. Minerva's grand plans hadn't worked, and it took hours to get the power to come back on. He'd felt like he had to give her the bed, but she refused, and he had laid awake in a half sleep for the rest of the night, his stomach rumbling from the rations that he'd insisted they share. A burning red sore had formed on his thumb from manipulating Minerva's crappy tools. They'd been able to unlock one of the door bolts, but couldn't get the final side arm to budge. The increasing heat in the pod didn't help.

"I really need to pee," Minerva said, nudging Toref fully awake.

"Go ahead, my eyes are still closed," Toref said, embarrassed.

She exhaled noisily. "Put the pillow over your face, man." She grabbed the pillow before he had a chance to do anything and stuffed it in his face.

He sat up and removed the pillow. "I'm not like Rusty; I don't treat girls like he does."

"You're friends for a reason," she said, walking the two steps it took to get to the toilet. She pulled the unit out of the wall, and Toref threw the pillow over his head. He hummed a short song until Minerva shook him to dislodge the pillow.

"You can stop your weird song now." She looked at him, her pink eyes lighter in the morning sun coming through the skylight. "What were you singing?" Her face softened a little, tiny freckles dotting her cheeks and pale neck, unlike the dotting of purple scales on the edges of Rusty's face. Hers looked more like stars.

"Made it up, I guess." Toref tried to recall the song but was stymied by the constellations of freckles on her face, enjoying how each small brown dot scurried across her pale skin.

The pod shook, and Minerva scurried over to the side panel they'd been working on. She handed him the tool, hobbled over to her tablet, and punched in sequences while Toref messed with the circuits again.

After a few tweaks, the door shuddered open. Rusty stood grinning at a bunch of Hybrid girls with magenta hair. "I knew we'd heave this thing right off."

"You're so smart, Rusty-man," the girls said in chorus. Beyond them stood the dusty hangar ceiling with algae and vines hanging down.

This wasn't good. If Rusty had helped, who knew if the pod would close again. Or how much longer Toref's quarantine would be extended when the Monitors found out. *School feels like a long shot now.* He looked back at Minerva, tapping away at her tablet, ignoring all of them. The two girls with Rusty stared at her, the tall one grimacing like Minerva was dirty.

"Dude, what's wrong? Come on, the Rust made you bust out of here!" Rusty grinned, his purple freckles dancing across his tawny face, black almond eyes glittering. He spread his arms wide around the girls. "Shh girls, we don't want to break his focus," he spoke in a deep-throated accent like Stencil, one of the top casino bosses, that made everyone except Minerva laugh. They'd seen enough holo ads with Stencil's ridiculous voice. Rusty held out his hand to help Toref onto the platform, but Toref turned around to let Minerva out first. She pushed past him and gingerly crossed.

"Not as I'd planned, but it'll do." She wiped her hands on her white uniform, acting like she'd settled on something.

What is she talking about? "What?" Toref asked, jumping across to the platform.

"Oooh, Toref, we're so sorry!" A green-haired girl teased and made kissy faces at Toref.

"We hate to interrupt your little love nest," another girl snickered and put her hand out to touch Minerva, who scooted away. Toref was about to say something, but Rusty clapped hands on Toref's back and gave him a manly hug before the rest of the gaggle of girls laughed riotously.

"Gross, get lost." Minerva shooed the girls away.

"Thanks. They're annoying," Toref said to Minerva, hoping she wouldn't leave too.

"I didn't know you two…were so close." Rusty bounced his eyebrows at Minerva, who crossed her arms, her face going beet red.

"I. Was. Helping. Like you asked." Minerva's jaw tensed. "Hacked the records so you can get into school." She crossed her arms.

Toref thought she was going to push both of them off the platform to their deaths. He needed her to be on his side.

"It's not…like…that." Toref wished he could admit he liked her. He stepped between her and Rusty so that he was at least blocking any more nonsense from Rusty.

"Yeah right, crafty mouse-man," Rusty jeered.

Toref puffed out his chest, like he'd seen Rusty do before a fight. "Don't call me that."

Monitor Xiu, her turquoise hair fluttering, floated to the platform where they were perched. She seemed to be the nicest of all the Monitors. But Toref was still wearing his red quarantine suit, and Xiu might have to punish him.

"Baldashian, Lum, Shao, you have ten minutes until you're expected at school." Xiu was smiling. That was unexpected! The early morning sun lit up her hair feathers that matched her pink eyes with flecks of sea-green. Xiu was the second Ungar to ever be employed at the Orphan Pods, he'd found out from Minerva the previous night.

"Toref, change your uniform, otherwise they won't let you past the array." Xiu threw dark blue jumpsuits at the three of them. "Don't look so shocked. I know Minerva tweaked you in. But if you don't hurry up, Monitor Briggs will find out. I can't bail you out once she gets burrs in her anus. Move it!" Xiu yelled and zoomed away on her hover disc.

"She's beautiful, you know?" Rusty was practically drooling. Toref and Minerva punched him simultaneously.

"She's old. You're gross." Minerva stripped off her grease-stained jumpsuit, her underwear showing the same stains. Toref tried to avert his gaze, even though he didn't want to. She didn't seem to care who saw her in her old underclothes.

Toref followed, changing as quickly as possible, hoping she couldn't see how skinny he was.

"You know you like me," Rusty leaned into Minerva once she was zipped up. She knocked him back into the side of the pod.

"I'll see you two at Registration!" She hobbled down the stairs two at a time, holding onto the railing in a way that looked painful to Toref. "Hurry!"

He watched the direction of her crimson hair and it calmed him to know all he had to do was follow her and he might know where he was going.

"Tell me you hit that." Rusty stepped in front of Toref's view of her. "Come on, man. It's okay, you can't carry your V-card around forever."

"You're wrong. I don't even know her, really." Toref wasn't about to give away his already burgeoning crush.

"So? She's cute. And we both know she ain't never gonna look at me the way she does you." Rusty elbowed him.

Toref felt a new warmth spread through his chest. *Should I even hope?*

It had been at least a year since Toref had been able to attend school. In Rif City, if you couldn't pay, you didn't go. His mother had been one of the teachers at the local school, before his dad died, so it meant they could always go for free. At least, when she was working.

It was a luxury now to be able to learn and not have to work the fields in the blistering sun all day. From what Minerva had told him, every kid has to wait anywhere from a few weeks to several months to attend school. It wasn't compulsory at the Pods, either. When he reached the school registration building, there were rows of juice packs and freshly baked bread in the far corner, next to a row of tablets and rolled papers.

"Is that real food, or am I hallucinating?" Rusty asked. "And what is that smell?"

"Butter, I think," Toref answered, his empty stomach rumbling.

"Definitely butter, hardly a zucchini in sight." Minerva smirked. She tugged them to the front of the line and no one protested. As soon as Rusty flashed one of his smiles, everyone quieted down. Every kid was dressed in the same navy jumpsuit, though some had patches and embellishments sewn onto their jumpers.

A canine Hybrid Monitor shoved name tags with a sticky backing into their hands and hovered over the crowd. "Eat up, fifteen minutes till class starts."

"Do they do this every morning? I normally have to steal them."

Rusty asked, before shoving a roll into his mouth and pocketing another.

Toref followed suit, making sure to grab one of the jam rolls. They looked like something from a distant dream. When he took a bite, bits of aili berry rolled down his chin. He stayed away from the zucchini muffins, which Minerva took extra helpings of.

"Well, I'll be off then, things to do, games to play, girls to pay. Or the other way around." Rusty flashed another of his smiles, but Minerva caught him by the collar of his suit.

"I didn't go through all this trouble for you to skip out." Rusty continued to squirm against Minerva's grip. "You can't make it on the outside without reading Stan and a little Hybrid Kesh." She let go of him, but by now Toref had stepped in to back her up.

He couldn't understand Rusty blowing this opportunity for a free education just because he wanted to play with dice and sticks in the dirt all day. "She's right, you know?" Toref threw in, trying to be helpful.

Rusty took a step back from them and dusted himself off, even though he wasn't dirty. "Who has more coin than the two of you together?" His face was taut, his eyes cold. All the charm had dissipated so quickly.

I definitely do not like this version of you, Rusty.

"So?" Minerva got closer to Rusty, their noses touching. "You think your stupid wit and perfect visual recall of games will get you out of trouble when you can't read? No way," she said.

"It's gotten me further than you, circuit-girl."

Minerva took a hold of Rusty's neck and Toref moved in, pinning his arms behind his back so he couldn't knock her over. "You want me to tell your pack of girls you have a catching disease? You won't get any action the rest of your time here."

Rusty stopped struggling and followed them when Toref let go. He didn't say anything to them when they entered the class bungalow. Toref shut the door behind them, the only light coming from the screen at the front. The entire room was cool and a robotic voice welcomed them.

"It's cold in here." Rusty smiled at Toref, something more genuine than his earlier oily manipulation.

"Shut up and learn," Minerva whispered.

Toref waited for the first video to start and bit off a piece of bread from his pocket before opening his school-issued tablet to take notes. *I'm finally here, able to learn again.* The previous days' madness attempted to cloud his mind with each word he wrote down.

You'll never find them, his mother's voice seemed to hiss, her emaciated body flicking back and forth in his mind as the memory of her betrayal taunted him.

CHAPTER 13

IDRIS

BLISS CASINO

Inside the casino, Dina steered us away from the gaming rooms and into a vast stone corridor with a tall glass wall where people waited to catch elevators. The two servants accompanying her walked away, and she flicked her hand upward. The circle of carpeted flooring we stood on moved beneath the floor with us on it, a type of elevator without any walls. Other floor elevators operated a few feet away from us as we descended through the floors.

"Whatever happens, you do not know me," Dina whispered, her jaw tense.

Like I could forget her. Or her father, Wiid. My pounding heartbeat settled a little. "I don't know why I'm here."

"That's good. Better than most," she said, a soft quiet settling over us as we passed lower and lower through the floors, the perfumed air of the casino giving rise to a musty aroma. Dina's tiny, heart-shaped face leaked no emotion at all, staring straight ahead, one eye seeming to flick over something, likely a lens enhancement for her owners to communicate with her.

I had four knives stashed on me, including the one at the end of my tail, which was tricky to trigger, but not impossible. I wished I'd practiced it a bit more with Shakratel's men.

The carpet elevator slowed. We reached the last level and the circle stopped short of a stone floor at the edge of an underground cavern of steaming water. At least five pools of water extended out for meters all around us.

"Whatever you do, don't mouth off," Dina said, a tiny corner of her mouth turning up before she soldiered on.

No promises.

The blanket of humidity hit me in the dank cavern. However, it didn't look like a place where someone would be sent to their death. On the rock ledge in front of us was a carved metal suspension walkway that extended across the entire network of pools. Dina shoved me off the elevator, and I stumbled onto the ledge.

She grabbed my arm and led me over the bridge system toward the largest pool, where a dark figure swam. Steam rose from the briny green-blue water, the walkway lowering closer to the surface. *What is that?* I was trembling. Every muscle in my empty stomach clenched and burned. Being fed to one of Whip's creatures was not a death I was prepared for, especially since I hadn't done anything illegal in the past two years. *Okay, maybe three weeks.*

A figure rose out of the water, and I broke from Dina's grip on my shirt before she hissed and shoved me against the back railings.

A tall woman with long purple hair rose out of the water. She lifted long, dark strands of hair from her forehead, revealing a series of horn bumps that extended halfway across her skull before her hair began. She was enormous and muscular in her black swimming costume. When two servants in white ran over to the woman, I knew I was face-to-face with Whip. *The she-devil herself.*

"You've interrupted my morning swim." Whip's voice was smooth, almost musical. Her eyes had a dead quality that dulled any light touching their light blue hue.

"You said to bring her here." Dina pushed me forward, and I stumbled closer to Whip.

"I hear you might have information on someone I'm looking for." Whip clutched my arm, her grip radiating pain through my limbs. "She hasn't had anything to eat in days. Fetch something now before she passes out." She let go of me and the relief made my head spin.

I was about to protest, but my vision was covered in black dots and my head felt like it was going to explode. Dina snapped her fingers. More white-clad servants arrived with steaming foods on gleaming silver trays. Was it a trap? Perhaps some of it was poisoned?

"Eat. You'll pass out if you don't," Whip said, pointing at the food. She didn't look like someone I should disobey ever, though I wanted to.

"I'm not eating it if you're drugging me," I said.

Dina uttered an audible sigh.

Whip just laughed. "I don't waste drugs on lowly cabbies with fake Gnasher IDs."

"My ID's real," I insisted. "I paid good money for it."

She gestured toward the food in front of me, and I decided the solid stuff was probably the safest, sticking to bread and cheese.

"There's plenty here." She gingerly picked up part of a fruit dish, but kept her eyes on me the entire time.

After a few minutes, my sight cleared, and the full luster of the blue-green water pools came into focus. Whip was settled into a metal chair that had been draped in a soft, white fabric and picked at the twenty different dishes in front of her, still assessing me.

"We always end up throwing away a lot of leftovers, so you might as well take what you like. Once you've answered my questions, of course." She grinned in a way that had nothing to do with happiness, unlike when Yura or Shakratel smiled. Whip's face turned up because she knew she could do whatever she wanted with me. I froze, wondering if this was the end for me, and possibly Pinu, too.

She stared past me, like she was inspecting an object. "You look a lot like a runaway textile slave, Idris Muskovarianlitu, from Brailesu Textiles," she said.

Tafla. My whole body went stiff, and I had to swallow deep, controlling every facial muscle so she couldn't see my shock. I kept my gaze steady on her while my pulse raced, my heartbeat in my ears and my stomach threatening to empty its contents.

"I'm sure there's loads of runaways from Brailesu. I hear they have all sorts of problems." I made sure not to look at Dina as my voice lowered. "That's the problem with *free labor.*"

I made sure to emphasize *free,* knowing Whip was guilty of enslaving her workers just as much as Brailesu.

"That so?"

"Don't have to worry about that as a cabbie." I folded my arms.

Whip smiled a little, "I see you know a bit more than the average cabbie here, making runs for my friend, Shakratel." She looked at me, letting that knowledge sink in.

"What do you want?" I didn't want to stay underground with her any longer than I had to, or let her know she'd completely spooked me.

She sniffed another dish and took a large bite out of the shell of a crab, crunching on all the hard bits like it didn't bother her. "Your hover is stolen, your Gnasher ID is likely not your real name, and for a month Brailesu has had a warrant out for a young woman who looks remarkably like you." A servant appeared and rubbed oil onto Whip's feet and calves. "You help me, and we forget about your fake Gnasher ID, maybe replace it with a real one and get the security drones off your back?" Whip surveyed the room calmly before turning back to me.

"Brailesu Textiles belongs to your rival, Stencil. Why do you care?" I asked.

"Right." Whip's eyes were cold.

"You don't care about fake IDs or stolen goods. All those things make you money." *Why was I arguing with the She-Demon herself?*

"Must be hard living so long on your own. Only a petrukian to keep you company."

I stiffened at the mention of Pinu.

Whip indicated for a chair to be brought over so I could sit across from her instead of standing. "I need your help."

I refused the chair. "How can *I* help you?" I tried to keep my teeth from clenching.

"I'm looking for a young man." An image of a young boy was projected on the screen behind Whip. "He probably looks like this now." The picture transformed into a teen boy around my age, with dark brown eyes, a thick smattering of freckles and bright, orange hair. "As you might be aware, Orphan Pods are off-limits to all bosses."

"He could be anywhere, except the Fringe colonies or factories. His birth name was Maximilian Lum. Hasn't been seen in years, and Stencil wants him."

"Never seen him," I said, my voice hard.

"That's not what I'm asking." A man bearing a cart of weapons approached Whip and helped her rise to stash an impossible amount of weapons on every inch of her body. "You might have heard that Stencil and I don't get along."

"I thought you were best friends to keep competition low," I said.

She grinned. "If you see Maximilian or hear about him, you tell me immediately." Whip leaned in closer to me after the weapons guy was done. "Once you send the message over, I could use someone like you here, if you get tired of taking Shakratel's scraps."

"You have a whole army of people," I said, waiting for the reason she'd singled me out.

"I suppose, but not someone like you. Brought up in poverty, like I was. There's something in you I recognize and admire, Idris. Think about my offer. You won't go hungry."

"No," I said, pulling my hat down lower to shade my eyes from Whip's intense stare.

"You can think about it."

A male servant approached and emptied a bag of what looked like a hundred or more worth of silver coins into my hands. I let the bag drop onto the smooth, stone floor.

Another circular elevator stopped and Dina arrived with what looked like a cabbie I'd seen from Whizz. He was a lot older than me, a musky odor following his approach.

Whip picked up the bag of coins and held them out to me. "Idris, you're going to need this."

"It'll get me killed," I pleaded. I didn't have change to break it into smaller, less obvious denominations.

"I'd say you have a few weeks to enjoy this. But, you leave it behind and I'll let my guards loose on you. They don't have my gift for kindness." She nodded to Dina, who brought the next cabbie forward.

I tucked the bag reluctantly into my inner pants pocket, the bulge hard to conceal on my leg, jingling as I walked. "Thank you."

"You tell me if you find Maximilian." Whip turned her attention to the cabbie who followed her through a door at the back of the underground cave. Two servants stayed behind with the remaining food trays. "You gots thirty second to take what you wan'." The shorter one declared in a bored tone.

I grabbed anything that would fit in my pockets, mostly sticking to fruit and bread that might last a few days.

When I was outside the casino, I threw on my sunshades. A servant stood by the open door to my hover.

"It ready for you."

I rolled my eyes. Shaking, I climbed up into the cockpit and slammed the door closed, my goal to put as much distance between me and that place as possible. I grabbed one of the baskets I used to keep coin in and set all the food in it. Opening the compartment where Pinu was hidden carefully, I found her curled up, fast asleep. My eyes watered with relief. I wafted a parabela over her beak, and she woke up immediately.

"Cheep, cheep, honk!" Pinu was ecstatic. She stopped when she saw my face. Pinu hopped into my lap, ripping into the parabela. I put the basket of food on her seat. "It's okay girl, we're going to Shakratel's."

I stashed the coin in the compartment where Pinu had hidden, and set a course for Shakratel's compound, when my radio dispatch started. "Pinu Courier, you're being scheduled for a run at the Orphan Pods. You got time on your skeds for a long round-trip run in the early morning hours?"

"Depends, what time they need me?" I asked, eager to get the hell away from the casinos.

"One at five a.m, on the dot. We've got two more pickups after that."

I considered how that would help me get out of Zeto even faster. "Five coins every half hour."

"Confirmed. We'll see you at dawn."

"Yes, see you then," I answered. Relief washed over me as we cleared the airspace above the casinos. We were on the path toward Shakratel's, steering us clear of the magnetic bands, even if it would have saved me 500 watts of energy from the batteries. I had some questions that only Shakratel could answer, and I needed a new Gnasher ID before the day was out.

CHAPTER 14

IDRIS

I stood trembling in front of Shakratel's desk. *You're safe now, stop shaking,* I tried to remind myself. He was flipping switches and typing into the console of the Gnasher relay machine to print a new ID tag.

"I didn't know what to do, Shakratel." I held my arms close to my body to bring some sense of stillness after the encounter with Whip.

He turned away from the machine, his usually pleasant face somber. I wondered if I had messed up and he was about to tell me I couldn't come back to the compound.

"You did nothing wrong. Whip called She-Devil for a reason, you knows?" He winked at me.

"What if I'm captured again?" I asked, then wishing I hadn't as another shudder rolled through me.

"You stay here, we figure something out. Maybe in few weeks, it time see the Fringes, like you talk all the time." Shakratel's light blue eyes were warm, his whole grey face crinkling.

I wrung out my hands, hating the feeling of not being able to keep my cool. "I don't have enough coin to leave." I pointed toward the bag.

"That's blood money, but it still doesn't give me enough for the long-distance flow batteries for long-haul flights."

He cocked an eyebrow. "You take passengers, we pay you. *We* get hover working wit' long-distance flow battery."

I crossed my arms. "You've done so much for me. I can't keep taking and not paying you back."

Shakratel rose up. "That's what family do, Idi."

I was about to mutter how I didn't know anything about that since both my parents were dead, but I didn't want to think of them, to even cross into that memory soup when my brain already felt so fried and sleep deprived.

Shakratel held out the new medallion to affix to the navigation console. "That should do, Idi. The old Gnasher ID I've retired. It harder for dem to track you." He handed the ID to me, his face creased with concern as he glanced out the window behind me. I looked to see what he was checking on, but there were only long prairie grasses swaying beyond the large orchid garden Yura and the workers tended.

"What keeps you here and not somewhere else?" I asked him. He had all the resources to leave and set up somewhere less corrupt.

He brought his gaze back to me. "I forced to fight in war, then defected and made this compound to help those also leaving army. I saw war ending before the real end. It not make sense go back to Myrel mountains. I got use to everything here. I want to take all the bad and try to make thing better, even if only on dis small patch of land. I owe Yura's mom, buried out in prairie after she step on land mine." His face went ashen and he plopped down, wiping his grey face with a rag.

"I'm sorry..."

"No be sorry, Idi. You family now. It time you knew. We all lost so much from stupid people with too much power killing and killing. Maybe you see dat only way through is make things better. Even if we do in little ways." He smiled up at me, clapping a hand on my back.

I placed the bag of coins from Whip on his desk. "Take them..."

Shakratel eyed the coins. "That be bribery money. We keep it on books for you. We make it right, don't worry so much, Idi. You come back here when you need something." He waited for me to make eye contact. "Whether you got coin or no. I hope you know dat." He handed me a key. "Dis your bunk room. It best you stay on compound."

Before I could thank him, the radio crackled on his desk. "Pinu's acting crazy. Everything okay inside?" Reggi asked.

"We comin' out. No worry, Reg," Shakratel answered.

The radio crackled again, and I put a tentative hand on his large, solid shoulder. "Thanks Shakratel. I appreciate..." I didn't know that there were the words to explain how I felt, both the relief and the quaking that ran from the tip of my tail to the top of my head. I was afraid that once I stepped out of his office, some other bad news would follow, or Whip's people would be waiting for me.

Shakratel clapped a hand on my shoulder. "You alright, Idi. You pick up dose Pods kids and come back here for good."

I nodded to him. "I'll go help Reggi with Pinu." Shakratel looked at me, like he was going to say something. I folded my arms around his wide back. "Thank you." I hugged him tight before letting go.

I darted out the main entrance. When I reached the hangar, Pinu was squawking at Reggi. He sat on one of his wheeled stools looking at the new blades on my hover.

"Nice job here," he said, his excitement at seeing me barely containable.

I felt that fizz in my stomach at seeing him again, and Pinu immediately calmed down, flying to my shoulder and pecking at my hat until it fell on the floor.

"Yeah, I replaced them myself. I should have let you do that. Took me forever," I admitted.

He glanced at the rest, wheeling himself along. I was glad he was occupied so I could just look at him and not worry that he was going to see my tail nervously flicking back and forth.

"I'm going to catch up on some sleep before making a run to the Pods. No fixing anything while I'm sleeping, Reg."

"I can run diagnostics, though, right?"

"Not if it means I can't take off in eight hours."

" 'Kay, Idi."

"I mean it, Reg." I looked at him under the hover, and he was looking right at me, like I held his whole world. I pretended I didn't see that, that his look didn't follow me all the way to my bunk room where I bolted the locks behind me, leaving Pinu to keep him company.

CHAPTER 15

TOREF

The next morning, Toref had lost track of Rusty after he'd left the barn, so he was left alone with Minerva. She looked up at him, like she wanted to say something and instead pointed at the schematic on her tablet, a beat-up looking old Monitor's tablet that was different from what they'd been given for class.

"How'd you get a Monitor's tablet?" he asked.

"I'll tell you, if you admit why you went to Rif City." Her pink irises were light in the morning sunlight, and a breeze blew her frizz of curls across her round cheeks.

Gosh, she is pretty, Toref thought. Couldn't they just get on with the schematics and leave that piece of family drama behind?

"Toref?" She crossed her arms.

She wasn't going to leave it. He told her everything that happened, only pausing halfway through to keep himself from crying.

"It was whatever your Mom's hopped up on, you know? If she'd been well, she would have told you," Minerva said, her gaze softening. "Don't try to leave again. You're lucky you're still alive." She turned back to her tablet, all business again. "Because I can code, I fix most of the Monitor's tablets, except Briggs. She's good at fixing her own stuff."

"Oh?"

"Rusty didn't buy it for me, if that's what you're asking." She pointed to the schematics and moved the tablet so it was closer to him.

Toref scooted in, trying to identify the pleasant aroma coming off her. Like a mix of butter and flowers. He wanted to know what made her smell so good. He stared at the mix of yellow and gold in her red hair. It wasn't all one shade of crimson, like he'd originally thought. The strands of curls were sprung tightly, some so frizzed that they looked like individual fuzz balls. She wrapped one strand around her finger before letting go.

He had to stop staring. "The green wires feed into the receiver, and the nodes there help to keep the receiver from frying when any sort of amplification is underway."

"You seen this before?" she asked, pointing at the yellow wires from the nodes.

"Definitely. I used to fix circuit board bugs." She handed the tablet over to him and he zoomed in. Monitor Briggs sailed over them, tutting when she spotted them.

"Come on, let's get to class," Minerva said, taking his arm. He enjoyed the feel of her hand on him as he leaned in closer to get a whiff of her hair again, trying to act very casual about it.

Rusty was already involved in a game of Ruga on the pavements outside one of the bungalows. "Time for class," Toref said.

Rusty looked up, then back at the game.

"Rusty, let's go." Toref put his hand on Rusty's shoulder, and Rusty shoved him off.

"It's too hard for me." Rusty's lips pressed tightly together.

Judging from the lines in the sand, it looked like they were only on round three.

Minerva groaned, bent down and swept the entire game. "You heard Toref. Come on, man." She pocketed the cards. "Game over. Let's go."

Toref leaned down to pocket the rest of the game pieces while groans ensued from the other kids: most wearing the blue school uniforms with a few green field laborer uniforms as well. Rusty's face glowed with a bright purple fury.

"What did you do that for?" Rusty yelled, the crowd quickly dispersing.

"You are the smartest idiot I know." Minerva leaned in closer, and Toref was afraid she was going to bite Rusty's face off. "Acting like all you care about is girls and gambling. But, you know what? I know the truth. Your *nukvit* won't ever be able to read, if you don't come with us now."

"All three of you are late for class—follow me to detention." Monitor Lagos spoke in his rumbling voice. His horns peeked out from his spiked hair and he flipped his sunshades down while he whizzed off faster than most Monitors on their levitating pads.

"My code makes that thing zoom," Minerva said, admiring the departing Monitor.

"That's because you like how he looks," Rusty said. "Didn't stop us from getting detention."

"Thanks a lot, man," Toref jostled Rusty so he tripped.

"I could have won!" Rusty whined, following the two of them.

"Class is way more important…especially if what Minerva says is true," Toref said softly.

"But we need that coin," Rusty insisted.

"I don't need your coin, I have my own," Minerva said smugly and hobbled in the direction of Lagos, who floated in front of the large communal bathrooms.

Lagos levitated back over to them. "To the detention bungalow. Let's go. If you're late again, you'll be scrubbing toilets."

Minerva turned back to Rusty, who was ambling behind Toref. "Why do you do these stupid things?" She pushed him toward the bungalow and almost lost her footing. Toref rushed over to steady her.

"What do you know about it?" Rusty said, dismissive.

A ferocious, feral energy stirred inside Toref, warming his full belly. "I know that my Mom almost killed me, that Hybrid gypsies were about to capture me and I escaped only to be dragged back here." He was almost out of breath, the weight of what had happened to him ready to spill out like deadly poison. "I think I know a lot more than you." Toref smacked the side of the bungalow, close to Rusty's face. "When's the last time you left this place?" He paused, the hot wind the only noise between them. Rusty refused to meet his gaze.

A shadow of a smile crept up one side of Minerva's freckled face. "No more nonsense. Toref's right, when they remove that console, we're all toast if we don't have some learning, my friend," Minerva said gently.

Rusty kicked at the dirt, crossing his arms, not moving. "Maybe I have a plan."

"Yeah? Well that's the first I heard," Minerva said.

Monitor Lagos zoomed in and landed, no longer pretending to not listen to the fight. "A little louder, please Rusty, because I want to hear this, too."

"The three of us bust out of here when I graduate," Rusty whispered, swinging his arms, eyes fixed on Lagos. He stuck his hands in his pockets, then ran them through his orange hair, looking more out of place than Toref had ever seen him. "I can't graduate alone, I need you two. Maybe we set up a business?"

"And we're your underlings?" Minerva put a hand on Rusty's muscled shoulder. "You can't do any of that if you can't read, Rusty. You know that."

"She's right," Toref said and watched Rusty's face fall.

Rusty sat in the dust, Lagos watching them all silently, like he was afraid something more was coming. Rusty was so quiet Toref didn't know exactly what to do. Minerva kept her arms crossed, squinting up at the cloudless sky.

The wind kept kicking up dust, blowing tumbleweeds that they had to kick away. Monitor Lagos opened the bungalow door and walked inside, leaving the three of them on the wooden porch alone. Toref knew he had to do something.

When he bent down to touch Rusty's back, he was crying. Not little tears, but big, choking sobs. Toref nodded to Minerva who hobbled through the bungalow door to Lagos, hoping that she could stall any scrubbing detail they were going to be expected to do for being even more tardy.

Toref knew what it felt like when you were at the end of your rope. He reached for the spare cloth in his pocket. "Here, man, it's alright. Minerva and I, we're here, we're going to help you. Just like you helped me with coin. There ain't nobody in this universe who doesn't know how to scheme, make people do things like you. Look, you even got Minerva running around, doing your bidding."

Rusty laughed, using the cloth to wipe his nose. "Thanks. I feel so stupid that everyone can read and I can't."

"There are plenty of people here can't read, Rusty," Toref pointed out.

"But, you and Minerva aren't those people," Rusty pointed out, wiping his nose before blowing it.

"Stop thinking you have to do it all yourself," Toref said. "Let us help you."

Rusty nodded and let Toref help him to his feet. "We better get inside. I don't want toilet detail for any of us." He looked up, tears still streaking his cheeks, the sun's glare in his dark brown, almost pupil-less eyes.

Toref saw the same pain he felt reflected back in Rusty's drawn face. It was a loss that he didn't know how to name or extinguish. He embraced his friend, rocking him back and forth like his dad used to when the tears had been the only way of letting go of whatever was bothering him, or his sisters. *I miss you Pops. You would know exactly what to say to Rusty.* A gulf of guilt rose in Toref as he thought about how he wished his mother had been the one to go first and maybe their family would still be together.

CHAPTER 16

TOREF

"Hey dude, it's been a week since you escaped. Why not have some fun to take your mind off things?" Rusty said, bringing both of them to the crowded arena at the edge of the Pods. So far, his plan wasn't working. Toref glanced over the racetrack below, unable to sit with the tension coursing through his body. Next to the arena lay the landing pad for incoming hovers dropping kids off, or transporting them out when they graduated.

He watched a tall, spiky-haired Hybrid girl with an enormous black bird climb into an old hover. *I can't believe that thing is still flying.* He clapped a hand on Rusty's shoulder. "What if I earn enough coin to hail one of those hover taxis? Maybe search for my sisters in Keto?"

Rusty looked over at where the girl's hover was taking off. "It's a possibility, but the casinos are big. Nobody will give you any information without coin." Rusty turned back to ripping up slips of old advert papers and writing numbers on them as kids came up to him.

"Oh." Toref knew he needed a solid plan, but this wasn't the place to try to formulate it. He tried to concentrate on the flicker of bodies speeding around the track below, dust kicking up. *Maybe this can keep me from being alone with all these feelings.* Now it seemed his emotions threatened to overwhelm him, a pressure in his chest hitching at his breath. He sat down on the warm concrete bench, rubbing his hands over the chalky surface.

"Skaters, two-minute warning." A Monitor called over the crackling loudspeaker.

Rusty handed out slips of paper to people in the audience to make their bets. Toref looked at the track, a few Monitors bopping up on their discs to float overhead. The slips of paper disappeared when they came close, though they were mostly watching the game and not the audience. Toref squinted and noticed it was all girls who wore flat metal skates strapped to their feet as they glided over the magnetic track. The girls circled, warming up before a gong sounded and they took their places.

Cheers went up when the gong sounded again, and the skaters were off, circling the track with terrific speed. Lena, his older sister, had told him about this type of interactive race-skating. Two girls on the black uniformed team passed the green uniformed girls. Their uniforms were cut-up with as much leg and arm exposed as they could manage. Tails poked through the end of the shorter bottoms as the longer-tailed Hybrid girls smacked the girls with them to knock them off balance or into another racer.

Toref scanned the crowd for someone familiar from class. His eyes caught on a puff of red hair at the bottom bleachers. Minerva. She was bent double, tapping on her thigh and peering intently at the skaters. She didn't seem to be cheering for anyone in particular. A whistle blew and the first race was over, with the next set lined up. Could he venture down to her without seeming completely obvious?

"Come on, last chance to make your bets. Win big this time, we've got some serious competition coming up in these last three heats!" Rusty called out next to him. "Okay, times up. Time to collect your winnings, folks from the last heat."

He stood in front of Toref, consulting his book to pay winners before collecting from losers. *He won't miss me.* As the crowd changed for the next set, Toref skipped over the benches set into the dirt-packed hillside, making his way through the crowd to Minerva.

A sigh went through the small stadium, and everyone on the track chattered while the teams handed over skates to the next heat's players. Toref glanced back at Rusty stuffing the coin into his pockets and watching him. A wry smile turned up at the edge of his mouth when Toref reached Minerva.

Toref hovered next to her, watching her freckled face set with a deep frown. He was afraid to disturb her mood.

When she turned to look up at him, her pink eyes were almost magenta, and she blinked back tears, quickly wiping her streaked face.

"Toref," she said simply. "Need something?" She wiped her face on the back of her hand before taking her tablet out of her long side pocket in her jumpsuit.

"No." He didn't know what to say. He couldn't help following where the buttons were too tight at her chest and she'd used a makeshift scarf sewn from discarded uniforms to cover it. She swept her hair back into ponytail holders, and he was amazed at how light her eyebrows were, almost golden. He lost all inhibition.

"You okay?" he asked, unsure if she was crying because of the dust, or something else.

"No," she said. "Which team were you rooting for?" she quickly asked before he could dive deeper into what was wrong.

"First time watching." Didn't he have anything better to say to her?

She smiled then, her crooked white teeth flashing. "Yeah, mag rolling's the best."

"You skate too?" he asked. *Oh, bad question. Why did I ask that?* "I mean, you rooting…"

Another tear tracked down her face and she wiped it away. Toref put out a hand, not sure where it would be okay to touch her, if she even wanted that. He reversed direction, running his hand through his thick, black hair instead.

"Nope. No skating for me." She pointed to her metal legs. "They don't have skates that will fit my legs, and it's hard enough to walk. I can't imagine skating…even if I'd really like to." She looked back at the track, like that was all she cared about. "I imagine it might feel like flying."

"Maybe I can make something…" Toref started.

"Nope, don't worry about it. We don't have the materials here." She smiled warmly at him. "And don't suggest gene tweaks either. Knowing the stupid stuff they have here, I'd end up with some crazy reptile legs and whatever else they're growing in their petri dishes."

Rusty appeared beside Toref. He threw his arms wide and came down to hug Minerva.

Toref was surprised she let him. Rusty held on a little too long, lifting her off the ground, even though she was a few inches taller than him.

She pushed him away. "Stupid. You wish." She tapped his face lightly, like Toref imagined his sister Penny would have.

"Awww, Minnie, come on." Rusty said, bouncing his eyebrows at her.

"Don't call me that. It isn't my name." She put the tablet back in her leg pocket and pointed at Toref. "I'll see you later at the barns, okay?"

She turned to leave before Toref knew what to say, watching her hobble carefully back to the pod hangar bay in the distance, the setting sun backlighting her halo of hair. *I need to make her a better pair of legs.*

Rusty looked at Minerva in the same way Toref imagined he was watching her. "I wish she'd pay attention to me like that." Rusty put a hand on Toref's shoulder. "She's never come to the barns before."

"She was talking to both of us," Toref pointed out.

Rusty raised an inky eyebrow, eyes glittering, and Toref was nervous under the weight of his gaze. "Whatever, man. She's the best girl in this whole miserable place. Ain't never given no man the time of day. No woman neither. She's all business, all school, all…everything." Rusty put a hand over his heart, sighing. "And that's why it's impossible for an idiot like me. I'll never get with a girl like that. A girl who knows her own mind. A girl who can see through what I am and still hug me." He handed over some coin to Toref, who had his palm open.

Rusty closed Toref's palm. "Get yourself a haircut so you're looking fine for when you see her later. If you get a chance to talk to her for longer than five minutes, take it."

Rusty set off toward the west fields and Toref followed, not certain if he was going to get that haircut or not, running his hand over his now bushy black hair. He stood up straighter, imagining what it would be like to feel Minerva's soft curls. He jostled the coins in his pocket and made a detour for the hair cutting shed at the edge of the planting fields. *I'm taking that chance.*

"We could catch one of the exiting hovers that drops off new arrivals," Toref suggested. They'd lasted a whole week in school without detention, but today had proved too much for Rusty and Minerva. They were busted looking at hover taxis instead of working on the reading lesson. *Now we're stuck scrubbing stupid-nukvit toilets.*

"We don't know when they're arriving," Rusty offered, scrubbing the wall next to Toref. Minerva sat below him, her mechanical legs thrown behind her.

Toref exhaled and stopped talking when he caught Monitor Briggs watching them with her yellow reptilian eyes. No chance they could keep talking about their plans with her around.

"Tafla!" Minerva muttered under her breath. At least she could sit while she scrubbed.

"Faster! Six more panels of tile to go," Briggs's brittle voice echoed off the bathroom walls. A few kids came in and, when they saw her, quickly scurried out.

"Discuss later," Minerva whispered.

Toref looked back at them and Briggs snapped her electrocoil whip in the air. Toref kept scrubbing the next panel, moving in tandem with Rusty, only stopping when Briggs was looking at her tablet.

A clanking echoed through the bathroom, and the familiar whine of another Monitor approaching on their hover disc resounded in the industrial space. They stopped scrubbing when Monitor Xiu came into view. "They need you over at the track for shift change. Looks like there's another arrival."

"Which taxi service did you use?" Briggs asked.

"Pinu Courier, they're the cheapest," Xiu answered with a smirk in her aquamarine eyes, looking down at Toref, like she'd overheard them earlier. *How did she do that?*

"Figures. That petrukian creeps me out, though," Briggs said with a shudder and headed off.

Toref stared up at Xiu. "Wait, is that the girl with the black bird?" He shot up, ready to run off to see if he could at least ask how much it would cost for her to take them into the city.

"Where do you think you're going?" Xiu asked, putting out a hand in front of Toref to keep him from leaving. She didn't have Briggs's whip, but the look in her eyes told him she meant business.

"I need to ask...if she can...because...my sisters." Toref tried to edge his way around Xiu. The look on her face stopped him.

"She's long gone by now, Toref." Xiu's round face peered at him cautiously.

"Can we hail her to come back?" Toref suggested. "Just for a few minutes?"

Xiu's tablet started vibrating, and she walked away to type on it.

"We'll get in trouble," Minerva said. "Besides, where are we going? Ask her to take us to one of the casinos, and then what?"

A new determination welled inside of Toref. His chest burned and he looked up at Xiu. Why not at least try to find his sisters by asking around? *Someone must have seen them. Don't most hover taxi pilots know each other?* "The only way I'm going to find out is by starting my search. We have to start somewhere."

Minerva stared up at him, her pupils tiny pinpricks in her light pink eyes. "Toref, Zeto City is huge. Maybe not as huge as the cities on the eastern end of the continent, but still big." She let her arms go wide, stretching her stumps out beneath her. "You see how we have thousands of kids here. Imagine trying to find your sisters in a place twenty times this size and no database for shortcuts."

Toref rested his head against the cool tile. Was it better to give up, to say they were lost so the pain inside him would stop? *No, there had to be another way.* "It might be impossible. But, I'm still going to try. I don't care how long it takes me to find them."

"You're not doing this alone," Rusty said, a certain resolve on his freckled face. "I'm gonna graduate from here in two months. We've gotta see what's out there for me anyway for work, so why not combine missions?"

Xiu floated behind them, a grin on her small, round face. "You three are impossible. Finish this wall and you're done." She folded her arms and leaned against her disc so she circled above them. "Talk to Lagos about your plans. He'll know the best way to hail Pinu Courier." She winked and took off.

CHAPTER 17

IDRIS

I didn't like picking up kids from the Orphan Pods—they reminded me of everything I was working so hard to run away from. While making my way there at the ungodly hour their dispatcher had scheduled me in, I immediately regretted it. Pinu cheeped happily, because she liked being on the go, but the nap I'd just woken from hadn't fully refreshed me. The Pods' landing lights were shabby, and there were all sorts of crop fields to confuse me as well as their hangar bay lights where the kids slept.

When I had to pick up chatty Pods kids, they reminded me of a connection with other people my age that I'd missed. I suppose that's why I hung around Reggi. He was the only one on Shakratel's compound close to my age.

Once I touched down, I promised myself I'd only wait ten minutes. If the kids seemed too romantically involved, I was ditching them. *No more undressed bodies in my hover, thank you very much.*

My stomach gurgled and twisted.

Might as well eat dinner while I waited for them. I reached into the basket on the floor with the last of the meat buns from Shakratel's. It boggled my mind how they made bread so soft without the meat filling seeping through the spongy bread. Pinu craned her beak, and I fed her little bits.

A soft knock came on the cargo door, and I turned to face three older teens standing outside the hover. I stuffed the last bit of bun in my mouth and chewed quickly, unlocking the doors.

A dark Ungar boy stepped forward, his steps tentative. "I'm Toref. This Pinu Courier?" he asked. "I messaged the dispatcher." He stopped and stared at me with a look I didn't understand. Two more kids stood next to him, seeming a bit older.

There was something familiar to the shock of the orange mane on the freckled kid next to Toref. I tried to recall where I'd seen him before, but I knew it was impossible…

"Do you remember me?" the orange-haired kid asked. "I'm only asking, because you look—"

"You a little young to leave the Pods?" I interrupted, jumping down to the ground. I remembered him now, from the day of my escape.

A pale Ungar girl with frizzy red hair and pink eyes took his arm, stopping his inquisition. "Rusty, stop." It didn't keep Rusty from grinning like we were best friends.

"How old are *you*?" Rusty asked, still trying to inch closer while Toref stepped in front of him.

Oh, that's how it is with you. I knew his type. "Old enough for a taxi license," I said.

"Oh?" Rusty pressed.

"I took young mods. I'm fifty," I lied, smiling a little to sweeten the deal. I could see where this was going, and I wasn't going to have any of that flirtation.

"I want to try those," Rusty said, and his friends groaned cause they knew I was lying.

"This is Pinu Courier. I need evidence you can pay the round-trip fare for three stops."

"Rusty, show her your coin," Toref said to him. Toref looked like the safest one of the bunch.

Rusty revealed a fist of silver coins. "Minerva, I'm not the only one paying," he winked at her.

"Yes, you are. You owe me." Minerva smacked him on the back as she and Toref climbed in. *Maybe she's my kind of person.*

Rusty tossed three coins my way. "A little deposit, eh?"

I closed the door behind him and pocketed them. *Some deposit, konshin.* "Locks, Pinu," I said as I climbed back into the cockpit.

I was ready to get this trip over with. I glanced back at the three of them, wondering what they were up to. In the cabin light, Rusty's face scales looked black. There was something unusual about his dark eyes, and I tried to recall what was feeling super familiar—beyond meeting him before—but the meter beeped and it was time for takeoff.

"Strap in, Pinu."

Minerva reached toward Pinu. "Is that a petrukian?" Before I could put down the chain barrier between the cockpit and cargo hold, she had her hand outstretched, and Pinu hopped down from the copilot's chair to nuzzle Minerva's hand.

"Pinu, we've got to go." I stared at the trio in the rearview mirror. "What are your three stops?"

"Petrukians stay with one companion for life, right?" Minerva asked, and Toref crouched behind her, staring at the bird and smiling. They were either so enraptured by Pinu that they hadn't heard me. *That, or they were a little stupid.*

"Destination? Meter's running," I demanded.

Toref pointed west. "Oh, Central District, maybe near Garnet casino?"

I looked at him. "You sure about that?" It didn't look like they had enough coin.

Toref stared at Minerva, but she was focused on Pinu. Rusty got closer and Pinu snapped at him. "Wait, I remember seeing a girl a month or so back with a bird like yours—"

"Rusty, leave it alone, it doesn't like you," Minerva said gleefully, and Rusty retreated to the back seats.

"Whizz District and then back to the Pods," Toref said finally.

"Okay, belt in everyone. We're off." I revved the engines and steered us into the air, trying to keep my voice even. I remembered Rusty, all right. He had hit on me the day I'd escaped. *Tafla, let this night be over already.*

Halfway there, Minerva peered down at her tablet.

I nodded toward her device. "You'll want to hide that or stash it when you're in the Central District. Most people don't carry those around."

She looked up at me, a worried look on her face. "Doesn't everyone have one?"

"Definitely not," I emphasized. "Hey, are you sure you want to check out the area outside of Garnet? Do you have something specific you're looking for?" I asked.

Rusty met my gaze in the pilot's mirror, and when his face caught the cabin lights, that feeling of familiarity came back to me. Not only had I met him before, he looked far too similar to the kid Whip had shown me earlier that day. The pattern of freckles that were closer to his hairline, the dark almond eyes and shock of orange hair all made sense. But the scales on his hands and neck were different from the photo.

"You sure you want to go to Garnet?" I asked again. They seemed too young and green for that scene. I didn't want another incident like when I'd picked up Samrah, Shakratel's niece.

"Rusty graduates in two months, we're looking for a place for a repair shop," Toref said, looking back at me with a look of recognition that felt eerie. I regretted picking them up already.

"What kind of repair shop?" I asked, adjusting the flight path away from any of the major casinos.

"Hovers, machines, maybe some comp tech," Minerva said.

"You'll have less competition in the Whizz District, or maybe in Azules Quarter," I said. I wasn't entirely certain this was true, but I also didn't want to be the one to deliver their friend into Whip's very eager hands.

"I don't think she likes me," Rusty said, smiling at me in the rearview mirror. His flirting skills needed some serious work.

"That makes three of us," Minerva replied, testily. Rusty tried to put his arm around her and she batted his hand away.

Pinu kept craning her head back to look at Minerva and Toref, who sat closest to her. Maybe there was something to those two. Whatever it was, I wasn't eager to get them mixed up in their friend's possible capture.

"Feel free to take a look at the south side of the city here, so you can get your bearings before we get closer to Whizz." My heart pounded in my ears, as I recited different things that I could tell Rusty.

Hey, I was just bribed by one of the casino bosses to bring you back to her.

It's been nice knowing you. By the way, there's a price on your head.

He seemed cocky enough to relish it, as he stared at his reflection in the cargo windows and arranged his mane of hair. In the distance beyond him, the lights of Stencil's three casino towers alternated between white and red.

"Hey, aren't we supposed to cut closer to the center of the city to reach Whizz District?" Toref asked.

The altitude alarm went off, and I felt the engines hiccup like we'd hit a bump, except we were hundreds of feet off the ground. Pinu jumped up to the dash and pointed a wing at the engine console. All the engines were fine, but we were still losing altitude. I had at least another 10 kms before reaching Whizz, by my calculations.

I looked to the east, where Shakratel's compound was, the lights of the nearby dam flickering. That was only 5 kms away, give or take. There wasn't enough light to see what was below. I readjusted our course. "Hold on," I said and made a tight right turn, setting course toward the dam and flipping up my navigational console. It flickered in and out.

"Oh no. *Tafla.*" Something electrical was going on. Blood

hammered in my ears as I fought against the wind to keep us on course to Shakratel's.

The battery alarm went off, and the lights in the cabin dimmed.

"What's going on?" Minerva said.

"Electrical short, I think," I said finally.

This wasn't possible. I'd kept the fuel cells charged for days. I'd even put down extra mounting plates to keep the panels stable during wind gusts that hit my part of the Scraggs. I was so busy flipping buttons and trying to reallocate power, that I almost didn't notice Toref and Minerva behind me. Pinu had raised the barrier.

"Stay away from my cockpit!" I yelled, our altitude continuing to drop. We still had another two kilometers before we'd see Shakratel's landing strip lights.

"You want me to co-captain?" Minerva asked, Pinu jumping up and down in excitement.

"They're not all operable, only the bits that Pinu can reach, and I don't have the time to tell you which ones." I kept my eyes on our controls.

Pinu kept cheeping and pointing with her wing.

"Pinu! Pipe down!" I yelled. "You both, get back so I can keep us in the air!"

The cockpit got very quiet, the only sound the gusts of wind blowing us about.

"Can I adjust your auxiliary power?" Toref opened the panel without waiting for my response. "This works, right?"

"Don't ruin my hover."

"They can fix almost anything," Rusty said, and something in his voice made me listen.

I have nothing left to lose.

"Okay, I'm going to see if we can't get some power back from your aux cells," Toref said, heading to the central circuit panel behind me in the cockpit.

I kept us steady as the air beneath us became choppy the lower we got to the ground. The engines were now working at half power.

"Your batteries are almost shot," Minerva called out.

I steered us closer to the ground, hoping I could slow us down for an emergency landing without stripping all the new hover blades in the process.

"How are things?" Rusty called out from the back.

"Shut up!" we all yelled at him.

My hands turned to ice as I steered us upward on the unsteady stream, trying to keep the nose even. "Just a few more kilometers." I heard a boost in the engines as Toref patched the aux conduits.

"Come on girl," I said to my hover. Pinu thought I was talking to her and snapped her bill with satisfaction. *At least she wasn't worried that we're going to plummet to our deaths.*

"I need to see those landing strip lights, please. Let me see those lights." It was pitch black and a thumping beneath us grew louder. The last thing I needed was to land in the middle of some gypsies' camp. They'd torch the whole hover before it landed.

The thumping got so loud that we had to land. The lights of the dam were now blinking to my right, which meant we were close enough that we might only have a half hour's walk to Shakratel's, if my navigation system was working well enough to tell me.

I brought us gently down. The wind blew us from side to side, and Minerva held steady on the copilot's side. The power blinked out, and we plummeted. My stomach dropped. I pulled the throttle back, the systems suddenly coming on after a zap sound from behind, where Toref was. Whatever was beneath us cushioned us as we landed with a final *thwack*.

"Goddess, help us." I tried to turn the engines over again, but nothing was coming on, not even the emergency lights. We were completely in the dark. "I'm so sorry you guys. This has never happened before." *At least not in the last three months.*

"I'm sorry we couldn't get her working to stay airborne longer," Toref said.

"That was thrilling," Rusty declared.

"Everyone okay?" Minerva asked from the copilot's chair.

"Need any good jokes?" Rusty asked, flicking on a tiny light.

Minerva did the same, and each of them was wreathed in a tiny light that was affixed to their breast pockets. Minerva hobbled over from where she sat, and I pushed the button to unlock the front doors. A burning smell enveloped the hover. I looked at the back exhaust vents to make sure there wasn't a fire in the engines.

I hopped out and landed in a crop of corn. The burning must've been from the force of the hover blades hitting the crops. *We are officially in the middle of nowhere with no light to guide us.*

Rusty hopped out next. "Finally! An adventure! Freedom."

"I'm so glad you're enjoying this." I was ready to hit him.

"We have to get back in forty-eight hours or they graduate us and we have nowhere to go, Rusty," Minerva said softly.

"Well, let's find our way out of here first, then we'll worry about getting this thing in the air again," Rusty responded.

I climbed to the top of the hover to get my bearings. Pinu flew up to settle on my shoulder. I could see the faint white-and-blue piloting lights for Shakratel's landing strip to the left of us. We were closer than I'd thought, but would still have to pay for a mag-tow. I'd never landed this far from rescue. *Whip's cronies must've done something to my hover.*

"Don't touch me, Rusty," Minerva said.

"I didn't, it was Toref."

"Rusty, I swear…" Toref climbed to the top of the hover where I was. "Can I help with anything?"

"Yeah, get your friend to shut up."

"Done."

He climbed down and I heard a loud "Owww!"

I had to get away from the three of them, they were already driving me crazy. I sent Pinu ahead to Shakratel's with a message in one of her claws.

I turned to face Rusty, eager to get the worst over. "You're a wanted man." I said to him. "And not in the way that you're hoping." Minerva and Toref started laughing before they realized I was completely serious.

At first, he looked at me like I was joking, a small circle of light from Minerva's tablet casting shadows across his grin. I let the silence do a little talking before I continued.

"Whip captured me and is offering a hefty reward for information about you." I relayed the rest of what I knew while he sunk lower against the corn, his two friends with their arms around him.

I really didn't like being the bearer of bad news, even if he was a pain in my ass.

When we reached Shakratel's, bits of corn silk flecked all over our clothes, Reggi greeted me with a smile and flick of his bushy tail. I hated that I couldn't help smiling back.

"We crashed," I said.

"I'll get the mag-tow, don't worry," he said, and for the first time I wanted to hug him, like really feel his arms around me.

Except, not in front of strangers.

"I think I know what's wrong with your hover. I can help fix it," Toref offered.

"That would have been a lot more helpful twenty minutes ago, when we weren't falling out of the sky," I said.

"We have to get back within the next day and a half, and it's not like there's another hover around here," Rusty said. "Probably the faster, the better, since Whip is looking for me." He looked up at the hangar. "What is this place, anyway?" He started toward the double doors, and Minerva pulled him back.

"Is there a way that another hover can take us back—" Rusty was cut off.

Toref held out his hand and both Minerva and Rusty went silent. "She needs our help. We get her back in the air and maybe figure out this mess that you're in Rusty...with Whip wanting you and all."

The entire hangar bay went silent. I heard a whistle behind me, and Yura stood there, smoking a feratik stick. "Idi! That hunk o' junk o' yours finally fall outta da sky?" She chuckled a phlegmy laugh and handed the stick to a woman who stood next to her in closer-fitting blue robes. "Come on, leave Reggi and mechs with you hover. I can see wee needs a-fatten' you up." Then she eyed the other three with me. "I see wees have a friend now, Idi? Welcome friends."

I looked back at Reggi. "Don't worry, Idi." He smiled widely, total confidence in his hazel eyes. "We've got this."

Yura waved her hands at Reggi. "Reggi, do diagnostic and let me know."

I was about to protest, but then I saw the look in Yura's eyes. She knew how I felt about him, or how he felt about me, and all the awkwardness. How it had kept me away.

"Come on, we might as well eat and make a plan," I said to them, gesturing inside. It was time Rusty knew what it meant to have a price on his head, even if I was in no mood to converse with him.

The smell of spicy soup and yams made my stomach rumble. It felt like there wasn't enough food in the world to fill the anxiety that was going to engulf me.

CHAPTER 18

IDRIS

The sky was brightening at the edges as dawn crept in. I wanted to enjoy the cool of the morning, the repair bay's thick sailcloth covering shading us from the sun for the few hours we had left to work before we'd have to retreat indoors. Fatigue seared my muscles, making my brain sluggish. I took the wrench from Toref and fastened the wheel lock back in place.

Minerva was still programming the new motherboard. "Toref, give me that wire and attach it here. Idris, can you thread that through the drive shaft?" she asked.

I took the thick black wiring and couldn't help staring at her stumps. *I thought my life was hard.*

"Okay, stand clear, I'm testing H1," Minerva said.

I scuttled through the cabin back to the cockpit to start H1. It turned over with no problem.

"Good, let's leave I,." Minerva said. I liked the competency in her freckled face, so ghostly pale against the dark concrete of the hangar bay walls.

As we kept working on the rewiring of my hover, I didn't want to admit how amazed I was with two extra hands cutting in half the work that would've taken Reggi and I at least a week.

Dai, di, di, dai, dai

Toref sang very softly, Minerva joining him on the chorus. I watched them subtly rotate around each other, so peaceful, working with a synchronicity I'd never experienced with another person.

"I'm going to get all the copilot's controls working," Toref said after I'd taken the last wire and fed it through. He hopped up to where I was inside, making his way to the copilot's chair.

"Only attach the stuff that Pinu can operate, otherwise it will be confusing for her," I said. At the sound of her name, Pinu roused from where she snoozed on her chair, flapping her raven wings.

Toref looked at Minerva, who shook her head. It looked like some discussion had already passed between them. "Your copilot's controls have to be fully functional," Minerva insisted.

I looked between the two of them, crossing my arms, feeling my face heating up. "Only if it will really save time," I insisted.

"That way, if you ever decide to have a copilot...in addition to Pinu," Minerva added, "you don't have to redo the wiring." Her face was so earnest, not pushy.

I had never spent this much time with kids my age, so I was understandably anxious about a plan that I hadn't decided for myself. *Is there another motive for them helping me?*

Minerva's earnest face and Toref's patient glance at me settled my stomach a little. "Okay, let's make it operable."

Toref held out his dark, smooth hand to me when I stumbled onto the workbench opposite him. I batted it away to let him scuttle under the hover on a wheeled bench.

"How'd you get this hover?" he asked.

"Don't worry about it," I replied. I didn't know if they'd report the hover to the authorities.

Minerva groaned and rubbed at the ends of her stumps.

"Is she okay?" I asked Toref.

"Oh, yeah, just phantom pains, right M?" He turned back to the last two engines that needed wiring.

Minerva pushed herself along on the rolling bench, her legs lying on the ground like expended toys. Pinu sniffed at them and before I could say anything, Minerva slid underneath with us.

"I don't understand how you operate this thing all by yourself, the repairs, all of it. It must be impossible to maintain," Minerva said in awe.

"Reggi helps with most of the repairs, and he's taught me a little bit." I tightened the last two connections. "How'd you lose your legs?" I asked abruptly, shifting the focus away from the curiosity I saw forming in Minerva's face.

"Fleshmarketers," she said simply, but there was a tension to her mouth I hadn't noticed before.

"Sucks, yeah?" I said.

Toref looked between the two of us with that somber gaze that felt so invasive. Like he knew more than he was saying.

I inspected all the blades, avoiding his gaze even though I knew they were all in working condition. "I'm done here. Anything else before I close the copilot's console and reattach the wheel?" I asked.

"No, go ahead, and I'll run the diagnostics as soon as the wheel's attached," Minerva said.

A few minutes passed with only the sound of her tapping on the tablet. It occurred to me that I hadn't ever thanked them for helping with the repairs. "I appreciate you helping. I'll pay you back before I leave for the Fringe territories, hopefully in the next few weeks or so."

Minerva's eyes went wide. "Why would you want to go there?"

"Get away from this pit, 'cept Shakratel's of course."

Toref tapped on Minerva's arm, nodding. A certain language between them that made me feel a loss, a pit in my stomach where I wanted someone to act like that with me. Though I knew Reggi liked me and I liked him, there wasn't comfort, just stress in the feeling.

It was my first time acknowledging that I was missing that comfort in someone, besides Yura and Shakratel accepting me.

Knowing me so well, in fact, that when I was in a snit, they would place a hand just so on my shoulder, like my mom used to with my Dad.

Toref rubbed Minerva's arm gently when she sighed and he simply took her in with those quiet, violet eyes of his.

When Minerva was struggling to make her way back, I reached for the handholds on her bench and brought her gently back to where I stood, with Toref pushing from the rear and scooting himself closer.

"The Fringe territories are really dangerous." Minerva said, sitting up with some effort and rubbing her legs. "You definitely can't go there alone with only your bird."

"Why?" I asked, watching her pink eyes flash with anger.

"I lost my legs in the Fringe territories because my parents sold me to fleshmarketers. If I hadn't messed with the fleshmarketers' equipment and hailed the Orphan Pods, I'd probably be dead."

"That was a long time ago," I said.

"I haven't heard word that things are any better now," she said, giving me a knowing look. "I know it's tough because of what happened with Whip, and judging by the bruises on your arms, there's a lot you're not saying." She sighed, looking up at the corrugated metal ceiling above us. "But it doesn't mean that it'll be any easier on the outside."

I nodded, looking out at the prairie grass billowing in the wind. There was more out there for me. Calling to me in a way that nothing else did. I had to hold onto my dream, even if it felt really far away at that moment. I had to believe that it might be different for me, especially if I completely left the valley behind and made my way to the ocean. "I can't stay here. Whip will come for me. I have to make sure I'm gone by the time she sends her cronies."

"—You're still a kid," Minerva pointed out. "You could come back with us to the Pods."

"Naww." It sounded nice, but that was too many people for me. "They'd take Pinu away and my hover, too. It would be too hard to adjust to another way of life. I want my own piece of land, plenty of water. That's all I need." I smiled at them, everything inside me feeling lighter.

"I know I'm Ungar, so you think maybe things will be different for you in the Fringe territories because you're Hybrid. It might be better to have at least one other person with you when you go," Minerva suggested, setting her tablet on the worktable next to her.

Reggi came into the bay, taking off his cap and grinning shyly at me. "You need anything? I'm not on shift for another hour or so."

Minerva turned to look at him, then me, her eyebrows raising as she stared at me, a slight smile playing at the corners of her mouth as my face heated up.

My stomach turned, and I couldn't look at him.

"Everything alright, Idi?" he asked, looking directly at me.

"We're all set, thanks Reggi," I said, my eyes trained on the shiny concrete.

Toref stepped in front of Minerva and me, keeping Reggi on the outside.

"I can't wait to get out of this stupid city," I muttered and sorted the tools.

"It's dangerous out there, Idris. I don't know if it's any better than what we got here," Minerva said.

"Three things: no casino bosses ready to torture me for information; fresh air, and plenty of water and land." I tapped the roof of the hover. "We have six more hours before we can test the battery charge. I'm getting some shut eye so I can fly."

The work lights were turned off as the sun came up, and I headed to my bunk at the back of the complex. My boots echoed on the painted concrete and I tried not to think about how much this was all going to cost.

When I reached my bed, I closed my eyes and I saw the image of Rusty from Whip's cave. If I turned him in, I could leave tomorrow. I'd have enough coin to buy a plot of land.

No, I couldn't do that. Not to him. Not to anyone.

I couldn't look Yura or Shakratel in the face if I did that. The casino bosses sucked all their people dry for their own purposes. I couldn't consign Rusty to that fate, not after picking up so many people trying to escape a once glittery and enticing life.

A flicker of Samrah's state when I picked her up—the bloody ends of her dress, the bottle being thrown at my hover—shadowed my attempt to sleep. I'd seen what they'd done to Samrah that night and how Yura had spent months getting her back to normal so she could work again. The bosses didn't do anyone any favors. Everything was poisoned here, and the sooner I got away with clean coin instead of blood money from the casino bosses, the better.

I settled back against my rice pillow as it shifted to conform to my head, my tail curling as though Pinu was beside me in the bunk. On cue, Pinu flew in, nestling into her spot inside my tail.

My parents had tried taking shortcuts, and it led to their deaths. When I left Zeto, I wanted to do it without feeling like I owed anyone anything. I turned on my side and let sleep overtake me, while Pinu's black form roosted at my side.

CHAPTER 19

TOREF

Toref watched Idris' long-legged frame exit the hangar bay. She walked like his older sister Lena, with a certain swagger that was all too familiar. The drawn look on Idris' pale face weighed on him, her yellow eyes filled with sorrow.

He didn't know how this was all going to work out, as the hours kept ticking by. If they were gone longer than forty-eight hours, there was a chance the Monitors wouldn't let them back in. As much as Rusty was confident they could earn on the outside, looking around Shakratel's compound, Toref wasn't ready to throw himself on the mercy of complete strangers to earn coin. He'd had enough of that in the scrapyard in Rif City, with barely enough to feed his family a meal a day.

He leaned against the hover's circuitry panels and lifted out the charred comp board, watching Reggi inspect the innards, his wispy moustache twitching as he looked at the fuseboard.

"We got enough spare parts on hand to fix the hover in a few hours if you and your girl can give us a hand," Reggi said.

"She isn't my girl. Her name's Minerva," Toref answered, then felt guilty for possibly making Minerva think he didn't like her.

"Yeah, whatever," Reggi said, winking.

So, this is how it's going to be on the outside, Toref thought. "How much do you think it will cost?"

"Anywhere from 500-700."

Toref coughed and tried to act like that kind of coin was normal.

"She needs new batteries, these ones were shot pretty bad by the electrical failure," Reggi said, looking serious. "We can also see what refurbished stuff Papa Moto's has on the other side of the valley, but it could take hours for the next stock delivery to Shakratel's."

Toref glanced back to where Rusty was playing at the gaming tables before he ran a few calculations, looking at all the machinery on hand, arranged in neat, rusty steel towers. He'd been hoping to get some answers about where his sisters were. There wasn't anyone here who could tell him anything. It felt like their orchestrated flight was all for nothing. They'd been away for a total of nine hours, according to his arm panel.

We need to get back by this afternoon.

He looked at the burnt-out wires. He had been trying to redirect the current and probably burned up Idris' batteries inadvertently. "Is there something I did wrong while we were losing power?"

"Maybe, but it's hard to tell. Once the cells are fried, they dead. They got no stories ta tell." Reggi pointed out, holding up the charred motherboard.

Great, I can't even get that right either.

Hours later, Idris walked in, her hair pulled all the way back, and Toref saw a fresh bruise on the side of her faintly striped neck. *If she were my sister, I'd protect her. Keep her away from the people who did this to her.* Her tail whipped out, flicking back and forth. She looked terrible and Toref stared again at more bruising on her exposed forearms. When he glanced back at her pale face, he wondered if she was his sister Penny's age.

"Idi, you got wiring problems—" Reggi said.

"Reggi, it's Idris to you. Only Shakratel and Yura call me that." Idris crossed her arms.

Reggi smiled up at her, like he was hoping to win her over, and she only recoiled. "Sorry, Idris. Your friends here can help—"

"They were my passengers," Idris emphasized, making Toref wince.

Maybe she didn't know how to make friends, Toref wondered.

"Well, everything else needs re-circuiting before you get her in the air. Without help, that's a two-day job. With help, it's a four to eight hour job, maybe less if they know what they're doing." Reggi left the panels open and wiped his hands on his apron. "I'll let you decide."

He took off without her responding. Once he was out of view, she kicked the landing gear wheels. "You don't have to help me. We need to get you guys another hover back to the Pods. Minerva said you have to get back by this evening."

Toref knew getting back in a few hours would solve everything for them, but nothing for her. If she were his sister, he wouldn't have abandoned her. *She looks so alone. I can't leave her with this mess.* "We have a little longer than that, we want to help." He paused, coming closer to her. "We also need to know more about what Whip told you about Rusty."

Idris nodded, her face still frozen in what Toref assumed was grief. She ran her hands through her inky black hair. "I don't know why she wants him, but it sounds like her archenemy, Stencil, has his eye on Rusty, too."

A few more people trickled in from a small hover taxi that took off right after landing. Most of Shakratel's clientele appeared to be field laborers, taxi drivers, and "modder" misfits that worked on the outskirts of Zeto.

Rusty and Minerva joined Toref in the hangar bay and peered at the exposed innards of the hover.

"I think I have a solution," Rusty declared. He was beaming, and Toref wasn't sure what to make of the ebullient look on Rusty's face.

"Let's hear it," Minerva said, folding her arms.

"They've got some game tables up and running, and I could earn a bit more coin to get us back and help with repairs...since I feel..." Toref could see Rusty trying to put on the sincerity act, when in reality he wanted an excuse to gamble. "...*Responsible* for your hover going down."

Idris looked right through him, almost like Minerva, but harder, more jaded. "What's in it for you?"

"We need your knowledge of Zeto." He deflated a little, looking around to make sure no one was listening in. "Especially how I can keep from Whip getting her hands on me, or any of the casino bosses."

"I told you everything I know." Idris turned back to the wiring, tracing the burned wires through the panel as she opened more panels. "If I were you, I'd ditch this city as soon as possible."

"Idris, hear us out. You're in danger, too. If we can save you coin, maybe that will get you to the Fringes faster," Rusty said.

Toref tried not to hold his breath. She seemed to be wondering if she could trust them. Rusty walked over to the drive shaft, and Idris shooed him away. "I need Minerva and Toref to help me. Do your thing inside, Rusty, and leave us alone." Idris glanced up at him before turning back to the repairs.

"You said I have a price on my head." Rusty didn't move. "That's why I want to help. You could have not told me and taken me straight to Bliss casino." He fiddled with his uniform in a way that Toref hadn't seen before. "How long before they figure out where I am?"

"Who knows?" Idris sighed and ducked out of the hover. "See these bruises here? That's from Whip and her cronies. I have to leave before they come for me again. Whatever happens, your secret dies with me."

Rusty looked stricken, all the color leaving his face and neck. He swung his arms, trying to act casual and light, but Toref knew that worried look coloring the edges of his face scales. "I'll be at the gaming tables if anyone needs me." He shuffled off before Toref could say anything to him.

What do you say to your best friend who might end up worse than the state they left Idris in? Toref started to walk toward him, to say something to comfort him, but he drew a blank. *Isn't it better for me to simply stay here and help get us back as soon as possible?*

Toref dove into helping Idris get her hover back in the air. He drew up a repair schematic based on what Reggi had told him. He leaned in to the open panels of Idris' hover, where all the comp units were ready to be ripped out.

"These need sequencing, right?" Minerva asked.

Idris shrugged.

"What does that mean?" Minerva asked, taking out her tablet.

"It means I don't know how to code, that's what it means."

"Don't get testy, just trying to help," Minerva said more calmly.

"None of it works, so I'd do myself a favor by ripping it out." Idris reached for a blue wire, starting to tug.

"Not so fast. I need to see what still works. Grab me that sequencer over there." Minerva pointed to Toref, who grabbed it for her before heading over to the circuit boards to see what he could rescue.

They were at it for hours before fatigue set in, and Toref knew he had to check on Rusty. Before he could, a short man sauntered up to the hangar bay. His pink skin glistened in the lights.

Idris raised a hand, "Ho, Sokil. Still paying too much for skin mods?"

"Better than roasting with fur you don't need, Idi."

"Still Idris to you, Sokil. Later." She didn't look at him when she spoke, her body tight, like when she'd spoken to Reggi. Toref noticed that Shakratel was the only man she seemed to be comfortable with. *I better keep a wide distance from her so I don't rattle her.*

"Time for a break," Idris declared.

Toref was afraid to leave the hover as it was, with all its guts exposed. "I can stay here."

"Leave it, nobody wants my piece of junk, Toref." She pointed toward the door that led into the rest of the building. It was cool inside, the corridor connecting with a larger cafe where several people milled about, even though it was eight in the morning. He could hear the sounds from the gaming rooms in the back. He walked through the cafe, narrowly avoiding waitresses carrying large fizzy drinks to tables in the gaming rooms. Every six feet, a narrow column held up the roof over their heads. Mirrors were attached to the columns, giving the room a larger feel.

Rusty called out to him from a raised table, "Look at the house special here!" He had a steaming plate of meat and vegetables over rice. "Shakratel's hedging some bets on me at the Ruga tables in a few minutes. Breakfast is free for us," Rusty bragged, stuffing food between his words.

"Great, I can't wait," Minerva said, grabbing a bite of his food.

"A champion needs to eat." Rusty reached for the meat she'd stolen from his plate, but he was too slow.

"Come sit, eat, and enjoy." Shakratel welcomed them to sit at the table with him, and Idris pulled up a chair next to him. Despite the cool temperature inside and ceiling fans circulating overhead, Shakratel was bare-chested, his stone-colored skin showing a variety of scars and scrapes. He thumped his enormous cane on the ground, and Toref realized he was staring.

"Knew I could get your attention dat way." Shakratel grinned. "I don't wanna get in you way of food, but dat friend of yours. He for real?" Shakratel leaned in. "He play big stakes, or he just young-stupid?"

Toref wanted to say "young stupid" but Rusty had never lost any game he'd played sober. "He's for real. He always wins. I don't know if that's good for business—"

Shakratel waved the waiter over. "You no worry my business. My business safe-good." He followed the waiter. "Eat. I come back in little time see Rusty play."

The look in Shakratel's light blue eyes scared Toref a bit. He tried to see what Idris' reaction was, but she was shoveling stewed vegetables in her mouth.

A half hour later, raucous laughter came from Rusty's gaming table. Shakratel watched without a single expression crossing his creased face, hands folded over his belly. It looked like Shakratel was personally overseeing the game, but the more Rusty joked, the more Toref was afraid he'd set the other players on edge. At least three of the men looked like they'd ascended out of the hottest volcanos of planet Janus. The small one started laughing once the die was thrown.

So Rusty was playing the idiot card. He'd used it when the stricter Monitors were playing him for coin on their off days. But, his idiot act would only work for so long. These guys looked like they killed people on good days and tortured small children on bad ones. *These are not the sort of men who fall for your cheap tricks, Rusty.*

A roar from the gaming tables made the whole room rise to their feet. The losing guy held a multifacet knife up to Rusty's neck, already drawing blood. Before he could slice deeper, Toref ran at him. Shakratel raised his cane and shocked the pink man. He dropped the knife, writhing on the ground, while Shakratel laughed.

"You look like a Drugian sludge, Ba-shok! Hey, look-ee friends at da show!" Shakratel was laughing so loudly the whole place joined in. Within seconds, the men were emptying their debts into Shakratel's hands and Ba-shok followed his friends swiftly out of the room. Two smaller bouncers holding canes like Shakratel's followed them out.

"You take rest, then you play more. How many rounds you got in you, Rusty?" Shakratel asked.

A deep ache and fluttering anxiety settled into Toref's chest and belly. They needed to get back to where it was safe.

"I can play all day, if I have to," Rusty boasted. But Toref saw the fatigue lines at the edges of his thin mouth.

"I think one more round would be best before we've got Idris' hover ready to go," Toref said.

Rusty stood up and put a hand on Toref's shoulder. "Come on, man. We can be away for longer. This is our chance—"

"Don't do this." Toref kept Rusty from moving, the cut still bleeding on his neck. "Look." He pointed at his injury.

"We need this win—" Rusty started, his dark eyes flashing with the glory of victory. "To find your sisters, to get out of here…"

"We need to get back to the Pods before they kick us out, and come up with a solid plan from there."

"There's no future at the Pods, Toref," Rusty pointed out, his voice softening.

"We can't just stay here either. It's too dangerous, Rusty. Too many people have seen you," Toref pointed out, his friend's body deflating.

A racer was watching them from the corner of the room. Toref didn't like the look on the man's face. He could be another person Whip sent to find Rusty.

"Come on, man. Let's get you somewhere less…visible," Toref said.

"Good idea." Rusty clapped him on the back. One of Shakratel's stocky bald-headed men, carrying a shock cane, followed them through to the hangar.

CHAPTER 20

TOREF

Toref bolted the last of the pilot's console in place. *Finally.* He glanced over at the copilot's controls, all up and running. *Thanks to me powering through.* Pinu flew from Idris' shoulder over to him.

"Cheep, meep." Pinu jumped on his shoulder, her claws digging into his uniform.

"Leave him alone, he doesn't have any food for you." Idris came through and held out her hand to Pinu, who didn't jump on right away. Idris' yellow eyes reflected the bright sunlight, and Toref sensed a sadness in her gaze as she waited for Pinu to rejoin her. There was a weight to how she held her tall body upright and stiff, towering over all of them, her face the only indication that she was younger.

"We need to get a move on soon, eh?" Rusty said, plopping down into the copilot's chair. He opened the compartment under the steering shaft and tucked a bag of coins in there.

"Not with you sitting there. Pinu might peck out what's left of your cheek," Idris said.

The aroma of faint smoke followed Yura into the hangar bay. Her long, crimson robes bounced with her as she moved, her chestnut hair loose down her back. "Rusty, my dear…" she called out.

"Uh…Hi…Yura…" Rusty stuttered.

"Oh, that's how it is, huh?" Toref teased Rusty, who blushed.

"Naww, my man." Rusty drawled before Toref pushed him out the copilot's door where Yura was waiting.

"You got it working very fast. Reggi may need a few more hand now," Yura took another puff of her stick, winking at Toref.

Rusty shuffled his feet. Minerva stifled a laugh beside Toref. *He's never nervous around women.* Toref hopped out of the hover to get closer.

"Yura…I…thanks for helping me…" Rusty bumbled.

"I not help you at all, Rusty. But do let me know when you're back again. It would be good to see you." She whispered something in his ear and waved her hand at all of them, the scent of the feratik stick wafting over Toref in pleasant notes of cedar and sage.

"We need to get them back, Yura. I'll see you in an hour or so?" Idris said.

Yura's smile softened as she reached out to embrace Idris. "Course. See you in an hour." She sauntered through the doors of the hangar and Toref couldn't help laughing at Rusty's embarrassed face.

Rusty stood there still staring at where Yura had gone. Toref was entertained by his friend being smitten by someone he'd likely never be able to have. Toref climbed into the hover last, leaving the passenger side door open, as Shakratel came out of the doors of the casino area, the sun glinting off the glass doors as they closed behind him.

Shakratel wore loose-fitting white pants, his chest still bare in the cool morning air. "You wanna comes work for me, you gots a place, right here." Shakratel clapped his hands on Toref's shoulder before clasping hands with Rusty.

"Thank you, Shakratel," Rusty said, meeting Shakratel's gaze with a respect Toref had never seen him show any adult, except Monitor Xiu.

"See you in an hour, Shakratel," Idris said, her voice soft as she waved to him. "Get the doors. Toref and everyone belt in."

Toref closed the door and the locks clicked. He swiveled his chair around so he could watch Idris pilot. Rusty leaned over with another bag of coin, but Idris pushed it back.

"I don't like owing anybody," Idris said.

"These are your earnings fair and square for taking us back." Minerva insisted.

"Nah, you helped with the repairs, so I'm in your debt." She drew up the throttle, and within minutes, the prairie surrounding Shakratel's compound became patchworks of orange and beige desert with a sliver of river shining below.

The cabin noise quieted as they coasted, and Toref leaned forward so Idris could hear him. "Are you absolutely sure that Rusty's the one Whip's looking for?"

"He looks an awful lot like him."

"How can I keep them from nabbing me?" Rusty asked.

"If you're serious about leaving the Pods, you could work for Shakratel, but you're better off leaving the first chance you get," Idris said.

Toref cleared his throat. "I can't go without my sisters. I have to find them." He watched Idris carefully, his next idea a small seed that he wasn't certain he could mention. *You don't ask, you don't get.* "Maybe we can all work together at Shakratel's?"

Idris turned back the throttle and looked at him through her mirror. "You all better belt up, we've got some turbulence ahead." She didn't say anything for a while. Toref felt his idea lingering in the air. The air was thick with the silence of nothing stirring except the engines keeping them aloft.

Idris looked at him through her mirror. "I don't work with people, 'cept Shakratel and Yura. It's just me an' Pinu. That's the way we started, and that's the way I'm going out of this world."

"We make a good team," Minerva piped up, smiling at Toref.

"Apart from Rusty's mouth," Idris said.

"He's solid, once you get more time with him," Minerva said, surprising Toref.

Rusty's mouth was wide open in shock at Minerva's words.

"Like I said earlier. It's just me and Pinu. Though I do like you more than most." She leaned over to stroke her bird, who cheeped.

Toref felt a small blow to his stomach, a creeping of cold throughout his abdomen that made him turn away. He'd thought for sure she might change her mind. After everything they'd repaired. *Maybe that's the problem. She doesn't know what it is to have a family, to have a chance at something better.* Toref glanced at Minerva and wondered if the day would come when she'd also leave him on his own? Could he convince her to stay, to hold on?

He leaned against the window, the Pods complex coming into view.

"What if we did repairs, beefed up your hover when you're off-duty, helped you make runs and protect you from Whip?" Minerva asked.

"Then you can make it to the Fringes faster," Rusty added.

"Count me out on going to the Fringe territories," Minerva said. "They don't care about slicing you up to earn coin, if it suits their fancy."

"They don't have to know I'm from the city," Idris responded.

Minerva leaned forward. "They'll know your accent." She fixed her gaze outside the window. "I'd rather die than go back there." She adjusted her metal legs and her face hardened. Toref didn't want to push Minerva to leave the valley, but it was looking more and more like their only option for keeping Rusty safe.

The lower they went, the closer to the Pods, the more he felt a spinning in his belly like a gathering hurricane inside him.

Idris kept her gaze fixed on the landing area outside the Pods. "I have one goal in my life: to leave this place. Alone. I don't want to disappoint anyone or feel like I owe you." She throttled back as Pinu set the landing gear and peered back at them, cocking her head from side to side like she wanted to say something.

"You have to adjust yourselves to the new reality on the outside, where no one cares about you," Idris said harshly.

"Shakratel cares about you," Toref pointed out and watched her soften.

"No one really cares about us in the Pods," Minerva said, squinting in the sunlight.

"That's not true," Toref said, catching her gaze.

They landed bumpily, but the landing gear held. Idris cut the engines and no one moved for a few seconds. Toref looked at Rusty's flushed face, his face scales darker against his bronze skin. Toref glanced at Idris. He wished there was a way to turn things around for her. For all of them.

Maybe, if we can hire her again, I can convince her to help us find my sisters, at the very least. I'll float leaving for the Fringe territories to Minerva again, help her to see that if we want to help Rusty, we can't stay here with him having a price on his head.

He looked at Minerva and felt that pinch in his belly again. If he had to, could he leave without her, now that he was getting to know her? How could he change her mind, too? He didn't care what she said. Staying here at the Pods, or even in Zeto, wasn't a good long-term plan. If he found his sisters, it was likely the bosses would be after Toref for payment. What if Rusty…the questions plagued his brain to the point that he had to get out of the hover. He shoved past Rusty, opening the cargo door to get out.

Toref stood by Idris' open pilot window. "Will you at least consider that you can get to the Fringe territories faster with us, if it comes to that?"

Idris hopped out just as two Monitors zipped out to the dirt landing area. Idris held out her hand to Toref and squeezed it harder than he'd expected. He thought he saw the corner of her mouth turn up, her eyes shaded by her sunglasses. When she let go of his hand, Rusty had helped Minerva out.

"Don't leave here again, unless it's to leave for good." Idris gestured toward Rusty. "Steer clear of Zeto. You're safest at Shakratel's or another Boom town to the south. You'll need more coin for the journey, but it could keep you out of danger."

Toref watched her slip back into the cockpit, rolling down her window. "I hope you find your sisters. Just remember, wherever they are, they may have changed since you last saw them. Be prepared for that, before you find them." She gave him a tight smile.

Toref felt that twisting again, radiating to his upper arms and thighs. It was hard to stay upright, the breath catching in his throat. He wasn't ready. He saw that in how she talked to him. Like she knew how bad it was, had lived it and was still struggling through the murk of suffering.

Rusty handed over a small stash of coin to each of them, patting his pockets to a bit of jangling when Idris took off, the air around them gusting dirt in their faces.

Toref waved to her as her silver hover rose in the air, quickly eclipsed by the floating figure of Monitor Briggs and her snakelike hair whipping back and forth. Lagos's beefy figure floated behind her, looking rather grim.

"Don't know how you got out, but you've got a lot of shifts to make up for it." Briggs tapped the side of her hover disc before pulling out a surge stick and shocking Toref first, who fell onto the dirt. It wasn't as bad as he'd thought, nothing like the pain of being separated from his family.

"I'll take the rest of your coins for safekeeping, Rusty," Lagos drawled, looking beaten.

Had Briggs hurt Lagos too? The other Monitors complained enough about Briggs that he believed it.

Rusty turned his pockets inside out and opened his shirt to reveal a handful of coins. His freckled skin shined in the sun. "That's everything," he said.

"There's more." Briggs shocked Toref again with an electric charge and he fell, coins rattling in his pants pockets. He could barely move.

If Toref thought it was hard finding his sisters, it was going to be even more difficult trying to earn that money back in time for Rusty's graduation. Minerva was still standing, and likely holding the bulk of the rest of Rusty's coin. Toref turned away from her so they wouldn't suspect anything.

"I've got two tablets I need you to fix," Briggs said to Minerva, handing her the beat-up tablets.

Minerva looked at them and neither appeared to be able to power on. "Toref has to do the wiring."

Toref watched the dissatisfied expression on Briggs's face. "He better be able to repair these, otherwise it's back to cleaning crew for all of you." She zoomed off, leaving them with Lagos.

Lagos walked over to Toref, standing over him, his horns glistening in the morning sun. "You three should have known better. I told you to be back before sunrise." He held out his hand to Toref. "You content to lay here and roast in the sun?"

Toref closed his eyes for a moment, Idris' warning echoing in his mind. *You have to adjust yourselves to the new reality on the outside...* In one great groan, Toref pulled himself to standing, a surprised expression crossing Lagos's face.

He didn't want to be all alone like Idris, unable to ask for help. But he wasn't about to accept defeat either. He had to figure out a way to get them out of the Pods and to his sisters as soon as possible. With each painful, wincing step through the entrance gates, Toref knew he was going to have to be the one to take charge on their exit strategy.

CHAPTER 21

IDRIS

After I dropped off the Pods kids, I realized I had never been away from the Scraggs for longer than three days. After a day spent with Toref, Minerva, and Rusty, the hollow echoes of my cave sounded different. Pinu followed me to the back of the cave, through the tunnel that led to the water cavern below. The high-domed ceiling reflected the dying light of the afternoon and it took a while to adjust to the dim light. Pinu leapt into the air and snapped at the glowing insects along the far side of the cavern walls. The last of the daylight coming in through the cracks in the cavern's ceiling bounced off the surface of the water. *For the first time in my life, I don't want to be alone here.* I promised myself I'd get the last of my stuff and head back to Shakratel's. I just needed a few moments to say goodbye.

When I walked back through the tunnel into my cave, a flowery scent mixed with spices floated through the air. Pinu immediately stiffened, flying up to the ceiling and growling. *We had visitors. Tafla.*

"Pinu, perch. Now," I whispered, and she flew to the nest she'd built in one of the ledges in my cave's ceiling. I inched along the back wall, keeping a distance between whoever was edging very softly around my hover. Their shoes clunked inside the cargo area. I inched close enough to be within reach of my toolbox. When I touched a metal wrench, a stinging sensation burned my hand, a sensation like a fireball passing through my body, the throbbing reaching a pinnacle before dying away. I slumped against the wall, my hand no longer holding the wrench, but still burning.

"Weren't expecting us?" A golden made-up Whip stood above me, two eel men tethered to an unhappy Dina who held an electrocoil whip. The eelmen's skin was a mottled grayish purple, their dark blue eyes staring as if they were permanently in shock. *So, Whip had her own personal electricity unit. How in the goddess am I getting out of here?*

I tried to think of a way to get up, but my body wouldn't respond. In that moment, another bolt jolted through me. Thunder boomed in the distance and I tried to push my arms up to sit, but I could only move my head away from her. Maybe if I didn't look at her, and instead concentrated on the circular marks on the cave's walls, I wouldn't hurt so much.

"Perfect day for a visit. My friends: Lutz and Putz. They love to be shocking," Whip purred softly, coming closer. Her heels went rat-tat on the stone flooring.

"Funny..." I wheezed out.

Dina stood the greatest distance possible from Lutz's and Putz's mortified faces.

"What...do you...want?" I gasped out. I was surprised my brain worked enough to put a cohesive sentence together.

"I haven't heard from you, and I don't like waiting for answers." Whip spat on the ground next to my face.

"So you thought electrocution was the way?" I asked, almost laughing with pain.

Another bolt coursed through me, weaker this time.

"It looks like you need a little more juice before you understand that this isn't a polite request, Idris," Whip said.

I didn't like the tone of her voice. "I'd rather die." My tongue felt thick, but I didn't want her to think that incapacitating me meant I would willingly take whatever came next.

Dina's boot rested next to my face. "Dying isn't a choice right now. You'll be fine in an hour." She still held tight to the trembling eel twins. I almost felt sorry for them, even if they'd unintentionally done this to me.

"Do you remember how things were in Brailesu?" Whip asked, her voice low. She crouched so that her gaze was level with mine, green eyes bloodshot.

"I don't. Memory erasure. Paid a lot of money for it," I said, trying to plaster a confident grin on my face that felt like it had been dropped in acid.

"I see, you're going to play hard here." She leaned in closer before an alert went off in her wrist console.

"Yes? He's been spotted?" She glared at me. "No, no, follow him. I want a full report as soon as I get back." She tapped on an ear device that seemed to be implanted. "I'm on my way, make sure to wait for me." She walked back to her sleek, red hovercar, pulling out a hover disc.

"Well, Dina, I leave her to you." Whip nodded to Dina who immediately looked like the obedient servant, but there was something different in her face, a paler look crossing her skin as Whip hopped on her hover disc and sailed out of my cave.

Dina let go of the eel twins, who relaxed. "Give Whip information or leave Zeto." Her face looked so concerned, something I'd never seen her father show.

"Yeah, well, that might be easy if I had enough coin. Believe me, I'd be more than happy to see the back of her for the last time." Some feeling returned to my burning limbs.

"My father...I wish he hadn't." She pressed lightly on my hand, and I jolted away, a terrible acidic feeling in my limbs as I rolled against the wall of the cave, another wave of pain making my stomach turn.

"Your father...was a pig," I whispered.

Dina dry laughed. "Yeah, he was. I killed him." I looked at her, the hardened cast to her eyes now making sense. "Whip found out and brought me to her casino." She looked out at the eel twins, not moving, her hover waiting behind mine. "She says you're the best pilot." She looked out over the Scraggs in the distance. "Don't give her what she wants." Dina's expression darkened.

Dina held her hand outstretched toward me, my last flight out of the factory. She was smaller in her beige cotton shift that barely reached her knees. Her other hand held the gear box for the hangar gate to lift and let me out. Did she expect me to take her with me?

"Get away from the gate. Close it and stop being foolish," Wiid said.

His hand remained on her tail as they walked away together.

I blinked it away. I didn't want to return to anything that reminded me of him.

"You're the only slave to escape Brailesu," Dina said, sniffing.

"What about you?" I asked.

"Whip took me." A flicker in her eyes told me there was more. "I don't care about my future, but in forty-eight hours if I find you again, she's going to make sure you never leave."

She walked away, dragging the eel-men with her. They scuttled across the floor, their soft shoes making muffled sounds before they disappeared into her hover. Slowly Dina's perfume faded from the air. *So Wiid still had found me, even if it was in the form of his daughter.*

I tried to turn over, but my muscles wouldn't obey me. If I'd still had my goddess statue, I would have prayed, could even without it, I supposed. I tried to roll, but to no avail.

Dear goddess, help me. Please. Get me out of here.

I'm sorry it's been so long.

I attempted to roll again. No luck.

If I couldn't move, how was I going to get away? Whip was the most powerful person, besides Stencil, in all of Zeto City.

A memory of my father, hands open in one of his history books, fluttered before me. I closed my eyes and saw him bent over the battered book, bombs going off in the distance, explaining how the Hybrid Wars started.

"We could have developed the technology to leave Janus, but we chose to

kill each other instead." Father closed the book and leaned in closer to me. "We had too many years of hating people who were basically the same, when it came down to their emotions, what they loved, how they lived." He paused, thumping the book and then looking at me with his soft, yellow eyes. "Don't become like them, our masters here. Always try to do the better thing, the thing that feels impossible."

He'd sat close to me, holding out the lamp he'd made from salvaged materials and stolen oil. I reached for him and the past melted away.

Instead, Pinu stood in front of me, holding a blanket in her beak. I passed out before I could feel the warmth of it insulating me.

I woke to rain pelting outside of the cave. Pinu was asleep on my belly. When I tried to raise my head, Pinu moaned. My stomach rebelled, and I turned over to vomit. My muscles shook as I crawled to get up. The image of my father swam before me.

Do the thing that feels impossible.

A new ache in my chest spread, and I wasn't certain I wanted to do what I had to. My spine felt like it was on fire and my head ached horribly. Using the hover to support me, I stumbled around the vehicle to make sure that nothing else was amiss, or that there weren't hidden creatures coming for me in a second round of torture. Pinu hopped along with a partially unwrapped grain bar.

"Thank you, girl." I stuck it in my pocket for later. I needed to rinse the acidic taste out of my mouth.

After a shaky trip to the water cavern, I packed everything I could fit in the hover. I managed three bites of the grain bar while Pinu helped carry what she could in her beak. I took one last look at the cave. It didn't feel like mine anymore.

I started the engines for Shakratel's and didn't look back.

CHAPTER 22

TOREF

If there was a special doom assigned to the lower lifeforms of Janus, Toref decided this must be it. He'd scrubbed the same five toilets, basins, and floors for the past twelve hours, but the Monitors wouldn't let up. Not even Xiu. *I'm done with this tafla.*

Minerva grinned at Toref and he felt a surge of hope inside him. He wasn't sure where it was coming from, he was so exhausted. "We'll be done in a few hours." When he saw Rusty's glare, he whispered to Minerva, "I hope."

"I don't know about that." Minerva wiped the sweat off her brow with her arm and exhaled.

Her arm touched his, the sensation so pleasant he was afraid to move away. He wanted to comfort her because she hadn't been the same since they'd come back from Shakratel's. But did she want his comfort, now that they knew their dream of working in Zeto was riddled with so many holes? He felt that at the center of their necessary escape was getting Idris on board to help them navigate their way out.

"If we convinced Idris, I think we'd have a chance to make it to the Fringes," he blurted out.

Minerva turned to him, her eyes flashing, "Count me out. I like

Idris, but I'm not going back." Minerva tried to stand, but slumped back against the wall, leaning against Toref. Her head dropped to his shoulder in a swift movement that caused all of him to flush with heat, her hair soft where it touched his neck.

Toref watched Minerva carefully; she looked like she was going to be sick, she was so pale. "We can't go back to where I was. That place…" She covered her face, bringing her forehead to her hands before leaning back against the wall, half of her hair shielding her face. "I still have nightmares about them…how they barely numbed me before they took my legs, like I didn't matter. I almost died, you know?" She leaned her head against Toref's shoulder.

Toref gently touched her hair, but she said nothing.

"I won't let you anywhere near anyone like that. I'd die first, Minerva." Toref said, reaching for her arm, but unsure how to touch her properly. "Tell us, help us understand."

"We've got all the time in the world, and we couldn't make this place cleaner if we wiped it with our bare asses," Rusty remarked, and they all laughed.

When she looked at them, Toref could see the tears in the corners of her eyes. She raised her head, grinning, then got quiet again, staring at the ground, her hands at her sides.

"My parents fled to the Fringes during the war. As Ungar, it was hard to find work and they were separated into different camps of work for Hybrid gypsies who promised they'd be able to earn their own patch of land. They had almost nothing when they left the valley, except their ability to program modules and fix stuff."

She looked down at her artificial legs. "When things were terrible and we hadn't seen my father for months, the war was still going on. At the end, my mother had to sell me. It was either that or let both of us starve." She sniffed and exhaled looking Toref in the eye, a hardness in her eyes that he now understood. "The fleshmarketers wanted to sell off pieces of me in the city for kids who lost their legs in land mines. So, they took me to the Hybrid camps on the outskirts of the Fringe territories, close to Zeto City, and they took my legs. They gave me something to drink that would numb the pain, but it didn't fully work."

She rubbed at her knees. "I was maybe six...in a bad way when they called the Monitors to get me. Apparently they couldn't get me to stop screaming. I was lucky I have a good set of lungs. They saved me from the gypsies cutting off my arms."

Toref put his arm around her, a horrible feeling of darkness rising in his gut. She rested her head on his shoulder again. "We're not taking you back there."

"I know we have to find a solution, I just don't yet know what that is, so I'm afraid of everything." Minerva admitted, wiping her face on her uniform.

"I remember when you came. You were either really quiet or really loud. Nothing in between," Rusty said, smiling. He moved to the other side of Minerva. "Don't worry, Minnie, we'll figure something out."

"Don't. My parents used to call me Minnie."

Rusty nodded his head and he locked eyes with Toref, who squeezed her arm gently. An unspoken moment between the two of them. Toref knew he couldn't let Minerva go through anything like that again. He had to find a way to talk to Idris again and work at Shakratel's, for all three of them to be safe and away from the clutches of the casino bosses. And then, maybe there was a chance he could find his sisters.

"Maybe I can become a Monitor. All our problems are solved!" Rusty said. "I'll make sure we can all live here forever."

They laughed, not saying what they all knew. There's no way, after years of harassing and making the Monitors' lives difficult, that Rusty would ever be allowed to work at the Pods. Rusty put one hand under Minerva's arm and Toref followed to help her stand.

"Come on, let's finish up here. Maybe we can get Lagos to beg Briggs for mercy on our behalf. I can't take another day here," Toref said. He steered them toward the awning. The sky was thick with dark clouds, the air heavy with the scent of rain.

Lagos raced back inside and jumped off his hover disc. "I think I heard my name. You three ready to join the rest of civilization?"

They helped Minerva follow Lagos out. Toref knew that he was going to have to ask Lagos for another favor, but wasn't sure what he could offer in return after they messed things up the last time.

If you don't ask, you don't get, Lena, his oldest sister, used to say.

There was no hurt in trying.

When he glanced back at Minerva and Rusty, Rusty still had his arm tenderly around her, helping her walk. Toref moved his arm around her waist, allowing more of her weight to fall on him. If he couldn't change things for his family, he could try to change things for the three of them. Lagos was key to getting a message out to Idris. Rain pelted them as they ran for cover in the cafeteria hanger ahead before the rain soaked the ground, all the dirt turning to mud and rushing into a mini deluge. *It's now or never*, Toref thought.

"The longer we stay, the greater the risk I'm going to be found here, within the city limits." Rusty rubbed his mane of hair absently while they sat in the cafeteria at the Pods.

"Why don't we get to Shakratel's and figure things out from there?" Toref asked.

Minerva nodded, not looking at either of them. She kept tracing the lines on the map, looking forlorn. Toref put his hand gently on her shoulder, waiting for her to shrug him off, but she didn't. Rusty raised an eyebrow, but Toref shook his head. Now was not the time for Rusty to tease them.

Why couldn't he like her without an audience?

"Minerva?" Toref's voice was so quiet, he wasn't sure she heard him.

"I know, I know. I just want you to be prepared for how it's going to be. I understand it might be easier in the Fringes now, if we decide to go, than what I went through with my parents selling me. But, nothing changes fast here on Janus." She tapped at her legs. "And if we want to leave, we're going to have to make me new legs at Shakratel's. These don't fit very well."

She settled in closer to Toref and turned the map to face him. "If we kept to the water route here and another one of us knew how to fly, we'd probably make it to the other end of the peninsula in a day or so. Remember, though, life on the Fringes is different. I don't think either of you is ready for that."

She closed her tablet and clicked on her pocket lamp, getting up. The tiny glow lit her slow amble away from them. Toref watched her go back to her pod, even though he was hoping she'd join them at the Reserve.

"I think she might just leave for Shakratel's. And that means we can probably get out of here for good." Rusty's voice had a tinge of sadness to it, his voice catching on the last three words. "I never thought I'd leave this valley." He stood up and clapped a hand on Toref's back. "Be careful with her, my friend." Rusty ambled through the dark, his night vision sufficient to roam around without a lamp while Toref headed to the radio relay station.

CHAPTER 23

IDRIS

Yura and Shakratel stared at me from across the metal table, the late afternoon sun glinting off the surface. Both of their normally jovial faces were a picture of dread after I told them about Whip and Mira's visit to my cave. I must have looked awful, even after consuming double the lunch I would normally eat at their place.

"You have to leave, soon as possible," Shakratel said.

"I don't have the flow batteries to make it."

Shakratel thumped the table, annoyance creasing the folds of his cheeks. "I tell you, I give you what you need."

Yura rubbed his shoulder, then gently lifted my fingers in hers. "They could have killed you. I surprise you not more sick from the shocking." She exhaled loudly. "Idi, it not safe."

"I know, I just feel like...I don't know. It's too soon. Look at all you've helped me with. I don't want charity." Something else was lodged in my chest that I couldn't say to them, the feeling forming still.

Yura let go of my palms and put her hands on both of my shoulders. "Maybe we just needs to help, and someday you help someone else. Life like that, you know?"

I didn't exactly know how life was like that. But I knew that Yura and Shakratel had certainly kept me alive when no one else cared. I looked into Yura's grey eyes, her face full of concern for me. Now that I had my chance to leave, I was afraid, terrified, beyond any word that could describe the deep quaking within me. They were my family now. And you don't leave your family behind.

Why had it taken me so long to realize that?

Now, I can't leave them. Neither can I risk their safety by staying.

Samrah, Shakratel's niece, sauntered over. She no longer wore the loose flowing robes that most of Yura's women wore. She had on a jumpsuit, much like a mechanic, and handed over a piece of radiograph paper before slipping out quickly.

"Ah, so you have a message from your friends?" Yura asked, like she didn't know what the message said already. Pinu swung down to sniff at the paper.

IDRIS. NEED YR HELP. HAVE PLAN TO WORK. MSG BACK IF YOU CAN TAKE US TO SHAKRATEL'S, POSSIBLY TO FRINGES. WILL PAY OUR WAY-TOREF, R & M.

"Great," I said, rubbing my face. Everyone had already decided what I was going to do.

"You can't go to the Fringes alone," Shakratel said, leaning in and looking over the message. "You need smart companion." He looked over at one of his guards who was approaching and whispered in his ear.

Yura stood up and stared through me, as though she was seeing something new in me. "We won't let you leave alone. It not safe, and we have friend who needs go with you."

This was new. I looked up at Shakratel. He gestured for me to follow him down to his office. As we continued down the hallway, I caught Reggi working on my hover, removing a silvery bit of goop from the pilot's door. Probably a tracker. He nodded to me before torching the device. So they had tracked me here after all.

"I'm a danger to you now," I said to Shakratel.

He waved a hand. "Only if you stay longer than a few days. For Whip, I'm small operator. Outside Zeto's city limits. She has to work extra hard to scoop up a fish like me. But, it doesn't mean she won't do it, if you stay. Plus, I take away you, the orange hair, and two of her old workers. She not like that, if she know it me. But, I deal with it." He had a wry smile on his face and gestured to the men waiting for him. "I not survive her war jus' to let her boss me now."

Two of his bodyguards came close behind me. They were about as wide as they were tall, and I was a full head taller than them. I picked up my pace when I felt one of them breathe on my neck. Shakratel was more silent than I'd ever heard him, the rat-tat of his cane the only sound as the scent of soup dwindled the further we walked away from the dining hall. Was I in trouble with him? He reached a stairway I'd never seen, tucked at the back of where we'd turn to go into his office. We descended one floor to a network of tunnels that ran underneath the complex. I took off my shades so my eyes could adjust to the dim light.

Shakratel turned several dials on the walls as we passed under flickering yellow lights. When a huge wooden door creaked open at the end of the tunnel, the aroma of wet earth and foliage swept me into the room. Shakratel gestured for me to go in first. I stepped in hesitantly.

It was dim with a warm light, like it was dusk, yet still cool and inviting. Green plants surrounded the small room and at the opposite side, on a long wooden bench, sat a large Manox Hybrid, bigger than Shakratel, on an enormous purple cushion reading a paper book. He didn't look up when I entered.

Unlike other Hybrids, he wore very few clothes and was covered in dark fur. When Shakratel called out to him, he turned his large sorrowful yellow eyes toward me.

"Ho, Jesik." Shakratel said. Jesik rose from the bench, coming over to clap his hands on Shakratel's shoulders. His ox-like snout moved into a grin, his teeth white and flat.

"This Idris, I call her Idi, for small-name." Shakratel grinned.

I wasn't certain what to say. I'd never seen a Manox up close. "Ho,

Jesik," I said, sticking to Shakratel's greeting out of respect. Shakratel gestured for me to sit down.

The guards closed the door behind them and bolted it from the inside.

"What's happening?" I asked.

Shakratel raised a stony brow and exhaled. "Jesik escape Stencil's casino. He need go Fringe territories in few days, hopefully with you."

I looked at Jesik and tried to imagine his enormous bulk in my hover. He'd take up at least two seats.

"Other Hybrid come here from Whip's casino, ask question. Guards had to scare her away." Shakratel gestured toward Jesik. "He keep you hover safe safe till you leave."

"Why did you leave the casino?" I asked. I wasn't sure I wanted to hear another terrible story, but I had to know.

"They want I be their punisher. I not do it and escape, but head guard come after me, and I kill him by accident." The look in his haunted eyes told me there was more.

The image of Dina holding the tether on the eel twins swam in front of me for a half second before dissipating. I knew that worse things awaited those who went against the casino bosses. But it didn't mean I could leave for the Fringes with a complete stranger.

"I don't know," I said honestly. The thought of traveling with four people sounded like a terrible idea. It was nothing like my original plan to fly solo with Pinu.

Shakratel folded his hands carefully, looking me dead in the face. "We have everything you need to leave in three days."

"We'll need more time to install the flow batteries," I insisted.

Shakratel looked from me to Jesik, who hung his head.

"It's not that I don't want to, I just need more time—" I continued.

Shakratel put up his hands and cut me off. "We pay."

Jesik threw down a bag of coins. I had to keep myself from getting even more riled up. Didn't they understand it was about more than money?

"Can we discuss this without—" I tried to gesture that I didn't want to hurt Jesik's feelings, but after looking at his hanging head, I knew that had already been done. "That's a year's wages, and you know that. I owe you so much, please don't let me forever be in your debt."

Shakratel leaned in to where I sat. "It expensive to leave Zeto. The Fringe transport hovers leave once a month, sometime not so much. Jesik pay me, I pay you with retrofit and flow batteries." He took my hand in his calloused one. "You know you can't stay. I wish you could." He pulled me into his huge embrace, rocking me from side to side. "Danger too high, Idi." He sighed. "For both us."

He sounded like my father in that moment. I hugged him back, holding as tight as I could before releasing him, gaze trained up at the ceiling. I couldn't look at either of them when it felt like everything was falling apart worse than it already had. Once I was certain I wasn't going to cry, I glanced at Jesik and his friendly ox-like snout. *I can't abandon him.* He was large enough to scare the crap out of anyone tailing me. He could haul stuff and help me keep the kids in line, if it came to bringing them across, too.

I need more time. But that wasn't something I had.

"You'll let me pay you back someday, if I take Jesik with me to the outer Fringe territories?" I asked, checking with Shakratel.

"Yes." Shakratel's wrinkled face turned up at the corners, and he put his hand out. "There is no debt, only a chance for better life for you." He squeezed my hand. "That good enough payment for me, knowing you safe safe."

I held onto Shakratel's hand, almost unable to let go of him, and wishing I had made different choices that had allowed me to spend more time with him. *Why had I been so eager to always be on my own with Pinu?*

When Shakratel let go, I held out my other hand to Jesik. "Can you take down anybody who messes with us, or do I have to be the one to scare the bad *tafla*?" I asked Jesik.

"I make sure no one touch you!" Jesik said, withdrawing his hand.

Shakratel laughed a throaty chortle and clapped a hand on both of us. "You no worry 'bout Jesik. He get his name, Jesik or Quick Giant, for reason. You see. You see." He gestured toward his guards, and they opened the door, slipping the coin purse into Shakratel's hand.

One of the guards walked ahead of them and another followed directly behind Jesik. Shakratel's cane clacked as they ascended upward. "We have racer boys with large hover to borrow so you get Pods kids today," Shakratel said.

"Today?" I asked. An excitement stirred in my chest over flying someone else's hover, especially one of the rowdy racers.

Yura appeared, her yellow robes billowing as she walked through the stone corridor. "So you leave us." She crossed her arms, the smile lines around her full mouth deeper than they'd ever been. Shakratel patted my arm and continued onward with Jesik and his guards. Yura gestured toward her dressing rooms. "I get you change of clothes."

I was puzzled, fingering the lapel of my purple jumpsuit. "These are clean."

"We need disguise for you."

I looked out at the window for Pinu, still circling the compound. The gentle swooping of her large black wings in the air made me wish I wasn't leaving. How did I explain that to Yura when that's all I'd talked about the entire time she'd known me?

"Come." She took my hand, and it was cool and smooth in my rough palm. I held her closer to me, following her down the corridor, imprinting in my mind the shiny bounce to her loose curls bounding up and down. I had to remember all of the precious moments I had with her.

One of her entertainer girls brought out a blonde wig and a cropped white top that showed off a lot more of me than usual. She tried to thrust an impossibly small pink skirt at me, and I snatched a pair of tight pants instead.

"I need pants to fly."

"Thank you. Off now." Yura shooed the woman out of the dressing cubicle that was draped with an array of outfits, like they were waiting to dress me over again. The tight grey pants were high-waisted and molded to my legs nicely.

"You must look different, so it not easy to tell it you," Yura said. She inspected me carefully as I swapped out my tops. She gathered my hair into a knot at the top of my head and grabbed a swath of red cloth and swooped it around my head, forming a complicated, but beautiful knot. "That will do."

"Thank you. I definitely don't look like myself now."

"That the point," Yura said, a small smile playing at the corner of her mouth. Her grey eyes betrayed no mirth at all.

"I don't want to go," I spurted out. "I'll miss you too much…"

She took both my arms, scanning all of me before gently putting her arms around me. She held me close, squeezing me to her for a long time.

There were tears in her eyes when she looked at me again. "I know it right you go. But I not want it. I imagine for long time you stop liking cave, you live here with us and do all the cargo runs." She wiped her eyes and I felt that stronger closeness with her that made it so much harder to leave, now that I knew I felt at home here. "I know it not a big, flashy life, but it a good life."

"And now it's impossible," I said, keeping my arm around her waist. "I never really felt at home in the cave, I just felt it was necessary. So, I wasn't taking advantage. I took forever realizing…" I let my voice drift off because I felt the pressing of the memory of the factory edging in from the corners of my brain. "I don't want to leave with strangers to the Fringes when I'm finally home here."

She took my hand and we stood there, hands rocking back and forth. She reached down and kissed my cheek. "I know you'll do the right thing, even if it tear both of us apart." Her heart-shaped face glistened as tears tracked down her cheeks.

I wiped my eyes. It was impossible not to cry if Yura was, too. "I will. I know it isn't safe for us," I admitted.

"A lot of people are counting on you. You can always come back, if you don't like it. By then, Whip will have cooled, or maybe we get lucky and someone kills her. Maybe even Stencil?" Yura shuddered a bit. "Maybe we get lucky and they kill each other." She threw her hands in the air. "Zeto City is saved!"

I couldn't help laughing. Footsteps clacked on the stone floors and Reggi peeked through at us. "I've got keys to one of the racers for you to try out." He looked at me, his gaze level with my eyes, despite my ridiculous outfit.

"You look nice," he said, then getting shy and wringing his hands before he placed the key fob in my palm. "I'll see you outside."

Yura crossed her arms and lifted an eyebrow. "Any other reason maybe you want stay longer?"

I shook my head and started back toward the hangar bay. I couldn't let her know that I'd miss Reggi more than I liked to admit, even to myself.

Outside, the heat shimmered down on me, the sun beating on my exposed midriff. I sauntered over to the borrowed electric blue hover. I pressed the lock release and Jesik showed up, seemingly out of thin air. "Where were you?" I asked.

"I ate, and then I wait." He crossed his hoof hands in front of his massive chest. "This outfit look stupid. You not choose this?" He kept his eyes even with mine.

The way he held my gaze made me like him instantly. "Yeah, it's a disguise."

"That make it maybe okay." The corner of his mouth turned up, and he gestured toward the hover for me to let him in.

It was definitely possible we could be friends with his no-nonsense attitude. "Get in and check that the copilot safety strap fits, otherwise I'll snag you a new one."

Jesik doubled up two of the straps on the two seats he sat on, and they barely made it over his middle.

"Wanna race?" Mussa, one of the racers, waved to me. He was

eyeing my bare midriff. I looked back to see if Reggi was around, but all I could see were his legs as he worked on my hover.

"You might regret this!" I said to Mussa, hopping in. Why not have a little fun on my way to pick up the Pods kids?

Mussa ran over to his hover and revved the engines.

Pinu hopped up and down in front of the copilot's door, and I pressed one button to open all the doors again. *Fancy.*

"Cheep, meep, cheep!" Pinu chastised me, and I opened the strap so she could belt herself in. Once she was settled, she looked over the new dials. Jesik was grinning from the back.

"Landing gear here, stabilizer here, and don't worry about the radio until we're done with this flight."

Pinu nodded and settled back.

Mussa revved his engines again, and I snapped down my sunshades. I throttled us back and we sailed out of the hanger, my stomach against my spine and my whole body rocketed against the pilot's chair. The g-force against my body was exhilarating. I almost threw us into a complete corkscrew loop before I righted us and headed toward the Pods.

At least I could fly something that knew how to zoom for once without worrying about breaking it.

CHAPTER 24

TOREF

Toref waited with his friends in the afternoon swelter. Field sprinklers whirring in the dusty green of the fields, the only sounds to break the gnawing silence. Doubts flooded Toref's brain. What if Idris didn't come? What if something happened to her on the way to the Pods? Or, if she changed her mind?

An electric blue racer blasted out of thin air and slowly came to a stop in front of him, Minerva, and Rusty. Its white-blue lights illuminated Rusty and Minerva's shocked faces. Toref wasn't sure the hover was for them until it landed, and Idris jumped out.

"Well, what are you all waiting for?" she asked, arms crossed.

A deep seizure started in his stomach and he had to exhale deeply to release it. *It's finally real: we're leaving the Pods.* He looked back over the complex, the stadium lights illuminating the dusty complex along with the occasional whirs of Monitors whizzing by on their discs. He never thought he'd imagine missing his time at the Pods.

"I don't know if I'm ready," Rusty whispered next to him, tugging at his orange mane.

"Don't let me be the brave one to step in first," Minerva muttered, pushing Rusty forward.

He took a step toward the hover, and Toref still held back. A Manox stepped out to let them in, his huge bulk towering over them.

"This is Jesik," Idris said dryly. "Our bodyguard."

Jesik got a pleased look on his furred oxface. "Come in, there's room for all." There was something warm and pleasant about him that Toref liked, and he felt himself involuntarily walking toward the hover. They weren't on their own, just the three of them. They had a whole crew now, didn't they? Why, then, didn't he feel better about leaving? *Is it the uncertainty about Penny and Lena?*

He looked up at his friends, Minerva watching him carefully, her mouth drawn in a thin line. *I probably have a better chance of knowing something if I leave this place, than if I stay.*

The gates leading into the main entrance of the complex were ajar, a chain loosely affixed around them. Monitors Lagos and Xiu's smiling faces peered through. They threw their discs down and surfed over the tall gates to join the group on the other side. Lagos held his beefy arms wide and wrapped them around Toref, squeezing tight.

"You take care of these two. I don't think we'd have ever gotten Rusty out of here alive if it wasn't for you and Minerva," Xiu said, her hair feathers touching his cheek as she hugged him next.

Lagos's crushing hug reminded Toref of his dad, on days when Toref was struggling at school. It was painful to allow Lagos to let him go, to know that those hugs wouldn't be freely available from anyone in the near future. That the future was this unknown invisible line stretching out in front of him.

Toref looked at the last two caring, living adults in his life. He wasn't certain how he'd go on, but he knew he had to. He put one last hand on Lagos and Xiu's arms.

"Thank you for everything." He wanted to say *I'll see you again. We'll stop in and see how things are going.* But he knew that would never happen.

When Toref glanced inside the hover, Rusty and Minerva had tears streaking down their faces. He had to squeeze between them once Jesik entered the hover.

"Belt in, people!" Idris yelled.

The doors shut automatically, and they were airborne within seconds. Zeto glittered to his left, the bright lights and red circular magnetic bands iridescent. The city seemed to call to him, to invite him to try to find his sisters in its terrible, garish light. He had to turn away and set his sights somewhere else. It was no good dwelling on what he couldn't change. He felt the warmth of Minerva's hand and he leaned into her, the softness of her head leaning on his shoulder, making his heart settle for the first time in days.

CHAPTER 25

IDRIS

I monitored the wary look on Toref's face, shadows moving underneath his purple eyes while we sat in Shakratel's hangar bay. He continued to work slowly on the flow battery connectors, but I could tell his heart wasn't in it. Minerva also watched him carefully, not joking or prodding at him like she had the day before.

I approached Toref, taking one of the wires he'd just connected and I threaded it through the console pegs. "Something's wrong," I said.

Toref looked down at me, let go of the wire, and sighed. "Yeah."

I leaned in closer to him. "Is it Minerva?" I asked. I knew she wasn't too hot about going to the Fringe territories.

"No." He leaned out, as if looking to see if anyone could overhear us.

"What is it then?"

"It's my sisters."

The way he said it—the shadows moving to his eyes, causing moisture to build up, but not spill over—I knew it was deep.

"I don't want to leave without knowing where they are." He sat down in the cargo area and told me everything that had happened to them. "It feels impossible to find them now. I mean, I don't even know where to look."

A crazy thought occurred to me. We weren't equipped to take on more passengers as it was. It was going to be a tight squeeze with Jesik all the way to the Thousand Lakes district where Shakratel felt it was best to resettle, but I also couldn't do nothing. If I'd had a chance to see my parents, even for five more minutes, I would have given up everything.

"I don't think it's impossible. Maybe crazy, but not impossible," I said, the idea still forming. Jesik had spent a lot of time in Stencil's casino. If Toref's sisters were there, he might know something.

"Come with me." I hopped out of the hover and waved for him to follow me into the dining hall where Jesik was helping the servers make breakfast. Samrah played a light tune on the tanaloon while Yura crooned along.

When I signaled to Jesik, he stopped chopping carrots and wiped his face on his yellow apron.

I let Toref talk.

"I'm looking for…" He started describing their appearance, and Jesik got very quiet. His large eyes went wide when Toref pointed out his younger sister's features and how she resembled him.

Samrah and Yura's song ended and Samrah came over to where we sat discussing. Samrah's face looked very somber as she looked at Toref, the daylight reflecting off his dark skin.

One of Samrah's thick eyebrows rose. "One of your sisters look like you?" she asked.

"The youngest, Penny. The oldest is much taller than me, very thin, with a beautiful singing voice."

"What does it sound like?" Samrah asked.

"Um…deep, low, and throaty, I think?" Toref said.

Samrah started to look a bit agitated. "Can you sing one of her songs?"

Toref began singing.

They say
You got mountains to climb
They say
You are losing time

When Samrah's face changed, an unmistakable recognition, he stopped.

"Lena?" she asked.

"Yes." Toref's whole body went rigid, and he stood up. I was afraid at that moment for Samrah to give him hope when we didn't know if his sister was still in that casino, or if she'd been traded.

"I knew her. Only a short time. She very, very good singer," Samrah said, her face somber. "I don't know if she still there. It not good place." She sighed and walked away to rejoin Yura on the stage. Toref started to reach for her before I pulled him back.

"Let her go, Toref. We'll ask her again in a few hours if she can give us any more details."

Toref hung his head. "I feel like I need to go there, even if I don't find them. Just to try." I put my hand on his shoulder, feeling his body heave with all the feelings that must've been coursing through him.

"I want to help, Toref. But I don't know how to get into the casino without all of us being in danger again."

Rusty sat beside us, grease all over his freckled hands. "We need you back in the hangar." He took one look at Toref and wiped his hands on his grey jumpsuit. "Hey, Toref. You get more information?" He swiftly was by Toref's side and embraced his friend after a few moments of them whispering together.

I let them talk it out, walking back to the hangar bay with a heavy feeling in my chest, my parent's faces floating in front of me.

CHAPTER 26

IDRIS

Hours later, Minerva rushed into the hangar bay, knocking over tools as she staggered against the workbench. I immediately ran to assist her with walking, assuming it had something to do with her new prosthetic legs. "I can't find Toref or Rusty." She leaned over to catch her breath. "They've been gone for at least a half hour or more."

I looked past her into the dining room, the fans whirling overhead and the sound of the game tables echoing beyond. "He's probably just in the back with the big gamblers, trying to steal more of their coin."

Her pale face flushed, her freckles looking darker. "I already looked. Jesik, too." Jesik quietly approached, his bulky demeanor a bit hunched, like he expected me to explode.

"Maybe they went exploring outside." I called to Pinu, who was perched in the rafters of the dining room, waiting for someone to let her peck at their scraps. "Pinu, come on. I need your help."

She cheeped and swung down, settling on my shoulder, her claws digging in. "Help us find Toref and Rusty outside." With a few beats of her large black wings, she was airborne and out the double latticed doors that led to Yura's garden. I followed her outside, the day still crisp and overcast. It looked like rain was on the horizon with high thunderheads gathering beyond the golden Scraggs in the distance.

Minerva lightly touched my shoulder. "I don't think they're here. We've been looking all over for them."

When I saw the way she looked at me, pink eyes wide, her mouth pulled tight, I knew that something else was going on. Something she knew a lot more about than me.

"Where do you think they went?"

She exhaled, settling down on a huge boulder with moss around it. "Probably one of the casinos to find out where Toref's sisters are."

"We don't know that for sure," I replied, hoping they were somewhere beyond the prairie grass, fooling around, like normal teenagers were supposed to.

Reggi bounded outside, his furry hair wild. "I saw them take off with Mussa twenty minutes ago. Sorry, Yura just told me you were looking for them. I thought they were just taking a short ride, otherwise…" he let his voice trail off.

"We have to go get them." Luckily I still had my disguise on. "There isn't any time to spare." I pointed to the only hover in the dock. "Reggi I need you to tell me what direction you saw them fly, anything to help us locate them fast."

"Get the landing gear ready." Minerva followed my instructions to co-pilot the racing hover we'd borrowed. I had to leave Pinu behind, and each of us were dressed in long, hooded robes that Yura and Samrah had put over our clothes. "You find them and get out of there fast," she'd said.

I adjusted the large sunshades Samrah had slipped on my face before I'd left.

"There!" Jesik pointed to a landing spot close to one of Stencil's casinos.

"How do we know that they're there?" I asked.

"If Whip is looking for Rusty and you, it's likely they wouldn't hit one of her casinos first," Minerva said. "They might be stupid right now, but not so stupid to go into Whip's lair."

"That's three casinos we have to search through," I grumbled, shifting down to make way for landing. "Landing gear, Minerva."

She was a pro, remembering everything I'd told her on takeoff. We landed without a hitch and were left staring upward at the sparkling red flagstones of Garnet, Stencil's largest casino.

"I hate this place," Jesik grumbled, going to open the door.

"We need to stay together, and one of us will remain in the hover at all times," I said. "I don't want it to get towed."

Minerva looked at me nervously. "I can stay, but if I have to fly the hover, I don't know that I'd do a very good job."

"All you have to do is get it in the air long enough for the security drones to leave," I said, patting her on the shoulder. I was hoping it wouldn't come to that. I wished Reggi weren't so strapped with my hover repairs because an extra pair of hands would have been helpful right about now.

The day was already heating up, and I hit the button for the cabin windows to come down a bit more and let in what little breeze there was. My stomach and limbs felt all aflutter. I did not want to run into Whip or her cronies again. I knew the chances were slim in her archenemy's casino, but still.

I scanned the crowded landing strip of hovers and spotted Mussa's lime green hover. "Look, there's Mussa's hover." My body was on such high alert that my leg muscles felt like rocks.

"What if it's another one that looks just like it?" Minerva asked.

"No one else would waste coin painting their hover that color. Keep an eye out for them if they leave before we find them," I said.

Minerva nodded and looked over the controls, like she was memorizing them.

"Don't worry, we're only going to go in for a few minutes, twenty minutes tops before coming back," I said, before whispering a quick prayer to the goddess.

Jesik gestured toward the towering revolving brass doors at the front, at least three times higher than me. Such opulence wasn't making me feel any more comfortable about going in. The minute we stepped through, Jesik stayed by my side, our hoods drawn over our heads.

"Where's the gaming room you'd expect someone like Rusty to be in?" I asked.

Jesik contemplated this, bringing a hoof hand to his snout. "Maybe not jus' gaming, but music?"

"Right, to the entertainment rooms, then." Jesik nodded and took my arm gently, leading me down a tall stone corridor with arched ceilings and an upper level of stained glass windows that let in the sunlight. It was especially cool inside, and it felt like normal life was hushed outside.

I didn't like the feeling. It was artificial and a lot was hiding behind the posh surroundings and perfumed air. We made our way through an atrium and into an arched doorway where players silently spun wheels and traded cards. Soft singing drifted in from the back of the room.

When we stepped in, I clocked Rusty's orange mane. I was ready to rip every hair off his head, but Jesik held me back. "No acknowledge you know, move slow-slow to table before approach."

He surveyed the room, and I counted at least six guards in the enormous space.

"It's a good thing Stencil's on vacation. Means things a little looser around here while he's on the coast," I overheard one guard say to another.

Toref looked up at us from the table he sat across with Rusty and guilt spilled over into his violet eyes. He nodded to the stage, and I saw a girl come onstage that looked like his description of his tall, willowy sister. She began singing and I had no doubt he thought he'd found her. The shocked look on Toref's face said everything.

CHAPTER 27

TOREF

Toref knew he had to be careful. He couldn't just announce himself to Lena. It was too dangerous, even if the guards seemed to be feeling calm with their big boss, Stencil, away on the coast.

Please let me get to her safely.

He crept around the perimeter of the gaming room, the thick carpet cushioning his every step, the air perfumed with jasmine.

The crowd turned when Lena sang softly, the tune soothing and strangely enchanting. Her voice crescendoed into a powerful vibrato that made Toref stop. Lena's newly purple reptilian skin shone from the warm amber light fixtures above while a guitar accompanied her.

"Keep moving," Jesik said, bumping lightly into Toref, surprising him.

Toref glanced back to where Rusty played, a sly smile on his face. The rest of the players were clearly annoyed with him already. That couldn't be good.

The song shifted and no one clapped. Guards in wrapper suits flanked the exits from the stage. They looked bored. Toref glanced at Lena again, her green eyes locked on his while she sang. She shook her head. Only a little, before looking out over the crowd, her face beaming, but her eyes were dead and cold. When her smile lifted again and she shook her head at Toref, he knew everything had changed.

Idris sidled up next to Rusty.

I have to make a move now, before they force me to leave.

When Lena finished the last song, she moved past the guards, who tried to keep her onstage.

Toref's biceps were held tightly behind him, Jesik whispering in his ear. "Don't talk her right now. Everyone watching."

Plenty of people were following her exit from the stage, but it didn't mean they were watching him. He pulled himself out of Jesik's reach and Idris immediately clamped her hands onto Toref's arm. "We have to get out of here."

"That's Lena, isn't it?" Rusty was beside him, nodding to her retreating figure walking past the guards who trailed her emerald dress that fluttered as she made her way through the northern doors in the gaming room. "She's beautiful..." Rusty followed after the guards.

Toref dashed out into the hallway after Lena. *This is my chance.*

Jesik jogged next to him, not caring that people were now watching them.

Toref darted down the three-way corridor, desperate to find the billowing emerald dress. His sister stood out from the hallway's red-and-gold diamond patterns. Her long face was drawn. "Lena..."

"Follow me," she said, and pointed at the stairway to the left of the elevators.

"What's wrong, why aren't you happy to see me?" Toref asked. *Why wasn't she saying how good it was to see me, how she missed me?* All the things he'd imagined she'd say when they were reunited? A hollow pit formed in his stomach.

Lena looked behind them, then up at a circular orb above them. Jesik followed directly behind her, blocking Toref from embracing her. Only the glimmer of the hem of her billowy dress gave any indication that any part of her was still alive in a way that he could understand.

"Lena, slow down. Please!" Toref called after her.

Idris followed closely behind Toref. "We're clear at the tail, for now."

Lena led them through several corridors before descending another flight of stairs. Toref was keeping track so they could make a quick escape.

"It could be trap," Jesik said, stopping behind Lena, who took his arm and tried to get him to follow her. Jesik didn't budge.

"We don't have much time. Please. I know where Penny is. You have to take her with you," Lena pleaded.

Toref was almost too shocked to say anything. They'd been here this whole time and his Mom hadn't said anything. *Why had she lied?* The thoughts were threatening to consume all rational thought. He focused on Lena's slight figure leading them down the stairs, any sense of her being a teenager evaporated, as if she'd taken his mother's place and suddenly become an adult.

The smell of barbecue wafting up the stairs made his stomach rumble. But, he was too sick with the knowledge that his sisters had been here for almost two months. Idris' previous warnings echoed in his mind, and he almost ran into one of the short, Hybrid servers holding platters of food to take up the stairs.

"She's in the food prep area, over there," Lena pointed. "I have to get back."

Toref took her thin hand before she could get away, "Wait! Please, Lena. I've been looking for you for weeks. I'm sorry I didn't find you earlier, I tried…"

"Don't." She snatched her hand back, acting as if his touch hurt. "It's Penny you came for. Get her and go."

Toref was afraid he'd hurt her. "I've been looking for you for so long. Please, Lena. We've got a hover, there's room."

The servers around them were moving quickly, and a few stopped to stare.

"I can't." She looked around, overdressed in the kitchen full of servers and cooks in jumpsuits and white aprons. "I'm not…good. They've changed me. What they've done, I can't undo. Nobody can.

Forget you saw me. I'll be dead soon anyway." Lena ran off, her dress one large billow of green, and Toref hated that when he lunged for her he only felt the swift rustle of the emerald fabric slipping through his palms. A familiar female voice called after her.

"Lena, get back here. I haven't seen you for days. I've got your favorite…" Penny's voice faded, sounding even sadder than Toref felt. When Penny caught sight of him, she sobbed, letting the small tray she'd been holding clatter to the counter she stood beside.

"Toref, I knew you'd come for us. Quick, we have to—" Penny embraced him and then she pulled him through a plastic partition, Jesik and Rusty following close behind with Idris slipping in front of them. Shouts broke out and the stampeding of feet told him they'd been spotted. "We've got to run, come on."

Jesik pushed them in front. "Lead the way up," he said to Penny, who Toref kept within arm's reach as she led them through the frozen area, partitioned by thick, plastic sheeting that hung from the ceiling. When they left the freezer area, two guards waited for them, stun guns pointed at Toref and Rusty. "You're not taking her." Toref growled, throwing his arms protectively around Penny, wishing there was some way they could run back and grab Lena, too.

Jesik bumped the guards into each other, stealing their stun guns and hitting them over the head with the back end. Toref grabbed one gun as the group charged up the staircase.

"This way to the lobby and outside," Penny called out to them.

Idris was waiting for them at the top of the stairs, a hood obscuring her face. Beyond her, an entourage of guards with different, sapphire-colored uniforms followed. Toref spotted an enormous woman, who resembled posters of Whip, sauntering down the corridor to his left, almost as tall as Jesik. *What is she doing here?* She was accompanied by a small Hybrid girl with purple hair. *Tafla, while Stencil is on vacation she thinks she can invade his casino.* Toref looked for another way out, a way to keep Idris away from that horrible woman.

"Oh no...we gotta jet," Idris declared. "Make sure you run for Mussa's hover!" She yelled before running through the revolving doors and outside.

Toref tried to whisk the rest of the group outside, but Rusty and Penny were frozen watching the entourage. Whip and the Hybrid girl stopped a distance from the group and pointed at Rusty. "Grab my son before they run, Dina."

Oh no, oh no! Not this now!

Dina took one step toward Rusty, snapped an electrocoil whip, and dragged him to Whip's side before Toref could do anything.

"You're all dead, you hear me? Don't come between me and what's mine!" Whip yelled at them, directing a swarm of guards.

Toref lunged for his sister, but he was too late, one of Stencil's guards had already grabbed her, dragging her out of Toref and Jesik's grasp. "Nooo!"

Toref tried to break past them to reach Rusty and Penny. "You can't take them!"

Whip stood in front of him, dragging him away, while Rusty looked back, his face covered in tears. "Don't leave me here!"

"Rusty, Penny, no!" Toref called out while Jesik lifted Toref over his shoulder. "We can't just leave them there, Jesik!" Toref pressed the charge button on the stun gun and shot a charge that sailed over Whip's head. Dina took a running leap at him and he shot again, hitting her with a bolt that made her crumple on the ground. They had to get out of there, but he didn't want to leave his sisters and Rusty behind, not without a fight.

Through the revolving glass doors, he caught a glimpse of Minerva piloting the hover. Idris flew through the next rotation of the doors with another stun gun and shot at the remaining guards.

Jesik jumped in front of Toref, knocking two of the guards to the ground. "We go now." He pointed to Idris' retreating figure. "Get in the hover."

When he turned around again, guards were still coming. Jesik kept firing rounds from the stun gun. Toref raced toward the levitating hover already in the air, and Jesik lifted Toref into the open passenger door and grabbed onto the landing rails while they levitated away from the gathering mob of guards.

"Come on, don't let go, Jesik!" Toref strained to pull Jesik inside. "Almost got you, Jesik." With one last heave, he slammed the passenger door shut behind both of them. Mussa's hover had already taken off ahead of them.

"I can't believe you did that to us!" Idris called out to Toref. "Fasten your belts, people, we need to get out of this airspace, fast." Toref looked at the fading red dot that was Garnet casino and he felt a horrible ache that he was so close to rescuing his sisters. Instead, he ended up losing his best friend and putting all of them in danger.

"I'm sorry, I was so…stupid," Toref said to Idris, who looked away.

"Strap in people, we're in for a bumpy ride," Idris said, flicking a switch. She throttled back, and when Minerva confirmed everyone was strapped in, they bolted out of the city center. They circled the squat and shanty outskirts of Zeto City for what felt like hours. Toref stared at the seemingly desolate city, a terrible gnawing in his chest. Now what? How can I ever apologize to them for getting Rusty captured and all of us now in trouble with two casino bosses?

"We've lost the trail of anyone who tried to follow us, I think it's safe to go back to Shakratel's." Idris' voice sounded flat and exhausted.

"What can I do…what can we do…?" Toref's voice trailed off, as he felt so defeated, so aware of his haste and how it brought everything crumbling down.

"We can't," Idris said. "We're now all wanted. There are cameras all over the casinos, and they'll save our image and have their cronies on the lookout for us. We have to leave for the Fringes so we don't endanger Shakratel."

Jesik scooted closer. "You heard Whip. She Rusty mom. Once Whip have you, good luck," Jesik said. "She's worse than Stencil." The smoke from the stackjoints rose in small billows below them. "Stencil bad guy, but he not enjoy hurt people like Whip."

Toref hunched over, putting his hands in his head. *How could I have gotten this so wrong?*

"Need more people to rescue them, Toref," Jesik said gently. He tried to touch Toref's arm, but Toref shrugged him off.

"You don't understand," Toref said, staring out the window, not looking at him. *I can't just leave them there in that awful place.*

He looked out the window, charting out in his mind how it would work, how many more people they'd need to storm in and rescue them. But, as he plotted it out, he knew that it wouldn't work. They didn't have the time, the manpower, and most of all, Lena had bolted when she'd seen him. She hadn't even wanted to be around him.

What had they done to her? How could my mother...

Every effort seemed to have some stupid setback waiting for him. He saw Penny in those final moments, those once chubby cheeks now flat and bony. *Why can't I get a break to help them?*

The city receded in the distance, and for once, he wished he could cut off his emotions like Idris, or be super strong like Jesik. Anything other than the gnawing pain that seemed to never stop inside of him, like a whirling, angry storm.

CHAPTER 28

IDRIS

I'd never seen Shakratel greet me when I'd landed before. We were in deep tafla, even deeper than I had imagined. He was flanked by eight of his bodyguards. When I got out, I rushed over to him, his face all furrows and grey wrinkles.

"Follow my men," Shakratel commanded, gently taking my hand.

"I'm sorry this happened Shakratel, it's all my fault," Toref tried to explain, but I put out my hand to hush him. Who knew who was listening and possibly spying on us from one of the casinos for some extra coin?

We were rushed through the hangar bay to Yura's back gardens.

Shakratel stopped, out of breath. "I never think it get dis bad. You gotta leave in a few hours. Soon soon, my child." He gestured toward the benches and tables outside. "Sit here, and I've set my guards around you. No one come here except Yura and me."

Minerva and Toref settled next to Jesik, looking more despondent than I felt.

"What happen?" Yura rushed into the back garden, flanking me on the other side and throwing glares at Toref. I filled them in on everything that happened.

Both she and Shakratel had deep circles under their eyes, looking as exhausted as I felt. Pinu flew to my shoulder and pecked at my ear, letting me know she was there. I smoothed her raven black feathers.

"So, they have Rusty? And Toref's sisters?" Shakratel asked, his blue-grey eyes tired.

"It happened so quickly." I wiped a sheen of sweat from my forehead. "There were so many guards…I'm surprised we got away."

He nodded, looking around the garden like he was making sure no one had snuck in to listen to us. "I surprise too. But glad, so very, very glad you safe here." He put a large palm on my forearm. "You see Whip?"

I nodded. "She said Rusty is her son."

Shakratel sighed and looked up at the ceiling. "Whip's son been in my compound. Now, that something. You think he know?"

I shook my head. "No clue. He didn't even want to go with her."

He brought me close, folding me into him. The minerals on his bare chest glistened, and I laid my head there. "We don't want her claim you, too." He held me out from him, with a look I'd seen him give Yura before, mouth turned down, his eyes misty. "We make sure they not take you. Two hours then, Idi?"

"Is Reggi almost finished with the repairs?"

"He say so…" Yura said, looking unsure. "Anyway, if it longer, that okay, you all need eat and rest a little before the journey."

A terrible lump formed in my throat. I knew we were putting them in danger, but it didn't make it any easier. I wiped an errant tear from my eye before clearing my throat. "If my hover and supplies are ready, we'll be gone as soon as possible," I said, trying to keep my voice from quaking. I didn't want Toref and Minerva to see how upset I was.

The moment had finally come, and I couldn't move a millimeter. I didn't know how I was going to be able to leave Shakratel and Yura so soon. I looked at Toref whispering softly to Minerva.

My pain was nothing like hers in losing Rusty. I'd had the advantage of years of being on my own. It had been hard, but…I looked up at Shakratel…I had him and Yura, at least.

"I wish I could pay you back." I wished I could have said *I don't want to leave you now. You're all I have.* The words were stuck in my throat.

I knew there was too much danger in my trying to stay longer. Per usual, the choice had been made for me.

Shakratel waved his hand, tapping his cane on the ground. "Naw, naw. You take Jesik and these two and make sure they safe safe, and that all that matter. Yura will rest happy that you all had new life chance. This not the end, Idi. More happy times will come."

I wanted to believe him.

He put a hand on my shoulder, tapped twice and took off through the main entrance. "You bolt behind me. Yura and the girls will come with food for you, then in few hours we get all supply you need to go safe safe."

"Should I follow you out?" I asked.

Shakratel grinned. "Rest for once, Idi. It been a big day." He paused for a moment, addressing all of us. "Maybe, too big for one day, so you all let some calm in. I know it hard, but try." I put a hand on his shoulder before embracing him. I didn't want to let him go.

Jesik followed Shakratel out and bolted the garden door behind him, his hulking figure somehow more serene than anyone else.

"Thank you, Jesik," I said, walking over to the long bench beside him. I kept my eye on Toref and Minerva, still furiously whispering. Jesik came to stand silently by my side, as though awaiting instructions, when Toref and Minerva approached us.

"What is it?" I asked.

"I just want to tell you how sorry I am." Toref looked askance and wiped away a tear that tracked down his dark face. Jesik tried to embrace Toref, but stopped when Toref glared at him. "I just wish there was some way to not lose Rusty and have my sisters with us when we leave."

"We have to leave, otherwise we put this whole compound in danger," I said.

Minerva took off her prosthetic legs, sighing. "I know, it just doesn't make it any easier. I'm terrified to leave, even though I know we have to."

I sat down next to her, drawing my knees into my chest. "Every minute we're here, we are putting everyone here in danger, even if we're outside of Zeto's limits." I sighed, looking up at the skies. "Those bosses will do anything to anyone, we are just pieces they feel they can maneuver on a Ruga board."

Toref sighed, pushing one of the orchids that had come closer to him away from his bare arms. "I just wish…there were some way…" he looked at Minerva, but she just shook her head.

"We can't help them right now. We'd need a huge group of people, and even then, it's a huge risk. You saw what your stunt got us."

I saw I'd been too harsh when Toref ended up in tears, Minerva scooting closer to put her arm around him.

"Look, once we get to a good community in the outer rim of the Fringes, we might find people to help us."

Toref nodded, resigned. "So we leave in a few hours?"

Minerva looked up at me, stricken.

"As soon as possible. I'll need Minerva to help copilot, and Toref you'll need to help with navigation."

Toref stood up, pacing along the periphery of the garden. "It's all my fault."

"Don't be stupid," I said. My head ached, and I really needed them all to shut up long enough for me to have just a little peace. When I saw the hurt looks on his and Minerva's faces, I knew I couldn't just leave the conversation there. These were people I'd be traveling across half of the continent with.

"I'm a former factory slave. Born and bred. I saw my parents die. Nobody but Shakratel, Yura, and my dead parents ever cared about me, besides Pinu." I looked up at the darkening skies, rain starting in the distance. "Maybe it will help if you start concentrating on what you have now instead of what you lack." I walked away, Jesik trailing after me to unbolt the doors into the dining area.

"I'd rather die than leave without my family," Toref said softly.

"Good thing this isn't up to you. Feel free to play hero when you aren't risking all of our lives. We're leaving in a few hours with or without you." I raised my arm for Pinu to come down from the roof. She waited until I was in the dining room before she landed on my arm. Jesik patted me on the arm twice before rejoining Toref and Minerva back in the gardens.

I watched them through the window. Pinu curled up on my side while Jesik and Minerva spoke to Toref. I'd forgotten how hope could strangle even the most innocent and well-meaning of people.

CHAPTER 29

TOREF

"Toref, we see you!" *Lena and Penny called out to him.*

In each hand they held out hotcakes as they ran across the ravines, jumping over boulders.

"Wait for me! I want a hotcake, too!" He ran after their dark figures quickly skimming over rocks, stopping to take bites of their hotcakes.

Penny stopped and handed him the last one in her pocket. When he took it in his palm, it was still warm.

Someone placed a blanket over him and when he awoke, dinner had been brought in by Yura and her guards. Jesik sang with Yura's girls as they passed around the plates of rice, crispy chicken, and parabela fizz drinks. Minerva seemed calmer, taking a seat next to Toref and even taking food from his plate, like at the Pods.

He stole a glance at Idris, and he got a short nod before her yellow eyes darted away. Would they ever be normal around each other?

An hour later, Toref couldn't help rubbing at the gnawing pain in his chest as he watched Yura and Shakratel hold onto Idris, her starting to pull away before they pulled her back into their embrace again. Tears streamed down all of their cheeks and after they laughed a bit, they finally patted Idris on the back and shooed her inside the hover. Toref was the last one standing looking at them, for a moment their visages interchangeable with what he imagined his parents would have been if things had been different. If he'd been able to actually say goodbye.

"Toref, it's time," Minerva called out to him. He had to remember that she was still here and that she was worth fighting for, even if he'd lost everything else. Maybe it was better this way, to fade away rather than having a finite goodbye.

He waved to Yura and Shakratel. "I'm sorry I put you in danger." They both clapped hands on him, but didn't say anything as he stepped up into the hover.

Idris looked back at Toref once he belted in, her eyes tear-streaked, and she gave him a tight smile. He nodded to Minerva, holding her gaze before she helped start the engines up as copilot.

As they flew away from the valley, the salmon and purple stone hills flitted by more quickly than Toref had imagined. He looked at the changing landscape below, now all grasses and occasional stumpy trees, waiting for it to change, hoping the details of the hand-drawn map would be visible in the hours it would take to get to their first stop. He had no idea how he was going to get back to see his sisters again.

When Zeto Valley was a small pinprick in the distance, he whispered, if only to himself. "I'm coming back for you." *I'll be more prepared next time, less of an idiot.*

"You alright?" Minerva asked him from the copilot's chair where Pinu sat perched on her shoulder.

"Yeah, let's keep on course, following the river until sundown," he said, consulting the pulse navigator he was in charge of. He watched the ribbon of silver expand the further they flew northeast, the magnetic resonators traders had embedded on their routes to avoid landmines from the war. The resonators would hopefully help them find their way out to the green hills of Dro-Ra and maybe beyond that.

"Roger," Minerva said, looking over at Idris, who gave a thumbs up.

Pinu was avoiding Toref, and he felt bad about it. She used to sit in his lap and curl up while Idris was flying. But now she was safely perched on Minerva's armrest, occasionally hopping between Minerva and Idris, allowing Toref a view of what lay ahead.

Jesik was asleep across three seats in the back. Idris started to sing, low and soft, and Toref recognized the tune from the night before. Jesik woke up, joined in, his deep bass voice rumbling. After a few minutes, Toref sang along. Then he changed the lyrics to a rhyme he used to sing with his sisters:

> *Fool you once,*
> *Fool you twice*
> *Three times*
> *Blind as mice.*

> *Ain't going back*
> *Ain't going forward*
> *Till I know where*
> *you've been, my love.*

The song's tune continued into a wordless melody, all three harmonized as Toref hummed along, looking at the landscape become gradually more green and lush, blue and green lakes reflecting the light of the sun and puffy clouds in the distance. *Maybe you need to start concentrating on what you have, instead of what you lack.* He felt his heart lift a little, and it seemed that perhaps Idris was right about some things. Just not everything.

CHAPTER 30

IDRIS

The emerald canopies and trees below were harder for Toref to navigate with the mists creeping in. He'd suggested to me that we could try flying around the forest, but it would tack on an extra two hours, and the danger of landmines was too great in that area, if we needed to take a break and land.

Toref looked up at me from the screen. "That's the last of the radio waypoint signals. We're on our own now."

"Thanks for letting me know. How are you Minerva?" I asked.

Minerva sat in the copilot's seat, wearily holding the controls while I snacked on roasted nuts and dried wild boar Yura had packed for us.

Yura. Would I ever see my friend again? She was more than a friend, I decided, she was my sister.

"It's so green," Jesik said from the back. He looked like he was swaying a little in his seat.

"You okay?" I asked Minerva again. I was going to need to take over for her soon.

"Navigator, it looks like we need your help making our way through the Misting Forests," Minerva said to Toref.

He glanced at the map Shakratel had given us. "Shakratel said it would take anywhere from an hour to three to get across the forest," Toref pointed out.

Jesik was still swaying in his seat. I didn't want him getting sick in the hover. "I need you to find a place for us to land to rest for a bit and take a bathroom break," I said.

"Do you think it's safe?" Minerva looked directly at Toref. "The mist is getting thicker." She looked genuinely worried.

"If you think we need to land, let's do it quickly, and where there's plenty of light," Toref said diplomatically. Minerva was afraid of Hybrid gypsies, but looking at Jesik, I knew we had to land.

Minerva put a hand lightly on Toref's arm before returning to the stabilizer, Pinu hopping on her shoulder. I jumped into the pilot's seat. The dark, tall trees had a thick mist that clung to them, and the scattered clouds turned into a thick, pea soup of cloud cover. Turbulence started within a few minutes, the tendrils of mist occasionally coming up and blocking my view through the cockpit's windows momentarily.

"Let's go a little higher," I said.

After a few moments, it was only getting worse. The dim daylight wasn't helping.

"It's going to be hard, if not impossible, to see with the mist. We can turn around and go the other route, or land while there's still light to see," Minerva suggested.

I veered out of the way of a tree and nodded to her. "We'll land for a few minutes to see if the mist clears. We can get a little bit of a break before taking off again. Landing gear."

Pinu jumped up and perched on Toref's shoulder. *So much for loyalty*, I thought.

We landed with a thump, and the lack of engine noise felt like a deep relief. I flung the door open and stepped onto muddy ground, the mist curling around tall pine trees that rose above us in every direction, a thick canopy blocking out the light. Blonde grasses grew in patches around them. Ferns and vines hung from the tall, spindly limbed trees with bushy tops. I'd only ever seen foliage like this in the Ungar murals all over the city.

"Great idea," Toref muttered, his arms crossed while he looked at Minerva's trembling figure.

"You're flying next," I said, pointing to the cockpit. I stomped into waist-high blonde grasses, eager to find a place to pee, then heard a rattle in the distance. I turned back to the muddy, moss-covered ground that Toref stood on. "There's something creepy about this place I don't like."

"Definitely," Toref agreed, zipping up his sweater.

Jesik seemed a lot less unsteady as he inhaled deeply. Minerva stood next to him, back pressed against the hover, while Pinu was still perched on Toref's shoulder. Jesik took a look at each of us, his eyes bloodshot, before tromping off into the thicket of trees.

"Wait, I don't think…" Toref started but Jesik had been enveloped by the mist. "Idris, where does he think he's going?"

I shot him a look. "Well, I can't read minds, but I think he's prob-ably taking a potty break, which sounds like a great idea. See you all in a bit."

Halfway through going to the bathroom, I heard singing. I searched for leaves before finishing and buttoning up my pants. The singing stopped. The mists circled and rose around me, and I wasn't certain if I knew the way back to the hover.

Toref appeared through the fog with Pinu flying close by before landing on my shoulder. "We need to go, sounds like Hybrid gypsies." He glared behind him. "Minerva's spooked and I don't want her more worried than she already is."

"Get her inside, then." *Why is he waiting for me to make a decision?*

I followed him back through the forest to my hover, Jesik standing outside looking fairly miserable from motion sickness. The mist morphed, shifting with the sound of singing coming closer. "I'll get the stun stick." Jesik lumbered inside, retrieved the weapon, and waved us ahead of him into the hover.

"It isn't going to be easy to take off in this weather, but I don't want to wait around to find out who is singing that awful racket," Minerva said, trembling.

"Go ahead inside, no reason to stay out here." I listened for where the singing was coming from. "Let's get out of here."

Jesik nodded his head once, his eyes hard. "Everyone inside. Now."

A cacophony of drums, rattles, and singing was accompanied by a growling. Glowing yellow eyes peered through the fog before materializing into five rag-tag Hybrids, all tall and fox-like, with plenty of fur.

I hissed, "Jesik, get inside. We're taking off. Minerva are you ready to pilot?"

"Sure thing, boss," she yelled back, the engines starting up.

Three grassy balls surged through the open door, and I rushed inside to avoid their trajectory. One ball smoked and when Minerva approached it, the ball unfurled and attached to her arm. I grabbed at the ball of grass that had a life of its own and ripped it from Minerva's arm, lobbing it out the window before closing it. Blood dripped down Minerva's arm, her face draining of color. "I told you nothing good happens out here." She started crying.

"Jesik, get inside. Now!" I yelled, bringing Minerva to the back of the hover to tend her wounds.

He launched off a few stun bolts before jumping back into the hover and slamming the door shut. He put one meaty hand on my arm. "We go, I take care of Minerva."

I jumped into the pilot's chair, Toref already in the copilot's seat, following bleats from Pinu. "Tell me where we're going," he said.

"There's not enough visibility," I said. "We're going to have to gun ourselves upward to avoid the trees." *Hopefully.*

The Hybrids beat on the hover, rocking us from side to side.

"I don't want to see what else they have in store for us, let's go!" I yelled. "Pull back on the landing gear once you see the treeline," I said to Toref. He kept us stabilized as I zoomed us into the air. The mists rose around us, and it felt like I could hear the cacophony music of the Hybrid gypsies awhile after we were fully clear of them.

"That was close."

Jesik coughed, and I came close to him, his whole body shaking from the encounter an hour earlier with the Hybrid gypsies. I looked for another blanket but mine was the only one left. I wrapped it around him and sat beside him. Minerva looked even worse, her arms limp and her skin ashen. I looked at her arm wounds, and they had a black rim around them. When I brought my hand near her forehead, she was too hot.

"We need to bring your fever down, Minerva." I rummaged in our med bag that Shakratel had supplied us with but it looked like Jesik had used up all of the anti-fever powders.

"Minerva's doing worse," I called out to Toref. Pinu joined me in the back, snapping her bill back and forth with displeasure before sighing. "We're going to need help in the next few minutes."

Jesik groaned mournfully while Minerva woke and guzzled the last of her water canister down. "Why do I feel so awful?" When I felt for her pulse again, it was erratic. Minerva slumped over before I could ask her anything else.

"Find a spot to land," I yelled at Toref. I ran over to the pilot's seat to survey the landscape. Dark hills rose around us with lush green growth at their bases. A wide ribbon of river wound around the hills.

"We have to find a settlement with people," I said as I took the copilot's seat. I flipped on my sunshades in the bright sun peeking over the hills in the distance. "Surely they'll have healers for Jesik and Minerva."

Toref turned over the controls to me, completely stricken, his voice shaking. "You're sure…the Fringe people…will help us?"

I strapped into my seat and started the pilot's controls, waiting for

Toref's signal that he was getting ready to land. "It's better than letting them die in the air."

"They won't die," Toref said.

I wanted him to be right. Sparkling in the far distance was the purple sea I'd hoped we'd land near, but I was going to have to ignore that part of our plan now.

Toref reached across and pointed toward where the rivers converged. "Between that set of black hills, the map says there's a village, Sai Lou Mori, to land."

It was difficult to find a patch sufficiently stable for landing and that looked inhabited.

"We're going to need to go lower," I said to Toref. "Tell me when you're ready for me to assist."

"I'm ready," Toref said, looking spent.

"Do you want me to take over?" I asked.

"Not yet, I'll let you know," he said, looking at the navigation board that showed us dropping elevation, which would mean we'd have to stay clear of the edges of those hills, especially if a wind gusted our way.

The afternoon sun was waning through the base of the hills. Cabins and wooden houses were on sprawling plots of green and brown patches of land with thin canals running between.

"Here, let's circle and land on that open space below," I indicated to Toref.

"Okay, you take lead." He switched the primary steering over to me, and I brought us into a gentle landing pattern. As we circled closer to the settlement, I overshot our landing and thudded to a stop outside the wooden gates of a town square.

Standing in front of the gates was a fox Hybrid girl. She approached and tapped on the hover, and I rolled down my window. She started haltingly in Hybrid Kesh, then she spoke again rapidly and fluently in Stan. "This is a closed community. You'll have to press on to Township Central, southwest. Twenty minutes or less from here, that way." She pointed with her staff toward the mounds and the sea I had been so anxious to see.

"We've got two sick friends," I said.

The fox girl shook her staff and pointed toward the next township.

Minerva wasn't going to make it much longer without help. *I'm not having another death on my hands.* I didn't bother to close the window, but nodded to Toref. He placed his hand on the landing gear. I brought us into the air again, long enough to soar over the wooden gates, and plopped us directly in the middle of the town square.

A handful of children came out of one of the large three-story wooden houses, followed by older children and several adults. The fox girl, clearly exasperated, hopped over the fence and stood in front of our passenger door. She moved back when Toref came out with Minerva in his arms. I shut down the engines and followed Toref to the largest house where the children were standing out front, while Jesik limped along.

"We need a healer. We were attacked by Hybrid gypsies," I said to a tall young woman with long sandy hair. She looked behind her and ran off.

"I hope someone else will help us," I said to a stricken Toref.

When a white-haired older woman emerged with the sandy-haired girl, followed by a bald, reptilian man, I relaxed a little.

"We bit by prairie grasses," Jesik said, indicating Minerva.

"Prairie grasses?" The old man's reptilian eyes bounced. "Darshana, get my kit. Gita, let's have the kids inside for chores."

"Come on, let our visitors have some space, you all can ask them questions later." Gita, the older woman, shooed the ten or so kids of various ages back inside. I couldn't help wondering if these were all their kids.

A large, very pale man—even paler than Minerva—stepped forward. He had dark, black eyes that looked even more sinister in his pale, very human face. *Was he Ungar with some strange modification?* "Os, they can't come in here with a sick person," he said to the old reptilian man. "They're obviously city runaways. We don't have room for them."

"Diarmaid, be quiet," Os said. "We've plenty of room. I'll check on these two, right here in the open. No chance of passing on whatever they have. Then, we'll quarantine them all. You can come with us, and make sure it's all done properly?"

Diarmaid didn't look happy, those black eyes twitching back and forth. I took several steps back from him. I knew his type, though I couldn't quite identify why. "No hovers in the town square, you know the rules."

Os put out a hand to silence him. "Let me do my work and you do yours. Cows'll need milking. Why don't I send kids round to help?"

Os whistled and a few kids came out and followed Diarmaid without further instruction. I was amazed at his ability to do that without raising his voice.

Jesik stood next to me. He put a hand on my jacket and then closed his eyes. "I don't feel good." He crumpled onto the soft, mustard brown dirt. I tried to lift him up with Toref's help, but we needed the rest of the kids to lift both him and Minerva. We followed Os, the old reptilian guy, and the girl with the sandy hair he'd called Darshana, who carried a large basket that was almost half her size.

They led us into a backyard, behind the three-story wooden house. The short, bright green grass was covered in blankets, and beyond that was a large stretch of land with wooden tables, chairs, and two ancient railcars. They laid Minerva on a blanket and Jesik on the other. Os set up a drip feed into Minerva's mouth and palpated her hands and abdomen before covering her in several layers of blankets, propping her thighs up on a thick cushion.

"We're going to need to tend them here. Fly your hover over to that patch by the rail cars. We need to check the rest of you for fever."

Toref nodded at me and darted over to the hover, engaging the engine and quickly landing with no bumps. I sat there on the grass, stunned. There were so many people milling about, it made me feel dizzy. Pinu had taken off and was soaring overhead like the party had just started. A gaggle of kids were watching from the second floor window in the roof, where the eaves met.

When Pinu came down to land on my shoulder, a few kids trickled outside and downstairs.

Os looked at them. "Shoo, you have cleaning up to do in the kitchen. You can visit with the petrukian and…"

"Idris," I said.

"Idris and her friends later." His voice was so gentle, yet commanding. I'd never heard anyone speak like this to children before. He reminded me of Shakratel, but with less spice. I had wanted to lie to the kids and tell them that Pinu bites, so they'd leave her alone.

Pinu pecked at the ground, finding tasty morsels within seconds. Os came close to me, holding out a thin metal rod attached to a stone that turned from grey to red to blue when he brought it close to my forehead and face. He then scanned the outline of my body with the stone. "You're in good shape, just vitamin deficient and need sleep therapy." He moved onto everyone else.

When he stopped at Minerva, he looked down at her metal legs, almost marveling. "Who made those?"

He looked at Toref, holding Minerva's hand and back to me, then Jesik.

"We need to adjust them, while we're here," Toref answered.

Os looked at all of us in awe. "Well, we are very lucky to have you among us. I'm guessing you have come a long way?"

I nodded and looked up at the crimson outline along the clouds in the sunset. *If only he knew how far all of us had come.* A sadness and longing for the familiar compound at Yura and Shakratel's coursed through me.

Book II

by Sarah J. Coleman

CHAPTER 31

TOREF

Toref looked at the tall, black, and green hills in the distance and was wracked with guilt over Minerva being so ill. *How could he have been so stupid, so they were forced to leave. Now she was sick.* The unholy green was so electric it almost hurt his eyes. A wetness in the air was noticeable with each inhalation. He had imagined, before they left Zeto, that once they touched down, some tiny sense of normalcy would return to his life. Except, he no longer knew what normal was, his stomach twisting in knots over Minerva's state.

She had never wanted to come here. *It's my fault that I pushed her. She would have been happier staying at Shakratel's, if that had even been an option.*

"Come on kids, you can introduce yourselves to Toref later," Gita said, her silver hair twisted into a messy, thick knot at the top of her head. Though she was much older than his mother, likely his grand-parents' age—if they'd lived—there was a strength to Gita that Toref felt. It was in the way she stood in a wide-legged stance and how the kids all obeyed her when she told the ten-plus gaggle of ages eight to nineteen to get to work. That care and concern was different from how most of the Monitors had dealt with kids at the Pods.

She called out to a girl with long, sandy hair that fell to her waist. Toref couldn't imagine that was a terribly practical length to wear one's hair.

"This is Darshana, my niece." Darshana didn't look at Toref. "Os is training her to be a healer. We've some sickly in the fields, so she'll help with your friends until Os comes back."

Gita gestured toward a railcar where Toref had helped Os and Darshana carry Minerva and Jesik. The railcar looked like something from before the Hybrid Wars. There wasn't any rack underneath it, and the original windows looked like they'd been replaced with large, circular windows that needed more seam glue, Toref could see, around the edges.

"What is it?" Gita said.

"I was just looking at the railcars," Toref said, making a mental note to fix that window when he had a chance.

"You'll stay in the red one until we're certain everyone is clear of whatever ails your friends," Gita said.

Toref peered at the white railcar where Minerva and Jesik were and strolled toward it. Gita stepped in front of him, blocking him.

"I don't want to leave them alone," Toref insisted. "It's my fault they're so sick."

A guy with a ponytail joined Gita in blocking Toref's way. "Snap fever ain't pretty." He held out his hand. "I'm Kalyon. My parents died of snap fever." Kalyon gestured toward the white railcar. "Pretty nasty stuff, so it's best to let them rest while the medicine works in their systems."

Kalyon had the same scales around the edge of his face like Rusty, but the rest of him was tawny and sleek, his straight black hair gathered in a leather thong at his neck. He was several inches taller than Toref and he couldn't help thinking about how casually Kalyon had mentioned his parents' deaths, like it wasn't anything unusual.

Darshana put a hand on Kalyon's shoulder and peered at Toref with violet eyes. "I'm sorry about your friends. I hope that we can help get them back to health." She gestured toward the other railcar. "If you'll come this way to the red railcar, I'll finish checking all of you." She held a stone in her hand and glanced back at Kalyon, but his gaze settled on someone standing behind Toref. When Toref turned, he saw Idris lingering outside the railcar, looking annoyed except when Pinu landed on her shoulder and took off again.

"That's some bird you have there," Kalyon said to Idris.

Idris only flicked her sleek black hair out of her face and said nothing.

Oh, Idris, Toref thought. *Did she always have to be so peevish?*

Toref followed Darshana to the railcar, and she placed a stone on each of their foreheads, asking them to stick out their tongues after the stone turned red.

"I think that's it. I'll check again tomorrow." Darshana took off to the white railcar and Toref followed her until she was inside, afraid that if something happened to Minerva, he wouldn't be there to comfort her. Or was that even what he wanted?

He inhaled the humid air again and smelled something different, a pleasant, sweet aroma. Gita approached with a young boy, around eight years old, with horns sticking out of his forehead. He handed them each a paper-covered disc.

Idris was the first to take it. "Soap! Finally! I can't wait to wash." She handed one to Toref who inhaled the incredible rose scent.

How long had it been since he'd smelled soap that didn't have the aroma of disinfectant?

The young boy came closer to Toref, sniffed, and then wrinkled his face like Toref stunk. "I'm Nalo. I'm supposed to show you the washing house. Gotta wash twice a day. Them's the rules. *And* you've got chores starting tomorrow. Nobody rides the free penny here." He glared back at Gita who just smiled at him, the corners of her eyes wrinkling pleasantly.

Okay, so this was normal Nalo behavior, Toref guessed.

He held out his hand in greeting to Nalo. Nalo came close again, sniffed, and sped off down the grassy yard. Kalyon laughed and Gita yelled at Nalo, eventually running after him.

"Nalo is the most energetic one in our house, so you'll have to excuse his craziness," Kalyon said.

"What's the wash house?" Idris asked Toref.

Kalyon looked mildly uncomfortable and pointed to a group of wooden sheds in the distance. Idris swished her tail about and Toref hoped she wasn't going to be annoyed forever. "It's…where…you know…you get clean." He was looking at Idris and suddenly Toref knew.

For whatever reason, Idris is making Kalyon nervous.

Toref looked at Idris. "Shall we?"

Idris pushed him, "I'm not washing in the same room as you! It's hard enough I'll have to sleep near you."

Toref flushed, his cheeks heating up. Another kid sauntered over to grab his soap from Kalyon.

They followed Kalyon past the small kids gathered outside watching Pinu soar through the air. A small forest lay beyond the washing wooden huts, their open top roofs letting steam out between the rafters.

"Pinu, bath time," Idris called out and the kids watched, trailing along behind Idris, as Pinu came in for a landing on Toref's shoulder this time, cheeping and pecking at his hair.

He looked behind, and Idris had a faint smile on her face. "Take her in with you, if you like, but don't say I didn't warn you. She's crazy in water."

It was just him, Pinu, and Kalyon. Kalyon looked down at his chest. "We're all the same underneath." He went inside, not waiting for him. Toref heard the sound of water and ran in, unable to stand his itchy skin a moment longer.

Toref kept hoping he could check on Minerva. It was difficult to sleep on the stuffed mattress on the railcar's floor. Between Pinu's snoring bulk to his left, and Idris moaning in her sleep, he'd had to get up in the middle of the night. He was afraid to step too far outside of the railcar and into the misty, cold night. He didn't know what dangers waited for people in Sai Lou Mori, especially after all of Nalo's stories the night before.

Something about rogue beetle teams, and wolves...or had it been llamas? He'd been too worried about Minerva to pay attention to all of it.

Idris sat straight up, Pinu rolling off her and over to Toref.

"What is it?" she whispered, not moving as she pulled her legs into her chest and rolled onto her side so she faced him.

"Couldn't sleep," Toref whispered, moving the sheer curtain aside to look out again on the dark outcropping of trees outlined by the half-moons shining above them. "I'm worried about Minerva...and Jesik. What if I hadn't gone to the casino..." He couldn't complete the thought, the anxiety swirling in him like a tornado.

"Toref, you can't change the past." She stretched upward. "Do you think they'll let us stay?" Idris asked, sounding younger, all the usual gruffness absent from her voice. Her black hair stuck up and the striped edges to her skin around her face were more obvious in the early dawn light without her hair covering them.

"Can't say," Toref said. He'd seen the weird looks from some of the villagers when he'd taken a walk in their wide dirt square the previous afternoon. Maybe their opinion would change when they saw that the newcomers could be useful. No one here seemed to be starving or dirty. They also didn't seem to have the same technology, but maybe that was a good thing.

He rubbed his sandy eyes. Part of him wanted to go back home, except he didn't know what that was anymore. This was supposed to be home, and as he looked out at the foreign landscape he wished he knew the answers to the ache he felt inside, or had some way of reaching Minerva, of helping her feel better. "Can we try to sneak in and check on them?"

"She'll get better. Don't worry, Toref," Idris said softly before turning away from him and rolling onto her side.

Toref laid back on his mattress, Pinu settling on his belly with a few snaps of her beak. He closed his eyes, drifting off as he softly pet Pinu's back feathers.

He was awoken with a start when the aroma of yeast filled his nostrils. A shadow stood in the railcar's doorway. Then the shadow morphed into three shapes that, as he blinked, became Nalo, Gita, and Darshana.

Toref stood straight up, eager to fill his stomach.

"Last day we bring you food, ponz," Nalo said, his hair sticking up around his tiny horns.

Gita glared at him while Darshana smiled, flicking her long hair behind her. "Language."

"Yours." Nalo's face fell and he put a basket of freshly baked bread and jars of jam and other foods into Toref's hands, following Gita out. Darshana stared at all of them, her violet eyes snatching at Toref when she looked at him. Pinu landed on his shoulder, and she stopped staring.

Gita came back and put a hand on Darshana's bare arm. "Darshana, come on, let them eat." She pushed her forward, and Darshana walked to the other railcar where Jesik and Minerva were. Gita gestured toward Toref to follow. He waited for Idris to wake. Her hair was smashed on one side of her pale face. She grabbed two rolls, handed one to him and followed him silently outside.

Once they were at the railcar that held Jesik and Minerva, Gita looked at Idris and shook her head. "It's best that only Toref comes in." Idris soundlessly ducked back out to the red railcar, sitting on the steps while feeding bits of roll to Pinu.

When the door to Jesik and Minerva's car opened, Jesik was standing. Minerva was asleep, facing them. She looked comfortable, Toref thought. Jesik, on the other hand, seemed to have a twitchy movement to his limbs as he paced in the small space that wasn't intended for his bulk, ducking beneath the low ceiling.

Darshana held up the stone to Jesik's snout and arms. It turned yellow, then back to grey. "No fever." She replaced the stone in her basket. "You're in a dangerous stage of the sickness."

"I feel better," Jesik said.

"That's why it's called snap fever," Darshana said quietly.

Gita gestured for Jesik to sit. "I've seen plenty of soldiers get right back to fighting and hours later, they're dead in their soup, after thinking they were over the snap fever. You need lots of liquids." Her lined face was severe, her bright blue eyes warm despite her warning.

"You can go outside, but not beyond the yard," Darshana instructed, writing a few notes in a thick, battered book she brought out of her basket. "Though you aren't infectious, we don't want the ignorant townspeople to get any ideas." She raised an eyebrow and Gita smiled at her.

Toref got the sense that there were a lot of divisions he was going to get to know fairly soon. "Why don't they know that it isn't contagious?" He glanced over at Minerva.

Gita exhaled, "Oh, they know that the snap fever is only contagious if the prairie grasses bite your skin, or you have an open wound that the grasses get stuck in, like happened here to Minerva." Gita frowned at Toref, "There's no way to get that into the dunderheads in town who know everything, most especially when the weather's going to turn, and all sorts of other nonsense we pay no mind to."

Toref laughed a little, and Darshana stayed quiet, looking nervous. She handed him a small flask, and he took it to Minerva.

Minerva woke, reached out toward him, her finger tracing his cheeks. "You have a round face don't you?" Her voice was husky. She blinked her pale pink eyes and a guilt settled deeper in his belly. *If she recovered, would she forgive him?*

"What happened to me?" she asked after she'd finished drinking the vial.

"I'll tell you when you feel better," he said, his stomach twisting. "Do you want to see Pinu?" he asked.

She shook her head.

Gita and Darshana took Jesik outside, leaving the door ajar, drawing a curtain in front of it that allowed some air to come in, but blocked most of the chill.

It was just the two of them now. *Do I have the courage to apologize for bringing her here?* Would it change anything between them? The need to divulge was greater than the pain that was holding him back.

"I'm sorry this happened to you." He stroked her back. "I know you never wanted to come, and my foolish actions landed you here."

Minerva looked up at him with her pale face that had delighted him from the first time he saw her. "Everything is not your fault, you know?"

Toref shook his head.

"I wish those gypsies hadn't attacked us, but I'll get better. Don't worry so much, Toref. We'll go back for your sisters and Rusty, you'll see."

Toref smiled a little, tears already forming in his violet eyes, tracking down his dark face.

"How's Idris?" she asked, her pale eyebrows quirking.

Toref grinned and she smiled back at him.

"Not much changed, then?" Minerva folded her arms, resting back against the bed's railing.

"I think that guy…Kalyon? The one with the ponytail, I think likes her."

Minerva's face colored with pleasure. "Ooh, now that's something exciting. I can't wait to see them in the same room."

Toref sat against the bed, careful to be respectful of her space. "She'll probably break his heart."

He turned around to see Idris standing behind him. She swung back outside, her tail swishing back and forth before he could say anything to her. Pinu flew over to Minerva's bed, and she reached out and stroked her feathers before falling back asleep. He sat there, waiting for her to wake. He wasn't sure how much Idris had heard and wasn't about to try to find out, especially if she was in a snit. *I seem to be doing everything wrong.*

He sat there, darkness swirling around him like a thick, painful fog the longer Minerva stayed asleep, her breath slow and steady. When the questions plaguing him about her recovery got to be too much, he bolted outside, hoping the fresh air would help.

"How bad is it?" Idris asked when she returned an hour later. Her thick, dark eyebrows were drawn together, her thin mouth in a straight line.

That's what he both hated and loved about Idris. She cut through all the small talk to ask the really important questions. Except, as he looked up at the sunny day and fast-moving clouds overhead, the shaggy, green trees swaying in the breeze, it felt like everything was moving around him too quickly. He wasn't ready to move at that speed, to spill everything out and feel the emptiness that might come after. A deep fear had lodged itself in his gut, that Minerva would not make it, that he'd have yet another disappearance on his hands, and he never got a chance to tell her how much he cared about her, even loved her, after everything they'd been through.

"It could be better," Toref finally said.

Idris nodded, thrusting her hands in her pockets, her yellow eyes not leaving his face. "Yeah, it could."

CHAPTER 32

IDRIS

At first light the next day, I awoke to Jesik's furry hand tapping my shoulder.

"What?" I rolled away from him, and Pinu fluttered out the door. Now I had to get up. Jesik sighed before opening the door to the railcar, letting in the wet, crisp air. Toref sat straight up, looking up at Jesik's bulk.

"Are you better?" Toref jumped up. He looked like he was eager to jet over and see Minerva.

It was clear from both his and Jesik's faces that I wasn't going to be getting any more sleep that morning. I sat up and pushed Toref aside so I could get out.

"You did that last night, too," Toref said, a wry grin on his face. "I must've been snoring."

"Why didn't you just shut up, then?" The mist rose from the grass outside the rail car. A cold breeze blew in, and I wrapped the quilted blanket I'd slept with closer around me as I leaned against the railcar's doorframe. My arms still felt frozen and stiff. Pinu flapped her wings and perched on Jesik's shoulder when he walked by. For a few seconds, I expected Yura and Shakratel to follow. *They're far away from here.* I backed away from the door to my bed, the cold too much for me.

"Everybody, it breakfast time." Jesik sniffed the air and took off, leaving the door wide open.

"Close the door, Toref," I yelled.

I had never been so cold in my life. Except in Brailesu Factory, and that was a different, gnawing, cement-laden state of cold. Pulling my blanket tighter around me, I realized I needed to get outside and adjust myself instead of brooding indoors. Unlike Toref, I closed the door behind me.

The frigid, wet air hit my feet first even though I'd slipped on my boots. My bare hands were exposed where they clutched the blanket. The breeze nipped at every bit of exposed skin. When I looked up at the mist-obscured black hills with green swirl patterns along their bases, I admired the green carpeting the rest of the valley. I wanted to feel as safe in this land as I had imagined I would. But, it still bothered me that I never told Yura and Shakratel they were my family, my true home.

I wished I could ask Yura what made those hills black, sit next to Shakratel and enjoy one of his stories from the war, instead of always feeling like there was a ticking timer going off to direct my next move. Here, time felt different, and I wasn't certain I liked it. The lush wetness of the fields and hills felt foreign instead of beautiful and familiar. I hated to admit I was terrified of the unknown.

I had wanted to be here for so long, and now that I'm here, nothing feels like I imagined. I didn't think I'd have to adjust to anything because I was pining so long for these wide open spaces.

The aroma of roasted ham and cooked vegetables wafted on the breeze from the kitchen that faced the yard where I stood. Through the window, I could see an older girl who looked a lot like Kalyon helping with three other kids in the kitchen.

Jesik bounded out of the wash house, his black fur gleaming. "Wash before breakfast, they say." He rubbed his head with a piece of cloth. A new pair of denim-looking trousers were around his waist, a pair of red suspenders holding them up. He snapped them. "Get on." He pointed toward the washroom, but I had no intention of getting even more cold before I ate breakfast.

"I washed last night, thank you."

Before he could say anything, I headed toward the back door, slipping past the kids in the kitchen and into the dining room that was laid out with platters of roasted vegetables, cheese, and fried bread. Three wooden tables with long benches already had kids sitting at them, none of them yet touching the food. This felt like even more food than they served at Shakratel's.

Jesik and Toref joined me at the table and once the final steaming tray of roasted vegetables came in, the little boy, Nalo, and the guy with the ponytail, Kalyon, joined us with a dark-haired girl, Litu, that looked like Kalyon's sister. Darshana sat at the other table and stared at me with her violet eyes, until Gita declared we could eat.

"Let us be thankful," Gita said, pressing her hands together and toward the top of her head.

All the kids repeated, "We give thanks!"

They politely took turns, but Nalo had demolished what was on his plate within seconds. Kalyon put his hand on Nalo's arm, indicating he could not leave, which made me smile. Nalo gave him an innocent look that Kalyon ignored, and I was afraid that Nalo was going to catch me grinning at his antics. Litu picked at her food, looking around and surveying everyone.

I dug into the root vegetables, attempting to eat the potatoes in small bites, as my first instinct was to eat as fast as I could. When bowls of spicy soup were passed around, Litu perked up. "I love this soup!"

"Are you Idris?" Litu asked. "The one with the bird?" Her smile widened into a toothy grin, the dark scales around the rim of her face similar to Kalyon's.

"Yes," I said.

"I'm Litu, Kalyon's *older* sister."

Kalyon rolled his eyes.

When I sipped the soup, it was only lukewarm.

Litu stood up, taking off a loose fuzzy green covering she wore. "You're freezing. Take my wrap. I've got more clothes upstairs for all of you."

Jesik frowned. "I no need more clothes."

Litu smiled at him. "Sospiru's fuzzy like you, and she wears clothes when the frost comes."

"The what?" I asked.

"Frosts, you know, the snow, when everything that isn't indoors freezes? That's when it gets really cold. Right now, it's fall, so we're waiting for the last of the grains to grow before we harvest in a week or so. It's good you're all here, because we need your help." Litu spoke with such authority that I wondered how old she was.

Kalyon finished his soup and smiled at all of us. "We're really glad you joined us." He looked over at me for a moment like he was going to say something and then stopped.

Litu stood and consulted a sheaf of paper from her pocket, calling out names and assigning jobs. Jesik took off in the direction of the fields to help with irrigation. Toref hopped off to do hover repairs. I stood up to follow him when Litu held out her hand to stop me. "We need you with the animal teams today."

"It's my hover—"

Litu consulted her sheet again, looking back at Kalyon who was helping clear dishes. "Oh, I'm sorry, I thought it was Toref's hover. Right. Toref said he could move your hover over to the fallow fields for repairs?" She made notes on her paper. "Kalyon will show you the herds and pack animals. Since you have a trained petrukian, I figured you would be good with him since we're short a hand today."

"I'd rather be with my hover," I said, trying to keep my voice even.

Litu turned away from me, like it was settled for me to go work with her brother. Gita and Os were already meeting with the younger kids. I hated that feeling of being stuck.

At least I wasn't being forced to work in the kitchen.

Kalyon walked over to me, folding his arms across his chest. I hadn't realized how dark his eyes were, so black. His entire smooth, angular brown face was turned upward, his long nose following a line of pleasantness wafting off him. He smiled, and it was making me even more uncomfortable.

"Why are you looking at me?" I asked.

"Because you look cold." his grin morphed into a look of concern.

"So?"

"I don't understand why you won't let Litu help you." He took the rest of the dishes, and I grabbed the silverware, depositing them with the younger kids in the kitchen before following him up two more flights of stairs to the attic. In the narrow room, there were various items of clothing, the aroma of wool pleasant. I wanted to stay in the warmth among all those pieces of cloth hanging from hooks in the wooden roof beams.

"I think these should fit. I'll see you downstairs." He started down the stairs and stopped. I had already thrown off the blanket around me, my midriff shirt showing off my pale, fuzzy navel. I don't know why I felt embarrassed when he looked at me. "Oh, make sure you pick dark, thick pants. We're going to get dirty this morning. It might be a three-wash day."

I didn't like the sound of a three-wash day.

I followed Kalyon uphill through the rows of alfalfa fields to a trio of large, wooden barns set against the rise of one of the black-earth hills. The barns looked more like a hangar bay for machinery than animals. When he led me to the side door of one of the pens, I was face-to-face with a pair of enormous beetles humming to each other and spinning around. They were double my height and five times my width. "What are...they?"

Though their humming was calming, they had ferocious horns protruding from their heads. I took several steps back until I was braced against the back of the pen, ready to jump if they made any sudden movements toward me. *They're terrifying.*

"Your first time seeing beetle teams?" Kalyon asked, looking delighted by the whole scenario.

"Of course," I said, cautiously. "We don't have these in the city, but there are other things that would likely scare you." *I don't want him thinking I'm some wimpy girl.* I pulled my woolen hat tighter over my head.

The beetles' exoskeletons shone with an onyx, metal sheen. When they turned, a clacking and buzzing sound arose, and their shells turned from black to an iridescent blue-green. They belonged in old Hybrid war stories, something for wielding destruction. My breath caught, heartbeat thudding in my ears. When Kalyon opened the pen to let a pair out, I darted out for the field.

Before I could catch my breath, a small figure rammed into my stomach. Little Nalo rolled on the ground in front of me, small horns glistening from his fuzzy brown hair. "Watch out, weird girl," he growled.

I leaned over to catch my breath, but when I saw the beetle team clacking toward me I sprinted until Kalyon shouted. "Idris, wait! You don't have to meet the beetle teams today. I can take you to the llamas and alpacas instead."

He ran to stand next to me, shielding his eyes from the sun, clearly out of breath. His black hair had come loose from its ponytail. Its silky, black strands swung in the breeze. I wanted to touch his hair, but stopped myself.

What am I thinking?

The beetle team pulled a metal frame behind them while Nalo spoke to them. Out in the daylight, they looked less menacing. I watched them for a while as they followed Nalo out to the field. He hopped on top of their ridges and sang to them while he rode, crouching between them, directing their movements with a thin string that hooked onto their antennae. He looked like he was having the time of his life.

Stupid kid.

Why had I been so scared?

For a moment, the whirring and snapping of looms was in front of me, the gnawing sound of their engines feeling like it would grind my bones to dust. Their sounds dissipated when the beetle teams cast their shadows over me.

That's why.

I'd seen enough people lose limbs or life to those machines.

The Beetle teams buzzed and clacked along the rows that were being fertilized, humming in tune with Nalo.

Now I felt extra stupid. Kalyon was still watching me, and I gestured for him to lead the way up the hillside to another set of stalls, though much smaller than the beetle pens. As we got closer to the base of the hill, I spotted rice terraces cut into the green hillside, stalks sticking up. A flock of orange llamas grazed alongside white alpacas. A few of the llamas, their large eyes blinking, came toward me and then darted away when I got too close. I wrapped my light blue sweater tighter around me, securing the leather belt.

"I think they like you," Kalyon handed me a bucket of feed. "Hold these out to them. They'll be your friends in no time." He pointed out the white alpacas running away from us. "The alpacas are shy. Pet them from their necks, so they won't spit."

I looked at the dazzling creatures and wondered what Pinu would think of them when she flew overhead, if she weren't too busy keeping everyone else company. I held out the feed to the gorgeous, jewel-eyed creatures.

Kalyon pointed to the ones nearest him. "The females here, Stringy and Genti, are our pack animals for transporting wool. See how furry most of them are? We have to shear them in the spring so we can spin the wool for clothes. According to Diarmaid, we're in for a long winter." There was a gentleness to his high cheekbones, the way he walked with a purpose that felt almost like a dance.

"Does Diarmaid know everything?" I asked, grinning.

He gave me a look that told me he was pleased with what I'd said.

"Amongst other problems with Diarmaid. Os always says to ignore him. The only thing we can do is be prepared, wait and see." He clicked his teeth at the animals, and I followed his lead.

There was a calm around him as he patiently held out the feed and waited for them to approach, a few loose strands of hair blowing across his sharp, light brown cheekbones.

More of the alpacas gathered, their long necks reminding me of swans. I scanned the skies for Pinu, but there were only sea birds, their white and black bodies soaring on the higher air currents.

"I'll leave you here with them, if you like. I usually bring lunch out here with me." He pointed behind him. "I've left some cheese, figs, and bread in the basket. If you get hungry, you can wander back to where it's stowed in the upper part of the barn, out of reach of Nalo."

"What if Nalo finds it?" I asked, knowing he was more than capable of eating everything in sight from what I'd witnessed earlier that morning.

Kalyon laughed, causing the alpacas to scatter away from us. "We keep him pretty busy. Nobody will bother you today..." his dark brown eyes met mine. "...unless you want them to."

Something hit me deep in my gut then. It was like what had happened with Reggi, but different, calmer, causing a heat to spread through my face and neck. He looked away before I could hide my blushing from him. He walked onward with more feed, approaching a grey llama that allowed him to pet it.

The animals circled around me as I stood there with my hand outstretched, getting closer and closer, and only a few nibbling the bits before prancing away. *This could take forever.* I had been so spoiled by Pinu's easygoing nature when it came to mealtimes. As I waited, I looked in the short grasses and saw something glinting in the sun. I put down the feed bucket and found a wide-toothed comb that looked like it was intended for the animals.

I held it up. "You want a comb?" One alpaca had already found the feed bucket, which I took away from it, so the others could eat the grains.

Another alpaca approached, with white dots on its face, trilling back in its throat and shaking its body. It had already had its share of feed and nuzzled my hand where I held the comb. I set down the food and combed its back fur. As soon as I had combed one, another stood in its place. I hadn't noticed that it was midday until the sun was high overhead, my muscles aching and stomach growling.

I looked over at the barn that Kalyon had pointed to, and he was waving at me, holding up the lunch basket.

What a strange person.

I put my hand on my flat stomach. What a light feeling I had inside when I looked at him. I wasn't certain I didn't like it.

When I got back from the animal pens, Toref was waiting for me, one arm around a sickly looking Minerva leaning on him to walk slowly around the town square. *She doesn't look much better.* Jesik stood with them, and stared at Nalo's herd of talking pigs grumbling by. Nalo stopped and glared at the group, his tiny face scowling. He wiped mud off his round face, only managing to smear it. "I don't understand why you newts aren't taking care of the whiny pigs instead of me." He poked Toref in the chest with his cane.

Toref looked like he was about to push him in the mud, but held back when we heard the pigs talking back.

"Horny boy, you too bossy, bossy," the pigs said in guttural voices.

I thought for a second it was the other kids playing a joke on us.

We stood in awe of the pigs, who continued to grumble, a few rolling in the abundance of mud in the town square after the midday rains. "We gotta take bath-bath, before dark-dark," they snort-spoke.

I loved the crazy things.

Toref laughed and Nalo waved his stick at him. "What ya starin' at? Never seen Walyun pigs?"

Minerva was laughing so hard she fell, and tears were coming out of her eyes. I had to pick her up and dust her off, clumps of dirt sticking to her red curls. The rest of the crowd of kids didn't look pleased with us. Nalo brandished his stick in the air after tapping more of the pigs along.

"Can we help?" Toref offered.

Nalo shook his head, a sinister grin spreading across his face. "Sexy tail can help." He pointed at me, and I stared at him like he was insane. I was too shocked to say anything, which was saying a lot for me.

"You're, what, like ten? Get on with you," Minerva said, taking Nalo's stick and attempting to swat him. The pigs grunted and took off without Nalo, who stood there looking peeved. He scowled at Toref again, seeming to think it was all his fault.

Jesik growled next to me.

"New people should be shuckin' pigs. Stupid big mouths," Nalo whined.

"Stupid big mouths," the flock of twenty pigs repeated. Kalyon kicked Nalo in the butt as he passed and Litu followed behind Nalo's herd.

"It's not fair," Nalo yelled, continuing onward.

The pigs echoed Nalo's words.

Kalyon smiled at me. "Some chores are better than others."

"Pigs are interesting. Small boy, not so," Jesik remarked, putting a twig in his large, oxen mouth and munching on it.

I could have hugged him.

CHAPTER 33

TOREF

*I*s this the moment before I'm going to lose her?

Minerva sat in a wicker chair in the spacious railcar, holding out her arms to Toref and Idris. Toref gratefully let her enfold him in her now thinner, but healing arms. *Why isn't she healing as well as Jesik?* Idris even let her hug her, despite looking rather damp. Toref was surprised Idris didn't say anything, but instead wrapped Minerva's blanket tighter around her. *Was it possible she was thawing after Minerva's embrace?*

Toref couldn't help worrying about Minerva, still so pale with light blue shadows under her eyes. Os stood next to the door, his bald, light green head gleaming in the lamplight. He reminded Toref of his father and how he would linger in a room to make sure everyone was okay. It was a watchfulness Toref now wondered if he'd inherited.

Toref walked over to Minerva, the jute carpet under his feet cushioning the sound of his footsteps. There was a spaciousness here, with only two beds, that his railcar lacked. He wondered, just for a moment, what it was like to lie on a real bed, but when Minerva started coughing, he let the thought go. *I wish she were well, and I was the one who was ill*. He drew her blanket closer around her and reached for the flask of water Os had replaced earlier.

"Is she worse?" Idris whispered to Os.

"I can hear you," Minerva croaked weakly.

"Oh. Sorry." Idris paused, her tail whipping back and forth. "How are you feeling?" She looked at Minerva earnestly and Toref couldn't help himself feeling a warmth for Idris, despite all her prickles. She obviously cared about Minerva's wellbeing, too. *That's enough for me.*

Idris took a seat at the edge of Minerva's empty bed. Toref took Minerva's hand, then swung her into his arms to carry her over to her bed. She stopped coughing when she took another sip of a small tincture Os gave her.

"I wanted you all here," Minerva started. "I'll try to say everything I need to, even though I'm bone tired." She sat against her bed railings, and Idris scooted over to give her more room so Toref could sit close to Minerva. "I will get better. Stop worrying about me."

Toref glanced over at Os, who didn't give them a reassuring look.

Idris folded her arms in front of her and glared at Os.

Will she get better? Toref thought.

"I know, Idris, you dreamt of coming here, and I'm glad you brought us here. I'm sorry I gave you all such a hard time. No matter what happens, we're safe here." Minerva leaned against Toref, and he squeezed her hand, wishing for a moment alone with her to apologize again. To explain how wretched he felt after everything that had happened the last few days.

"You all look so worried, but I want you to remember how it was before." She took a deep breath. "No one wants to stay where they have no choice. I feel like we could have a really good life here. So, please don't hold back, because I'm still sick, okay?" She looked at Toref and tears fell down his cheeks.

"I need you to get better. To hold on, Minerva," Toref said, putting an arm around her.

Idris had tears tracking down her face. Minerva held out a hand to Idris, and she scooted closer to Minerva, putting an arm around her.

The door to the railcar creaked open to reveal Jesik's snout. He quickly closed the door, but not before Toref called out to him.

"Hey, Jesik. Come in."

"I'll go get him," Idris said, wiping off her face and calling Jesik back inside.

A smile crept across Os's light green face and Toref saw a warmth in his grey eyes he hadn't seen before.

Jesik stepped inside and sat on the last wooden stool available in the small railcar. "I just want say hello to Minerva...to say...I hope you better soon...and dinner ready." He nervously twitched his hands, until Minerva nodded to him.

"Thanks, Jesik. I think I might actually be hungry today. I wanted you all here to tell you that I think we need to try to find a way to get the others we left behind." She looked at Toref. "I don't want to leave Rusty and your sisters there, if we can help them—"

Os stood up and walked over to them, handing Minerva her dinner tray. "I think that's enough for today, Minerva. We need to get some soup in you."

She waved him away. "I'm not done."

"Minerva, you need rest. Say what you need to tomorrow," Toref urged her.

"No, Toref. I want to say it now."

Os offered Minerva more water and she drank a small glass before continuing. "Idris, Toref will be a good friend to you, if you let him. Toref, I need you to listen to what Idris tells you as you plan to return to Zeto to get Rusty and your sisters. Everyone here, even you Idris, has a good heart."

She reached toward Idris. "You let them love you, okay? I'm going to hug you now and say goodbye." She reached out for Idris, who took Minerva's hands, her yellow eyes filled with tears and an expression of grief around her mouth Toref had never seen. Idris held onto Minerva for a few seconds before letting Toref embrace her.

"I want you to let yourself love—even if you're suffering, Toref." Minerva said, her smile weak.

A stone lodged in his chest. "Please, Minerva, hold on...don't leave me. I..." His voice caught.

Was Minerva saying goodbye?

Toref held onto her as long as he could before Os ushered them outside, closing the door behind him. His face was grave. "I don't think Minerva is going to make it through the night."

"No. It's not possible..." Toref covered his face, unable to look at any of them. "She's doing better. Please Os, I can't lose her."

Idris glanced at Toref. Her eyes were bloodshot, and she was a little sunburnt. "What am I doing here?" she whispered, hugging her arms to herself.

Toref moved closer to Idris.

"I'm not saying she won't live, but I want you to be prepared, if she doesn't." Os paused for a bit, watching his news sink in. "I'm going to talk to you next week about the rest of what Minerva said. About going back. But, for now, just enjoy any time you might have left." He put a hand on Toref's shoulder. "We'll begin the healing singing for her. We won't stop trying to get her better."

Toref watched him depart, a low tune wafting through the air from Os, while Idris' tail whipped back and forth furiously. "How can he say that. Like this happens every day?" She made a fist into her palm. Jesik put a meaty hand on her shoulder, and Toref was surprised she didn't hit him.

"I'm going in to stay with her," Toref said, unable to be outside where they could all watch him in his destroyed state. Every step back into the railcar felt weighted, like he no longer was here, but halfway to that dark place he'd been before with each loss in his life.

Once he was inside he fastened the door behind him. *She can't go. Not now. Not before...* He looked at her sleeping, her breath slow and regular. "Minerva, I love you." He knelt beside her bed. "I hope you can hear me because I'm going to die if you don't make it. Don't leave me all alone here." He clutched the edge of her bed. "Please hold on for me. I love you so very much, and I'm so sorry this all happened."

The waves of turmoil rose in him, a black tide of sadness, pushing at him, constricting his breathing until everything went dark.

A night like this
We can imagine

Os continued to sing softly, his voice low and melodious as he walked through the rest of the village.

Opening like a flower
Despite the freeze…

Something deep inside Toref stirred, a soft, weighty comfort washing over him from Os's tune. Only seconds earlier he had felt so lost and torn inside.

Kalyon and his sister Litu entered the room holding two white candles. Both of their raven black hair was undone and it spilled over their shoulders. They joined in Os's song, a bright halo of light around all of them. When they stopped singing, a great ocean of sound rang in Toref's ears. His heartbeat thudded, punctuating the ocean's roar. It wouldn't stop and it shielded him from the sounds of everyone around him, those waves crashing and breaking, his heartbeat the only other discernible sound.

It wasn't until he heard Idris' voice, and felt the wood floor underneath his face, that the ocean sounds stopped. He was lying on the cold floor, his breath trickling back into him.

"Toref, did you hear anything I just said?" Idris threaded her arm through his.

He sat up to catch his breath, sweat pouring down his face. "No, I'm sorry." He looked up at Minerva in her bed, peacefully asleep. For now.

The waves churned in his belly once more.

"I know you're worried, but she's okay," Idris said, stroking his arm gently. She set her cheek on his arm in a way that days earlier he would have thought she was ready to do some evil to him. *I don't deserve her touch. I left my sisters and my best friend behind in a horrible place.*

She held him closer. "Nothing is set. She will get better." Idris' voice was light and gentle.

"What if you're wrong?" he asked, bitterly.

Idris held him there. It was like she knew that he wasn't certain he could walk two steps on his own and yet was afraid at the same time that he was in so much need of her. *How much more loss can I take?*

CHAPTER 34

IDRIS

I couldn't believe that Minerva could be gone by morning. The memory of her pale face, her limp, red curls waxen under candlelight sunk me. It was my fault she got so sick. She didn't even want to come here, despite everything she'd said.

Yura's chiseled face swam in my mind. She felt further away than ever before.

The air was heavy around me in the dusk, and the smell of rain still in the air made me miss the desert and my parents. I felt a deep, dark presence clinging to me, and I didn't know where to turn.

I longed for the warmth of Shakratel's compound, the independence of my hover and being able to zip around, almost at a moment's notice. Minerva, Toref, and Jesik were now the last links to that life. If Minerva died, one of my last tethers to Shakratel and Yura would feel like it had been severed. *If they knew I couldn't keep her safe, what would they think?*

I don't know how I'm going to continue. I knew I had to, but at that moment I did not want to keep putting one foot in front of the other. A heaviness settled into my muscles and bones, making every step harder.

Why does this always freakin' happen to me?

I needed to glide along on the breeze, like Pinu, as if nothing mattered. But I was petrified that if Minerva died, I was just that much closer to being all alone in the wilderness of Sai Lou.

The clattering of dishes that signaled dinner was ready made me bolt out the front door, my breath misting in the cold. I had to get away from everyone, so I followed the pathway I thought I recognized, through the fields up toward the barns and alpaca grazing area.

The soft strumming of a tanaloon crooned in the distance. I kept running away from the sound, past the barns and up the hill toward the rice paddies. The sky was heavy with clouds, the sun already dipping below the hills in the distance. I walked behind a small copse of trees at the base of the hill, beside the last barn. I trudged to a fallow field where the soil was dotted with a large group of flat-backed rocks that stood in the center of the undulating grasses and dandelions.

Overhead, among the dark clouds sweeping past, the sky was a deep fuchsia and gold, streaked with purple. A flock of black-faced seabirds yelled "skew, skew, skeeewww," in a throaty chorus. I looked below to the buzzing of bees and hornets hopping between the dande-lions and grass. Minerva might never see any of this again. All the noise of the living things spun around me. When I looked back at the lanterns glowing in the windows of the cabins in the valley, I knew I couldn't walk back, even if my stomach was empty. I looked up at the sky to see if the seabirds would fly by again.

There was only the occasional flight of small songbirds. I wondered if Pinu, too, would take off for these skies on her own someday, or if everyone, like Minerva and my parents, was destined to leave me?

A hornet zipped through the air for a large bird to swoop in and eat it, half its carcass dropping to the ground before I caught Pinu snap-ping up the remnants. I hoped it wouldn't make her sick.

She settled on a rock next to me, hopping up and down excitedly.

"That's something I've never seen before." Kalyon's voice startled me, and I looked up to face him, standing in the field, dandelions blowing around his feet.

"We're not used to having plenty to eat." I wondered how long he'd been following me. I tried to relax, my heart thudding.

"She'll be useful to have around when we're harvesting fruit," Kalyon remarked. "But, you don't want those hornets close to you. Their sting is painful, especially the pink ones."

"Oh they have colors?" I looked at the rest flying away from Pinu's snapping beak. The last of the light was dying in the sky, and the dual moons were rising.

"Here, try this." Kalyon held out a bit of grass to me. "It tends to keep the hornets away from close range. They hate the smell."

I wrinkled my nose, until I saw him chewing on some of the grass. It smelled like lemon and peppers. I took a bite on a blade, then when it settled my stomach a bit, I took a few more. The seabirds came back as I munched on the grass, my stomach calm for the first time in hours. The black-faced birds called out to each other, "so, so, so, so…" Pinu watched from where she perched beside me.

I fixated on the sky so I wouldn't have to look at Kalyon, hoping that my heart would stop fluttering up and down.

"It was a hard day, for you and Toref…I think," Kalyon finally said.

"It was." I accepted another blade from him, and he sat on the other side of me, his face illuminated in the moonlight.

There was a wetness to the air that made me wonder if it would rain again soon. "The birds sound so different when the sun goes down," I said awkwardly.

He looked at me, like he was going to say something serious, and then his wide mouth turned up. "To keep predators from easily identifying them. At least that's Litu's theory." He sighed, stretching his arms upward before letting them settle awkwardly at his side.

"Gita is worried about you and I'm…also…worried." He looked at me with those black, almond eyes. I felt myself drawing internally closer to him, but also ready to dart away.

"There's nothing…to be worried about. I just needed to be alone for a little while. I'm not used to so many people and it gets…"

"Overwhelming," he finished.

"Yes," I laughed, and he chuckled beside me.

"I have to share a room with Nalo until I turn eighteen, so I know how that is." I liked how he said it without any annoyance.

"Imagine hearing Jesik snoring every night, or Toref talking in his sleep," I said, twirling the last bit of grass. "I need Minerva healthy… so…I have…another female ally."

The bird calls echoed, some metallic, others high and whispery as the clouds rolled in, occasionally covering the moons.

"We could stay out here all night," I said suddenly. *Nobody would know.* The thought delighted and terrified me. I knew next to nothing about him.

Kalyon drew out a long length of shiny cloth. "We're in for a storm." He came closer to me, but stopped abruptly a few inches away, like he was waiting for me to bridge the distance. He shook out the cloth that reflected an amber light, and he draped it diagonally across half his torso. Before he could explain, fat rain droplets soaked us. Pinu took flight, and I held his arm while we trudged through the mud.

"You can get closer to stay dry," he said. The mud soon came up to our knees, and I tucked under his arm, helping to hold the oil cloth up. I had to focus on keeping in step with him, my arm around his waist to stay warm as the air around us cooled, the rain pelting us.

"Didn't it already rain earlier today? What is this?" I asked.

"Act two," he said, laughing. He was enjoying this a little too much. Kalyon inched closer to me, not in an intrusive way, but it made it easier for me to hold onto him. He draped his arm around my shoulder to keep the cover in place, rain soaking every bit that wasn't covered by the oil cloth. There was no lightning or thunder, just the incessant pelting.

"We'll be there in a few minutes," he insisted.

It felt like it took ages to reach the house. Kalyon yanked the door open, and Gita was standing over a teapot by the fire.

Gita cleared her throat. "Idris, use my room to change."

I heard murmuring as I changed into the warm clothes in Gita's room, the pants a little big, but comfortable. I didn't want to feel that pressing in my chest for Kalyon. But it felt like there was a warmth where his hands had been around my shoulders, my hand remembering the feel of his waist and the brush of his straight hair against my face. *Was it impossible to feel that, especially with everything that needed sorting out inside of me?*

The house felt strangely quiet for a few seconds before the murmuring started up again.

Some things I had to see through, no matter how painful or unjust. Would Kalyon's courage lift me out of my sadness? I was tempted to avoid him, regardless of the racing of my pulse whenever he was near. That was biology, wasn't it? Nothing deeper.

I came back into the living room with tea already set out. Kalyon rubbed Pinu's black feathers down with linen scraps. I saw that flicker in Kalyon's eyes when I sat across from him.

My pulse picked up again and for once, I chose to stay and sip my tea slowly across from him. Thoughts of Minerva and Toref drifted back in as my body warmed up from the tea.

CHAPTER 35

TOREF

Toref awoke the next morning to the sound of jubilant singing. When he stumbled with Idris and Jesik out of their railcar, Minerva was standing on her metal legs outside smiling weakly.

She's alive! She's okay!

He couldn't help throwing his arms around her, a weight within him lifting in the early morning sun. Idris joined in hugging the two of them.

"You're okay now. You're okay," Toref said.

Jesik pranced around them, his large body casting a shadow over us each time he made a rotation around the trio. Toref finally waved him over. "Get in here, before I decide I'm tired of hugging these two."

Everyone laughed and it felt good to breathe so easy.

A week later, Toref followed a grumpy, hairy Diarmaid into his hangar with Idris and Minerva, who looked on with suspicion. Diarmaid stared at them with his black eyes like he'd never seen Ungar before or he was afraid they'd steal his stupidly ancient hovers.

"I have a shipment of rice that needs to go out to the port tomorrow. My hover ain't working. You think you can get her running for a two-hour round-trip flight?" He crossed his large, hairy arms.

Toref had never seen anything so old. "It looks like she's going to need a lot of work." Toref didn't mind working on it, but I had a feeling we were not going to get it running and would have to use my hover instead.

"We'll work on it," Toref assured Diarmaid, who looked back at Minerva for confirmation.

"We'll take a few hours and let you know, okay?" Idris said, her voice low.

Toref knew he had to keep things light after Minerva's recovery. He had been a live wire all morning since they assigned her chore duties.

Maybe all of them had been live wires for quite a while.

He tried to silence his own swirling thoughts by following Minerva's instructions. "Let's take a look at the motherboard, wiring and…" he looked at Idris, who shook her head.

"The comp units on this are probably blown, but we can look, just to be on the safe side," she grinned, and it felt good to be back in the thick of repairs again.

After a half hour, Minerva went out to collect water and came back with mud splashed over her face. Toref stopped his work on the next board to rise to greet her. This was the moment he could get closer, as Idris had stepped out to go get more materials. The minute he took a rag out of his pocket to clean off her face, he felt that lurch inside him that something was changing very quickly. He held out the cloth to the rain and then inched further out, the rain pelting his head, rivulets tracking down his face and into his eyes.

Minerva took both his hands in hers, letting the rag drop to the ground. Someone sang from a nearby cabin and the music blended with the pattering of rain. She pulled Toref close to her, kissing both his cheeks and closing her eyes. *Oh that feels nice.* The water poured over them as he brought her closer and kissed her full on the mouth, drawing her further into the hangar.

Wow. Kissing her is like magic.

He heard footsteps and drew away, watching for Diarmaid, who might yell at them for not working on his busted stuff. Idris approached as Toref savored the moment of their gentle ascent into finally admitting what they were, albeit without words.

"Go. I'll finish here," Idris said, shoving them away.

They walked uphill from the hangar, holding hands, giggling and looking like two fools who needed each other.

Was such a thing possible for Toref?

Idris found them the next morning in the barn next to the pig stall, asleep in the hay. "Get up, it's breakfast time!"

Toref brushed himself off before helping Minerva with the clumps of hay all over her sweater. *What had we been thinking?* It wasn't like they had hair that hay easily shook out of. Everyone would know what they'd been up to.

Idris put her hands on her hips. "What do you think you're doing? Os has been asking for you."

Nalo stood behind her, already leading the pigs out, who were grumbling again.

"What do you think you doing?" The pigs repeated, except much louder.

"You missed breakfast, ya flat-heads," Nalo called behind him, shaking his cane at the pigs.

They repeated him in a snorty chorus.

"They are so annoying," Toref whispered, and Minerva held out her hands for Toref to help her back into her legs.

Toref helped her strap them in and Idris watched them with a grimace. He lifted her to a standing position. She kissed him, right there, in front of everyone, like it was nothing.

Could he be so bold again?

He watched for the pleasure flushing Minerva's cheeks. Toref lifted her off her feet and carried her for a bit, while she squealed happily. *So this is the life we were meant to have.* He couldn't help another, darker feeling tugging at him that Rusty and his sisters couldn't experience such happiness, too.

CHAPTER 36

TOREF

A MONTH LATER

A t first glance, Toref thought, harvesting rice seemed fairly easy. The stalks came out of the cold water easy enough. After his first row, though, his back was aching and Idris' earlier grumbling about how annoying it was, now made sense.

Everyone around him sang while they harvested, some echoing the last three lyrics of each line.

Carry me over the hills,
Beyond the dark earth I see
The shining lakes beckon me home
Away, away, from dear Mina Li...

I'm longing to see the purple shore
The windswept skies so clear
It burns me to the core
To be so far, yet near

Carry me over the hills...
I'm happy, my friend, not alone

To see you beyond those hills
Of our home, beloved, home.
Our home, beloved home.

He'd hoped that harvesting the rice stems would take his mind off thinking about his sisters and Rusty and how much he missed them during the long harvest season days. He tossed the plants in the basket for the beetle teams to separate. Minerva still wasn't well enough to stay upright for the twelve hours everyone had spent in the paddies for the past month of harvest season. Once they were finally together at night, he was too tired to do anything other than snuggle with her before he passed out.

He looked up at the carapaces of the beetle teams as they clacked along, humming with little Nalo sitting cross-legged on their backs. Toref moved closer to watch the small-eyed creatures humming along on their thin, furry legs, towering over him. The beetles seemed cooperative in a way that sometimes humans hadn't quite managed, except when they were singing with each other. And man, was there a lot of singing here.

It was almost nonstop the past few days. Was it the lack of electronic entertainment, he wondered? He moved to the next row, adjusting the basket tied to his waist. The singing ceased when a whistle shrilled across the paddies. Toref kept thinking about the last stanza of the song "I'm happy, my friend, not alone..." it was worded so strangely. The sun was now high in the sky, and it felt like he couldn't move, his legs burning every time he moved them. Everyone stopped, and his team moved toward the whistle calling out at intervals.

Os waved for Toref to follow the rest of the kids back to the barns.

"Lunchtime break, everyone!"

Jesik handed the reins to the beetle team he'd been following back to Gita. "We go?" Jesik asked Os.

"That's right, Jesik. Everyone eats now." Gita gestured for Jesik to follow her solid figure back toward the barns.

Something about how Gita ushered Jesik into the barn made Toref remember his mother before his father died and how Lena, his oldest sister, had bossed them all around when they were slacking in the kitchen. Penny used to get so mad.

"Who does she think she is?" Penny whispered, her round cheeks going tight with anger.

"I'm the one who makes you the sweet cakes you like, so you better listen to me," Lena called out.

"Damn, how does she hear me?" Penny muttered.

"My eagle ears, my dear," Lena said, her thin face going wide with a toothy smile showing the tiny gap in her two front teeth. She smoothed back her frizzy bangs and kept her hands on her hips.

Toref would give anything to go back to that time. It made it hard to fully enjoy what he did have in Sai Lou, with the exception of his time with Minerva.

"We can't leave Rusty and your sisters there to die," Minerva had said weeks ago.

How do I attempt the impossible when I can't even keep my own emotions in check?

It felt like the more knowledge Toref gained, the more it overwhelmed him with the weight of the impossibility of changing any of it, especially as the weeks stretched on. *But I have to find a way—without risking everyone's lives again.*

CHAPTER 37

IDRIS

TWO MONTHS LATER

T he winter winds and snow blew in daily, forcing us all indoors. That morning, Gita, her fuzzy silver hair threatening to escape her bun, woke Kalyon and I up at sunrise to trudge outside with Nalo to feed the alpacas and check on all the team animals. When I saw the sky darken and snow falling on the hillsides in the distance, I knew it was time. "Hey let's go back to the house, before the snow makes it impossible to see."

Inside the warmth of the large, wood-paneled house, music sessions and daily stretch-meditation had started. Gita was running music practice while Os stretched in the opposite living room with five kids. Since the music had already begun, I dragged myself into Os's space. Everyone was following his series of stretches and humming. Kalyon moved over and Litu waved for me to take the empty spot on the floor. We sat down, bringing our knees into our stomachs and rolling back and forth. I heard coughing from the front, and Minerva wheezed from where she was seated on the ground.

"I can't continue," she whispered.

I bent over to lift her up the stairs to the top floor room we now shared with Litu in the "girl's suite," as they now called our side of the attic. We'd essentially taken over the southern attic, which had originally been used for storage. I took down a sweater from the pegs for Minerva.

Minerva looked at something behind me. "Could I wear the blue wrap Litu made for you?"

It was my favorite, but I hadn't told anyone that. Kalyon had picked out the color weeks ago when Litu was showing us how to dye the alpaca yarn. When I wore the wrap, it made me think of him, even though I tried every day to avoid the question of why I thought of him, why I lingered in the barns with him once the snow came...all those reasons piling up and torturing me, especially if our conversation extended beyond a few minutes.

I didn't need to have what happened with Reggi, that awful awkwardness, repeat again.

I eyed the wrap and saw a green one that might suit Minerva better. "Why don't you take this one, it looks like it will fit you better."

Minerva smiled slyly at me. "I see how it is, Idris. You want to keep your stuff nice for..." She didn't say his name.

"You've got it all wrong, Minerva," I whispered. The door was still open.

"Maybe I do, and maybe I don't." She grinned, her face jubilant with that wisdom she always seemed to have.

I handed her the green wrap, and she wrapped it around her, closing the edges with a large pin. I grabbed my blue wrap, fastening it around me tightly.

Thundering started up the stairs and I knew it was Jesik by his footfalls, Toref following close behind. The scent in the room changed to a piney maleness that pricked my nostrils, and I took a step back to let them into the cramped room, pulling our drying clothes to the side.

"Snow?" Jesik asked, his ox snout turned up pleasantly.

Toref clapped his hands. "Come on, we don't have evening chores, and we might as well enjoy our midday break outside!"

"I've already spent hours outside in the cold," I said. "No way."

Toref sat next to Minerva, lying back on her bed. He pulled the covers tight around her and opened the curtains, a patch of sun coming through the window. I was glad to see that nothing seemed to dampen how much they liked each other.

"Let her rest, you two," I said and shooed them out, following them down the stairs to the next level where most of the boy's rooms were. Jesik and Toref now shared a room with Kalyon. They grabbed their gloves and scarves. Jesik didn't bother with anything more than a sweater and denim overalls. Kalyon sat on the bedroom floor stringing a tanaloon.

"Snow...Toref. Come. On. You like it! You know you do!" Jesik opened the large window that looked out on the fresh falling snow. Toref put his scarf around his neck and was about to leave the room when Jesik picked him up and threw him out the window. Toref laughed and landed in the snowbank below. "Get down here, Jesik, and get a taste of your own medicine!" He lobbed a snowball at Jesik.

Jesik shoved himself out the window, hooting, and yelling until he landed on the same bank.

I watched the two of them running about, throwing snow at each other like lunatics. I couldn't help laughing at them, though I had no intention of leaving the warm house.

Or Kalyon.

I closed the window and locked it to keep the draft out.

Kalyon was struggling with re-stringing his instrument. *I could leave him to it*, I told myself, but I couldn't quite get my feet to move. *What was I supposed to say to him?*

A girl downstairs sang in harmony with Gita. The girl's voice was beautiful. I leaned out into the hallway to listen. When I glanced back at Kalyon, his eyes immediately met mine, a sense of longing there I hoped I wasn't imagining. Was it because of the song? I leaned back out to listen, not wanting to know what those eyes said, avoiding the question there.

My stomach felt like it had dropped out and everything in the room had gone still, crystalline. I couldn't hear anything other than the whooshing of my breath and the exhalation of Kalyon only a few inches away from me. This tension in my chest was different from when any other guy had looked at me.

"I can help you string this, if you want," I said, moving closer, tempting the feeling to recede.

"You can play?" His eyes lit up.

"No, but it's my favorite instrument. I can be handy, when I want to." I took the tanaloon from him, his hand lightly brushing my arm. He lingered by my side, watching me tighten the screws with the string attached properly at the end, using some of the resin glue to keep the ends attached to the wooden pegs. Once they were all attached, I plucked each string, all of them badly out of tune. When I looked up, his brown arms were close, his lean muscles showing beneath his flannel shirt.

"What?" I asked.

He tied his long black hair behind him. I wished he'd left it down. "I can teach you how to play. I'm not amazing. I can play as much as any git in Sai Lou. The real pro is Diarmaid." He raised a thick, black eyebrow. "We don't ask him for lessons, unless we're desperate."

I laughed, because I knew how Diarmaid was, especially about wanting us newcomers gone.

Kalyon tuned the strings and slid down the boxed platform of his bed, patting a place on the rug for me to sit. I was eager to make the strings sing. I held the long neck of the tanaloon and inhaled Kalyon's woodsy scent.

"You're holding it by the wrong side, so it'll make it hard to mirror the correct chord fingering." He adjusted the base of the instrument so it rested across my right shoulder and hip, demonstrating how to pluck the strings. He was closer than he probably needed to be, demonstrating the chord with his arms around me.

After a few tries, I had something almost resembling a melody. Kalyon sang along to the three chords, his lips close to my face, helping me adjust my fingers. I fumbled, and he started again, making sure I was in the right place before continuing to sing.

"I'm just a lonely man
Living here, on the land
Earning my keep, I try to see
Beyond the sun's set where I'll be.
But, all I see is your face,
In the clouds, my dear
All I see is your face
In the clouds, my love.

Kalyon was singing to me. I didn't know what to do, so I stopped playing. I wanted to be closer to him, but I didn't know how. It would require me surrendering the instrument. It felt safe and secure in my hands. A small snippet of Wiid appeared in my mind before I brushed him away.

He isn't allowed in this moment.

I looked at Kalyon's full lips. I had seen people kiss before, but how...?

He closed his eyes for a moment, leaning back against the bed. He was only a few inches away from me. All I had to do was touch his arm...I stood up and put the tanaloon on his bed before I made a mistake. My gut clenched as I walked away, a deep grey washing through me in not being able to touch him.

"Thank you," I said when I reached the landing.

I had to discharge that welling inside my belly that wouldn't stop, so I stepped outside with Kalyon's jacket around my shoulders that afternoon. It had been the first coat I could find, and I let the crunching of the snow on my moccasins beat out a rhythm to keep myself from thinking of him, though every other thought made me think of the height of his cheekbones, what it would be like to touch them...No...I had to think of something else. Then a new thought crept in, about how the light touched the tiniest freckle I'd found at the corner of his chin the other day.

I continued walking until the cold seeped through my moccasins and my feet were almost numb. I spotted Minerva in the kitchens. She had an apron around her. That was probably the only place I was going to get warm at this time of day, especially if she'd already fired up the ovens.

When I'd hung up his coat and changed into a fresh pair of socks, I headed to the kitchen, closing the wooden door behind me, the warmth immediately flooding my face. Minerva was slicing tomatoes. Several pans cooled on the brick tables next to the ovens.

"One more dish to go in. You want to cut the rest with me?" she asked, her pale face smiling pleasantly.

I took over peeling the potatoes and slicing them up. All the thoughts I'd been trying to avoid while walking in the cold came flooding back to me. I couldn't talk about Kalyon in the open here. But Minerva was smart, she might catch on to what was bothering me if I said it in a way that she understood.

"I wish I understood how cooking really worked," I said.

"What are you talking about?" Minerva put a hand on her hip, inspecting my face before her pale eyebrows lifted into acknowledgement. "Ah." She checked on a pan of stuffed tomatoes with rice already in the oven.

I joined her by the oven, soaking up the heat. "I don't know how you learned to cook all this stuff. It feels like I'm catching up every day I'm here." I reached for one of the rice balls and took a bite.

"The dill is the secret," Minerva said. She wiped her hands on her apron before handing me a tray to put in the other oven.

"I wish I could understand how all food worked," I said, cocking an eyebrow.

"Anybody can cook," she said with a sly smile.

"Not me. Never done it in my life, probably never will."

Minerva leaned into me, "I can teach you how to cook, but the other stuff, you'll have to ask Gita about. However, you're a detail person, you'll pick it up." She patted my arm like someone who had seen a lot, even though she was only a year older than me.

I leaned against the countertop, continuing to peel the last of the potatoes, enjoying the feel of the skin peeling back against the sharp knife. "I've learned that a person can't be too many things. I can pilot, I can fight, I'm good with animals. Those are my limits."

Minerva cocked her head to the side, grabbing the potatoes from me. "You don't think you can change?"

I looked at Minerva and remembered a moment with my mother, sitting inside one of the hovers she was fixing.

"Love is real, Idris. I know you've seen how Wiid and the other overseers are. That isn't love. I want you to remember that love is different. What I felt for your father. That was and will always be love." She kissed the ruby statue of the goddess and handed it back to me.

I sighed, feeling that stone in my stomach that came whenever I had to change, and it didn't feel like my choice. But, what if I chose to love? What if…

"I'll always be this way." I took one of the grilled peppers from the pan and took a bite. Minerva stood there waiting for me to finish my thought. "Nobody really changes. My parents didn't, even when their survival demanded it. I changed just enough to survive—and that's the reason I'm stuck either flying or mucking out the animals."

Minerva handed me a cooked ball of rice with a meaty sauce center that I loved. I took a bite, sauce dribbling down my chin before I caught it and wiped it off. "How did you do it?"

"I let circumstances change me," Minerva said. She coughed loudly, a deep rattle that I knew meant she was done for the day. I took the grill pan from her hands and fetched a glass of water. She didn't stop coughing after two glasses, and Gita came down, looking worried. "You're going to have to finish dinner preparations, Idris, because everyone else is at their evening chores."

"Litu!" She called out into the living room.

"Litu's at the loom!" Litu yelled.

"I'm coming," I heard Kalyon say.

I panicked, staring at the abundance of food we'd need to get out. I felt bad I'd shooed out the kid who'd been helping Minerva earlier. I couldn't cook at all. There were still two more pans that needed prep and baking before the first shift of young kids showed up.

"You chop, and I'll do the seasoning?" Kalyon asked, but really he was telling me.

"Please, I have no idea what to do," I said. He looked at me like he knew, but wasn't chastising me. There was that calm to him that washed over me.

My mind pinged between worrying about Minerva and this new blooming inside me thanks to Kalyon, and settled on cataloguing how close Kalyon and I got to each other. Me avoiding eye contact and acting busy. Trying to keep that armor up that kept all the other guys away. But when I snuck a glance at him, he immediately met my gaze.

Could I let myself like him?

What if I was wrong? There was that gnawing worry that he was an awful person. An image of Reggi floated up, followed by Wiid, and I pushed them both away. No. It had to stop sometime, why not with him?

When we finished cooking the last pan, Kalyon handed me a rag, our hands touching for a moment, his fingers lingering by mine. I let his thick fingers caress mine for half a moment, before I wiped the sweat out of my stinging eyes and sat on the far counter to catch my breath. A group of kids had already come through to dish up and it was dark outside. The window was cracked to let in some ventilation from the heat of the ovens.

"You ready to eat?" he asked. Kalyon looked down at me, with an openness in his lovely face that made me want to throw my arms around him.

This madness feels completely comfortable.

He'd already dished up a plate for me, and I followed him out to the table, accepting an extra helping of toasted potatoes and tucking in so I didn't have to say anything. Once I was halfway done I bolted upright, the tension killing me, the need to touch him overwhelming.

"I'd better check on Minerva. I'll be back," I said.

"Should I keep your plate warm?" he asked.

I pretended I didn't hear.

When I came back, he was the only one left at the table, looking at me like his life depended on my being there, his gaze so warm, his mouth full. He pointed to the kitchen where he'd kept my plate warm, and I followed him wordlessly inside.

He moved closer to me, taking my hand and kissing my knuckles before turning my palm around and kissing the center of it. A warmth spread through me that made my legs relax in a way I had never experienced before. Everything around us had a soft glow when Kalyon released me to get the plate. I sat back on the counter to finish my food, and he didn't touch me as we cleaned up. This new state both thrilled and frightened me because I had no idea what to do.

Or if there was anything to do, when I felt this full of warm air and strange, fleeting thoughts.

I turned toward him, one hand outstretched toward him, needing him again. Kalyon took my other hand and brought it to his cheek, before placing both hands around his neck, pulling me that much closer. We stood like that for a while, almost swaying, before Nalo burst through the two of us, like nothing was going on here at all.

"Stupid kid," I said.

CHAPTER 38

IDRIS

The cold air stung my exposed cheeks and hands. I had been avoiding Kalyon for days. Minerva kept badgering me that I stayed at the stables too long. When Kalyon had come around to check on me, I'd left the stables quickly, in a hurry to avoid him when he came on shift. My body ached with the need to be near him, but I couldn't bear thinking about what might come next, how it might all crumble if I had a flashback. It was too much for me.

I'd even asked Gita to change me to hover repair, but she'd refused. They didn't have enough hands, as it was, to attend to the animals. She'd looked at me, like she expected me to spill my guts, like they all expected me to.

I wasn't going to. Not ever.

"I see how he looks at you, Idris," Minerva had said two days after the whole him-touching-my-hand thing.

I'd turned over in my bed, wanting to ignore her while knowing she wouldn't let me. "Yeah, well, maybe I like it."

"So, do something and tell him," she'd chided.

"Like you tell Toref stuff?" I sat up and looked at her in the dark, a sliver of moonlight illuminating her frizzy halo of hair.

"Don't make this about me," she said softly. "I know bad things happened to you. But, there's something good about him. Even I can feel it."

I'd told her about Reggi, in a moment of weakness, so it wasn't like she wasn't aware of what had come before. Almost nothing. She didn't need me to tell her about Wiid. It was written all over me. Damaged goods coming from a long line of damaged goods.

Minerva sat up, rubbing at the ends of her stumps. "It can get better, you know. You can trust him, at some point, when you're ready…if that's what you want."

I came over to her side of the bed, watching to make sure we weren't waking Litu. "I don't know. I like him, I do…it's just… I'm so terrified. And that fear feels more powerful than all the good things I feel for him."

Minerva held me against her and I wished I could cry, to let out all the horrible that came before so that there was room for this feeling for Kalyon. When Litu woke us in the morning, I had fallen asleep curled up next to Minerva, her cozy quilt covering both of us. Her soft hands were comforting on my shoulders.

Pinu circled above me, not touching down. To her, in midflight, it was like the cold was something fulfilling and refreshing instead of numbing every thought in my head on the ground. In between Pinu shifting her long, black wings, I imagined Kalyon's smile, his flashing white teeth, the way he took my hand to show me which string to play on the tantaloon. The fact I'd liked it.

What if I allowed him in?

A smile played at my lips involuntarily and I let it, looking up at the milky sky again, Pinu circling and circling.

To be that free. *What would I do with such freedom, and would I even appreciate it, if I stopped being afraid?*

Once the house was in view, I stepped into a series of deep footsteps in the snow around its wooden exterior. I heard the crunching of snow behind me. When I turned, Kalyon was approaching, his black hair sticking out of a grey woolen cap. Minerva was behind him.

"What's wrong?" he asked, coming close, but not embracing me.

"I was watching Pinu, making sure she doesn't fly too far away." I looked up at the bright circle of the sun peeking through the thick cloud cover. "I was thinking about freedom...how I wish...I...could know you...better." I stared at my moccasins for a moment, frozen, afraid of what came next.

"I want that too, Idris," he said, a soft smile playing at his full lips.

I stepped back, though my hands ached to hold his. I needed to see that he could be gentle with my terribly scarred heart, but I was still terrified that I'd read everything wrong. "There are no secrets in this house, are there?"

"Sadly, no. Once someone is...you know...everyone eventually knows," he said softly, taking one step closer to me, the snow crunching under his feet.

I felt bad, until his toes were right against mine, Minerva still watching us, her shawl tucked around her. I looked up into his long, thin face, those eyes so warm as he took my hands. "You're cold, let's get you inside." His palms folded around mine as he tucked them into the pocket of his snow poncho.

I found myself unexpectedly grinning, the warmth of his touch surging through me and squashing all the fear.

"I'll follow you inside in a minute," I said, looking past him to Minerva and planting a small kiss at the edge of his jaw.

He grinned, his uneven white teeth flashing as he stepped through the kitchen door, closing it softly behind him.

Minerva rushed to me, taking my cold hand, hers still warm. She folded me into her ample chest, and I felt the tears that hadn't come days ago finally fall. It felt like a river of sadness was flowing out of me.

"Finally, Idris. Freakin' finally." She drew circles on my back until I was ready to go inside.

CHAPTER 39

TOREF

Toref sat by Diarmaid's hover console, sneaking glances at Minerva while reattaching the wires that Gita had mistakenly clipped. He'd need to solder the other wires in order for the drive shaft to work properly again. However, his mind was occupied elsewhere, trying to say something meaningful to Minerva, to get her to look at him, but also worried someone would see him wanting to be closer to her.

"This is really old tech," Minerva said, artificial legs off, her pant legs sitting halfway empty on the floor where she was spread out with her tablet attached to the nav console. "I don't even know if I can update it." She looked up, grinning at Toref with her *I want to kiss you* face that he loved.

He leaned into her, the scent of soap on her skin, but stopped halfway to her lips. Gita was humming somewhere nearby, rooting around in the vegetable garden. He still didn't feel comfortable touching Minerva openly around other people. (Even though Idris had caught them in the barn all those weeks ago.)

That felt like months ago, instead of weeks.

Idris catching them had only made him more reticent. It wasn't embarrassment, but the need, with so many kids around, to feel like their relationship belonged only to him and Minerva.

He looked back at the wires, his breath catching, and he knew he needed a break. He thought back to the plan he and Minerva had been talking about: to go back and rescue Rusty and his sisters. His heart fell as he considered it and all the risks it posed, to all of them.

"What's the matter?" Minerva whispered.

He looked out the dirty windows, glancing for any sign of Gita. "I just feel uneasy. I don't know if it's that I don't know if we can get this up and running in time for planting, or if it's something else." *Can I share my feelings?*

Minerva scooted closer to him, helping him feed another wire through the drive loop. "What if it's all of it? Our lives have changed a lot. I find myself waking up sometimes, still thinking I'm back at the Pods, a Monitor hovering over me asking me to fix their tech for the thousandth time." She put down the console. "I really miss Rusty. He was a brother to me, to both of us."

Toref felt bad, like it was always him complaining about things and here was Minerva, trying to be cheery, rarely complaining. *Am I a weight on her?* Their life here was incredible, but there was always that shadow lurking in the background. A deep guilt still pressed on him for having gotten away while his friend and sisters suffered.

Or was it that he always wanted more, never quite satisfied, especially when he and Minerva were together...no, he couldn't think about that right now. Why couldn't he just appreciate her—all that red hair, those beautiful freckles on her round cheeks, her soft skin—without wanting it to go further?

He leaned in, her soft lips touching his.

"Hate to interrupt you, but I was wondering..." Gita's voice boomed over them.

Toref gasped and whipped around to Gita smirking, the lines in her face turning up pleasantly. Unlike Os, she didn't seem to care that they were kissing while they worked. "I wanted to check on the progress and see if one of you wanted to run these to Litu for our supper?"

She held up a basket of potatoes and turnips. There was another dark orange vegetable with spikes that Toref couldn't identify. "What's that?" he asked.

"Chaya root. Great for spicing up soups and stews. I think Litu knows what to do with it." Gita looked behind her, her face still jubilant. "Or, at least I think she'll find out once she cuts it open. Very pungent, but tasty!"

Toref detected something else in Gita's expression. She had something more she wanted to say that she was working up to. It was the way in which she was a little too cheery, the corners of her wrinkled, pale mouth turning up in a way that didn't feel quite natural.

Minerva looked from Toref to Gita and started to hook in her artificial legs. "I need a stretch. I'll take those to Litu."

Toref leaned toward her. "We can do it together, right Gita?"

Gita shook her head. "Actually, I wanted to see about the hover, Toref…and some other things." She nodded at Minerva. "I'll see you in a few."

Minerva took the basket and was off, waving back at Toref. When Gita turned to face him, Minerva blew him a kiss. He struggled to keep his attention on Gita.

"You can't hide what's going on with you and Minerva from me, eh?" Gita smiled and perched on the wooden bench with a groan. "It's good to see young love here in Sai Lou. Winter is long here, and you're all settling in very well." She sat next to him in the open cargo doorway of the hover. She groaned as she wiped her hands on her legs. "Getting old is hard, but I have to say…there's a wisdom you can't trade for anything."

Toref looked at her, still stalling, like she had something more to say. "Are you afraid that Minerva and I are….um…"

Gita got very calm. "That is a concern, especially as you're both so young and have been through a lot. It can mean that feelings get intense, and over time those feelings change as things get better. Sometimes the relationship can change too."

He considered this, looking out at the fields stretching in front of them, the cloudy sky one large swath of grey with no sign of deviation, with the exception of shaggy pine trees and black hills in the distance. "I think Minerva has been through worse than me. At least I remember my parents being normal and caring for me. I don't think she had any of that."

Gita exhaled, putting her hand on his forearm. "Be careful. Take it slowly. That's all I'm asking. When you feel like you have to take things to another level, talk to Os or me. I'm hoping you'll wait awhile, but relationships are different for everyone."

Toref knew that from observing the weird dance of Idris and Kalyon every day. *I'm thankful that's not my relationship with Minerva.* But he knew how afraid he was, every time he reached for Minerva, every time he wondered if this would be the moment she'd reject him, that she'd say she wasn't interested anymore, and then he truly would be alone.

I wouldn't know how to handle that.

"I see you've got a lot going on there, Toref. And you're missing your family, still."

It had been a few weeks since he'd talked to Gita about going back. He looked into her green eyes, the color of a new blade of grass, her face lined with wrinkles, and yet that feeling of youth that she radiated.

"I still feel like we need to go back for them, I just don't know how," he heard himself say quietly, like he was afraid that saying it would make the possibility disappear. That fear crept out of its shadow place, from where it haunted the edges of everything he did.

He looked up at the sky again, trying to discharge the terrible feeling that shook his frame.

"Are you certain you want to take the risk of going back?" Gita asked. "It will take a lot of manpower, and we could all get captured in the process." Gita put a hand on Toref's shoulder. "I speak as someone who fought in the Hybrid Wars, who saw people die. I know Whip and Stencil, I saw how heartless the two of them could be when they were fighting on the same side." Her eyes darkened, no longer jade green, the folds in her face falling. "Now they have rival casinos."

Toref felt there was more history there in her life than he could begin to imagine. "My best friend, Rusty, was captured, and if my sisters can't be found, we can at least help him. It feels like I can't live my life here without at least trying to help them. If we can create a good plan, even just do reconnaissance to see if it's possible..."

Gita stood up, brushing dirt from her pants and sweater. "I know that you want the people you love to be here safe with you. But sometimes what we want isn't the best thing for everyone. You're part of a larger family with Os and I, if you want to be, and that means that going back doesn't just affect you anymore. It would affect all of us, especially the rest of the kids here if we try to rescue your family and we lose part of our family in the process."

A pit settled in Toref's stomach, a weight settling in his limbs while he looked at her for a while. She was right. The risk of such a rescue operation crashed inside of him, clanging about in his insides. The dark pine trees swayed behind Gita, and he knew in that moment that he couldn't give up on his sisters and Rusty. Yes, she was right, it would be difficult, but there had to be a way. Something new had sparked within him, and he had to press the issue, even if it meant upsetting the delicate balance in Sai Lou. "I have to try, Gita," he said softly, meeting her gaze. "If we can get enough of you to help us."

"Let me talk to Os and see what he says." Gita nodded once and ambled away.

CHAPTER 40

IDRIS

The violin leapt with a winged sound that lifted me from where I sat. It sounded so ancient and airy, like a seabird soaring above all the creatures stuck on the ground. Kalyon inched closer, his arm around my back, the fire in the hearth crackling behind us.

I leaned against his shoulder, a white and black tendril of my hair falling into my face. Kalyon tucked it behind my ear. That single touch, before he settled back into the cushions of the platform where we were squished between Jesik and Minerva, made me nervous. Minerva's hands entwined with Toref's.

Why was it so easy for her?

Was it because there was nothing left to be taken away from her?

I didn't dare sneak a glance at Kalyon. The stirring feelings got worse when he wasn't around, the dreams after the kitchen incident the previous day: of him putting his hand on my face and coming close…the rest I didn't know. The mechanics of it, the possibility that if I kissed him wrong, he'd never touch me again. And there was the chance of getting caught kissing by the others in the house. *Nightmare.*

I inhaled the pleasant sandalwood aroma of him as he shifted his weight, his arm closer to mine, not asking, not grasping, just there. A comfort I hadn't expected.

The violin held onto the last note, slowly singing itself to silence. No one stirred and chatter slowly filled the room as the lights burned in their lamps along the dining room walls. It was a strange feeling to be so comfortable, Pinu roosting in the alcove above the violinists. I wished in that moment I could share this with Yura, talk to her about him, get her advice.

Kalyon swiveled around to where he was directly in my line of sight. There was a fullness to his lips that I hadn't noticed before.

"I've never heard anything so beautiful." He put his arm behind me, like he wanted to wrap it around my waist. "You?"

"It was more than beautiful. It was like I was flying." I blushed when I said the last part. It sounded so fanciful, not like me at all.

"You're right." He leaned into me, like he meant to say more, but waited when I didn't say anything. "What?"

"What?" I asked.

"Are you...I mean...is everything okay?"

"I probably need to stand." I needed to get away from him, from the magnetic pull I was feeling. If I stayed put, my mind would keep trying to figure out a way to get him closer. *They can't all see me like this.* But then the violins were playing in my head again. Like it was something that I had no control over, the music influencing me, even if it was gone.

A violin started up again, and I wasn't going crazy.

In one swift movement, I yanked his shirt sleeve and dragged him with me to the hallway, where the music was still audible. It was cold on the floorboards, their creaking accompanying our footfalls, and once we were out of view of the kids, I pulled my sweater tighter around me, fastening my scarf. He leaned in, his red scarf already untied. It fell to the floor and I reached for it.

"No, let it be," he said, holding my waist.

I touched his wrist and he took my hands, a fizzle inside spreading through every part of me. His eyes were so dark I couldn't see his pupils in the lamplight. He took my scarf and threw it to the floor beside his scarf. The music started up again and the violin was breathtaking in its depiction of a bird call, another related melody starting again. He looked at me expectantly, his lips slightly parted.

"The music…I've always…Pinu and I always loved it. It's the thing that kept us going when I escaped."

He shifted closer, one arm on the doorframe, his other arm snug around my waist. He was waiting for me, I could tell. My heart was going to burst out of my chest if I didn't calm down. Maybe talking would help.

"To hear it now. It's like a dream, and I feel like tomorrow I'll wake…and be back in the factory, except my parents are still dead. Or, I'll be back in my cave and Whip is coming after me."

Both of his arms were securely around me. It was ever so gentle, and I looked up in his eyes, an understanding there I hadn't expected.

"When I hear this music, I never want to go back. I want to stay safe…I'm talking too much, I know I need to stop, but…"

He brought me closer, his body asking before his knees were touching mine. Like there was no cloth dividing us, nothing to keep us apart, though we were so different. I let him enfold me in his arms, our feet moving gently in rhythm with the music. He was so peaceful and I was so full of needing him, like a powerful, surging tide.

How could I tell him this, would he want to keep holding me, if he knew?

I released myself from his arms, though he still gently held onto my elbows. "You see…I'm not used to being around people. There were endless people before I escaped and then…after…just Shakratel's compound once a month spending time with Yura and him and my passengers. Passengers are almost all annoying, never there for long…"

Kalyon smiled, looking at where Toref and Minerva were folded into each other.

"Yeah, except Toref and Minerva. They were passengers who became like family."

Kalyon raised an eyebrow, smiling. "You're not talking too much, you know? I want you to know that."

"I'm glad I'm here, even if I don't know how to be here, how to enjoy and just live and not be worried about the next bad thing."

He let go of me, his hand outstretched toward me, like it was my choice what came next. Having that choice meant everything.

I took his hand then, feeling that I couldn't continue, that my words weren't enough in this moment. His hand didn't feel like I'd expected, rough, yet gentle, not holding me in place, but barely a weight to my palm.

He tried to come closer, but the music had stopped and like a fragile string, the moment was broken. The cold was seeping in. I needed to get away from everything I felt when he was too near like that.

"Idris, don't go," he said.

"I'm tired and cold."

"I'll walk with you." His footsteps pounded after me as I made my way toward the front door.

"No, don't worry, I'm fine. I'll see you tomorrow."

And like that I knew I would regret letting go of him, just like I did everyday with Yura and Shakratel. *I never got to tell them they are my family.* The minute I stepped away, I wished he had walked with me, that I wasn't so painfully difficult. How could I unravel so many years of being alone to let him in?

Was it even worth it?

I walked up the hill and slept in the barn that night so it would be easy for me to start my shift the next morning. What frightened me about Kalyon wasn't his gentleness, but that fire that I knew all men had. I had seen how men had grabbed Yura. How Wiid assumed my mother and I were his property. One day whistling through his teeth, everything normal at the looms and then tomorrow, *bam.* I was shoved to the floor and he was grabbing at my waist, pulling me to him, Dina looking on, tail flicking nervously.

At least Yura chose who touched her. There's that consolation.

I knew that fizz when Kalyon touched me meant something I didn't understand. Something other people probably understood. My body primed to create more ways for hands and feet to meet. And after that, I didn't know. That lack of knowing was absolutely terrifying. At some point, I'd fold to the moment where I surrendered to his dark eyes and let him in. Then I'd be like all those other women.

"Idris," Kalyon called out.

The crickets were so loud that I could almost pretend I didn't hear him in the stalls.

"Idris, I need your help."

There wasn't anywhere for me to hide behind the beetles. I arranged the mud pies and stirred them up so the worms were easier for the beetles to find. The beetle teams knelt and groaned. Strange that I was more scared of Kalyon than them. I opened the corral and latched it behind me.

"You forgot the other latch," Kalyon said, reaching across so our shoulders barely touched.

"Sorry," I said, reattaching the outer latch. All it took was one errant sheep to break the beetle teams' delicate legs.

"I didn't see you all day. You hungry?" He looked at me, like he was searching for something, almost a worry flickering across his dark eyes.

I hugged my arms to myself—the cold biting at my skin since I'd forgotten my outer coat. Now I wished I'd brought it.

"You okay?" he asked.

"No," I said, and I looked into his warm almond eyes, daring myself to admit that I was afraid, to see if my words could sit well with him in a way they hadn't with anyone else. He folded me in his arms, and when he felt me shivering he wrapped me closer to him. His hands were careful with me, not searching or prodding.

He let me go when I shifted my weight on the heels of my feet.

"Can I give you my sweater?" he asked. In that moment I didn't want his sweater, I wanted him—and I was afraid of how I could stand so close without touching him.

"Yes."

He took off his outer coat and I held on, the warmth inviting me closer to him. Once the sweater was off, I folded myself into his arms. His flannel under layer was even warmer, and I laid my head to his chest, while his lips gently touched my cheek.

"Oh, Idris."

"Kalyon, just hold me, please. Nothing more."

There. That wasn't so bad.

"I will. I will hold you as long as you want me to." He brought his arms tight around me. "You can tell me, you know. You don't have to keep everything inside."

All the fear I'd been holding onto dissipated like a grey fog slowly lifting. He brought his sweater around us, the neck large enough for both of us to fit inside the body. We stood there in the groaning barn with the beetle teams munching around us, humming faintly.

If I could have, I would have frozen us there forever.

We walked along the pond bordered by tall, thick-trunked trees. We had to hike for over an hour to reach a spot where the hillsides that dotted our valley flattened out. It was hard to believe that anything lived beyond those steep green and black hills. I glanced up at the grey sky above, and it calmed me. There had been so few grey skies in Zeto. Nature was much louder here than we could ever be.

"You're quiet."

"Yes. When I'm not mad about something." I flicked my tail out and caressed his hand.

I wanted him to be here with me. I also needed to know about his past, where he came from. I squeezed his hand and let go. "I never got to hear your story of coming here," I said. I felt bad when I saw him wince, his face pained as he rubbed his hands over his prominent cheekbones.

I took one of the baskets he'd been carrying and placed it over my shoulder, my tail helping to balance it as we continued to the large rocks bordering the lake. When I touched one of the rocks it was warm.

"Litu and I escaped the snap fever and Hybrid gypsies on the plains."

"How did you find Sai Lou?"

"We almost died getting here. No hovers for us, just traveling on foot."

I looked at him while he pulled his long hair away from his face, tying it back into a knot. His hair was longer than mine. I reached for the long strands, enjoying their silkiness for the first time.

The morning sun broke through the clouds and his warm, brown face turned toward it, a dimple forming in the corner of each cheek. That smile. It could light twenty lanterns.

I fixed my gaze back on the basket, rooting around for what he'd packed. Kalyon reached his hand out for the basket.

"What would you like?" I asked.

"What do you have?" he smirked.

"You packed the basket, silly," I giggled. His touch had a different weight as I handed him a boiled egg. His fingers lingered on my palm before taking the egg. I set the basket between us, a necessary distance as I felt a gentle thrumming between us. I was scared that I would kiss him and do it all wrong.

"You were saying about your journey…" I said.

"When Litu and I recovered, we decided to stay and become part of Os and Gita's family."

"Like I felt like I was part of Yura and Shakratel's family, at least for a while."

He handed me a piece of bread, his hand touching me again. "Do you still miss them?"

"I do. I wish they could meet you."

In that moment, my chest fluttered and my breath caught. I could only stuff my face with food and wait for the subject to change, because I hadn't ever considered anything beyond getting to safety and starting a new life.

What did I know of love and what it meant, other than watching the ruination of too many lives as a result of it?

I looked at his face again, so warm and kind. I brought both hands to the sides of his face, letting his lips bridge the distance. A small fire ignited in my belly when he kissed me, his lips brushing mine in soft strokes. His hands taking my face in them.

"I like this moment with you, Idris. I don't want to ever hurt you. What I feel for you is real, I'm not messing around."

I kissed him again. It wasn't quite enough, so I let my tongue linger at the edge of his mouth. He laughed then, and it felt like our bodies could speak in a way our words couldn't.

It was thrilling to be alone with him, the lake water calm and pristine as he pulled me closer to him on the warm boulder. I had no desire to do anything other than enjoy my mouth on his.

CHAPTER 41

TOREF

The air was heavy in the morning, a dense fog hanging over the fields when the sun crept between the hills. *I wonder how my sisters and Rusty would feel about that fog, if it would feel like some mysterious, magical thing to them, seeing it for the first time?* Toref knew it was planting time soon, and he had a narrow window of time to make his case about going back to Zeto before summer came. Once the heat hit, it was too hard to fly long distances, at least using the old hovers they had.

The nyphid rooster crowed, and he hopped out of bed. Everyone else was still sleeping as he slipped out of his room where Kalyon snored and down to the kitchen, wrapping his moss green sweater tight around him. He could hear the sizzling of something in the pan. When he walked through the dining room into the open kitchen door, Jesik was standing over the stove cooking eggs and a battered griddle cake that they used to eat in Rif City.

He turned around, clutching his hairy chest. "Sorry, you scare me."

"I should have said something." Toref looked around to see if he could help him, but it looked like he'd already done most of the cleaning. Then a thought struck him. *It isn't his day to do breakfast.* "Why are you up so early? Isn't it Kalyon and Idris' day to cook?"

As he watched Jesik turn the griddle cakes, contemplating the question, he was caught up in a memory when Penny, his youngest sister, had been cooking the exact same breakfast before their father died.

Penny beamed at him from the two Bunsen burners on the kitchen floor as she turned the griddle cakes, lowering the flame for the eggs before covering both of them.

"Couldn't sleep." She looked at him with identical violet eyes to his. The corners of her mouth lifted. "Mom and Dad already left for work. Get Lena up so we can eat this mess!" She lifted the lid and turned off the burners. "I made too much, like usual."

She took a bite of the griddle cakes and he ran over to the front room floor to wake Lena, who groaned and turned over, opening only one eye to look at him.

Toref shook off the memory and went into the pantry to grab the syrup and think through what to say to Jesik about going back to Zeto. He searched along the walls of the pantry, finally finding the syrup in a large dark wood canister with a metal mouth that allowed the syrup to pour without spilling, if it tipped over.

He wished he had such a device that could keep all the emotions he felt about his family and his future from spilling over, plaguing his mind and never letting him go. Bringing the syrup to the table, he could see that he wasn't alone.

Jesik was already eating the griddle cakes, the eggs completely separate from the cakes. He was like Minerva, who hated for the syrup to touch the eggs, preferring sweet and salty things to stay separate. When Minerva came in, her hair still mashed against her face, Toref brought her a small dish to dip her cakes in.

"You remembered," she beamed at him.

"Thanks for making these, you know you didn't have to," Toref said to Jesik, enjoying the familiar taste and extraordinarily sweet syrup.

Jesik looked out at the dewy fields in the distance for a while, eating and not saying much before turning back to Toref. "I needed to remember something good." He took another bite and grinned.

Pinu flew in and sat next to Minerva, who stroked her. Pinu pecked at the bench, her polite way of saying she wanted food. "Do you think Idris will mind if I feed her a little?"

Toref looked behind him to see if she was anywhere around. He couldn't remember what they were allowed to feed the petrukian. "I think a few bits won't hurt, maybe just without the syrup or eggs."

"Alright, here you go, you big glutton." She stroked Pinu's black feathers and she cheeped happily after pecking at a few pieces of the griddle cakes.

Os came bounding down the stairs, and Idris ran into the house, slamming the front door behind her, her black-and-white striped tail flicking about as she darted toward the kitchen. "Sorry I'm late to start breakfast."

Os followed her inside. "You make enough for all of us?"

Jesik looked guilty. "Sorry, I…" He looked over at Toref.

"You can have some of mine, if you like." Toref offered Os his plate.

Os surveyed the two of them. They weren't supposed to make special meals for themselves. It was a waste of the grain.

"I knows, Os. I not do it again," Jesik said. He started to take his plate in, and Toref followed. Jesik hadn't finished his eggs yet. "Most who settle here take an oath not to go back to Zeto City. If they break that oath the twin council decides if they can stay."

Jesik took one look at the leftover eggs and nodded toward Os, who happily ate them.

Minerva was finished in a flash and joined them outside. Jesik deeply inhaled the crisp morning air while the sun rose above the hills in the distance. Pinu flew out with them, taking to the early morning skies.

"This is my favorite time of day," Jesik said, bringing his grey sweater tighter around him, cinching the enormous leather belt. They walked past the fallow fields, small shoots of green already sprouting up after the winter snow.

"I want to go back, to try to rescue Rusty and my sisters," Toref said, watching Jesik's snout move into a frown as he scratched his head. They kept walking side by side, the silence like an ache in Toref's chest.

"I not live with myself if I not know what happen to your sister and Rusty," Jesik finally said after several minutes of walking in silence, the mist slowly rising from the ground. "I think for going back. It danger, but I not like leaving them behind when we now strong and have more people can help."

"I feel the same way, even though I know it's a big risk. So we have to be careful," Toref said, and they stopped. He looked up at the determination in Jesik's face, how his wide mahogany brow furrowed. *He believes this is important, too.* "We have to convince Os and Gita to help us keep everyone safe, if we can go back."

"I help with layout of casinos. I there for years and know things," Jesik said softly.

"But, that might have changed..." Minerva whipped around the corner. She took Toref's arm. "It doesn't mean I don't want to try. But it's not something we can do alone."

Jesik's face went taut, that jovial expression at breakfast gone. "I help you. We just try." He held out his hand, turning slowly and stopping in front of Toref. "Just look at how beautiful it here. Our life so good."

Jesik clapped his arm around both Toref and Minerva and sighed, looking up at the sky brightening as they stood at the edge of the field.

Toref felt his heart swell with relief, but also anxiety. It wouldn't be easy convincing the others, especially Idris, to use their hovers. But the feeling he had of soaring—of hope—as Pinu flew in long, looping circles above them, seabirds calling to her from a higher elevation, felt like a sign that better days were possible for them. "All we can do is try."

∾

Toref and Jesik found Os in the basement lugging seed up the stairs. He took one of the sacks from Os and laid it by the stairs.

"No, that one has to go up to the kitchen level for tomorrow's planting," Os said, stopping to take a breath. "I think I might be getting too old for all this hauling." He smiled, his green forehead wrinkling pleasantly.

"Jesik and I can do all the carrying for you." Toref took advantage of the break, clearing his throat and feeling the sound echo off the stone walls of the cellar. "Can you help us go back to Zeto...to get my sisters and Rusty?"

Os groaned and sat on a nearby barrel.

Jesik folded his arms, taking a step closer to Toref.

"If you leave Sai Lou, the rest of the residents might not let you back in," Os said. "That's not my biggest worry, it's all of our safety."

Jesik looked troubled. "I not like Zeto. I know it danger, but to leave three kid there, when there chance like here. It seem not right." He hmphed for emphasis, and Toref was happy for his support. But he could also see where Os was coming from.

Os stood up, rubbing his lower back, "If you go back, you could be branded oath-breakers. You'd be entirely on your own. It's happened before." He spread his hands wide. "You see all these kids without parents? All the kids Gita and I care for?"

Toref wasn't making the connection. "What does that have to do with going back to rescue three people?"

Os leaned into Toref, "You sure we can get them out of there without losing or severely injuring our family members here?"

Toref thought back to the first rescue attempt when they had just been winging it. "If we have enough people, enough planning, we can at least do the reconnaissance to try, or realize it's impossible and come back home." He felt a deep pang in his chest and caught his breath before the tears came. "I can't live with myself if we don't try."

Os's face became very severe, his mouth drawing into a thin line. "I want you to really take a look at all the kids we have here, whose parents said they were coming back after they went back to get one more thing in Zeto, to bring back a cousin, a friend…whatever it is, and they never came back. We had ten kids when you came, we now have four more." He turned to Jesik, "You don't quite count as a kid anymore, my friend."

Jesik bowed slightly. "I know it."

"Life is good here because we follow the rules and don't exploit people. All these kids here? Their parents were oath-breakers. We haven't heard from any of them. Not once. I assume they're all dead. Or got captured."

Toref took a sack of rice from the pile. "We're all coming back." He looked at Jesik and Os, the stony expressions on their faces. "Please help us keep everyone safe that we care about." He lifted the sack up and left the cellar, knowing that he was definitely going back, with or without Os's blessing.

Toref stewed about the conversation all day, keeping busy moving sacks of seed after lunch, helping Idris round up the alpacas, trying to keep her from launching into a tirade when Nalo kept dropping the shears. Toref thought the eyes of the alpacas and llamas reminded him of how Lena looked when they tried to rescue her: afraid and wild.

Once everyone in the barn was busy shearing, Toref cleared his throat. "There's something we need to talk about…"

Only Nalo looked at him, almost letting go of the baby alpaca that butted against his arms to get away.

"Careful, Nalo," Kalyon warned, sweeping his long hair out of his face.

Nalo held the animal more firmly while they cut away at the excess, downy fur.

"I want to go back to Zeto," Toref said. "It's time to rescue our friend and my sisters."

Kalyon crossed his arms and looked at Idris who refused to look at either of them, and ignoring little Nalo raising his hand like he wanted to say something.

Toref waited for a moment, to allow anyone to speak. When no one did, he continued. "When I spoke to Os about going back, he said that we might be branded oath-breakers, and that it's dangerous, which you all already know."

"That ain't true. We leave all the time and come back for trade," Nalo said, letting go of the baby alpaca when the last bit of it had been sheared.

"Nalo, that's different. We're going east, not west to the old cities." Kalyon said. "Why don't you round up another baby for us?" Nalo walked very slowly toward the pen, looking eager to listen in.

"Os is afraid because he's a war deserter, along with Gita. He knows that if you go, you'll need him because he's an old war strategist. But, if he gets caught…you're all in much bigger trouble," Kalyon whispered.

Toref helped Kalyon and Idris hold the animal while they sheared along the tops of its legs. "What if at least five of us go: you, me, Idris, Minerva, Litu…"

Idris' face fell, shadows darkening her cheeks, her tail whipping out nervously. "Count me out, Toref. I do not want to have to deal with Whip and Dina ever again. Remember: I'm the one who was almost killed by those eel twins, not you."

"So you'll leave our friends there to suffer?" Toref asked.

Something in her face changed and she looked at Kalyon, like she expected there to be some answer in his face. She looked down, her tail flicking about wildly before Kalyon put a hand on her shoulder.

"I don't want anyone to suffer, Toref, you know that." She paused, looked down at the little alpaca. "But there are too many ways this can go wrong," Idris said softly. She let the animal go once Kalyon gave her the signal, and something in her changed, a realization dawning on her yellow eyes. "Maybe if I can see Shakratel again, say what I couldn't to him and Yura, that would be worth it for me."

Os and Gita had joined them in the barn, their arms crossed, looking grumpy.

"So, you're talking about going back," Gita said, unfolding her arms and taking Os's hand in hers.

"Yes," Toref said, looking at all of them. "Who's in?"

"I am, and I'm sure Idris will join me, along with Litu." Kalyon said.

"Jesik's in," Jesik said.

Gita looked at Os, and she took his hand, holding it firmly in hers. "Well, Os, you have enough for a small militia to go in there and show our old enemies some good fighting." Her wrinkled face was turned up in a smile.

Toref smiled a little, not certain that this was real. "Who is your old comrade?"

Gita exhaled noisily, her breath blowing her grey bangs off her forehead, and looked up at Os. "I'll let Os tell you about Whip in the old days. I'm here to collect Nalo to tend the pigs."

Nalo jumped up. "I'm going too, right? I mean you need another pilot, right?" He hopped up and down, and Gita pointed back to the house.

"Pigs," Gita said firmly.

Nalo looked back at them, his small, cherubic face smiling from ear to ear. "And then you'll tell me what happens."

"Promise," Kalyon said.

Nalo yipped and was off, a storm of dust clouds following his small, running figure.

Toref looked at Idris, her large, yellow eyes fearful. "I guess this means we'll use my hover and one of your crappy ones, too." They all laughed and started drawing out plans in the dirt.

CHAPTER 42

IDRIS

I looked at the plans squiggled into the dirt. Five circles represented the five major casinos and the outlying areas, minus Shakratel's compound and the Scraggs.

"We need to land at Shakratel's if we have a prayer for any of this to work," I said. My heart lifted, imagining the happy looks on both Shakratel and Yura's faces when we landed, when I could tell them how much I missed them.

Toref met my gaze and nodded. His dark forehead was a series of furrows as he squatted over the drawing in the dirt, filling in Shakratel's compound to the west of the city's limits.

Now that we were going back, something opened up inside me, a window to my past that maybe needed closure. Or, a stream that needed diverting. I glanced at Kalyon who was sitting against the back of the beetle pen, deep in concentration. They needed to know him, to know that I was okay, better than before.

I pointed at the center of the dirt drawing of the casinos. "We have to do some reconnaissance before we rescue them. It's the only way to make sure your sisters are still in one of Stencil's casinos."

Toref nodded. "It would be great if we knew which one."

I looked at the circles, so easily marred by a breeze or an errant hand. *I wish it was so easy to topple the empires of those slaveowners masquerading as casino owners.*

I reached behind me and bumped into Kalyon. He took my hand gently, almost asking permission, and I shook my head. Not in front of everyone. "What about Diarmaid and some of the others in town finding out?" I asked.

Kalyon came closer, our shoulders touching. "They can't say we're all oath-breakers if six of us go."

I watched Os's bushy eyebrows rise, before he rubbed his bald, light green head, like he was trying to carefully shield his concern. "They can, and knowing Diarmaid, he probably will. You newcomers haven't taken the oath yet. There hasn't been time for a ceremony, and we wanted to make certain this was where you were going to settle for good."

"So, if we go, we're not causing you more trouble?" I asked.

Os grinned, small gaps appearing where he'd lost teeth in the war. "Some trouble is worthwhile, if we get your friends back. We've lived around Diarmaid a long time. He's always looking for something to complain about."

I looked at Kalyon, a new determination rising inside me. "I'm definitely settling here." I gave into a goofy grin I was certain was spreading over my entire face, just for the pleasure it afforded me when Kalyon grabbed me around the waist.

Os stared at us for a while, like he wanted to say something wise, but wasn't entirely certain what that was. He pointed with his toe toward the scratchings in the dirt. "Most would say there's no way a small group could rescue one, let alone three people deep inside of Whip and Stencil's casinos." He rubbed his scaled head. "But, something of the old life is creeping inside me, and I want to try." He stalked off, leaving us alone in the barn, the late afternoon air cold as it breezed through us.

I checked all the beetle pens while everyone else departed. Kalyon gave the last of the grain to the alpacas and watched me, like he was expecting me to say something profound.

"What is it?" I asked.

"I never thought Os would help you guys. I mean, not like this," Kalyon said, bringing his hair back into the hairband before we tromped through the fields to the big house. "It isn't easy for him to discuss the past. I've heard him and Gita talking about how he was a strategist during the Hybrid Wars. He worked for Whip, and Gita was special operations, mostly dealing with hand-to-hand combat. They lost everyone they knew, except each other. That's when they defected. When people died, Os took it personally because they followed his battle plans."

Kalyon's face held a grief that I knew I was only seeing the beginning of. It made me wonder how much his sunny disposition hid his old sadness. I put a hand to his cheek, and some of the shadows dispersed.

The sun glittered on the new buds pushing through the fallow fields. It would only be a matter of time before those buds were plowed over for whatever Gita was planning to plant there. I wondered if we were like those buds, being plowed over for something better and not understanding our part in everything until we were forced through the strainer.

No. I can't think like that.

I held Kalyon's hand more firmly.

Things are different now.

I closed my eyes for a few seconds, seeing Zeto City, Shakratel's compound, my cave, and then the thought that had only been a glimmer, a sliver of something not quite formed, came to me.

"I am glad we're going back. So you can meet Shakratel and Yura," I said.

"I'll be glad to see them in person," Kalyon said, beaming.

"They're not like anyone you've ever known." I put my arm around his waist.

"I can believe it, because you're not like anyone I've ever known." He planted a soft kiss on my lips.

I laughed and followed him into the kitchen. It felt good to let him in, while Pinu fluttered to land on his shoulder.

Shakratel's white stucco and terra-cotta tiled compound shone in the sun. It seemed so much bigger than I had remembered as my hover touched down outside of Reggi's side of the repair hangar. Excitement welled through me. I couldn't wait to jump out and hug Yura. I looked at Minerva copiloting where Pinu would normally be, and I missed her terribly. Minerva squeezed my arm before unstrapping her safety belt, Toref already waiting to help her through and into her metal legs.

"Home, sweet, home," I said, and felt a rush of warmth in my face. I was shaking, I was so excited.

Before I had a chance to open my door, Reggi was waving at me like a lunatic as he rushed in. Kalyon came around to my door and took me by the waist at the exact moment that Yura appeared, tears streaming down her face. "You back, Little One."

"Yura, my family. I missed you so much." Tears streamed down my face as I reached for her.

Kalyon let go of me so that Yura could hold me to her, her soft robes folding around me in the cool breeze. She stroked my now long hair. *It's so good to be home again.*

"It grow so fast, Idi. You even taller. Why you back? You miss us so much?" Her voice was shaking as she held me close to her again, her skin glistening in the sun when she pulled away.

"I wish we were back for longer. We're just trying to get our friend and Toref's sisters back."

A growling started behind us and the rat-tat of what I was certain was Shakratel's cane. He was arguing with one of his bodyguards, but the minute he spotted me, he stopped. I'd never seen him look so shocked before. His wide face was furrowed in an angry expression that didn't soften when his eyes met mine. I stepped forward, and Yura held onto me, not letting go for fear I would disappear, I think.

There was a thick silence, the only sound a whine of a drill in the hangar three bays over. Even that stopped after a moment.

"We had to come back, Shakratel. I needed to tell you something. Something I didn't say before."

He kept staring at me, saying nothing, until he started laughing, his face breaking out into the jubilant smile I knew so well, and I ran to him, almost knocking him over. I was now taller than him. "Idi so big now!"

I felt for the first time that he was the father I had lost and that all the ghosts from my past had met and merged here in the desert again. "Thank you Shakratel, thank you for being my family." I held him close to me in a tight embrace.

Shakratel followed me out onto the landing strip to take in everyone, nodding to Os, Kalyon, and Litu, who were obviously Fringe from the homespun clothes and easy expressions on their faces that city dwellers rarely wore.

"Welcome! Let's get you all inside now. Whip and Stencil been extra sensitive since you gone, and I no take chances. Reggi, bring the hover in and use cover." Shakratel ushered us inside where the fans in the dining hall blew warm, earthy air around. I had to take off the sweater that would no longer be necessary here, even if it was the middle of winter in the desert.

We sat down to a large meal, and Shakratel sat directly across from me after talking with Os for a while. "I glad you come, kids."

"We couldn't leave Toref's sisters and Rusty there," I said.

Toref smiled at me with a certain relief that relaxed his face.

"They can't find those two without big group. But, I too worry worry your safety. It get worse day by day. I think of packing up and moving north, maybe back to Myrel, even if there's little nothing 'cept rock and more rock." Shakratel looked at all of us with that wisdom I appreciated.

"I don't want to make things unsafe for you," I said.

He laughed. "Oh, dat ship sail, Idi. Casino bosses never like me, but dey like supplies I get dem. Dey leave me alone little longer." Something in his face made me think that things were worse than he was letting on.

"We're planning on running some surveillance first to figure out where my sisters and Rusty are," Toref said. His dark face looked pained. He'd been quiet the whole way here, like he was spinning all the scenarios in his head.

Yura placed a firm hand on my forearm. "Well, you all eat up and rest a bit." She looked at me, her hand cupping my cheek. "We so much catch up on and so little time." She nodded in the direction of Kalyon. I only had to smile for her to know what was happening. She kissed my forehead, and we sauntered off together to talk in her orchid garden where no one would disturb us.

The next day, I watched Reggi, Kalyon, Litu, and Os take off for recon with Minerva. Toref and I had to stay back because it was too risky that we'd be recognized. It was only a few hours, I had to remind myself, but it was hard to watch them fly away while Toref and I worked on the decoy paint job that would keep the scanners from identifying my hover.

"I can't believe something like this will work," I said, looking over at Toref, his face golden brown in the afternoon light.

"Oh, if Minerva says it will evade scanners, she's right," Toref said.

I finished the last stroke on the section of the hover's nose. "You worried about them finding your sisters?" I asked.

He stopped painting, his eyes wide with grief. "Yeah, or that they won't find them at all, and I never had a chance to say goodbye."

Without thinking, I threw my arms around him, paint fumes

wafting off both of us, and let his tears fall silently onto my jumpsuit collar. We stood like that for a while, until I heard the percussion of Shakratel's cane coming our way.

"They'll know something, maybe in a few hours, and then we'll go from there, okay? You're not alone," I reassured Toref.

Toref nodded, his purple eyes looking almost magenta from crying. "I know, it's just the knowing that scares me. The petrifying feeling that they're both already gone, and I waited too long to come back."

I rested a hand on his round shoulder. "Yeah, I know what you mean. But, there's no way we could have come any earlier, Toref. At some point you have to forgive yourself." I sighed, looking out at the dusty horizon. "Or it will consume you and never let you live the good life you have in front of you."

They'd returned from the reconnaissance looking rather tired, but determined. I could feel the waves of panic wafting off Toref. I glanced over the plan Toref and Os had drawn up after they'd located Penny.

"That'll be our first stop," Toref said.

Rusty and Lena weren't visible in any of the casinos they'd visited. I handed it back to Kalyon, and he tucked the plans into his breast pocket.

"I can't believe we're going to do this tomorrow morning, that I'm going back there," I said, nerves rattling through me.

"I'll be with you the whole time." Kalyon took my hand and squeezed it before settling his lips at my neck. The others gathered up the plans and sauntered off to the cafeteria.

Kalyon walked with me over to the edge of Yura's orchid garden where two swings hung from the roof of the dining hall building. We sat in them, our legs dangling over the stones, as bats and birds snapped at glowing insects. We swung there a while, until I heard Os's voice beckoning us back to join the group.

"Not yet," Kalyon whispered, taking me into his arms, rubbing his hands over my ribs. "I want you to know what I feel for you. That it's real, and that if something happens tomorrow, you'll know it's you I choose."

I kissed him before pulling him close to me, feeling that deeper ache for something we hadn't done yet, but I knew I wasn't ready for. I looked into his dark eyes and felt a trust threading through me that went beyond my deep bond to Shakratel and Yura. "I choose you. But, more than that. I love you." I paused, checking that he wasn't wincing. Instead, he flashed a beautiful grin, his eyes sparkling. "I hope it isn't too soon to say that."

Kalyon put both his hands on my shoulders before bringing me close to his chest, where I heard his heart beating steadily. "I love you more than I can say."

I was brimming with happiness for that moment of stillness with him, certain that what we had was real.

As I looked over the dying light on the distant Scraggs, I wanted to remember that this was the last time I had to look over the city of my previous imprisonment. I hoped I could liberate Rusty and Toref's sisters in a way that I couldn't set my own family free. And in some way, I would exact my own revenge on the city bosses who had forced us to live that way.

I took Kalyon's warm hand in mine and led him back inside where Os and the others were waiting for us.

CHAPTER 43

TOREF

Toref gazed at Idris in the purple velvet performer robes Yura lent her. She did look completely different in her alluring outfit, despite her sour face.

"I'm not going back to the casinos looking like some tart," Idris insisted, crossing her arms, the deep plunge of the robes showing even more of her chest.

Kalyon was grinning like a fool, his ears perked up. Toref wanted to laugh, but Idris caught his eye.

"Wipe that smile off your face now," Idris demanded as Kalyon turned away, laughing. *Brave man.*

"No one will recognize you like this," Yura said, her voice low and sultry. She let out a whistle, and Toref backed away from the simmering Idris.

Os climbed into Litu's hover in a dark cloak over a white suit. Toref could see that Os was not at all comfortable with this arrangement. "The sooner I get out of this thing, the better." Os flipped the cloak back, hiding his earpiece under his suit, then stashing a few weapons and a stun stick that he strapped to his leg.

Toref took the other stun stick and hid it with a Velcro strap along his calf, getting ready to board Idris' hover that Reggi and Kalyon were piloting. If he weren't so nervous, he'd tease Idris about not being able to pilot her precious hover.

Yura and Litu continued to surround Idris. "It's acting," Litu said softly to Idris, flipping back her wavy black hair.

"You're. Not. Helping," Idris replied.

"Neither are you." Minerva stood above her, her eyes flashing. "If we want to rescue our friends, this is what we have to do." She attached the body wire to Idris' upper arm.

Toref reached for Minerva's hand, taking it and kissing it before she enfolded him in her arms. They stood like that, her pink eyes catching the morning light before the others cleared their throats.

It was time to test the equipment and let her go help Litu pilot the agro hover. He knew that, but he was a bundle of nerves, worried that he was risking too much. Toref backed out of the hangar and spoke into the microphone, testing it out. "Can you all hear me?" They all replied as Idris hopped into Litu's hover, playing with the receiver while Minerva fired up the engines.

Idris gave Litu a thumbs up, and Litu hopped into the agro hover, its top rusted and dented from years of wear and tear. "Okay, your radio packs are good for about two hours, and then we have to get the hell out of there."

Everyone nodded at Litu's announcement before Idris and Os climbed in with her, followed by Minerva. Toref watched them go, Minerva blowing him a kiss. Why did she have to look so beautiful at a time like this?

I will make sure we all get back safe, Toref promised himself. *But can I promise that to anyone, least of all myself?*

Jesik gave him two thumbs up and grinned at Toref. For a moment, it felt at least on the edge of possible.

Kalyon waved to him from Idris' hover. Reggi hopped in to copilot. Toref concentrated on the map Os had drawn, superimposing itself in his mind over the morning cityscape of Zeto City still waking up. Jesik loped into the hover ahead of him, strapping in, and Toref realized this was likely the last time he'd see his birthplace like this. The sunlight glinting off the red and orange rocks, the outskirts of the city between Shakratel's and the casinos yet another obstacle to fly through before they were in the heart of Zeto City.

"Come on, Toref," Reggi called, Idris' hover's engines roaring.

Toref knew he had to go. He needed to finish what he'd started. Hopefully Rusty and his sisters would forgive him for waiting so long. He closed the passenger door behind him and hopped into the copilot's seat.

Jesik patted Toref on the shoulder before strapping in. "We can do this, Toref. We were made for it." He looked back at Yura and Shakratel waving at him from the ground, and Toref felt strength surging through him as they pulled away toward Stencil's casino. With Jesik by his side, they would rescue them. He just knew it.

Toref drew Jesik's cloak down over his large head so that only his friend's ox snout was visible, Jesik's eyes glowing in the dim light of Flame casino's entrance. This was the last place Penny, his youngest sister, had been seen from their recent recon. If they found her, they were bound to also find Lena. When they walked past the thick white pillars holding up the arched ceilings of the entranceway, the lights brightened, the rich, red tapestry on the walls glowing in a way that made Toref feel like he was being lulled into an artificial calm.

"Keep going, I can still see the two of you, and you need a longer lead in case security is tracking us," Os said through the headset. "We're going to keep an eye out for both Penny and Rusty. Once we spot them, start the diversion scheme we created last night."

"Don't stop and look at stuff, that's how we're going to get caught. Or they'll try to keep you there to spend all your coin," Idris whispered. "Make a path to the kitchen off the big gaming room, like we planned."

Luckily, Toref only had about 50 coins, which wasn't enough for more than three games. He increased his stride to keep up with Jesik. Despite Flame's cooling system, perspiration gathered at his forehead and the base of his neck. His palms were itchy, and every step felt like pins going up his feet. He figured it was nerves, but still, he needed to be in control, the brother who would rescue his sister, not some wimpy kid who couldn't help her the last time he'd had the chance.

"You two still there?" Os asked.

"Confirm," Jesik said. "I with Toref, we moving through Flame." He pointed toward a stone archway that led them through the exterior of the casino's gaming rooms, half full with people walking about listlessly. "Let us know when you close to big room where Penny spotted yesterday." Jesik said, letting his cloak slip back a little.

Toref immediately brought the top of the hood back down over Jesik and nodded in agreement, his blood pressure rising as they made their way through Flame into the next casino. "We're entering Amber now." The red walls and carpet gave way as they passed through the stone archway to Amber's purple and maroon plush interior. The stone corridors were all curved and what had seemed to be a main passageway broke into multiple rounded corridors they had to choose from. *How are we going to find them in this massive place?*

Toref stopped and looked at Jesik. "Which one?"

Jesik also looked stumped. Light shone in from the passageway they stood in where a large dome with stained glass windows reflected the sunlight above. Trellises of flowers and fruits grew from balconies lining the sides of the passageway, perfuming the air. Toref plucked one of the ripe cherries.

Jesik swiped it out of his hand and dropped it to the floor. "Not for us. It make you too sleepy." He handed Toref one of the nutritional cubes from the pocket of his cloak. "No eat anything here. It danger."

Toref put the cube on his tongue. "Thanks, my friend." He patted Jesik's arm and spotted Idris and Os following through the corridor. "Let's go up to where we can get a better sense of where their entertainment rooms are," Toref said into his earpiece.

"Confirmed, go ahead. We'll follow," Os said.

Toref knew he shouldn't look back, to try and get a glimpse of Idris in that dress, but he did. Os quickly whisked her out of sight down one of the curved corridors. Jesik took him by his sleeve across the floor to the elevator that brought them to the next set of balconies above. He had to keep his head in the game, but it was hard with so much to distract him.

A yellow uniformed Ungar stepped out of the elevator, vines lining its interior walls. "Which level?" he asked in clipped Hybrid Kesh.

"Entertainment rooms," Toref said.

"Which ones?" the Ungar closed the elevator's woven door across them and hovered his fingers over the buttons.

Toref heard music very faintly, an idea of describing Lena forming that might lead them to her faster. "Where the music is best. I heard there's a wonderful woman singer who has purple skin…"

"Well, many of our singers are purple-skinned. It's the rage, you know?" the Ungar replied, hitting two buttons as the elevator ascended swiftly.

Toref felt his stomach lurch as they moved upward, wondering how long it would take before he found Lena, or if finding Penny first would lead them to his oldest sister.

"I suggest starting on this level and then working your way to the bottom. The midday entertainment is always the best." The Ungar's saccharine smile did not reach his pale pink eyes.

Once Toref and Jesik stepped off the elevator, music played across the balcony. He and Jesik followed the guitars. They entered a sparse stone hall where the music on the stage was ignored by cloaked people playing at circular tables with pebbles and cards.

"We're on the top level in one of the entertainment rooms to the right of the elevators, but it's empty," Toref said. "We're moving on."

"We're on our way," Idris said.

"We're two levels down from you, Toref. No one in the entertainment rooms matches your sister's description," Os said.

A woman's voice echoed across the stone hall. Jesik turned toward the sound, looking at Toref. They followed the song out of the room and into the open atrium of balconies overlooking the levels below. Several vines partially hid alcoves where people were paired off. Toref followed Jesik down the stone stairs, searching every level.

They reached the ground level where they'd first caught the elevator and looked back up at the balconies above them, the stained glass dome letting in the harsh light that felt like it was searing through him, burning him for even trying.

"We're going to need to go on to Garnet casino," Toref said. He was afraid he'd missed something, but when he looked at his clock, they'd already been searching for a half hour.

A stone sign pointed the way toward Garnet casino, and a glass atrium of water divided it from Amber, the entire glass aquarium stretching out several yards. Below was a moving platform and an underwater glass tunnel.

Jesik stepped on the moving platform first, and Toref followed behind him. Fish in sapphire and canary yellow swam above them in the curved glass of the tunnel, while women with webbed fingers and fin-feet swam among the manta rays and sharks. Toref stared at the half-naked women, checking their features for any familiarity, but they were all too pale and small.

"Those be fish people. Lena and Penny not there." Jesik dragged Toref onward. "Let's find Penny where we see her yesterday." When they reached the other side of the tunnel to Garnet casino, there was a fifty-piece brass band playing on an elevated stage surrounded by the water. *How is it possible we haven't seen them yet?* A sense of hopelessness rose in Toref's throat. Everything was varying shades of yellow in the garish, open-air surroundings. Unlike Amber, there were no meandering levels or curved corridors. Above them, a series of open-air balconies ascended upward in a spiral to a fountain that was built into the vaulted glass roof. "This is going to take forever."

Toref skirted the brass band, pretending to look at the single-player wall games on the outskirts, all the while searching the band for any female players or singers. They all appeared to be Hybrid and Ungar males. Not a single woman in sight.

"Toref, where are you?" Idris asked, her voice crackling in his earpiece.

"We're in Garnet on the ground level where there's a band."

"I can hear it. Move upstairs, we're following," Os said.

Toref turned and saw Os make his way out of the tunnel. Toref followed Jesik upstairs, following the gradual loop of the sloping ramps that circled the interior of the building. They checked each room as they made their way upward, his calves burning from the exertion. He had to stop and get water, checking with Jesik before sipping from the fountain.

"Water usually okay. We know in half hour, if not," Jesik confirmed, not taking a drink himself.

Great. That did not make Toref feel better. A crowd was coming out of one of the rooms toward the top, and Toref left the fountain to head toward that room, sticking to the wall as people surged through. *Could Penny be here?* The room had double doors that had been shut, and a man in a white coat stopped them as Jesik reached for the handle. The guard had a long, scooping elephant nose. "Gnasher ID or Casino ID to go through."

Toref looked back at Jesik.

"Do I know you?" the elephant man asked Toref.

A loud, booming voice spoke over the man. "I'm so glad we arrived in time," Os bellowed, holding Idris tightly to him. Her pasted-on smile did not reassure Toref. He had to look away from her, waiting for the moment to slip in with Os.

"My dear, are you ready?" Os spread his hands wide and clapped them on the elephant man's shoulders. "Shall we proceed through?" He slipped several coins into the man's pocket.

"Of course, sir, right this way." The man opened the double doors, and Os continued to prattle on to him. "Such a daring cut, this suit you're wearing…"

Toref and Jesik snuck in with him.

Os and Idris chatted up the couples at one of the tables, but as Toref looked around the room, there didn't seem to be the usual assortment of games. Instead there were just numbered cards in stacks. The stage at the back had a group of women being dragged across it. Music was piped in, and the people in this room did not appear to be there for the usual entertainment.

Three more women took their places on the stage, and the last one to enter was pushed. She had large cheetah-like spots across her skin. She was so small, she could have been a child if it weren't for her mature face and full lips. She took a few turns, and the crowd cheered, some holding up numbered cards that two uniformed women at the front took note of.

A Lutana Hybrid spoke in rapid Hybrid Kesh from a podium at the side, closest to Toref. She switched to broken Stan, "good lute playing, singing, all dances, four languages, and lovely in clothes."

Toref looked at the line of women on the stage: mostly multi-hued Hybrids, only one pale-haired Ungar in the whole group. His eyes skipped over them, looking for anything familiar. Several of the reptilian Hybrid women were bald; all walked with thin chains attached to their feet. Nausea rose in his stomach from the state of them. *How could someone do this to another person?*

He snuck a glance at Jesik, who shifted his head toward the curvy bald one. Her skin was a shiny purple, and there was something familiar to the curve of her cheeks. Toref came a little closer. Jesik snort-sauntered over before Toref realized.

It's Penny.

He was ashamed that Jesik had seen her before him. She wasn't staring at anything, just swaying where she was chained.

"Found her. She's the third...from the right...on stage." Toref whispered in his earpiece, trying to keep his voice from shaking.

"That's going to be tricky," Os said.

Toref glanced in Os's direction, and he nodded. Os had his cards held up, like he was playing along during the auction like everyone else, but Toref saw the sadness in his expression. This was not going to be an easy retrieval. Toref inched closer to the guard at the end of the stage and saw that he had a key in his hand. If he could get it...

Penny took the stage, and Os became more animated, while the rest of the crowd watched him.

"He doesn't have the coin, we're going to have to do something," Idris whispered into the earpiece.

Toref knew they needed to cause a distraction to get her out. "We're going to have to do the decoy now," Toref said. "Os and Idris, make sure that you create the distraction for us to get out. I'll grab the key from the guard and take Penny. Jesik will guard us."

"Roger," Idris said.

Idris and Os immediately shouted at each other in the middle of the table.

"She's not worth that much, don't waste your coin on her!" Idris screeched.

"Don't tell me what to do, woman, I'll spend my coin as I see fit. Choose someone else if you don't like her."

They kept arguing over how much Penny was worth, stopping the auction while a few from the audience left. Toref's heart thudded in his ears. *I have to do this.*

Toref nodded at Jesik. Jesik hit the elephant guard in front of him while Toref grabbed the key from the guard's waist, dashed onto the stage, and lunged toward a listless Penny, grabbing her manacles. "I'm here to free you, sis."

She didn't say anything, her eyes blinking rapidly at Toref. He pressed the key to the lock on her ankle chains, freeing her from the rest of the girls. Jesik swept her up over his shoulder, and they darted toward the door where two guards were passed out, a flurry in the room as the crowd surged out.

She's safe now.

Another white uniformed guard appeared at the door. "You can't take her. The auction is still on."

Toref pushed him out of the way, shooting him with his stun stick while Jesik bolted ahead of him, firing at the other guard. He missed. Os and Idris came from behind and hit the guard, who crumpled to the carpet. Jesik ran to the exit, Penny over his shoulder.

Toref bolted with them until they got to the bottom floor, where he threw his cloak over Penny as they exited out the main doors to the hover landing pad. She was so still on Jesik's shoulder, obviously drugged to be kept compliant. "We're taking you home, Penny." He had to believe that they'd get her safely back home again. He took her hand, which was dark purple and clammy in his. He didn't let go of her until they were outside the hover Reggi was piloting. He helped Jesik load her gently into the hover.

"Where's Lena?" he asked his sleeping sister.

She opened her eyes briefly, her mouth dry and ashen. "She's gone, Toref. Long gone to heaven with Papa and Mama."

Toref's stomach clenched, his breath caught while tears coursed down his face. *Lena couldn't be gone.*

More guards poured out of the building, swarming around Os and Idris. They were too far from the agro hover, which was already in the air above them.

"Get inside, now! Hurry!" Jesik called out to them, while firing off shots at the guards who got close enough to grab his robes.

Jesik pulled Os and Idris in as they were airborne, the door still open. The guards were yelling at them while Toref belted in Penny, who slumped against him. *She's safe*, he had to remind himself. But he couldn't help feeling like a hole had been torn in his chest.

"We'd better stay in the air until we get the all clear from Minerva and Kalyon in the agro hover," Idris said, directing from behind the copilot's seat where Kalyon was.

Toref looked at Penny wrapped up in Jesik's cloak, too glassy-eyed.

"That did not go according to plan, at all," Os said, wiping perspiration from his bald head.

"Sometimes, you have to wing it, and that's all there is to it," Idris replied.

Toref edged closer to his sister, watching for any signs of her getting worse. Jesik handed him a water canister that Toref brought to her mouth. They'd have to flush whatever drugs they'd given her from her system.

Toref couldn't believe that Penny was all that was left of his family.

Could they rescue Rusty or would he be gone, too?

Penny leaned against him, her head resting on his chest, eyes still open and unfocused.

"You're safe now, Penny. Stay with me, please, lil' sis," Toref whispered to her.

"Brother-man," she whispered weakly.

CHAPTER 44

IDRIS

I tried to pretend I wasn't listening to Toref's conversation, like it didn't bring back haunting memories of my last moments with my Mom, while Reggi steered us toward Bliss casino.

I hope that this last stop won't cost us everything. I wanted to turn around, go back to Shakratel's, and be done.

I watched Toref's hunched figure holding his remaining sister through the rearview pilot's mirror. My heart sank with the recognition of that loss. Penny was definitely drugged, and I didn't know if Toref was prepared for who she was once the drugs had left her system.

I turned my attention back to landing spots around Bliss, not able to keep my nervous brain off Penny's situation. She might have been in captivity too long. I didn't know if Toref was ready for how much she'd been through.

"We have a lot of nice people waiting for you in Sai Lou. We're out of here forever, as soon as we get my pal, Rusty," Toref said to Penny.

"I'm glad you found me," Penny said. She slumped against the window.

Kalyon helped Reggi land us with a slight bump. Os nodded at me. I was going to have to go back into Bliss, face whatever was waiting for us there, even if I didn't want to. I was the only one who knew the way to the only place Rusty could be after all our surveillance turned up nothing. Whip's lair.

"Toref, you'll stay here with Kalyon and Reggi. They'll make sure you get everything your sister needs," Os said. "I'll stay on the radio with you to watch Idris and Minerva's backs as they go in with Jesik."

I watched Reggi land next to Litu and Minerva's hover. He climbed out with me, and we just stood there on the landing pad taking each other in. What if something happened and we couldn't say what we wanted to each other?

He took my hand and that moment of touch sufficed for whatever words we might have said.

"Jesik and Minerva are coming too, right?" I asked.

"I'm coming," Minerva said, tightening the connectors on her artificial legs. "Let's get this over with." She looked up at the tall glass building. "This place gives me the creeps."

The light blue blocks of glittering stone in Bliss Casino's front edifice gleamed in the morning sun. There was a small bustle of activity in and out as they began their shift change. It was exactly what we needed so that their security guards were less alert. I slipped one of the stun sticks in my pocket and watched Jesik pocket two more. He placed the grey hood of his robe over his head.

I looked down at the deep V plunge of my dress and couldn't wait to change out of the entertainer robes. I took one last look at Kalyon, and my heart leapt.

Minerva grabbed my upper arm, and I looked into the steady gaze of her pink eyes, her face unsmiling as she matched my pace. She didn't let go of my arm, even as we made our way up the stairs. Os and Jesik flanked us, like they were our bodyguards, and it felt better to return here knowing I wasn't alone.

The high glass alcove doors swung inward as we walked through them, all the brass on the tables laden with white and blue orchids swaying in an air-conditioned breeze. Everything felt hushed and quiet in the perfumed air. I looked to my left at the workers milling about during the shift change and found the circular floor platforms that served as elevators down to where I had met with Whip.

"We need to all be on that last circle in the carpet there, you see it?" I instructed the group. Os stood there in the lobby nodding at us, his wrinkled face stoically still. "You'll let us know if there's trouble before we come back?" I asked him, making sure my body radio was still working.

"Yes, go quickly down there and get back as fast as you can." He left us alone next to the floor elevators.

Once we were close enough to not fall off the platform in the floor, I pressed the floor button and we descended through the basement levels of the casino, the walls quickly changing to solid rock.

Once we travelled through solid rock, I knew we were coming close. My heart thudded in my ears, and my breath exited in shallow bursts. The elevator jerked to a stop behind an outcropping of rock. I stepped onto the cavern's uneven rock flooring, the humidity of Whip's water cavern making my nose itch. Jesik pressed in close behind Minerva and me. In the far corner, near the largest pool, someone was smoking a long pipe, arguing with someone else. The smell was already giving me a headache. As soon as we came closer to the sound of their voices, I signaled for everyone to pull back so we couldn't be seen.

Minerva immediately took cover behind the rocks, folding her body against the cavern as we followed suit.

"You will get yourself upstairs this minute. They're all waiting for you in the gaming room I made especially for you to oversee!" a woman screeched. It sounded just like Whip, but more pathetic.

I peered around the corner for just a few seconds to witness the person she was speaking to blow a pillar of smoke in her face.

"It's Rusty!" Minerva whispered, sneaking up behind me. *Goddess, let them not see us from up here.*

"I didn't bring you here to waste your life," Whip said, taking Rusty's pipe, her tight, black pants clinging to her muscular legs as she circled around her son.

Rusty snatched the pipe back. "I had a life before I came. You stole that from me." Rusty took another puff from the pipe. "So, if you don't mind, I'm destroying my brain's memories of that life."

Whip took a step closer to him. "Your friends weren't going to get you anywhere." She gestured around her at the cavern. "Where are they now?"

Rusty took a step closer, his face red with anger. "They were my family." He poked her with the pipe, and Whip took a step back. "I'm done here, fixing all your games."

"If you don't cooperate, I'm torching Shakratel's compound," Whip leered at him.

"Do it already, then. Isn't it enough that you destroy people's lives every day? And for what? More coin? More than you could ever spend in one lifetime," Rusty spat out.

Minerva crawled closer to the rock's ledge where we were watching. I followed a few steps behind her.

Whip took a step back, her face lightening. "I tried to get the pilot… the girl," she stumbled over her words, whispering something else and out of my peripheral vision, Minerva stood up. I was afraid to say anything. The only sound around us was the water trickling down into the cavern.

Rusty inhaled a long drag from the pipe, his glassy-eyed stare scaring me.

"What is it that you want? What haven't I given you?" Whip begged. I had never seen her look so pathetic.

Probably an act. Please, Rusty, be smart enough to see through her.

"The one thing you can't give me: my freedom," Rusty said. "You can't ignore me my entire life and then bring me back here, expecting me to appreciate this lavish life built on the backs of slaves."

"Stencil was going to…"

"Right, because he was going to use me. Whatever, it doesn't matter. Your political games aren't interesting." He threw his hands up. "I believe I've been cured of ever wanting to play any game ever again." He took a short bow in Whip's direction. "Thank you, dear mother."

Whip's stance hardened and she walked toward a glass door at the far side. "You're stuck here till you change your mind." The doors automatically opened when she waved her palm in front of them before she stepped through, and they thunked behind her.

"We have to go to him." Minerva started toward him, but Jesik held her back. I motioned for us to continue taking cover behind the outcropping of rock surrounding the perimeter.

"Only one of us should approach him," I said.

"Minerva can go. We stay behind, only come close when you signal," Jesik said, despite the terror I saw in Minerva's eyes.

"What if he doesn't want to go with us?" she asked.

"Raise your hand as a signal so we can get out of here," I said, the thought suddenly taking hold in my body. Minerva inched forward, her whole body quaking. It made me want to trade places, but she was much closer to Rusty than I was. I watched her walk-run toward Rusty's despondent form, and Jesik and I were quickly on her heels.

By the time we were on the lower level, Minerva had already reached Rusty. I was expecting them to do something, maybe embrace, but instead they stood there, staring at each other. She threw her arms around him and for a moment I froze, watching them rocking back and forth, Minerva's red hair covering Rusty's face.

"We're taking you home," Minerva finally said, releasing him. I was hopeful that was the end of it, and we could get out of there.

Rusty took one look at me and winked. *Oh tafla.* There was something of the kid I remembered in his bloodshot eyes as they welled up. "It's good to see you, Idris. Let's peace out of here." He nodded to Jesik, who quickly flanked us. We started toward the way we'd come in, but Rusty stopped us. He took Minerva's arm and dragged her over to the sliding glass doorway, that old sly grin I remember creeping over his freckled face. "We have an express way up and out of here."

When we reached the ground level, several guards, plus Dina and Whip, were waiting for us.

"Tafla!" I cursed.

I fired at the guards with my stun stick before aiming for Whip. It only glanced off her shoulder, making her bolt toward me. *Where is Os?* Just as I thought it, Os was there, blocking Whip from grabbing me. I dragged Rusty with me through the revolving doors and out to our hover, where Kalyon was firing off his stun stick at guards who were trying to get inside. A clattering of feet followed after us while I fired behind.

Minerva was flanked by Os, and Whip was hot on their heels. "Hurry up, head for Litu's hover!" They sprinted ahead.

A weird clunk hit the side of my head, and I looked down to see what it was: a ruby stone goddess statue rolling in front of my feet. I reached down to grab it. Dina was following, holding the tether to the eel twins who scuttled along with her. A strange smile played across her face.

She'd had it all this time.

"You can't take him. I can end all of you, right here, right now. Shock them already, you little bitch!" Whip screamed.

Os looked at her incredulously, closing up the hover as he and Minerva were airborne in Litu's hover. I was only a few feet from Kalyon and my hover.

"Yes, ma'am. Gonna shock them that deserve it!" Dina said to Whip.

Oh tafla, she's coming for me again. I ducked into the hover.

Dina simply nodded at me before yanking on the eel twins' tether and releasing a stream of electricity at Whip, who fell like a heap of rags at the foot of the stone stairs.

"What?" I exhaled. I couldn't believe it. Dina had turned on Whip.

Dina grinned at me, swinging the tether before shocking Whip again.

"Go! Before more guards come!" Dina yelled, releasing the reins. "Take me to Shakratel's. Please." She looked at me like she had that last day at the factory.

I was shocked back into the present, still reeling from her bold move. We had to get out of there. "Get inside, before I change my mind."

I spotted Jesik smashing the remaining guards heads together. "Come on, Jesik, leave them." I felt a zap in my left leg from one of the guards' stun guns when I reached for the handrails on the hover. I tucked the goddess statue into my pocket. No one was going to take it from me again.

Another guard fired a bolt that glanced off the bottom of the hover. One more charge and it would fry the electrical system.

"Get in the air," I yelled. Jesik bolted to the hover, hanging from the landing rails as we went airborne.

I watched another bolt pass in our direction, and Dina fired her stun stick at another guard aiming at us. He went down.

Dina kept firing until everything became a speck that disappeared on the landscape below. *The goddess was watching over me, after all.* I had never felt so amazed in all my life.

"Thanks, Dina," I said, totally exhausted.

I grabbed onto Jesik's meaty palm with Dina and Rusty's help and dragged Jesik all the way into the hover. Reggi steered us away from the city. Kalyon put his arms around me. I leaned against his chest.

"You headed for Shakratel's?" I asked them, still catching my breath and in no state to fly. *Dina had saved us.*

"We'll be there in about fifteen minutes," Reggi said, looking at me through the pilot's mirror.

"Anybody pursuing?" I asked.

"Nope, clear skies."

"May it stay that way," I said, lifting the goddess statue and kissing it before putting it back in my pocket.

I sat there, unbuckled in the cargo area of my hover, my mind replaying Dina shocking Whip, saving my life and still unable to comprehend it. Something inside of me—an old wound, a scar from the past—loosened, and I found myself breathing more freely than I ever had before.

When we touched down at Shakratel's, I knew we couldn't stay long. My heart soared and ached as I watched Yura's curls bounce while greeting us, her robes undulating around her.

"We got two out of the three…" I embraced her, finally feeling that we were safe. "…and a new helper who probably wants to share all of Whip's dirty tricks and vulnerabilities with you."

Yura looked over at Dina, and Shakratel's guards immediately flanked her.

As I took Yura's hand and we waited for Shakratel to emerge, I reminded myself that this might be the last time I would see them for a long time. I needed to find a way to be okay with that. Kalyon took my hand, and I let the security of his touch, of this moment, be enough for all the pain that had come before.

Rusty and Toref climbed out together, the two friends embracing as tears coursed down their cheeks. Penny stood stunned, her face still pale as she leaned against Toref to stay upright. At least there was an upside to the rescue, even if Penny was unable to recognize that right now.

I threw my arms around Yura and Kalyon, trying to hold on to the few hours we had left before we would have to leave again.

"Yura, will you let Idris take this dress back with her?" Kalyon asked, a wry smile on his face.

"Never gonna happen," I said, trying not to smile when Yura's eyes lit up.

CHAPTER 45

TOREF

Toref looked at Penny's lustrous, now-purple skin and green eyes. He tried to reconcile this new Penny with the old one. She pulled the blanket closer to her round chin and pointed with one arm toward Sai Lou's hillsides that were now in view through the hover's window. "Is that where we're going?"

Lena is dead.

He heard it echo in his head.

We are all that's left of our family.

He had to be strong for Penny. *I can't let her see how destroyed I am over Lena.* His last memory of Lena looking tortured in that green emerald dress floated in front of him for a few seconds.

I have to focus on the sister that I do have, the one who is here. He met Penny's gaze and wasn't sure if he saw something relax in her tense expression; maybe it was faint relaxation around her mouth, prematurely lined from lack of nutrition, he suspected. He needed to concentrate on how her bright green eyes crinkled at the corners when the sunrise's orange and fuchsia streaks spread across the sky, lighting up the green hillsides. As they came closer to Sai Lou, Toref spotted a new dotting of wildflowers across the closest steep hills to the south. He felt a pinprick of warmth at the idea of showing her everything in their new home.

Rusty put his skinny arm around Toref, a familiar smile twitching at the corner of his weary, freckled face. "Thanks for all of this, man. I owe you."

"Yeah, pay up, I know you got coin," Toref joked, squeezing Rusty's arm as they both looked out the window at the lush green hills below them.

"Seriously, I thought I was going to lose it when I found out Whip was my mom. After all that time..." Rusty ran a hand through his short haircut. Toref thought it made him look a lot younger than he did when he had a wild mane.

"She won't be bothering you again, that's certain." Toref smiled when he thought of how Whip was attacked by those same eel twins she'd inflicted on Idris all those months ago. *I hope she didn't survive that shocking Dina gave her.*

"Almost there. Belt in everyone," Minerva called from the cockpit.

Toref made sure that Penny's belt was still attached and put his arm around her.

Jesik smiled at him, his ox snout going wide with pleasure as they encountered turbulence, circling closer to the homestead. "I wanna sleep for a week," he said softly.

Os patted Jesik on the shoulder. "Me too, buddy." He craned his neck to look out the closest window. A small crowd had gathered at their landing spot in front of Os and Gita's house. Half the Sai Lou community was waiting for them.

"Well, it looks like we're going to have a bumpy landing," Os said as they touched down on the dirt circle. He threw the doors open as soon as the engines were turned off, and the humid air swept into the cabin.

Diarmaid stood gloomily at the front of a cluster of people that Toref recognized from passing or trading supplies. Diarmaid's wife, Noona, perched next to him, her long dark hair pulled back, looking even more upset than Diarmaid. Their five unnaturally pale children ran about until she yelled at them.

They slunk back to cling to their parents' legs. Toref kept Penny tucked behind him, not wanting Diarmaid's brood frightening her. Rusty jumped out ahead of him, ever ready to take on whoever was against them. *Some things never changed with him.*

Gita surged out of the house with the rest of the kids, Nalo at the lead. "Did you get them? Can I see them?" His questions seeming to never end.

Diarmaid stood apart from Gita and Os's kids, and there was something shadowy about him that Toref was trying to pinpoint.

Kalyon stood awkwardly next to Idris, holding her hand behind their backs. Jesik helped Toref scoop Penny up in his arms, Rusty flanking him. Toref was worried Penny wouldn't want Rusty near her, especially given how Rusty usually was around girls. The minute Minerva touched Penny's hand, Gita's gaggle of children swarmed around, and Jesik put her down.

"We're back together! We're together! We did it. You're finally here!" Minerva exclaimed, pulling Penny out of Toref's arms and wrapping her in her sweater, clutching her tightly.

"Careful," Toref said to Minerva, trying to keep a brave face as tears coursed down Penny's round cheeks.

"I'm glad you're here," Toref said to Penny. "I'm sorry it took me so long."

Penny smiled a little, looking so much like Toref's father in that moment. Toref kept an arm around his little sister, now a fraction of an inch taller than him. "Me, too." Penny leaned into Toref a little as he led her toward the house. "Never letting you go, Penny. Never out of sight."

Toref glanced back at Rusty, who looked a little lost. His orange hair curled in the humidity, a slightly tamer version of the mane that he'd had at the Pods. Jesik walked with Rusty toward the house and Toref clapped his hand on Rusty's back, Minerva taking Penny into the kitchen.

"Brother-man, you're home now," Toref said to Rusty.

Rusty beamed, the freckles on his face bouncing. Toref couldn't remember a moment when he was happier. Singing started inside the house and soon several kids were joining in, Nalo's small figure zooming about with infectious energy.

"Whoa, Nalo, slow down little man," Toref said to Nalo.

Rusty embraced Toref once they were in the kitchen, Minerva joining them and kissing Toref on the cheek. "It's settled now. We're family. You, me, Penny, Idris..." Rusty winked at Minerva. "Maybe Minerva too. You know, if she isn't trying to kick my *konshin* every day." Rusty rubbed his chin. "You two gonna get married?" He put a hand on both of them, drawing them closer as Minerva looked into Toref's eyes, a thread of desire stirring through him.

"The way she looks at you is melting my cookie!" Rusty said before Minerva smacked him on the arm. "Ah, the good old days, Minnie."

Toref started laughing, and soon they were tearing up as they held onto each other. Penny watched Nalo dart about in the corner of the kitchen, and pointed out the window to the backlot where Kalyon and Diarmaid were in a heated discussion.

"Do you want to check on them?" Penny pointed outside to where the crowd had grown.

Toref wasn't going to get in the middle of that. Idris stood a way off from them, Litu by her side.

Best to leave them to it, he thought. He reached into the bread pantry and saw that Nalo had beat him to it, serving up bread and cheese to his sister in the dining room. *That little beast*...he hoped that Nalo wasn't going to practice his flirting skills on her. Judging by their laughs, it was quite possible that's exactly what he was doing.

For once, Toref was going to let it be. He was content to join them at the table and watch Penny's green eyes light up for the first time since they returned. *Maybe things will be better than they were before.*

CHAPTER 46

IDRIS

A small group had gathered around Diarmaid, who was still arguing with Os and Gita, but I stayed a few paces away. When Diarmaid raised his voice, the younger kids skittered off to the house.

"He has some serious problems," I said.

"I think ours just doubled, thanks to Diarmaid and the elephant brothers," Kalyon said, indicating with his head the two elephantine male Hybrids standing behind Diarmaid.

I had met the tall, pale elephant brothers when I had first tried to train their beetle teams with Kalyon and Nalo. They farmed on the far eastside of the valley. They had to be pretty upset about something if they were coming all this way to talk to Os and Gita. Or Diarmaid and Noona had stirred up quite a few of the settlers about all of us leaving.

At one point, Gita cracked her electric whip, usually used for herding the sheep and cattle on the far pastures. The crowd disbursed, and Os yelled after the departing settlers: "We're not oath-breakers."

"Not according to township rules," Diarmaid fired back.

Os shook his head. "I'm not arguing this with you. Get off my property. We'll settle this at the tribunal with the twin council."

Gita took Os's arm and looked up at him with affection I'd never seen before. *Maybe they meant more to each other than just cohabitants helping kids*. They sauntered through the front door. I stayed outside with Kalyon after everyone else went inside.

Thick clouds gathered above us from the south. "Looks like it's going to rain in more than one way."

Kalyon looked up, then smiled at me. "Maybe. We'll see." He sniffed the air.

"They can't kick us out of here, can they?" I asked, holding his hand.

"They can do whatever they want. But it doesn't mean we let them." He brought me closer to him, arms winding around my waist. "Diarmaid is a mean sucker. He's living with serious war injuries and lost his whole family to snap fever. He got a new wife, new kids. He's scared." Kalyon looked tired from everything we'd experienced the last few days. Those new shadows appearing in the hollows of his high cheekbones made me want to comfort him. I brought him closer, kissing his forehead and cheeks.

"Can he make us leave?" I asked, a new fear coursing through me.

"No. We aren't oath-breakers. Everyone in this valley knows how Diarmaid is. Victory goes to those with cool minds." He gently kissed me, his lips lingering against mine. He looked up at Os and Gita's house, the place that finally felt like my home. "But we're going to have to keep a watch over the homestead tonight." He kissed my neck and face before leading me toward the engraved wooden door.

"I'll help you with whatever you need," I said, taking his hand, but not yet ready to go inside to whatever cacophony awaited us.

Os stepped outside, looking for us. "It's going to rain soon, let's get you all fed." He had a new look on his face, and if I didn't know any better it was almost a fatherly determination.

"Os, I'm sorry we made things difficult for you," I said.

He stopped for a moment, hand on the front door, his wide, scaled brow settled into a calm expression as his grey eyes met mine. "No. We did this because we wanted to. Diarmaid has been waiting for a moment to pounce. If it weren't now, it would have been something else later. At least I'm young enough to still fight him and likely win!" Os flexed a muscle, his green scales bright in the fading sunlight. That look of determination on his face made me miss Shakratel.

It starting drizzling, and a cool wind blew in. Kalyon put his arm around me as we shuffled inside, the aroma of bread and cheese making my mouth water. Os took both Kalyon's and my hand, clasping them. "This is your home now." He looked at both of us with such intensity that I couldn't look away. "Someday, you'll do the same for others."

When he said that, I felt there was a chance that, at some point, I would feel completely settled here. Maybe all that had passed in Zeto City would become a healed bruise that could fade to a distant memory.

Hours later, we shuffled across the village square and into a drafty, wooden tribunal room, full to the max. Several small children were running around, and I wondered when they'd kick the noisy creatures out. Ungar twins, an adult male and female, at the front clapped two round stones until the room was silent. "We only have thirty minutes to vote on Diarmaid, elephant brothers, & etc, on behalf of the settlement of Sai Lou Mori, raising issue with oath-breakers Os & etc."

The male twin unrolled a scroll and started reading. "Please remember that we define oath-breakers as those who leave the settlement for fifteen full days or longer and take up residence in Zeto City."

"Secondly," the female twin continued, "They eschew our way of life. Thirdly, they use their commerce in the city to misappropriate the goods of the settlers of Sai Lou Mori, and refuse to adhere to the settlement's governing body and allocations of land, property, goods, animals, and distribution of needs over wants."

The twins looked over the assembled body. "At this point, we wish to dismiss all present under the age of fifteen."

Diarmaid and Noona protested and the elephant brothers hooted, but the twin judges were unwavering.

Toref sat down next to me, where I was perched on Kalyon's lap, because every chair in the place was taken. There were a few places available up at the front closer to Diarmaid and his brood, but I wasn't going anywhere near them.

"Diarmaid, based on the evidence you are presenting, there's nothing indicating oath-breaking here," the female judge said.

Diarmaid stood closer to their table. "Look at how many children Gita and Os have in their care."

"Very considerate of you, Diarmaid," Gita remarked, her wrinkled face impassive, but her blue eyes were aglow with a heat I'd never seen before.

"It does look like they have exceeded the usual standard allocation of ten children per aged adult over eighteen years," the woman said, looking at papers before her.

Os pointed to a section of the page, "Here you'll see that our new family members are all over age thirteen, plus Litu, Jesik, and Rusty are over eighteen, so they are considered adults."

"But, but…it isn't right!" Diarmaid sputtered. "They left without permission."

The two twins narrowed their eyes. "This looks personal, Diarmaid."

Diarmaid stood taller. "What if they bring more people?"

The twins looked to Os and Gita. "Are you planning to regularly return to Zeto City?"

A strange hush went through the room.

"We are not," Gita said, but then she caught a look on Os's face. "But that does not mean that if we were to rescue children in the future, that we would not come here, before the committee, to get approval."

"But what if they do it again?" someone shouted from the crowd.

"As far as I can see, no law has been broken, no harm has come to the community, and these proceedings are finished." The twins rose and a hush fell over the room, no one stirring as they left. Something inside of me was set free, like the last bit of tension had finally dissipated, and I stood up as the room cleared.

Kalyon held onto my waist, waiting until the dusty room was empty, before turning around to face me. He leaned down to kiss me full on the lips. I hadn't realized how much tension I had been holding, afraid we'd be forced to leave, until that moment. I let myself enjoy his sweet, tender kiss.

"I'm glad we don't have to run off. It would have been awkward climbing through the mountain passes with the alpacas, goats, and llamas," he said.

"Silly," I said, swatting his arm.

I gazed into his mirthful, perfect black eyes, tracing his high cheekbones with my fingertips. He was so beautiful, I wasn't certain I deserved him. "We would fly with the alpacas, goats, and llamas."

Kalyon laughed at me.

"What?" I asked.

He took my hand, and we meandered back home. "Animals don't do well in hovers. We'd have a mess on our hands."

"We already have quite a mess on our hands."

He looked up at the yellow-gray sky. "That we do, my dear. But I would rather be in a mess with you than spend another second alone." His face was so open, his gaze so warm, that any doubts I'd had flew out of my chest, like ancient moths. I was truly free in the moment with him.

I looked into his face, his dark eyes searching all of me, his mouth slightly open before it was on mine again.

In that moment, the change I had been so afraid of was here. For the first time, I knew that it wasn't weak to feel wanted and to desire that from Kalyon.

I put my arm around his waist as we walked on. The rain fell in warm, fat drops that soaked us through before we got home.

Once we were in the dining room, the fire crackling and everyone talking in the kitchen, he lifted me up and spun me around and around. I didn't want him to ever put me down again. When we were both dizzy from spinning, I fished the worn goddess statue Dina had returned to me out of my pocket and placed it on the stone mantel over the fireplace where it would reside safely, I hoped, for the rest of our lives.

I uttered a small, silent prayer of thanks to her before I let him lead me into the kitchen where Toref and the others were waiting.

CHAPTER 47

TOREF

Toref tried to catch his breath as he hiked with Minerva up the last leg of the winding mountain trail. He had been worried that her new legs wouldn't be up to it, but she kept insisting she was fine. Now she was walking faster than him! Up this high, he could see all of the distant green hills, blue rivers running between them for hundreds of miles in every direction. *We're finally here*, he thought, gazing affectionately at a flushed, but absolutely stunning Minerva.

Penny, Jesik, and Rusty were still behind him. In the six weeks since Penny's rescue, she'd slowly shed some of her shyness to spend time with the whole wild household. He watched her beam at Rusty, who was catching up to her. She was the first person that Toref had noticed Rusty never teased, even acting shy and polite around his sister. He was afraid that Rusty really liked her and that brother-man was about to get his heart broken.

Penny ascended the last bend in the footpath, taking Rusty's hand to pull him over the ridge. *Good for her, letting him in*, Toref thought. Everyone from Os and Gita's house wore bright yellow scarves that Litu and Jesik had made. Toref took Minerva's hand, her soft skin pleasant in his callused palms, and walked over to the caldera at the top of the mountain where a deep, clear pool of water spread out before them. Dark green and orange fish flitted about in the water while electric blue dragonflies whisked overhead in the bright, turquoise sky.

Toref watched Rusty guide Penny into the caldera, Jesik holding onto her other hand. Rusty's hand lingered until she released it, but she didn't appear unhappy. She was looking at Toref with her now faded green eyes. "Why did you wait to show this to me?" she asked Toref.

"It's first time, us new kids," Jesik said.

"Besides it was too cold before today to come up here, except for you, my fuzzy friend." Toref clapped his hand on Jesik's furry back.

Gita raised her hands to get their attention. "We've brought you all here for a special ceremony officially declaring you to be in mine and Os's clan forever."

"Even after our old bones go to rest in the earth," Os said, winking at Gita. She pulled him close to her, planting a kiss on his cheek.

Toref came closer to Minerva and she kissed him, her wild curls covering half her face. He didn't have to hide his affection for her from his sister, now that Penny had accepted Minerva.

"We ask the old timers to form a circle around the new timers, here in the pool," Gita instructed. "Make sure you take off your shoes."

Rusty splashed in first. "Shoes? What shoes?" and threw his moccasins at Toref, who pushed him down into the water. The rest of the kids fanned a circle around Toref's new family.

"Now, old timers, look into the eyes of your new family member and repeat as you pass each person and clasp their hands, 'I am yours and you are mine, from the tops of these hills to the end of time,' " Os said.

They all repeated the words until everyone had gone around the circle.

Litu started singing with a voice so powerful that it hit him in his belly. Her low alto moved the rest of the group, and soon the rest of the women joined in. With the next verse, the boys harmonized. After their voices died away, Penny sang. It took a few moments before Toref remembered it was one of their father's songs.

They say…
You got mountains to climb
They say
You are losing time
But I say, I pray
that you'll stay right here,
in my heart…
Yes, I pray, you'll stay
Right here, always here,
in my heart.

After the first repeated verse, Minerva, Kalyon, Jesik, and Toref echoed the ending notes, and soon everyone was singing, even Idris and Rusty, who couldn't sing to save their lives.

My family is finally together.

The thought kept repeating itself again and again in Toref's mind.

My family is together. His sister and Rusty were safe. He imagined his parents and Lena standing there with them, not as the broken people who'd gone out of this world, but the whole people he'd grown up with until tragedy had turned their lives sideways.

Penny stopped singing on the final line and embraced him. "Thank you, Toref."

She held him tight before letting him go, walking over to Rusty to hug him. He stood by her side while she embraced everyone.

They remained on that mountain that overlooked the entire verdant valley, bright with new growth, while puffy clouds sped overhead. Idris and Kalyon called out the cloud's shapes before they reformed into something else.

"Bunny. No, cactus."

"That isn't a bunny, it's an elephant!"

Toref stood in the water, holding Minerva's hand while she led him across the caldera so they could see the purple ocean sparkling beyond the rows of sharply pointed black hills in the distance.

"Someday we'll swim in that ocean," she said before kissing him again, and he savored the feel of her lips under his tongue.

Toref leaned in to enjoy the pleasure of her mouth, lifting her up and swinging her around. "How about we make our first trip in the new hover there?"

Her pink eyes sparkled in the sunlight. "Only if you swim with me."

"Let's all swim naked!" Rusty burst through them.

Minerva snorted at Toref's shocked expression. Why couldn't Rusty just let them have this moment?

"What's naked?" Jesik asked, and everyone burst out laughing.

The End

DID YOU ENJOY ORPHAN PODS?

A few sentences on Amazon or
Goodreads helps a lot!
E-mail us at murasakipress at
gmail dot com with your
published review and join our VIP
list as thanks for your time!

**PLEASE
WRITE A
BOOK
REVIEW!**

THANKS FOR SUPPORTING INDEPENDENT ARTISTS!

Acknowledgments

This book has been a long time in the making! There are so many friends, family, mentors, writing teachers, and colleagues who made this story possible. I must first thank the children I worked with who shared their stories, their heartbreak, and their joys. They are the inspiration for the found family in this story and the deep loyalty you see in Idris, Toref, Rusty, and Minerva. I'm grateful to the many talented folks, named and unnamed, who made this story come to life, most especially Kara Stockinger, feedback partner, colleague, friend, and masterfully inspiring; Shelley Weiner, my mentor at Gold Dust Mentoring who walked me through the first and second drafts of this novel; Rowan Hisayo Buchanan for her feedback on the third draft as my tutor at the Faber Academy; Billy Cotter; my wonderful editors: Nancy Knight & Heidi Asundi; cover designer Sarah J. Coleman; Patreon & Cup of Coffee supporters Andy Bailey and Yalonda Wilhoite; my feedback partners and classmates Marina Mustieles, Aye-Tee Monaco, Ishita Fernandes, and Antonia Protano Biggs; my friends Sarah Jobst, Danielle Merket, Cynthia Pierron, Pat Gower, Jennifer Merrill, Kellie McCants, Lara Yu, Maggie Gentry, Annie Williams, Roanna Flowers, PJ Hoover, Fran Carpentier, Nani Ackerman, Niki, Alex Herrera, and Dan Soulia; my family; and my husband, Joaquin, for his unwavering support and love, y la familia en Mexico, especialmente Mama Vicky, Efren, y Marisela! Muchas gracias!

Thank you, dear reader, for buying this book!

ABOUT THE AUTHOR

Photo by Laura Dalava

Britta Jensen's debut novel, *Eloia Born*, won the Writer's League of Texas 2019 YA Discovery Prize. Subsequent publications include a sequel, *Hirana's War*, *Ghosts of Yokosuka*, and *Orphan Pods*, the first book in a new series. Her short stories have been published in a number of anthologies, including the most recent *Mixed Bag of Tricks* and *Castle Anthology of Horror, Femme Fatales*. After living overseas in Japan, South Korea, and Germany for twenty-two years, her multilingual, cross-cultural heritage influences her writing in myriad ways.

She now lives in Austin, TX, with her husband, where she is working on the sequel to *Orphan Pods*: *Bones of Our Ancestors*. Britta has taught writing to adults and teens for the past twenty-two years, and edits books with The Writing Consultancy and Yellow Bird Editors.

Get free writing advice by joining her mailing list and access bonus content on her website www.brittajensen.com.

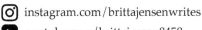 instagram.com/brittajensenwrites
youtube.com/brittajensen8458
patreon.com/brittajensenwrites

www.ingramcontent.com/pod-product-compliance
Ingram Content Group UK Ltd.
Pitfield, Milton Keynes, MK11 3LW, UK
UKHW041848200225
455370UK00002B/2